Enough to make her hair curl . . .

Jackson Scythe splayed his big—tan, long-fingered, ultra-masculine—hand on the door, opening it wider to allow my entry. As I took a tentative step forward, letting my imagination wander to ways he might use those hands, he passed me a brown paper bag he'd had tucked into the waistband of his jeans.

"What's this?"

"Barf bag."

I tried to hand it back to him. "No, really, you're not all that bad."

That earned a double quirk of the eyebrows and I could've sworn a twitch in a smile muscle or two. But he wouldn't let me score the last point. "You ever seen a dead body?"

"No," I admitted.

"Then you better keep it."

Praise For Laura Bradley and

The Brush-off

"With a clever plot, high style, and razor-sharp wit, Laura Bradley makes a grand debut with *The Brush-off*. This is one you'll definitely want to keep on your reading shelf . . . perm-anently."

—Maddy Hunter, Author of *Top O' the Mournin':
A Passport to Peril* mystery

"It's easy to predict that . . . Ms. Bradley's immense talent will gain the recognition of a Tami Hoag or an Iris Johansen."

—*Affaire de Coeur*

THE BRUSH-OFF

A HAIR-RAISING MYSTERY

LAURA BRADLEY

POCKET BOOKS
New York   London   Toronto   Sydney

This book is a work of fiction. Names, characters, places and incidents are products of the author's imagination or are used fictitiously. Any resemblance to actual events or locales or persons, living or dead, is entirely coincidental.

An *Original* Publication of POCKET BOOKS

 POCKET BOOKS, a division of Simon & Schuster, Inc.
1230 Avenue of the Americas, New York, NY 10020

Copyright © 2004 by Linda Zimmerhanzel

ISBN: 0-7434-7111-3

First Pocket Books printing May 2004

10 9 8 7 6 5 4 3 2 1

POCKET and colophon are registered trademarks of Simon & Schuster, Inc.

Illustration by Ben Perini

Manufactured in the United States of America

For information regarding special discounts for bulk purchases, please contact Simon & Schuster Special Sales at 1-800-456-6798 or business@simonandschuster.com.

This is for my
wild angels,
both in Heaven
(okay, you guys with wings, I'm finally listening!)
and on Earth . . .

Donna Drayton,
the friend who can read my mind.
Pam Morsi,
the colleague who won't hear of me giving up.
Paige Wheeler,
the agent who cattle-prods me.
Christina Boys,
the editor who gives me smiley faces in the margins.

And, of course, I couldn't forget my hairdresser,
Jay Askin, who patiently withstands three
hours of questions every six weeks.
(Oops, guess it's not a secret anymore
that I'm not a natural blonde!)

I couldn't have done this without y'all!

I hope we make somebody laugh. . . .

Keep up appearances; there lies the test;
The world will give thee credit for the rest.
Outward be fair, however foul within.
Sin if thou wilt, but then in secret sin.
                              —Charles Churchill

THE BRUSH-OFF

one

"IT'S STUCK!" HE WAILED.

Eardrums cringing, I pulled and pushed and squirmed harder just to avoid hearing any more of his contralto whine. Finally, red-faced and panting, I looked at the reflection of our contorted shapes in the mirrors surrounding us and had to agree. It was stuck. Which meant *we* were stuck. Together.

"Damn it," I mumbled, more to myself than to him. It was my fault I took the job. He'd told me exactly what he'd wanted, and I knew I couldn't do it. I told him I couldn't do it. But when he begged and whined, I'd agreed just to shut him up. Later, I'd tried to call and cancel, but he'd started in on how I was "The Best" (yes, including the capitals) and he didn't want anyone but me touching him . . . well, flattery works even when we know we're being buttered up. I was no exception, though I was still wavering between refusal and acceptance when he dealt the fatal blow. He had to remind me his wife was my best friend. Now, how could I say no?

This was why, I answered myself, with another

stomach-clutching look in the mirror. I took a deep breath and got realistic. "I'm going to have to cut it."

"No! Reyn, no!" His bawl dissolved into a sob. Tears quivered on his fleshy cheeks. "You can't cut my hair! Not my precious . . . *mi pelo muy bonito*—"

"Mario, I'm sorry, but I don't think we have any choice."

I tried to pry my cramped hand from the sticky handle of the brush, but it was no use. I'd thrown out my back with my last attempt at getting the round boar's hairbrush loose from his long, baby-fine strands when I put my foot up on the back of the chair to try to yank it free. So here I was, my denim broomstick skirt hiked practically up to my hips, one foot stuck between his back and the chair, the other dangling toward the ground, my chest draped—a generous verb, admittedly, considering my barely-B-cups—across the top of Mario's head, and my right hand attached by mousse, hairspray, and volumizer to the brush. My other hand was no help, being inextricably tangled in hair that had turned the consistency of half-dry molasses. Needless to say, I couldn't pull with all my strength. Still, never one to give up easily, I gave it one more weak yank; he squalled. With a frustrated sigh that was an ounce of self-control away from turning into a whimper, I relaxed my arms, making the muscles along the right side of my spine tighten frighteningly. I knew from experience those muscles would freeze in place, and I'd end up looking like the Hunchback of Notre Dame for the rest of the week. The handicap was good for better tips but frankly not worth the extra money.

"Why is this happening to me?" Mario sniffed. A tear dripped from the end of his nose onto the front of his mauve smock.

I thought of telling him the truth—that he was a vain idiot. But I held my tongue, mainly because I could qualify for that moniker myself, at least the *idiot* part. "Well, Mario, I *did* tell you I'd never used these products together before, let alone so much at one time . . ."

"But—but it's the only way I can get the volume I need." His liquid brown eyes met mine in the mirror with an anguished look that reminded me of my dogs when I don't let them in out of the rain.

He was never going to achieve the volume he wanted, but I wasn't about to tell him that. Not while I was within earshot of that ear-splitting, whiny wail. I wiggled the fingers of my captured left hand and began to feel them earn a measure of freedom. The throbbing pain in my back grew more insistent.

"I think," I began cautiously through clenched teeth, "I can get this hand free." I eyed a pair of scissors within reach.

"Oh, yes," he enthused, tears forgotten. "Then we can get some water. Maybe that will loosen it up."

"I can't reach the water, but I can reach the scissors." I tried to tone down the hopeful lilt in my voice.

"Aye-yi-yi-yi! Don't do it, Reyn. I'll tell Trudy, I swear I will."

I sucked in a breath and got ready to let loose on him. Someone beat me to it.

"Mario? You'll tell me what? What are you two *doing* down there?" a tentative soprano called from down the hall as we heard my front door, heavy with its beveled glass, clank shut.

Our eyes met in the mirror. His registered relief. Mine, abject embarrassment.

"Trudy?" Mario quavered. He turned his head toward the door. Or tried to. Our precarious positions wouldn't quite allow it without him taking half of my body with him, which he tried to do but only made it about a quarter of the way.

I should've been grateful to be rescued, but the fact that it was Mario's wife doing the rescuing completely squelched my relief. Why me? No one else on earth would go through the rest of her life making sure neither one of us forgot this horrible moment in time.

I had visions of being hounded every day by this embarrassment. I could be a poster girl for *Just Say No . . . to Overstyling.* Didn't they teach us to know our own limitations (and those of our customers) in cosmetology school?

"Where are you?" Her voice was getting louder—a dreaded clue that she was obviously headed in the right direction. *Damn.*

"Down here, Trude, in Reyn's chair." Mario was crying again, this time for joy. And I always thought the phrase "drowning in emotion" was an exaggeration.

Trudy appeared in the doorway, and I craned my neck just in time to see her mouth fall open and her hands bury themselves in her shimmering copper tresses. "Jesus, Mary, and Joseph, save me . . . and spank my heinie," she breathed while tracing the sign of the cross—forehead, chest, right breast, left breast.

Trudy was a Catholic with style. I admired that, although not as much as usual right at that moment.

"What's happened to you two?" she demanded after intoning a modified prayer for religious absolution.

"What does it look like?" I muttered with a surly glare at her via the mirror.

Trudy closed her mouth and opened it again. She

shook her head and licked her raspberry lips. She rubbed her fingers with their raspberry-tinted nails over her eyelids. She smoothed down cotton-candy-pink silk over her buxom bustline. I wasn't quite sure cotton candy went with raspberry or that raspberry didn't clash with the highlights in her hair, but I wasn't opening up those color debates now. Finally, she said, "I wouldn't venture a guess."

"Very funny," I retorted, seriously eyeing the scissors as a weapon now instead of as an escape route. Trudy had recovered from her shock, and the twinkle in her contact-created aquamarine eyes hinted at the infectious giggle-snort I loved so much when we were laughing. At something or someone else, that is.

Mario, weakling that he was, had held his tongue, no doubt in the hopes that I would talk us out of the sticky situation. Seeing I wasn't going to try, he gave up his silence. "Trudy, *mi corazón*, Reyn threw out her back."

"While doing what, pray tell?"

"Trude, I wanted that look that I was talking to you about, you know, that early-nineties Michael Bolton/Julio Iglesias combination. It's just so romantic." He tried to crane his neck to look at me. "Trudy calls it a variation on a faux hawk. Get it? Not a mohawk because of the long hair." He looked back to Trudy. "But the lift and height on the crown, the curls . . . I wanted to surprise you for your birthday." Mario's eyes brimmed with so much earnestness I almost regained my sense of humor. Almost.

"Julio and Michael, huh? How come it looks more like Lyle Lovett, then?" she quipped with a straight face that broke into a grin the moment she finished the sentence.

Here came the giggle-snort.

Actually, it took longer than I expected, a testament to the fact that Trudy was really trying for restraint, although not hard enough. I knew I should be damned grateful she wasn't jealous, that she wasn't thinking the worst—that I might have been in a clinch with her honey. But frankly, if she'd even entertained that idea for an instant, she wouldn't have been my friend for long, because Mario was so far from someone or something I'd want to be swapping spit with that I'd be seriously insulted if she even imagined it. Besides the fact, of course, that I would never do that to a friend. Except maybe a friend married to Harrison Ford . . .

Mario bowed his head, taking me with him and stretching my back. "Argh," I moaned.

"Oh, *Dios mío,* Reyn. I'm sorry," he sputtered, throwing his head back up, sending me off-balance, teetering off the edge of my stool, taking my hands and his hair with them. Mario screeched in pain. Trudy dove to grab me, or so I thought. She grabbed my arms instead, trying to save her husband's hair as my body continued its date with the floor. My body stopped in midair, and the excruciating tightening of my back prevented me from feeling anything in my shoulder when the telltale *pop* announced the sickening moment it dislocated.

Frantically, muttering a combination of curses and prayers, Trudy freed my hands as I collapsed onto the floor in a heap of misery.

Mario was crying. I felt a wave of comfort at his sympathy until I saw him patting the tangle of his silky jet-black hair and realized he was crying over the mess his coif was in, not the mess my body was in. Trudy jumped into his lap. They snuggled and nuzzled, and she sprinkled his face with kisses as I battled against the wave of nausea that threatened to dirty my just-polished oak floor.

"What do we have here?" asked a familiar voice with a smooth Mexican-American accent flavored with just a hint of affected aristocratic nasal. "If I'd known you were into this kind of thing, I could have sent you some more business, Reyn."

Head on the floor, I looked upside-down at the underside of the chin of the king of the beauty salons in San Antonio.

"You missed a spot shaving this morning," I croaked.

Ricardo threw his head back and laughed deep, low and toe-curling. It was his sensual signature and, I was convinced, the main reason he'd parlayed a mini beauty empire in our burgeoning South Texas city. It sure as hell wasn't because he could do hair. I'd always thought all his clients resembled teased Pekinese when they emerged from his enclave.

Not that I'd ever tell him that. His business acumen was unsurpassed, as was his power in certain circles, the styling salon circle being one of them. We'd once had a comfortable boss-and-employee relationship, one in which we argued but retained a mutual respect and a certain chemistry. After I went out on my own, the relationship evolved into a friendship that was contentious but close. Still, I knew he could and would blackball me in an instant if he wanted to. I valued honesty more than was probably good for me, and I wasn't always tactful, but occasionally I recognized when diplomatic skills were required. Now was one of those times, I told myself.

"She's not so bad off if she can use that rapier tongue of hers," Ricardo said in an aside to Trudy and Mario.

"My tongue's not what's hurt," I muttered, still surly.

"And what is, *pobrecita?*" Ricardo paused for dramatic effect. "Besides Mario's hair."

I sucked in a breath through clenched teeth and was briefly grateful that I was disabled. It kept me from unwisely wiping that smug grin off Ricardo's unnaturally beautiful face.

"She hurt her arm," Trudy put in generously. She said it without looking at me, as she was still in Mario's lap, fussing over his hair.

"My shoulder, actually," I corrected, feeling my blood begin to boil at the injustice of it all. I was doing my dumb friend's dorky husband a favor, which only got me into excruciating pain and was still the butt of every joke. Where was the justice in life? "I think it's dislocated."

Ricardo's brilliant grin—upside-down—made me dizzy. Why was he happy about my painful predicament?

"You're in luck, my dear Reyn. I can fix that for you."

Before I could get the "Sure you can" out, he'd reached down, scooped me up with deceptively slender arms, and done something indescribably painful in a bear hug that left me suddenly relocated. My ligaments protested mightily, but I was able to move my right arm. I wouldn't have to cancel tomorrow's appointments after all. Then the muscles in my back barked, and I was in pain again. A different pain, admittedly, but pain all the same. When you start cataloging the differences between throbbing aches and stabbing aches, you're in trouble, period.

Mario and Trudy looked at Ricardo in amazed and undisguised admiration. "Where'd you learn how to do that?" Trudy asked.

"Ah." Ricardo waved one manicured hand at the pair. "I used to be a paramedic. In another life."

"Dios mío." Mario's eyes widened. "You're reincarnated?"

I shook my head. I couldn't believe I'd let this doofus talk me into anything, his wife being my best friend notwithstanding. Trudy flushed to match her lips and nails—raspberry red with embarrassment; it felt nice to pass some of *that* around. It was also nice to know that while love had made Trudy blind, it hadn't deafened her as well. Ricardo was regarding Mario with an air of condescending patience. "No, Big M, I was a paramedic before I found myself, before I realized my mission was to create beauty, instead of to heal."

Leave it to Ricardo to glorify doing hair above saving lives. He almost had me believing the swill. I was tasting bile again. I cleared my throat.

Suddenly, Ricardo's eyes hardened, and he bored a serious look through each of us in turn. "That revelation was careless of me. I want you to forget you know about that; it would ruin my image."

He was right about that. The legend of Ricardo was that he came from a moneyed, aristocratic family from Mexico City and had been the lover of every Mexican president's wife before he left to seek his fortune in our humble town north of the border. I knew the truth (except the paramedic thing), that he'd grown up in the poorest neighborhood in South San Antonio.

Orphaned at thirteen, he'd worked his way through high school doing anything for money while living like a transient, eventually to become one of the richest businessmen in the city. For the longest time, I could never figure out why he wouldn't be proud of what he'd accomplished. But, of course, I'd been naive. Older and more cynical, I now realized he might not have accomplished what he had without the legend. San Antonio society matrons didn't like the idea of a hardworking southside boy doing their hair and charging $200-plus for the favor.

"Reyn?" he demanded, breaking into thoughts I hadn't realized had drifted so far.

"What? Uh, sure, Ricardo. Not a word." Flexing my stiff fingers, I nodded distractedly along with Trudy's and Mario's eagerly bobbing heads.

"I can always trust you, Reyn." Ricardo smiled as he ran a finger along my jawline. "You're a good girl. Can't run a business worth a black bean, but you're a good girl."

"Gee, thanks, Ricardo," I huffed, planting my hands on my hips with barely a wince at my back's clutching response. "Just because I don't have my own personal empire doesn't mean I'm not a good businesswoman. Maybe I don't want to have twenty-five stores. Maybe I like life simple."

Ricardo laughed in pure disbelief. "*Pobrecita!* Maybe if you started sleeping with your clients, you'd have an empire of your own."

"No, thank you." I grimaced, more at the thought of him sleeping with the crones I'd seen in his chair than at me doing anything with any one of my customers.

Ricardo shot an amused glance at Mario before he looked back at me. "I don't blame you, Reyn."

I bit my tongue to keep from laughing. After all, I had to live with Mario and Trudy nearly every day. Ricardo's visits were few and far between.

"Maybe I'll have you run the salons when I retire," Ricardo offered with a strange light in his angular amaretto-colored eyes.

"I'll be too old to do you any good by then, Ricardo. You forget how well I know you; you live for that business. You're not giving it up until you have one foot in the grave." I dismissed his fantasy with a flip of my hand, then I winced. Even that hurt.

"Reyn, it will be much sooner than you think, so consider it. I'm serious." He glided over to my three-tiered tray of tools, fingering the pair of scissors and tapping his sleek black Italian loafer on the floor, while looking out the nearby window. "There's no one I would trust more to make sure my customers are taken care of while I yacht around the Mediterranean for the rest of my life. I have enough properly saved and wisely invested so that you could lose money with the salons and it won't matter."

"Gee, thanks," I muttered.

"Need a boat boy?" Mario chipped in hopefully.

Ricardo smiled lightly but kept his gaze focused out the window.

Something about the secret in his eyes made me uncomfortable. I wasn't sure if the shadow I saw there was sorrow or defeat. Perhaps he was tired of building his way up from scratch; he had sacrificed a lot—no close friends, no wife and kids. Maybe he wanted to take some time off to explore all he'd missed. Or was something more sinister at work here? I glanced over at him again and decided I wasn't buying. Ricardo always did have a flair for the dramatic that complemented his selfish streak. Here I was suffering with a killer back, and he had me worrying about *him*. Enough was enough. I was tired and wanted to go upstairs to my bed and crash.

"Why'd you come by, Ricardo?"

He turned to look at me, the half-smile still on his full, sensual lips. His striking black eyebrows arched.

"You mean, besides to offer you the chance of a life-time?"

"Besides that." In the mirror, I watched as his finger-tips toyed with the sharp tip of the scissors, then pressed it into the pad of his thumb. Hard. The cuticle of his nail turned white. I watched for blood. Maybe he wasn't as cool as he appeared on the surface. What was going on?

"I need to borrow one of your brushes," Ricardo answered. "The new metal round with the pick, for a special client I have coming in tonight."

"You must have a thousand of those at your shops," I pointed out mulishly, suddenly tired of trying to figure out his mercurial moods and odd innuendos.

"Ah, no," Ricardo said, frowning. "The supplier, he got me angry, hiking prices only for my stores and not for others. I refused to buy anything else from him or use his products, yet he does carry the only metal rounds that really work on certain hair types."

"I thought you'd stopped styling."

"I still have about a half-dozen of the old clients who started when I started. I reward loyalty. They keep it quiet, otherwise I'd have hundreds demanding the same treatment. How exhausting that would be."

With an affected sigh, he shook his perfectly proportioned head of burnished black hair, thick and brushed back off his forehead to flow smoothly and curl at his earlobes. It was a style I well knew was cultivated for the best impression. Medium-length dark hair on men bespoke ultimate success and an even-tempered personality, according to a Yale-sponsored survey that was well circulated among hairstylists.

Out of the corner of my eye, I saw Mario studying it with tangible envy.

"I just sold my last one at the front this morning, and the rep won't be here until Wednesday. But you can take mine," I offered, heading gingerly to my supply tray. "I really don't use it as often as I used to when they first came out."

Ricardo stepped back to give me access to the tray but intentionally kept within my space. It irritated me. I'd spurned his advances years ago when we'd first met, and he'd never stopped—in unspoken ways—trying to prove how irresistible he was. I guess he thought one day I'd give in to his charm. The truth was, I considered him too slick to be attractive, too put-together to be my kind of man. I guess I like my men rougher and tougher. Give me a country cowboy over a couture king any day. I thought of Ricardo as a big brother, a friend, a mentor. He had given me my first job in the business a decade ago. I'd do a lot for him, but not *that*, and not because of his charm. I'd help him because I respected him and I owed him.

Trudy led Mario to the sink, wet his hair, and squirted about half the bottle of shampoo onto his head. I had visions of unending bubbles cascading over the sink and onto the newly cleaned wood floor. Of course, I had more important things to worry about, like my back, and getting everyone out of there so I could go to bed. I kept casting baleful glances at the floor nevertheless.

"Reyn, this is a mess," Ricardo observed with disdain as he began going through my cabinets. A blow-dryer fell out, bouncing off his shoulder, the end of the cord catching on his belt loop on its descent. "Everything so clean and neat on the outside, yet here, behind the scenes, complete chaos. You disappoint me." He plucked the metal tooth of the connection off his burgundy silk trousers and let it fall to the ground with a clatter.

I shrugged. It hurt. I glared. I wasn't about to explain my lifestyle to this prima donna of perfection. He'd never understand that I liked to shove stuff under beds and into cabinets. What were dust ruffles and cabinet doors for, anyway?

Ricardo had moved around the cabinets to the door that hid the utility area where I kept brushes to be cleaned and towels to be washed. I also kept the door closed. Another mess hidden.

"If the cabinets grossed you out, I wouldn't go in there," I warned.

"Normally, I would take your advice," Ricardo said from behind the cabinets. "But I need that brush. Now. You know how I despise tardiness, and I'm close to committing that sin."

Just as I realized my supply tray did not, in fact, hold the brush in question, I heard the door open, a conde-scending groan, and then his triumphant "Ah." I was in the process of straightening inch by painful inch when I felt Ricardo's trousers brush by my hip.

"You're a true *amiga*, Reyn. I owe you one."

By the time I'd straightened enough to look at the doorway, he was down the hall. I stepped into the cloud of Polo that followed ten steps behind him and wrinkled my nose at its cloying tanginess.

"No, I owed you double for your last favor," I yelled as the front door swished open.

"*Bueno*, so you still owe me one," he said as the door clunked behind him.

I turned my gaze to Trudy, who had, with only a small lake of bubbles at her feet, washed all the goop out of Mario's hair. She tenderly dabbed at his dripping tresses with a towel, as if they'd been critically wounded.

Resisting the urge to roll my eyes, I smiled instead. "All done? See you later."

Trudy shoved the swell of her raspberry lower lip out in a pout. "I thought we might stay, have a glass of merlot, talk."

"Oh, no. Your husband has done enough in one day. Sharing a glass of wine might require EMS."

Mario issued a small wail of protest. "Your back is *not* my fault."

"You're right, Mario, we can trace it to when I said yes. Now, scram."

"Ah, don't be that way, Reyn. Let us at least get you settled in, help you up the stairs," Mario insisted as he heaved his semi-flabby bottom up out of the chair. I wondered, not for the first time, why my best pal had chosen this man as her husband. Made me downright terrified of the Big L. What had my father told me when I was fourteen? *Reyn-Reyn, you can't choose who you fall in love with, so let go, and leave it up to fate.* This is not a good feeling for a control freak. Geez! No telling whom my funky heart would pick out. So far, I was still waiting to find out. Looking at Mario now, I was eternally grateful that my true love was still a mystery. Certainly, my Prince Charming couldn't be any worse than this?

I waved my hand toward the front door, and, grumbling all the way, they finally left me in peace, locking the door behind them.

My mind returned to Ricardo. Why had he really come? Did he have a hidden agenda, or was I psycho-analyzing something that I should take at face value?

A whine—this one from the backyard and of the canine variety—called me out of my reverie. I hobble-slid

to the door at the opposite end of the salon, which led
to home. It wasn't until after I'd let the dogs in, fed
them, then dragged my own dogs up the stairs and collapsed into bed that I remembered. The brush in the
utility room was the one with the plastic pick that, in a
fit of frugality, I'd sharpened to clean other brushes and
tools in my salon. Oh, well, too late now.

If I'd only known how right I was.

And how wrong life was about to be.

two

SOMEONE STUCK THE ELECTRIC SCREWDRIVER INTO
my right ear and drilled, the motor pulsing with a
strangely familiar, regular rhythm. *Pause, buzz, pause.*
Adrenaline spurted into my veins, making me realize
the urgency of needing to do something. *What?* I asked
myself through the fog infiltrating my mind. *Get away
from the drill,* my brilliant self replied.

I nestled deeper into my plush pillow. But the drill
didn't go away. No telling how many times the damned
phone rang before I realized it *was* the phone. As soon
as I did, I reached for the handset on the nightstand and
collapsed back onto the bed in pain. Someone had taken
the drill to my back.

The phone kept ringing.

What kind of person dreams about electric drills?
Carpenters? Building contractors? Hard-up women?
Hard-up women dreaming about carpenters?

Setting my teeth on my lower lip to offer pain a momentary distraction from my back, I sat up, again reached
for the receiver, collared it, and fell back onto the mattress.

"Urgh," I moaned, squeezing my eyes shut against the crimp in the cramp in my back. "Yul-lo?"

"Reyn," a masculine voice, made nearly eerie by its soft weakness, breathed in my ear.

"Hello?" I demanded strongly now, ready to call my fictitious husband "Claude" into action. He always seemed to get the cranks off the phone but quick.

"Reyn." The voice, weaker, rang a few familiar bells in my head this time.

"Ricardo?" I peered at the clock across the bedroom but couldn't make out the glowing digital numbers. It looked like 33:44:22 to me. I blinked, and it became 234:432. One of the dogs put her forepaws on the bed next to me and licked my face. Oh, great, dog spit would clear things up right away.

"Reyn. I need your help."

A thread of fear and the whisper of resignation in his voice sent me shooting up in bed despite my back. "My help?" I parroted dumbly. "In the middle of the night?"

"Reyn . . ."

"Ricardo!" I yelled, waking all the dogs. I could sense their attention in the pitch black. "What do you need help with? Where are you?"

I heard a peculiar sucking sound and wondered if Ricardo were drunk. He certainly didn't sound like his usual sober, arrogant self. Although I'd never seen him have an alcoholic drink, much less overindulge, I didn't know him all that well anymore, and I certainly didn't know what he did with his "valued and loyal" customers, one of whom he'd been meeting last night, tonight, whatever day and time it was. I squinted at the clock again.

"It's late. Too late." His voice had dropped to a near

whisper. "I just want you to remember what I said today. You get the salons—"

"You win the lottery after all, Ricardo?" Having decided he was indeed high on something, I was waking up to my smart mouth. "Listen Reyn . . . *peligroso* . . . to wonder." He paused with a tortured groan, and I tried not to think what had caused that. Or who. My hard-up-woman imagination filled in the blanks as he let out another heavy sigh before saying, "Be careful."

I knew that comment was meant for his companion, who was doing something likely featured on the Playboy Channel, so I didn't respond. He was quiet for a moment, and I thought he'd hung up or perhaps had been otherwise distracted. Then he whispered, "Take care of what's mine. The proof . . . it's there . . . in the pudding . . ."

It wasn't like Ricardo to use a corny cliché, but I didn't give it a passing thought. Then.

Suddenly, I was sleepy again, and my back was clutching up. "Ricardo, I appreciate the sentiment, but I have my own business to run. I like my little business. It's not much, but it's mine. And there was that 'black bean' comment of yours . . ."

A wheeze interrupted my independent-woman lecture. "Promise . . . you'll . . ." he choked out.

I wondered for the first time if Ricardo were sick. I might as well humor him. He probably wouldn't remember he'd even called by morning.

"Sure, Ricardo. I'll take care of everything for you. Now, I've gotta go get some beauty sleep. I need a helluva lot more just to look half as good as you do."

I waited for his reply and got none. Patience isn't one of my virtues and certainly isn't a word I even understand in the middle of the night with canine halitosis breathing on me, particularly while talking to a drunk, high, crazy, or horny once-upon-a-time boss, while my back was thrown out.

"Good night, Ricardo. Sleep tight."

I threw the handset back into its cradle, eased gently back into the bed (this seemed less excruciating than my earlier flop), and pulled the covers up to my chin. By the time I shut my eyelids, I was drifting back to Dreamland, hoping to avoid the tool-wielding Sandman this time, unless he had some X-rated plans for that tool that involved me.

The next time the phone rang, no dreams interfered, and I was able to recognize the ring for what it was. My eyelids wouldn't peel open, though, and I had to roll over onto my side to do the blind man's grope for the handset. My back felt pretty darn good, I noted with pleasure. That extra slab of Ben Gay, applied with a back scratcher stabbed into a sponge, must have done the trick.

"Hello," I answered cheerily.

An unfamiliar baritone rumbled some indistinguishable rush of words into my ear, made more indistinguishable by the fact that Beaujolais was sticking her big dog tongue into my other ear. I swatted her away just as I heard, "And who is this?"

My spirits plummeted. An anonymous crank first thing in the morning. That was worse than being awakened by a familiar one in the middle of the night. I sat up gingerly and called in my invisible reinforcements.

"Claude!" I screeched, half into the handset and half out. Pretty convincing, I thought.

"Please tone it down, ma'am," warned the caller with a decidedly impolite inflection on the polite term. "Your name's Claude?"

"No. Claude's my honey."

"Can you tell me, was it you or Claude who talked to someone at Ricardo's Realm on Broadway last night?"

Words caught in my throat for a moment. This was not a voice I recognized as someone who worked for Ricardo—too much bass, if you get my meaning. He never hired anyone who'd compete for the affections of the ladies. Yet there was something professional about his tone.

I'm rarely at a loss for words, so I recovered quickly. "Who wants to know?"

I think my directness set him back for a moment. There was a bit of a pause where I hoped I'd persuaded him to set the receiver back in the cradle. No such luck. "I need to know who called Ricardo last night, ma'am."

"Who's 'I'?" By now I was pissed off, but so was he, even if he was trying to mask it in politeness. I was beginning to get the hint that this was no crank caller. I wondered what he was trying to sell.

He blew a big breath that sounded like a hurricane in my right ear. "Let me talk to Claude. Please, ma'am."

Oh, a male chauvinist salesman. I'm not sure that was better than a crank caller. "He's not available at the moment. And if you're selling something, we're not interested."

"The only thing I'm selling you, ma'am"—he nearly choked on that last word—"is a trip to the Bexar County cooler unless you begin to cooperate."

A trip as in vacation? Something about the place rang a bell. A new resort? One of those chic restaurants over at the trendy Quarry Market shopping complex? But I was digressing. Back to the subject at hand. Who was this guy? And what was this insistent, hard-sell attitude?

Where did he think he was calling, the Bronx? This was friendly San Antonio, Texas, mister. Wait—how did he know Ricardo called me, anyway? Had telephone tracing technology become so common that any telemarketer could get hold of it? I felt fresh anger building. There are few things in life I hate more than telemarketers. I looked around for a pen to write down the company name. All I could find were some fingernail clippers and a Q-tip. I poised the little cotton wand like a pen—hoping the pose would make me somehow sound more threatening—and asked, "And with *whom* am I supposed to be cooperating?"

"Ma'am." He sighed heavily as if *I* were the one who woke *him* up. "I apologize. I identified myself at the beginning of our conversation, but it's, ah, early. Your 'whom' is the police. SAPD. I'm afraid you're *required* to cooperate with me."

Oh, *that* Bexar County cooler.

Just as my mouth fell open, "I Feel Good" screeched from across the bedroom. James Brown on my customized alarm, designed to shock me out of bed in the right frame of mind every morning.

. . . you know that I would now . . . do, do, do-do, do-do-do . . .

"That Claude now?" he asked.

I ignored his heavy sarcasm, not only because I'd been caught in a lie—by the cops, no less—but because my mind was galloping off in a thousand different directions, and I was trying to keep up with eyelids that still refused to open fully.

. . . I feel good . . .

"Sounds like someone had a good night," he observed. Could you despise someone you didn't even know? I wondered. Someone with this deep and rich a voice? Even politely pissy, he sounded pretty damned sexy. With a flush that seemed to precede conscious thought, I remembered him blowing into my ear—more accurately, into the phone and into my ear, and, to be fair, it really was a sigh of frustration. But if a pissed-off sigh was that good, just imagine what an amorous sigh would do to me.

"Well, it wasn't me," I snapped, suddenly irritated with the implications of my own thoughts as well as those in his tone. He was sneaky, this detective, couching his pointed sarcasm in ma'amy politeness. Plus, I didn't like the fact that he could evidently read my hormones long-distance. "How do you know I was talking to Ricardo last night?"

"Ma'am, I'm a detective; I'm paid to figure out these things. Plus, when we got here, Ricardo was holding the phone, and your number's the one it rang on redial."

"Great investigative work," I muttered with a frown at the image of Ricardo sitting in his office chair, snoring, holding the phone for hours. Had he been drunk enough to pass out? I hoped he'd gotten dressed after his lady friend left. Maybe he'd called so I could drive him home. What a jerk I was.

How *right* I was, and I still didn't know the half of it.

"And why didn't Ricardo hang up the phone?" I finally asked, hating to hear that my vain friend, so concerned with appearances, would end up with his customers titillated by an embarrassment in the *Express-News*'s gossip columns.

"Because he's dead."

As I punched "end" on the phone, I looked around through the pale yellow morning light streaming through the windows at three pairs of eyes staring at me in questioning sympathy. The dogs always sensed my moods but must have been dumbfounded by the mixture of horror, grief, disbelief, and guilt swimming around in my head, clogging my throat, and congealing in my stomach right then. All they knew was that it was something they'd better pay attention to.

"Girls, Ricardo's dead." I winced at the finality of my words.

Beaujolais, recognizing me in a weak moment, snuck a paw onto the bed and licked my hand sympathetically as she inched the rest of her eighty-five-pound body onto the mattress. As if I wouldn't notice. I noticed, all right, but right then, I didn't much care.

"What if I had talked to him longer, really tried to understand what he was saying to me? Would he be dead now? Why did he call me? Why didn't he call 911? Why didn't *I* call 911?"

Two blinks and a yawn didn't qualify as an answer, but somehow it was comforting.

That's why I had dogs—they were someone to talk to. I have no respect for people who talk to themselves. With a mouth like mine, I had to use it regularly, or I was afraid the words would come out in an indistinguishable rush to the first person I ran across in the morning. I consider my dogs a community service.

The two youngsters, Chardonnay and Cabernet, three-year-old sisters, yellow and black respectively, followed me into the bathroom. Their mother stretched out on my pillows.

I stripped off my oversize Lyle Lovett "Fat Babies Have No Pride" nightshirt and jumped into the shower before the water warmed up. I figured the blast of ice water would serve me right for choosing sleep over sticking on the phone with my friend . . . former friend . . . *dead* friend. I put my face into the stream from the showerhead, letting it take my tears down the drain. I cried through the shampoo and sobbed over my leg shave. I eschewed touching up my bikini line as too dangerous in my current frame of mind. I stepped out of the shower, feeling cleaner on the outside but without managing a Pontius Pilate on the inside.

After toweling off quickly, I pulled on some of my utilitarian cotton panties and unmatching—frayed, faded, toad-green polyester (hey, it was on sale!)—bra. I thought of the times Trudy had berated me for wearing ugly underwear. No one but the dogs see my underwear, I'd argued. She told me it didn't matter who saw it, you knew what you had on, and it changed your whole attitude on life. Her theory is that women who wear sexy underwear move sexily, thus radiating sensuality. Translated in my case, it meant I clomped around, moving like my plain yet useful panties, radiating—no doubt—pragmatism. I told her they just got covered up with clothes, anyway, so if they did the job, their looks didn't matter. She told me I was a disgrace to the beauty business, that beauty should come from within. I told her she was right about the latter but that I didn't consider underwear to be within.

Only half-naked now, I gently tugged open my closet door to consider my footwear. Or, rather, bootwear. I wear nothing but boots—unless I'm out walking the girls, that is. Then nearly three hundred pounds of dog requires some athletic shoe traction. All other times, though, I'm booted. I have forty-seven pairs of boots. My sister Pecan calls me Cowgirl Imelda. She ought to be more understanding, considering it's partly her fault. As a child, I had to wear all the holey shoes and scuffed-up boots handed down from my four older siblings, two brothers and two sisters. I never owned a new pair of any footwear, which sparked in me a burning desire for a brand-new, shiny pair of boots—a desire that was not fulfilled until I left home at eighteen.

But that one pair was not enough. I'm sure I have an obsession that would qualify some enterprising psychologist for a million-dollar federal grant.

And I don't care.

I must point out that San Antonio is not really a cowboy-boot-wearing town. Not like Houston and Dallas, that is, where every third person has on a Stetson and Justins or, depending on what part of town you're in, Luccheses or Dan Posts. It's not like that here—except in February, rodeo season, when every high-society babe pulls out her alligator pointy-toes—so my year-round boot fashion did sort of stand out.

I considered the carefully arranged (the only part of my life that was organized was my boot collection), custom-made three shelves of leather and various other animal and amphibian skins. What was appropriate for a crime scene? For mourning a friend? Plain, not lace-ups, as they might convey the wrong message. The black lizard pointy-toed gals with the silver trims beckoned, but I surely didn't want the blowhard cop thinking I'd dressed up for him. Those indigo maroon kangaroo numbers called from the second story, but I ignored them. After all, why was I letting his fantasy-inspiring voice determine my choices when he probably had a doughnut overhang above his belt and considered his gun proof of some deeply hidden masculinity? He had been exceedingly polite when my misunderstanding had tested his patience, but that didn't win many points with me.

I chose a somber pair of Justin Ropers and yanked them on.

The phone shrilled again. I stared at it; the dogs stared at me. I was expected down at Ricardo's main salon on Broadway to talk to Officer Charming, "Asap," he'd instructed into my stunned silence. I hate people who turn acronyms into words, as if I didn't have enough reasons to dislike this guy, anyway. Calling with the news that Ricardo was dead and waking me up to do it were numbers one and two on the growing list.

Maybe the caller was he, saying I wasn't required after all. They'd wanted me to arrive to give the positive ID. They knew who he was; Ricardo had been the object of media attention enough over the years for most of the city to know him on sight. But there were "procedures," the copper had said, brooking no argument. There were a dozen people closer to Ricardo than I was, who saw him on a daily basis, who could give the ID, but that's not a referral someone would thank me for later. I did have a business to worry about, after all, a business in which appearance and discretion were just about everything.

"Hello." I picked up after the tenth ring, giving in to curiosity.

"Guess your back's not any better this morning, huh?" Trudy surmised from my snarly tone.

"It's not that," I began as the tears resurfaced, my mood swinging from grumpy to grief-stricken in a second. "It's that . . ."

"Now, Reyn, don't be embarrassed about last night. I won't tell a soul."

Sure, I thought, *you with the biggest mouth west of*

the Brazos River. Then I felt immediately guilty that I'd harbor an ill thought about a friend lucky enough to still be living. "No, it's not the Mario Hair Debacle. It's something worse."

"Worse? What could be worse? I spent another hour at home last night getting out all the tangles."

"Oh, Trudy." I tempered my tone. Now was not the time to lose my temper. When had getting angry with her ever worked? I considered the most delicate way to tell her. The silence stretched on.

"Spit it out, sister." Trudy wasn't big on patience, either.

Okay, she'd asked for it.

"Ricardo's dead."

A squeal and a thud were the only responses I got.

three

IF I HADN'T RECOGNIZED THE SQUEAL ON THE OTHER
end of the line as Trudy's standard prelude to a faint, I
would've seriously wondered if another one of my friends
had died while talking to me over the phone. As it was, I realized I hadn't been considerate enough, hadn't asked if she
was sitting down before I blurted out the truth. I knew very
well she was prone to fainting. I called her name a few times
into the phone and then Mario's name. I even yelled to her
that I was wearing ugly, mismatched underwear, thinking
that might drive straight to her subconscious and rile her up.
No such luck. I reluctantly gave up. I had places to go, a
dead friend to identify. I'd have to get back to Trudy later.

I pulled on a black sleeveless bodysuit and a long
straight jeans skirt. With a whistle to the dogs, I ran down
the stairs, accompanied by their tapping nails on the hardwood steps which made each descent sound like an indoor
hailstorm. I opened the door, and they filed out in various
stages of enthusiasm. I planted my right Justin below
Beaujolais's tail to push her out, slamming the door shut
and flipping the dead bolt.

After passing the refrigerator without a twinge, I stopped at my Bunn to grind some coffee beans and do the three-minute brew. I told myself it was to fortify me for the task that was to come, but the fact was, I was addicted. I can't think of anything that would make me give up the first cup of coffee in the morning. Except maybe that vitamin salesman who'd moved in four doors down. Man-oh-man, did he have some sexual charisma. Of course, we were destined never to meet professionally, he was bald, and I wasn't ever buying vitamins—waste of money if there ever was one. I really wasn't the sort of cookie-baking neighbor who could just stop by with a plate hot out of the oven, so my only hope of meeting him was if one of my dogs left a calling card on his lawn, and that wasn't the best of circumstances in which to start a romance.

With that downer adding to my depression, I climbed into my seven-year-old white Chevy crew-cab truck and made the five-minute drive to Ricardo's main salon. The sight of the gold foil sign bearing his name didn't make me want to cry as I'd anticipated; it made me numb. A uniformed policewoman—uh, police officer; my New Year's resolution is to try to be more politically correct—stopped me as I turned into the parking lot.

"I'm sorry, ma'am. You can't come in here today."

"I'm Reyn Marten Sawyer. One of your detectives called and asked me to come to, uh, identify the . . ." I cleared my throat, only to have my voice sound more like fingernails on a chalkboard than it had before. "I . . . I was a friend of Ricardo's," I finished clumsily.

She glanced down at her notebook. "We were told to expect someone named Claude."

"Very funny," I muttered under my breath.

Her porcine eyes narrowed at me. She planed a pair

of sturdy fists on equally sturdy hips clad in that ultra-flattering blue SAPD polyester. "Excuse me?"

I cleared my throat again. I was beginning to sound like I had a problem with hairballs. "Claude. That's my nickname."

"Oh," she said, suddenly disinterested, and waved me through. I saw her talking into her walkie-talkie as I pulled the truck forward.

Perversely, I was disappointed at her acceptance of my think-on-my-feet answer. I wanted to give my brain another test to distract me from what awaited behind the double smoked-glass doors of Ricardo's Realm.

The parking lot was full of San Antonio police cars and dark Crown Victorias which either also belonged to police or were an odd coincidence among early-morning customers. I drove around for a minute before I settled on a space between two trees. Ricardo had taught me that anything associated with your name would reflect back on you, and his parking lot was a fine example. He'd planted expensive full-grown oaks and fragrant mountain laurels, and instead of putting in rows of parking spaces, he'd slipped them between trees at odd, aesthetically pleasing angles. It gave the impression of a trip to the park rather than a beauty salon. It also provided cover if you were leaving after just having your eyebrows and mustache waxed.

I got out of the truck and locked it. The police presence wouldn't deter a car thief. The ones in San Antonio had no fear and weren't subtle enough to recognize intimidation.

As I walked slowly to the salon, I looked at it as the police might. A four-thousand-square-foot box, all shiny gold metal and dark, tinted glass. Even the concrete outside the shop had been stained black. This was where I'd had my first job out of high school. I'd come from the country to the big city to go to college with a measly scholarship and no money. I'd gotten my cosmetology training back when I was still living in Dime Box, my hometown, but hadn't had any experience beyond giving too-tight perms, pouring blue rinses, and teasing old ladies' hair to twice the height of their heads. Ricardo was legendary even back in Dime Box. I knew he didn't hire anyone with less than five years' experience. Ten was the average. He was a perfectionist and a brutal taskmaster. Hairstylists were usually independent contractors, all working under the same roof, paying for rent and maybe pooling for a receptionist, but most had to pay for their own supplies and managed their own time. Not in Ricardo's shops. His stylists were employees, and starters took pretty low pay for the honor. But I wasn't easily intimidated. Gran always told me I had more guts than a sausage factory and just as much sense. Not a terribly flattering portrait, but those guts got me the job and out of Dime Box. Either that or the fact that Ricardo wanted in my pants. Either way, it paid for my business degree at Our Lady of the Lake University. And Ricardo got more than he bargained for businesswise . . . and less in the personal department. I think it was a fair trade.

The memories made me misty again.

Sucking in a deep breath, I yanked on the gold-plated door handle and nearly fell on my butt.

The heavy door suddenly swung out, and as I stumbled and fumbled to get my Justins under me, I looked up and saw a pair of jeans-clad thighs that made me feel suddenly and intensely feminine and vulnerable. I resisted the melting sensation south of my navel as inappropriate at a murder scene, but my lets still turned rubbery just when I needed them most. Grabbing the door handle for support, I straightened and felt my back tighten up. So much for the Ben Gay. I bit the inside of my cheek, finally regained my balance, and met the eyes that belonged to the thighs.

Arctic blue. I immediately thought of the ice packs in my freezer. Then I saw the burn behind the ice and revised it to dry ice. Icy and smoking at the same time. Those eyes and the sardonic turn of his lips—an intriguing mixture of thin upper and full lower—were just enough to immediately dissipate the mush in my gut and make my hackles rise. I just wished he could see them. Visible hackles were just one of many things I envied in my dogs.

"So, where's Claude?"

Damn.

I'd found the prince of anti-charm who'd offered me the all-expenses-paid vacation behind bars.

I reminded myself I wasn't supposed to like him. It was really too bad. On the phone, he'd had a natural tendency toward arrogant smart-ass. In person, he looked like he could make a woman undress just by thinking about it. My gaze flicked across his broad chest and flat abdomen. He'd never downed a doughnut in his life. It would've made things a helluva lot easier if he'd had a Krispy Kreme addiction.

Not that someone upstairs planned to make my life anything but more difficult over the next few days.

Steeling myself against my raging hormones, I refused to acknowledge the knowing look in those dry-ice eyes and stared right back. "Oh, Claude. He couldn't make it."

"That's a shame. I was looking forward to meeting him."

"Sorry I can't say the same for him."

We played another game of stare-down chicken. I'm happy to say that he looked away first. I'm sorry to say that he looked away to give me a toe-to-top eyeball appraisal.

"You don't match your voice. At all." The rumble in his voice hid any connotations that may have helped me figure out whether that was a good thing or a bad thing.

He did. Match his voice, that is. I wasn't about to give him a compliment, though. In fact, I'd finally noticed something on him that was less than perfect—his hairstyle. The hair itself was pretty awesome—a thick, rich blond with a rusty undertone that might have been the inspiration for a chemical color we use called Sahara Sunset. His wasn't colored; I could see it beginning to gray rather attractively at the temples and wave around the ends because it was too long. Now, if I had graying, overgrown hair, it would look frumpy; on him, it was just sexy. Go figure. I couldn't tell whether it was an overgrown version of the trendy ultra-short cut with a front flip, which would tell me he was confident and egotistical, or a poorly done medium-length cut, which connoted an intelligent conservative who tended to be narrow-minded. Hmmm. Was he a salon man too busy to get a trim or a cheapskate too confident to worry about style?

Usually, I can read people's hair a lot easier than this. I think pheromones were muddling my brain.

"No," he said, clearly baiting me. "I was expecting someone quite different."

I itched to ask, but I knew he wanted me to, so I didn't scratch. Instead, I fell back on propriety, holding out my hand. "I'm Reyn Marten Sawyer. And you are?"

As he took my hand in his, his brows quirked up, and I could see I'd surprised him. I guessed he was accustomed to using his sex appeal to control all his conversations with women. Ha. Gotcha.

The silence stretched on for a moment before he finally closed his fingers around mine. "Jackson Scythe, ma'am. Thank you for coming so quickly." His grip was strong and confident and held my hand a second too long, which also made it arrogant.

I let him hold on that extra second, which made me a pushover. So much for the gotcha.

"Hey, Lieutenant, that your wit?" called a voice from inside the salon. "Get her in here so we can bag this guy."

Jackson Scythe let go of my hand and splayed his tan, long-fingered, ultra-masculine hand—which felt good and looked even better—on the door, opening it wider to allow my entry. As I took a tentative step forward, letting my imagination wander to ways he might use those hands, he passed me a brown paper bag he'd had tucked into the back waistband of his jeans. It was warm.

"What's this?"

"Barf bag."

I tried to hand it back to him. "No, really, you're not all that bad."

That earned a double quirk of the eyebrows and I could've sworn a twitch in a smile muscle or two. But he wouldn't let me score the last point. "You ever seen a dead body?"

"No," I admitted with an instant rock dropping into my stomach and the realization that the verbal sparring and my naughty daydreams had only delayed the inevitable.

"Then you better keep it."

He walked into the room, letting the door go, and it was either follow or get spanked by a hundred pounds of glass. The activity level inside the salon was reminiscent of Ricardo's busiest days. Tears pricked at the corners of my eyes again as I saw the action was of uniformed cops milling officiously, plainclothes detectives searching through supply trays, and technicians spreading fingerprint dust over all the gold chrome and glass. A jar of dust spilled out onto the polished black marble floor. I didn't see a body.

"Over here," Scythe called from the doorwary to Ricardo's office. As I walked slowly to where he stood, I drew in my mind's eye the room as I remembered it. Rectangular, probably a thousand square feet, it took up nearly a quarter of the salon. It was a cold, sleek, high-fashion, soulless room that reflected more of his "image" than of the real Ricardo. It had floor-to-ceiling glass on the outside wall, floor-to-ceiling mirrors on the remaining walls. The gleaming black marble floors looked slick and seamless enough to be a venue for the Olympic figure-skating team. His gold chrome (at least, I thought it was chrome; knowing Ricardo, it could've been gold plate) and black leather styling chair, for the exclusive styling seminars he held there, stood alone against one marbleized wall. His gold chrome and glass-topped desk, Scandinavian-style sling leather chair, and several sleek black leather love seats took up the opposite wall. He had a telephone on a black chrome and glass table in each of the four corners of the room and one isolated in the middle of the room. I never had figured that out. I wondered now which phone he'd used to talk to me.

I was about to find out.

Scythe stepped back as I approached. The morning

light through the smoky glass turned the whole room an odd, otherworldly, metallic silver, and there in the middle of the floor was Ricardo, sprawled facedown, telephone receiver in hand, with a very familiar brush sticking out of the middle of his back.

four

"MY BRUSH!" I CROAKED.

Okay, so it wasn't the smartest statement I've ever made. The cops might never have known that I owned the murder weapon. My fingerprints weren't in any criminal data bank. I really was going to have to work on this impulse honesty thing.

"That's *your* brush?"

I could see I'd surprised Lieutenant Jackson Scythe for the fourth time that morning. I allowed myself a small shot of pleasure at that thought, not that I was keeping count or anything.

"At least, I think it's mine." Uh-oh. I'd backed up too late. My qualifier only intensified his interest.

His eyes roamed over my hands, my bodysuit, my skirt, my boots, in a detailed survey—different from his earlier perusal. He was using his cop's eyes now, after using his man's eyes to appraise me earlier. I swear, it was laser vision—sharp and hot, cataloging things on me I know I'd never recognize. I had nothing to hide, but I took a few steps closer to Ricardo to escape the scrutiny.

As I did, I caught sight of movement above me, and I looked up at the ceiling, where I met my own eyes in a mirror. This was new since I'd been in the office. An entire mirrored ceiling? It afforded a better view of Ricardo's body, although I doubted that had been his intention.

But what had? I wondered.

Even with my attention turned upward, I received no divine reply, just heavy, silent attention from the guy next to me, who carried a gun, an attitude, and barf bags. All I was getting here was more questions, no answers, and a lot of hassle. Digesting that last thought sent a shot of guilt through me. How could I resent this with a bloody friend lying at my feet?

After I issued a cleansing sigh, my eyes left the reflection and returned to the real thing. I was surprised that the sight of Ricardo didn't make me as tearful as the police-ridden salon did. Somehow, I could feel his spirit gone from his body a lot easier than I could imagine it gone from the place.

Scythe's attention was palpable behind me. "What makes you think the brush is yours?"

I found I couldn't turn around, couldn't let my eyes leave Ricardo's body. I considered tap-dancing around the truth, but that had never been my style—more because I'm not organized enough to keep up with a string of white lies than because of some lofty morality. My gran calls it Reyn's Lazy Righteousness. She claims you've got to be real smart and willing to work hard to be a good liar and not get caught. I'm not sure which of the two she doesn't think I qualify for—I'm afraid to ask. If you have the impression my family is opinionated, you're right. They make me look downright diplomatic.

"I think it might be mine because Ricardo came by my salon yesterday to borrow a brush just like this," I finally answered.

My hand moved in the direction of the brush, reaching to pluck it up and examine it, until I realized what I'd been about to do. I recoiled with a shiver of revulsion.

"Why would he borrow a brush when he has twenty-five salons and surely hundreds of brushes of his own?"

My gaze glued to the blood congealing around the base of the brush, I repeated the reason Ricardo had given me. I tried to ignore Scythe's powerful skepticism which drew an invisible question mark in the space between us.

"So who was he meeting?" Scythe asked.

"He didn't say and I didn't ask."

Crouching down, but not reaching out this time, I studied the brush. Same brand as mine. Used, not new. The pick was buried in his back all the way up to the shaft of the brush. No way to tell if that was my pick until it was . . . extracted.

"What I don't get is, what's on the end of that brush that'd croak a guy?" A hulking man jumped toward me from the corner of the room, and I flinched. I hadn't noticed him before, but the mirrors reflected the trees from outside and the cars, and my subconscious must have written him off as one of them. That could be the only explanation, because he certainly was big enough to earn special notice everywhere except on a football field. Check that. Maybe a bowling alley would be more accurate, considering his girth. He chomped chewing gum and smacked up right beside me.

"Never seen anything so fu . . . uh . . . effing weird.

And I seen a lot, lady, a lot." As he double-smacked in exclamation, I caught a whiff of Juicy Fruit that suddenly overwhelmed the fresh metallic scent of Ricardo's blood and the underlying odor of hairspray.

"A pick fits into the bottom of the brush," I explained, looking back at Ricardo's body.

"So?" *Smack. Smack.*

Nausea suddenly welled up in my throat. The edges of my vision blurred.

"You okay?" Scythe asked.

His intuitive question caught me almost as off-guard as my sudden reaction had. I had to concentrate on the facts, or I was going to give in to shock. I refused to give Scythe the satisfaction of being right. Clearing my throat as if that was the only reason I paused, I gestured to the brush and continued. "The pick's pointed, made of hard plastic, about six inches long, and it looks a little like a thick ice pick. These brushes are made of a hollow, round metal core and are designed to be used with a blow-dryer. The dryer air heats the metal, which sets the hair in a curl. The pick's used to separate the hair in a workable hank."

I finished in a rush of words as tears threatened to compete with my nausea and dizziness

"Whatever happened to curlers and a helmet hair dryer?"

"We still use those, but contemporary styles are more natural, less structured." Both men's eyes began to glaze over, but I plowed on, happy to be distracted from Ricardo. "This method—the blow-dryer and the brush—produce a looser, more natural-looking curl. Sometimes when a customer is only looking for a little extra body . . ."

Oops, bad choice of words. My gaze dropped back to

Ricardo, and for the first time I really noticed the blood that had flowed over his silk shirt was already dried, stiffening the cloth. That, more than anything else I'd seen so far, made me sad. He was always so fastidious. My palms itched to take it off and put him in a clean Prada shirt.

"The pick's sharp enough to bury in somebody's back? That's fu . . . effing scary," Gum Smacker groused.

"Well, it's not usually that sharp." My inappropriate honesty again.

Lieutenant Scythe stood at my other elbow and looked down, way down, at me crouched near Ricardo. I couldn't see him. I *felt* his focus. I cranked my eyes as far back as they could go; I wasn't about to twist my tightening back. I still couldn't meet his eyes. Just as well.

"What do you mean, 'not usually'?" he asked finally.

Leave it to ole Jackson to cut to the heart of the matter. I thought for a minute I was going to get away with my careless statement.

"Well . . ." I began. "You see, the brush that Ricardo borrowed was my cleaning tool."

"Hawh?" Gum Smacker scratched his head.

Scythe said nothing.

"I sharpened the pick so I could use it to clean the other brushes and blow-dryers and tools in my shop."

"Sharpened? With what?" Scythe asked quietly, ominously.

"A kitchen knife."

"Doesn't your profession have tools you can purchase to do that cleaning?"

My invisible hackles rose at the patronizing way he'd said a "profession," kind of the way he might refer to the world's oldest profession. Apparently, he accorded them equal respect. Like none. I forced my urge to argue back down in light of the obvious suspicion in his tone. "I'm cheap," was all I said.

Gum Smacker snorted. Scythe's left eyebrow half quirked.

"Right," Scythe muttered, turning away. He spoke to his companion. "Fred, I think the print tech can lift the latents now."

"Yeah, enough of this jacking around."

Fred Gum Smacker ambled off.

"Who's that?" I asked.

Scythe turned his intense focus back on me. "My partner, Fred Crandall. You ought to be honored. He doesn't tone down his swearing for just anybody. You probably remind him of his daughter."

I tried to imagine a feminine version of Crandall and shuddered. Jackson Scythe had definitely *not* just delivered me a compliment. In the absence of hackles and bared teeth, his statement deserved an eye-to-eye challenge. I balanced on the balls of my feet and tried to use my quadriceps to stand. It didn't help much. I unfolded like a rusty old picnic chair. I felt the burn of dry-ice eyes.

"What's the matter with you?"

"My back went out yesterday," I grumbled, rolling my head and gaining a little relaxation in my neck. My back refused to give, though.

"Oh?" Only his right eyebrow shagged up. I was beginning to recognize that eyebrow movement as an alert to suspicions, as opposed to his half-hitch twitch on the left, which indicated surprise. Give me twenty more minutes with this guy, and I'd have him completely pegged. "How did you hurt your back?" he asked quietly but not softly.

"By driving my brush into my friend's back, that's how," I snapped, irritated that he'd suspect me and tired of putting up with his cop psychology. One look at the well-hidden laughter in his face told me he never really did suspect me. He was just playing with me—the old cat and mouse—and that made me even angrier. "What kind of cop are you? Don't you want to take my confession?"

Crandall snorted. "Your confession of what? Getting a bad haircut?"

I looked in the mirror at the asymmetrical bob I'd coached one of the stylists at my shop through just two days before. I liked it. My hair swept straight down from a left side part to brush my right shoulder, tapering up around along the nape of my neck to the left side, where it just brushed my earlobe. Anyone could see it was a stylish statement. Maybe it was the color that was distracting him. I had to admit the shade, called red wine, was really closer to a cherry Coke and didn't particularly complement my fair skin. It tended to bring out the freckles sprinkling the bridge of my nose. I knew I shouldn't have tried such a risky color, but being naturally blond was so boring. Sometimes I just had to break out.

"Watch it, Fred." Scythe's voice was low, but its warning was not.

"What, hotshot? Maybe we've found our motive. If Ricardo cut her hair to look like a flying saucer, I'd call that motive for murder."

"I apologize for my partner; he's of the old school. I think your hairdo"—his eyes roamed over me, head to toe again—"suits you."

Scythe delivered the comment in the same impassive way he said just about everything else, which made it hard to tell how it was meant. There were a lot of ways to take what Jackson Scythe said.

"Alejandra, a stylist at my shop, gave me this cut," I answered neutrally, watching as a fingerprint technician shuffled in, unpacked a little kit and began dusting powder over the plastic end of the brush in Ricardo's back. My brush. A shiver slithered down my back as I forced my body still. Scythe's eyebrow barely flicked, which I suppose meant I wasn't entirely successful at achieving pure stillness. Or maybe he was telepathic.

"There goes your motive, Fred." Scythe dismissed his partner before turning back to me. "Your shop. Where's that?" He pulled his notebook out of a front inside pocket of his sports jacket.

"In Monte Vista, on the southwest corner of Magnolia and McCullough."

He wrote that down. I didn't know whether that was good or bad.

"What's it called?"

"Transformations: More than Meets the Eye."

His Bic stopped in midair, and his eyes shifted their focus from the page to meet mine. "Is that the name or a social statement?"

"Both. Books have subtitles, why can't stores? Beauty's about more than what's on the outside, although what's on the outside can change the way one feels on the inside." *Except for underwear,* I almost added, then stopped myself. I didn't need to have that argument with Jackson Scythe. *Not yet, anyway,* I added slyly.

"Whoa," he said, holding up the last three fingers of the hand holding the Bic. "I'm not equipped for a philosophical discussion right now. I'm just here to solve a murder which, no matter how complicated, promises to be less of a bog than a beauty debate with a woman who could clearly outargue me from its every angle."

How did he issue a compliment and a criticism in the same sentence so damned smoothly? It effectively tied my tongue, which was well practiced in pithy rejoinders. I hadn't been this self-conscious since high school. "You sound just like my aunt Mavis," I muttered under my breath.

Unexpectedly, Jackson Scythe chuckled. The skin along the nape of my neck tingled in response to the conservative rumble, the rusty essence of which made me think the lieutenant didn't laugh often. That the fingerprint tech nearly dropped her kit was another clue.

Scythe cut it short at her wide-eyed stare. He cleared his throat. "Sounds like aunt Mavis has her priorities in order."

Like *I* didn't? I wondered suddenly if Jackson Scythe kept *his* cabinets organized.

"Speaking of priorities, hotshot." Crandall reappeared, lumbering into the room and pausing for a few juicy smacks. "You have to decide when to talk to the vultures. They're setting up camp."

"Great. They can wait all day for my 'No comment.' "

"Ah, you gotta give 'em more than that," Crandall argued halfheartedly.

"The hell I do."

"We're not really gonna be here all day, are we?" Crandall reached into the rear pocket of his polyester slacks and pulled out another piece of Juicy Fruit. He unwrapped it, slowly, reverently, as if it were a precious gift. Everyone in the room watched, except the fingerprint technician, who seemed only distracted by the unusual. Like that chuckle of Scythe's. Hearing it again in my mind's ear, I stopped my body in mid-shiver with a stomp of my foot. I was getting sick of this guy's effect on me. He glanced at me and went back to reviewing his notebook. I couldn't help noticing the cute cowlick where his wavy hairs met his neck. It was something he couldn't see unless he held a second mirror behind his head, and he didn't seem the type to do that. For some odd reason, his cowlick made him seem more vulnerable to me. *Good girl,* I thought, grasping at whatever worked to keep me ahead in the head game were were playing.

Scythe glanced up from his notes. I smiled like I had a secret. He half hitched his eyebrow. Oops. I shifted my gaze back to a safer subject, Crandall, who was winding up his gum ritual. He wadded up the silver foil, flipped it over his shoulder, and added the piece to the wad in his mouth. It made me wonder if it was a continuous piece of gum, set aside at night like a watch, only to be popped back into his mouth again in the morning.

I watched Scythe walk over to the desk table and use the butt end of his Bic to shift around the papers on the glass top.

"Know this stiff's last name?"

Crandall's insensitive question startled me out of falling deeper into some kind of hormone-induced trance.

"Yes," I answered cautiously as I racked my brain for his surname.

"Yeah?" Crandall snorted. "Everybody but me and Jack here knows about this guy, but nobody knows his last name."

"He liked to go only by his first name," I responded distractedly.

"Like Madonna, that nutso?"

Cocking my head, I considered his comparison. I hadn't thought of Ricardo as aping Madonna before, but you couldn't look anywhere for a better miracle marketer, that was for sure. I nodded. "Yeah, like Madonna. Or Cher, I guess."

He flapped his notebook within an inch of my nose. "Hey, don't go knocking Cher. I like her."

"Uh, okay." I tried to imagine this gum-smacking, insensitive, foul-mouthed, paunchy, redneck tough guy as a Cher fan. Go figure.

"So, you gonna tell us his last name, or we gonna have to pull it out with tweezers?"

"Speaking of tweezers," said another plainclothes cop who walked through the office door, opening and closing the tweezers in my direction like mini crocodile jaws. I didn't want to think of what he was going to do with those.

"His name was Ricardo Montoya," I blurted.

The tweezer cop joined Jackson Scythe at the desk, plucked up a few hairs, and put them into a plastic bag before walking out.

"Know anybody who had a beef with Ric?" *Smack. Smack.*

"No." I shook my head. "But I wasn't as close to Ricardo as I once was. We were old friends, we ran into each other occasionally, by accident or when one of us wanted a favor . . ." Scythe appeared to be ignoring us, reading over the papers in front of him. But I knew he was listening closely. I could feel that intense focus. He thought he was tricky, but he couldn't fool me.

"Favor? That wouldn't be sexual favors, would it?" Crandall asked with a leer that compressed his face into layers of gray-brown fleshy folds.

Guess I didn't remind him of his daughter anymore.

"No, it wouldn't," I snapped a little too vehemently. Scythe looked up, met my eyes neutrally, and looked back down.

"Why? Was Ricky here a *hoto?*" While looking askance at the body, Crandall emphasized the Tex-Mex word for *homosexual* in such a way that he thought was cool and I thought was ignorant.

"No," I said too forcefully. "He was not. He had lots of . . ." What would be accurate while not too telling here? Sex? Girlfriends? Female bed partners? "Dates. With girls. I mean, women."

"You one of those 'dates'?" Crandall put in knowingly.

"No." I kept to myself that it wasn't for lack of trying on Ricardo's part. I was getting smarter. Surely, the cops would've seen somewhere in my rebuff a motive for murder. I had enough trouble having apparently furnished the murder weapon.

"What's this 'old friend' sh . . . uh . . . stuff, then? I mean, was he your old man's bud or something?"

"Yes, perhaps Claude knew him," Scythe offered from across the room. I wondered why the Claude farce seemed to bother him so much. His verbal shot flew on past Crandall, who wrinkled his forehead for a moment and decided figuring it out wasn't worth the effort.

"I don't have any old man," I retorted, ignoring Scythe's comment.

"So." Crandall smirked. "You and Ricky here really weren't old *friends*, then, were you?"

His point was slowly beginning to dawn on me, like the sun through a foggy day in Transylvania.

"Why? Do you think a woman can't be friends with a man unless she knows him by association through a husband or she goes to bed with him?"

"Right." Crandall double-smacked with pleasure at his universal wisdom.

"Then you're an idiot."

Jackson Scythe emitted a heavy sigh but didn't look up. Somehow, I sensed the sigh was directed at me instead of Crandall.

Crandall couldn't have been more surprised by my attack if I'd kicked him in the groin. He blinked and looked for an instant like he might cry. A teary redneck Cher fan. I was disgusted to find regret welling up in my throat. It derailed my feminist lecture. "Look," I said to Crandall. "Ricardo gave me my first job out of high school, let me have flexible hours to finish college. Then he lent me seed money to get my salon business started, which I've since paid back, with interest that he didn't ask for. He is—was—what I call a friend. I don't give a damn what you call it."

Crandall had recovered rather quickly and, ignoring my sentimentality, zeroed in. "Why the hell would he bankroll the competition?"

"You don't understand." I shook my head, then explained. "Ricardo didn't have competition."

"What d'ya mean? There's a barbershop on every corner. A haircut's a haircut."

"That's not true." I glanced at Scythe, whose attention intensified a few degrees.

"Ay-yi." Crandall dismissed me with one paddycake-shaped, hairy hand. "You're just saying that because you're a barber."

"No, I'm saying it because I know the business, and I knew Ricardo. Our hair is very important to us. A study done by a Yale University professor not long ago backs that up—within the first three seconds of meeting someone, we develop a first impression entirely from that person's hair."

"Nuh-uh," Crandall argued as he looked in the mirror at his own Marine-issue style—dishwater-brown hair clipper-cut on the sides with number ½ blade complete with flattop.

I continued, "That's what the study said, and I believe it. Think of how differently you might approach a witness who has a bleached mohawk versus one who has a natural brunet bouffant. People will go through a lot to stick with a stylist. I know women who flew in from around the state just to get their hair done every six weeks at one of Ricardo's salons. A lot of us have that kind of customer loyalty. But Ricardo went a step further. Going to Ricardo's was more than a trip to the beauty salon; it was a social event, and ultimately a bragging right."

That silenced the room for a moment. Then Crandall snapped a bubble in his mouth. His eyes were lit up like he'd hit the jackpot. I didn't know I'd been *that* convincing. "So, sounds like you have plenty of reason to be jealous of him. Your beauty shop's not doing as hot, huh?"

I fought the urge to give a lesson in the difference between jealousy and envy to this lughead who thought anybody with a pair of scissors could style hair. Instead, I answered the question. "My salon is doing just fine, thank you. I admired Ricardo's business acumen, but I wasn't envious of it."

Scythe, who'd been following the conversation without comment, now asked, "What did Ricardo say to you over the phone?"

"It was jumbled and didn't make much sense. His voice sounded weak, but I thought it was because . . ."

Scythe's eyebrows rose, way too slowly to be considered appropriate. He knew it, too. "Because?" he finally prompted.

"Because I thought he was with a date."

"You heard someone else's voice?"

"No, I guess I just assumed it, from his reputation and the breathlessness of his tone."

"You have an active imagination."

If you only knew, I thought. A light in his eyes sparked as if he did know.

"So, he never confirmed he'd seen anyone that night, not even the client he was expecting?"

"No, he said something about danger, about pudding, and about me taking care of what was his."

"What did he mean about danger? Was he specific? Are you two into some dealings together?"

"I don't know. No and no."

Scythe stared at me a beat longer, then turned to Crandall.

"Make a note to check with the doc about pudding in the stomach contents."

My eyes stole to the clock set in the center of Ricardo's mirrored ceiling. It intrigued me; I'd never seen anything like it. Its foot-long gold chrome hand showed just five minutes shy of seven-thirty A.M.

"Damn," I muttered. "I have an appointment coming in, and no one's there to open up until eight."

Jackson gauged me with a look, then sent some telepathic message to Crandall, who gave his gum a break to grunt and shove his notebook in the outside pocket of his 1970s polyester navy-blue blazer, the elbows of which were polished to a tacky shine. I wasn't sure whether his grunt was assent or indigestion.

"So, I can go?"

Crandall smacked and nodded. "Yeah. You know the drill."

Drill? What drill? The only drill I knew about was the one in my dreams, and surely Crandall wasn't referring to it. I stole a look at him and dismissed the thought. I tried to catch Scythe's eye, but he was reading a piece of paper on the desk. I could feel him taking in our conversation on another level, as if he were storing it for future contemplation.

"No," I admitted carefully. "What drill?"

"Don't leave town. And don't go trying to do a chemical peel on those fingerprints. We're gonna require those at a near juncture in time. Unless you've done some business with us before. Then that won't be necessary."

My heart banged up against the bottom of my throat. I pivoted from the smirking Crandall to meet Jackson Scythe's eyes. They'd warmed to a polar summer. Maybe I wasn't in trouble after all. "We go through a process of elimination on fingerprints. Ricardo's. Yours. Anyone else you can think of who might have touched the brush at your shop before Ricardo took it?"

I shook my head, feeling a little lightheaded with relief. Why had I been so tense? I didn't have any reason to feel guilty. Guess I just didn't trust the justice system to spare the innocent.

Scythe left the papers on the desk and walked up to me, pulling his wallet out of his back pocket. Lucky wallet. He extracted his business card and handed it to me without a word.

"Great, I'll add this to my little black book," I mumbled.

The icy-blues moved a few degrees closer to the equator. "You do that."

"Now that all the pleasantries are over, hotshot, let's get to work," Crandall grumbled as he ambled over to the desk. He sucked in a bubble.

"Hey, get away from there, Crandall," the fingerprint tech piped up in what sounded like an angry Chihuahua's bark. "You're spraying gum spit all over that desk. Steer clear until I'm done, or I'll be using this brush on you."

Everyone was making jokes about the brush—even me—and I suddenly felt the tears welling up in my eyes. Blinking them away quickly, I swallowed the lump rising in my throat. What a time to get emotional. Scythe would think it was a sudden onslaught of guilt.

"I'm real scared," Crandall groused, but he did move away from the desk to study the phone in the righthand corner of the room. "Why'd he have so many phones? I hope to hell they all aren't different lines, or we'll be knee-deep in fu . . . uh . . . effing paperwork."

I'd been watching Crandall hard, in order to get my grief under control, but I suddenly realized Jackson Scythe had been watching me. "Well?" he said.

What was he after? I looked down at my left hand, which I'd forgotten was holding the barf bag. I handed it, unused, back to him. It was the perfect way to lighten the moment. I forced a dazzling smile. "Thanks."

"You keep it. Never know when it might come in handy."

What did *that* mean? He still looked expectant, if a six-foot-three great stone face with dry-ice eyes can show such an emotion.

Though not usually patient, I found myself standing there, not moving a muscle, just to bug him.

Finally, he cleared his throat. "I was hoping to get your card, *Miz* Sawyer."

I flashed a grin—a real one this time. "I thought you guys were Big Brother, had all citizens' vitals in a data-base."

"We don't always like the trouble of searching it, and we often don't have the time when we need an answer to something."

"I'm worth the time and trouble," I threw over my shoulder as I walked out the door in the wake of his dis-belief, the Chihuahua's giggle, and Crandall's Juicy Fruit snort.

I know it was stupid in light of the power of his position and especially in light of his gorgeousness, but I couldn't help myself. Pomposity and arrogance wrapped up in testosterone do that to me.

five

JOLIE DUPONT'S GOLD LEXUS WAS IN THE CRAMPED six-car parking lot off McCullough, next to my house, but I hadn't seen her standing at the main door of the salon. Nor was she at the back door, which led to the living quarters section of my old home. I didn't want to incur the dogs' mournful gazes through the kitchen window, so I parked the truck and walked along McCullough to unlock the door to the salon. I glanced down at my Cinderella watch and saw it was twenty minutes after seven. Damn, the day's schedule was shot to hell. Especially if Jolie had lost patience and had walked down two blocks to the Bake 'N Brew for a cappuccino and a croissant. She'd return in the middle of my eight o'clock and expect to be worked in.

I fished for the keys I'd absentmindedly thrown back into my cavernous black leather tote. Far from vogue, it resembled a Mafia wife's shopping bag. I'd tried other, smaller purses and wound up putting as much in them, so that it looked as if I were walking around carrying a sausage on a string. Finding stuff in there was hell, too.

So I gave up fashion and carried the tote around with me, along with all the necessities, including a battery-powered curling iron in case I needed a touch-up or ran into a customer who did (don't laugh, it happens more often than you think), dog biscuits in case the girls were with me, and pepper spray. Ever since I bought the little canister after our neighborhood flasher opened his coat for me, I've been dying to use it to spray him where it hurts. So far, he'd denied me the fun by hanging out (literally) nine blocks north, nearly to where Monte Vista becomes the incorporated and exclusive city of Olmos Park. He must've been ready for a couple of square meals and a bed. Those Olmos Park cops would collar him for stepping foot in their city limits. He'd have to do a lot more than showing his hot dog to get the attention of the SAPD. They had gangbangers, drive-bys, domestics, and chop shops to worry about. Not to mention a dead hairdresser now. A homeless flasher wasn't tops on their priority list.

Not that Monte Vista was slumming it. It was one of two historical residential districts in San Antonio, featuring two dozen long, wide-street blocks and hundred-year-old homes, including many multimillion-dollar mansions. Mine wasn't anywhere near that caliber, but I was proud of what I'd done with it. My chest puffed up with enough pride to turn my B-cups into Cs as I stepped on the newly buffed limestone steps that led to the wrap-around porch. When the seventy-nine-year-old daughter of the original owner keeled over dead from a stroke while going through junk in the attic, her heirs just wanted to get rid of the run-down mess. I bought it for $102,000 (the price included a lot of that attic junk that cleaned up pretty well), and, with the help of my big brothers over one long, hot summer, I'd renovated it back to a two-story jewel that the appraisal district valued at three times the purchase price. Good thing I could write half of it off as a business. And good thing that business was holding its own, or I'd be in trouble.

Pressure. The knot was building between my shoulder blades as I thought about paying bills and a $50-a-week customer I'd kept waiting and was now missing. That led to thoughts of Ricardo and his promise to let me run his fortune-making salons, which led to images of his dead body and not only a friend but an opportunity gone. I embarrassed myself at the mercenary thought, but there was something bugging me about the outlandish offer that I would have never considered had Ricardo been alive.

And I still couldn't find my keys. I yanked my hand out of the tote and dumped it out just as a figure ran at me from around the left side porch. I jumped against the column as my body electrified with what had to be the last of my twenty-four-hour supply of adrenaline. A flash of red jeweled pump skidded on the plastic cover my of checkbook, landing its owner with a thump, a skid, and a squeal on the front steps.

"Jolie?" I unlocked my muscles, peeled myself off the column, and leaned over to offer her a hand up. I scanned her for injuries; the businesswoman part of me couldn't help but wonder if my liability insurance covered customers slipping on checkbook covers on my porch.

Ignoring my hand, she scrambled up—no small feat, considering her pencil-thin linen skirt—and nearly knocked me over with a tackle hug. I thought at first she was trying to strangle me for being late or for nearly breaking her neck.

"Oh, Reyn, Reyn, you're alive!"

She pulled away to hold me at arm's length. Her White Diamonds whooshed up in the rush of air between us. Her sleek, classic bob dyed Sunlit Linen bounced up and down as her eyes went top to bottom and back as if she were looking for missing parts. Finally, her dark doe eyes settled on mine, and she smiled, her brilliantly whitened teeth taking up more than half of her heart-shaped face.

I finally found my voice, which was the only part of me that I'd been missing—as far as I knew, anyway. "Of course, I'm alive, Jolie. Why wouldn't I be?"

She nodded and shook her head all in one motion, the highlights in her hair flickering and the diamonds in her ears flashing. "I heard about Ricardo on the radio on the way over here this morning. Terrible. Then, when I got here and you weren't open, didn't answer my knock or my ring, I got worried. You're never late. Never in the ten years I've been your client. I finally decided to call and got your answering machine. Then I thought I'd better look in the windows to be sure something horrid—like what happened to Ricardo—hadn't happened to you." Jolie paused to shudder.

"A beauty salon serial murderer?" I certainly hadn't considered that, and I didn't now. I mean, what would prompt someone to do that? Flunking out of beauty school? Having one too many bad dye jobs? Snorting one too many perm chemicals?

"Well." Jolie dropped her hands from my arms to her hips. "It's not *that* far-fetched. The world's gone absolutely *loco*. Plus, I was rattled over the news of Ricardo, and then you had to go do something completely uncharacteristic. My imagination ran away."

"Really, it was sweet of you. I'm sorry I made you worry." I leaned down to stuff my things back into my bag. Jolie's slide into first had dislodged my keys, and I plucked them from between two porch floorboards.

Jolie recovered her red, blue, and yellow Liz shoulder bag from the front walk and clucked over the skid marks. She climbed the five porch steps and handed me the checkbook, which had slid into the front flower bed. Lord knows what else was flung hither and yon. I made a mental note to do reconnaissance later.

I could hear the salon phone ringing as I fit the key into the front door lock. I looked through the beveled glass of the front door to see if the caller would leave a message. But no red light went on. A hang-up. Just as well. I had to hustle to get Jolie's color and style done before my eight o'clock arrived.

Jolie followed me into the foyer, closing the door behind her and then walking into the rest room to change into a smock. I flipped on the lights and looked around at my salon, suddenly struck with the contrast between my shop and Ricardo's. His ultra-modern, cold, and clean. Mine old, warm, and cluttered. An unmatching assortment of antique chandeliers lit the rooms, an odd collection of Chippendale, Duncan Fife, and other old furniture I couldn't name filled the small waiting room and sat scattered in the halls that led to other stylists' and nail technicians' rooms. Frayed Oriental rugs, which I hoped looked tasteful instead of just old, carpeted the polished oak floors in the hall and waiting room, which were paneled in oak stained a lighter shade than the floor. Each room was papered in mock antique paper, my only requirement being that people had to be featured on the paper. Not as easy as it sounds. Just try looking for it sometime. Flowers and animals, no problem, but people on paper—that was rare. What does that say about modern society? All of what customers saw in my salon—that wasn't "junk" from my attic—was collected mostly from flea markets and estate sales over eight years while I worked for Ricardo, went to college, and dreamed of owning my own business.

I'm a real believer in visualization. The power of the psyche can make dreams come true.

Now, looking at the salon, I wondered if it was also my subconscious that tried to make my shop look so much different from Ricardo's, and if so, why?

"So, where were you?" Jolie asked as she clicked into step behind me and we entered the last room on the left, my room. She settled into my chair while I went through the door to my adjoining office and dumped my tote. I snatched up a smock and slipped it over my bodysuit and skirt, snapping it together as I walked. As I passed the laundry room on my way back, I tried not to think about Ricardo there just hours ago and what I could have done to prevent his demise.

"I was at Ricardo's," I said as I mixed up Jolie's color.

Her doe eyes widened in the mirror as they met mine. "But how'd you hear about it so soon? It had just come over as a news bulletin when I pulled up here."

"The police called me and asked me to come identify the . . . him."

"But why you?"

I shrugged, hoping it looked convincing. I knew whatever I said would be spread through certain zip codes quicker than a broadcast news bulletin. I had to be careful. "Just got lucky, I guess."

"But you haven't worked for Ricardo in two years,

Reyn. How much do you know about him and his business now? Or is it someone from his past they suspect?"

"I used to know Ricardo well, Jolie, but we've been too busy to see much of each other lately. As for whom the police suspect, I don't know for sure . . ." *Besides me, that is.* I kept that part to myself.

"But why did the cops call you?" she pursued with a terrier's tenacity. "You must know something. They didn't pull you out of his appointment book, did they?"

Trudy knew how to get the truth out of me, that was for sure, by intimating that I'd been Ricardo's lover.

As I pulled on my thin vinyl gloves, I tamped down my urge to deny it vigorously and considered how much to say. She'd surely hear about Ricardo's visit. Trudy and Mario, sensation seekers that they were, would milk being there for all it was worth no matter how much I might beg them to keep quiet. "Ricardo stopped by last night. I guess the cops just wanted to talk to the last person who saw him alive. I mean, not the last, because that would be the person who . . . uh . . . did it."

Possibly in more ways than one. I recalled his reputation for sleeping with customers. Could they have *done* it and then she did him in with the brush? I wondered whom Ricardo had the appointment with that ill-fated evening and wished I had asked him. A crime of passion—wasn't that usually motive number one?

Jolie widened her eyes again, blinked, and pulled her lips down over her teeth. A warning bell went off in my head. The only other time I'd seen Jolie hide her prominent teeth was when she'd sneaked off to another stylist to get her bob trimmed and I'd guessed it at her next appointment. What was she up to now? I did a quick survey of her hair. No other stylist this time; her style had my mark all over it. Her behavior had to have something to do with Ricardo.

"Who do you suppose it was?" Jolie whispered, even though we were the only two in the salon.

"I don't know." I began sponging color onto her roots with my pressurized squeeze gun. "You have any theories?"

"Me?" she shouted. The sudden change in her vocal volume startled me, and I spurted too much color out of the gun at once. I grabbed a towel before the purplish lotion began oozing down her forehead. She modulated her voice with a forced casual tone as she continued, "What would *I* know about it?"

"You did go to Ricardo for a long time before you started with me," I pointed out. Jolie's defection was something that always intrigued me. At the time, I was fresh on the job in Ricardo's salon, and to have one of his clients request me was an incredible honor that I was afraid to question. As time passed, it got more and more difficult to broach the subject. Plus, I'd always thought of it as none of my business. It didn't stop me from being curious, though. Especially now.

"For nearly fifteen years," she admitted wistfully.

"I've always wanted to ask," I began carefully, feeling like I was tiptoeing through a minefield. I should just leave this alone, but my mouth rarely listened to reason. "Why did you start coming to me? I know my brilliant talent dazzled you, but I also remember you saying something about finding out that Ricardo knew your best friend from way back."

Jolie didn't chuckle at my weak attempt at humor. She pressed her lips more tightly together. I was really hoping to see some teeth here. I could only think of how I was going to do without this fifty bucks a week.

Pressure knotted again, tweaking his brother Pain in my back, who hadn't been heard from in a while.

I checked to make sure I'd covered all of Jolie's roots with the color, then I put the squeeze gun down on my tray and began peeling my gloves off.

"Who is your best friend, anyway, Jolie?"

"Celine Villita."

"I remember her," I said. "You brought her in once to have me do her hair when her stylist was sick or out of town or something."

Suddenly, Jolie moved her jeweled shoes from the chair's bar to the floor and spun around to face me. "Reyn, you wouldn't be trying to nose around and find out what happened to Ricardo, would you?"

I hadn't been—at least, not consciously—until that moment. I felt the shock or grief or whatever that had been holding me numb for hours lift, and sounds and images filled in—Ricardo's strange offer to run his salons the night before, his middle-of-the-night call for help, my bloody brush sticking out of his back, an arrogant cop's suspicion—and for the first time I began to take his murder personally.

"Reyn," Jolie warned, tipped off, no doubt, by the determined look in my eyes. Or perhaps I radiated determination. I hate to admit it, but one way or another, I'm as transparent as glass. This could be another reason I can't lie for beans.

"It just bugs the hell out of me." I forced the nonchalance into my tone. "He was a good friend."

"So, go do the rosary, send flowers to the funeral home, but stay out of the investigation. It'll be best for everybody if you just keep out of it."

Them's fighting words. My perverse personality

doesn't take to being told not to do something. It virtually guarantees that I will do that self-same thing.

After all, I reasoned as I smiled reassuringly to Jolie and spun her back around, Ricardo died before I could even up the favors.

I still owed him one.

six

DISTRACTED AS I WAS AFTER JOLIE LEFT, WELL coiffed but still ominously hiding her teeth, I made it through a morning full of appointments with no major insights from my customers regarding Ricardo's demise but no major disasters, either. Of course, one incident could've qualified had it not been for my quick-thinking nail technician. I had Mrs. Reinmeyer in my chair when Inez, a pal of mine who styles at Ricardo's Huebner store, called, telling my receptionist that it was an emergency. It wasn't, but it became one when Inez told me the gossip was that Ricardo swung both ways, was AC/DC, or liked to do the horizontal boogie with men and women, whatever you might call it.

My right hand—which was doing a touch-up with the clippers at Mrs. Reinmeyer's nape—slipped north rather suddenly, leaving a distinctive track through her sprayed silver curls. Mrs. Reinmeyer gasped, the receiver slipped off my shoulder, crashing onto the floor just as Daisy Dawn Washington walked by. She took it all in in one glance and, being the quick thinker that she is, exclaimed, "Oh, Miz Reinmeyer" the thick syrup in her East Texas accent completely hid the put-on in her tone—"you *smart* thing, you. You're getting one of those new tower styles."

"Tower styles?" Mrs. Reinmeyer and I echoed together.

With a warning glance at me, Daisy Dawn continued, smiling in admiration at my eighty-year-old client. "Oh, yeah, didn't Reyn tell you? They're all the rage in L.A. right now. I saw at least four gals at the Oscars with them tower 'dos."

"You did?" Mrs. Reinmeyer was brightening as she sneaked peeks in the mirrors, so I decided to play along, calculating the damage control I could manage on her style while making it look like I'd planned it that way. I swallowed my horrified apology and smiled reassuringly at Mrs. Reinmeyer.

Daisy Dawn nodded. "Sure, I swear Olympia Dukakis and Angela Lansbury had towers. Maybe Michelle Pfeiffer, too, although I can't be sure about that; the camera moved too quick for me to tell."

"Oh!" I heard Mrs. Reinmeyer's pancake makeup crack as her mouth curled into an unfamiliar smile. Truth be told, it looked a little scary.

"A trendsetter in our midst," Daisy Dawn whispered reverently, pausing a few seconds for effect. "Just imagine."

"Well." Mrs. Reinmeyer warmed to the praise, bless Daisy Dawn's lying little soul. "I did tell Reyn I wanted something *different* and *daring*."

She did no such thing. She'd stomped her scrawny purple-polyester-pantsuit-clad body across my expensively restored wood floor, complaining about her last cut and set as she had every single month she'd been my customer. Now, finally, she had something *real* to complain about, and she wasn't doing it. Go figure. If I'd only known, I would've given her a mohawk years ago.

"Now, Reyn, finish up," Mrs. Reinmeyer ordered with a twitch of her starched shoulders, having fully regained her superior attitude. "I can't wait to see the girls at bridge drop their teeth when I walk in with a *tower*, especially Marge Kelley. She's always so hoity-toity after her seasonal trips east to Bloomie's."

The irony of the image was too much for Daisy Dawn, who was biting down hard on her magenta-glossed lower lip. She patted Mrs. Reinmeyer's liver-spotted hand with three-inch talons that were amazingly natural. I never could see how she managed to put nails on others with nails of her own that long. "Go get 'em, girlfriend."

"Cool," Mrs. Reinmeyer answered, trying out the word the kids had resurrected from the sixties—one that she'd certainly only ever used to describe temperature. Daisy Dawn didn't let her silent laughter loose until she was down the hall, well out of Mrs. Reinmeyer's line of sight. Her dark Rastafarian braids shook, clicking the beads at the ends together merrily.

I owed her one.

If I wasn't careful, I was going to owe everyone in San Antonio favors. For some reason, that thought brought to mind Lieutenant Jackson Scythe. I wasn't *ever* going to owe him a favor, as he'd have to apologize for his arrogance first, and I doubted *that* would ever happen unless he was under the influence of some mind-altering drug. Or in a haze of lust brought on by the company of a naked woman.

And I wouldn't be that naked woman unless he apologized first.

The-chicken-or-the-egg dilemma. Probably the undoing of most potential relationships.

Quickly, before she regained her senses, I trimmed the hair on the right side of Mrs. Reinmeyer's head to match the left. And, to be perfectly honest, it left her with a style that would be more at home on a *Star Trek* set than on an old western, so maybe it was more chic than I knew.

Still grinning (a scary sight even without her scalp showing), she paid cash, shed her plastic smock, and left humming a turn-of-the-century tune. It's not what you're thinking—not turn of *last* century like Enrique Caruso, but turn of this one, Butthole Surfers. I'm telling you I meant what I said to Scythe at Ricardo's. Changing your hair can change your life. I just hoped I hadn't accidentally changed Mrs. Reinmeyer into an eighty-year-old headbanger.

Suddenly remembering the abandoned Inez, I scooped up the phone. A mechanical voice told me to hang up the phone and try again. I did, but the receptionist read a message Inez had given her which—because of the obscenities—I can't repeat here, no matter how much useful Spanish it might teach you. Suffice it to say that Inez considered my priorities skewed, and if I wanted to put my client's welfare over her gossip, I wasn't worth talking to anymore.

So I was left with a stunning piece of unsubstantiated gossip that may or may not have been true and may or may not have had something to do with Ricardo's murder but most certainly was something I had to investigate.

● ● ●

It was just after noon, and I was a henna away from lunch, when my first opportunity to clarify Ricardo's sexual proclivities walked through the door. Sherlyn Rocca, Transformations' current receptionist, called down the hall for me in her nerve-grinding New Jawzee accent (I'm not prejudiced against Yankees, understand, but she did put more mouth into her words than I did). Now, I have a state-of-the-art telephone system, being of the mind that communication is one of the bedrocks of the beauty business. People on a quest for self-improvement have no patience for busy signals or dense stylists who don't strive to have SHE LISTENED AND STROVE TO PLEASE carved on their headstones. I did my utmost to fulfill that motto (Mrs. Reinmeyer notwithstanding), while paying for the best technology to take care of the former. Or that was the theory, anyway. The weak link in my communication system was the human element, and until the techno-nerds of the world come up with an affordable robot receptionist, I'm sure this will be my cross to bear.

Oh, I can feel my good Catholic friend begging for forgiveness at my blasphemy. *Forgive me, Trudy.*

Anyhow, Transformations has seen ten receptionists in two years, at an average rate of a new one every two months. Now, that's a lot of time wasted in hiring and training, not to mention the mass of dreaded W-2s every January. I'm not a bad boss, and I pay a little more than the going rate, including a discount on salon services, so there's no excuse beyond the obvious.

My luck sucks.

This was my first thought as Sherlyn, a relative veteran at two months, three weeks, four days, and counting, flounced down the hall, if one can flounce wearing lavender iridescent high-heeled tennis shoes that weigh at least thirty pounds each. Honestly, Sherlyn's talented that way, so she pulled it off. It's in other areas she got shorted when God was passing out abilities, brains and common sense being the first two that come to mind.

There I went, a second blasphemy in as many minutes. Maybe I'd set a world record before the day was over, and then no one could say I was a total failure.

"Miz Marten Sawyer." Sherlyn paused to glance at herself in my mirror, running her pinkie nail, which sported a hand-painted nude on fire-engine red, along the edge of her lower lip to fix a renegade bit of purple lip liner. It was meant to match her shoes, I suppose. She smiled at her reflection and rebent a piece of her platinum spiked hair. "There you are."

I wasn't sure whether she meant me or her lock of hair or perhaps that bit of errant lipstick. I didn't ask, having learned through experience that asking would elicit an explanation I did not need, or particularly want, to hear. I also refrained from asking why she hadn't paged me instead of flouncing but chalked it up to another waste of breath. I watched the client in my chair work to keep her mouth from dropping open as she took in Sherlyn's mile-long legs and the orange bandanna tied around her hips that was supposed to serve as a skirt. I suppose the shock could have come from the clashing kaleidoscope of color Sherlyn refracted from head to foot, but more likely, my client was about to go into cardiac arrest over the obvious fact that Sherlyn wasn't wearing any underwear, unless it was amazingly one-sided. It was my fault, surely, as I did not think to include undergarments in the dress code I outlined when she was hired. Sometimes I give people in general way too much credit.

"Miz Marten Sawyer," Sherlyn repeated, insisting on using my middle and last names instead of just my first, despite my clarifications to the contrary. I wasn't sure whether she was really that formal or whether the four extra syllables were just another excuse to listen to her own voice, as she was its biggest, perhaps only, fan. Cats copulating came to mind when Sherlyn opened her mouth.

"There's a woman out front who says she wants to be worked in, but it looked to me like you're full for the day, so I told her to take a hike."

Both the client in the chair and I cringed. Praying this was a figure of speech and not a direct quote, I willed control into my voice. "What did this lady need done?"

"Hey, I didn't say lady, cuz that woman out there sureazhell ain't no lady." Mercifully, Sherlyn pulled up at the horrified look on my face, but not without a pout. "Anyhows, she wouldn't tell the lowlife help what she wants, she gotta talk to you."

"I don't have the time for anything today," I confirmed as Sherlyn's pout was replaced with a smug smile. "Did you offer her another day or time?"

"The only thing I was offering her was a knuckle sandwich." I opened my mouth to intercede, but she'd soldiered on. "But then she starts some lame story about being desperate cuz her hairstylist got killed, or some such crap. Like I'm gonna believe that. Right! I mean, the dog ate my homework is a helluva lot better sob story, and it's like *so* not happening!"

Pushing past Sherlyn, who'd found an ear in my henna client (I'd have to remember to give the poor woman a discount) and was continuing with her critique of acceptable excuses, I rushed to the reception area. A tall, wide, yet flat-bodied woman with heavy, straight black hair blunt-cut just above her last rib stood eerily still, her eyes focused on the center of what Trudy calls my Indian-from-India rug (I think *Oriental* covers the style in general, but Trudy went shopping with me when I bought it and wants people to know it's a real home-made import with hand-tied tassels and all). My visitor was dressed in what uncharitably could be called rags, but on closer inspection was a collection of vibrant silk scarves sewn together into a tiered dress that was very likely bought from the window of a hip (and pricey) boutique in Alamo Heights. Neckwear had graduated from accessories to stand-alone apparel without my knowledge. Or approval. Imagine that. Mr. Blackwell, where are you when we need you?

"I'm Reyn Sawyer," I said, perhaps a little too force-fully as I hurried up, hand out. "Can I help you?"

She looked up quickly, her black curtain of hair falling back to reveal a lovely, ageless face, her skin glowing and unwrinkled, either proof of youth or bely-ing decades. I've always wondered why Asian women never look anywhere near their age. The children look like ultra-wise miniature adults, and the adults look twenty when they're sixty. I've never been able to figure out if they are blessed with more inner peace than I am or just better skin.

Probably both.

Her only mistake seemed to be in wearing more makeup than she needed. Midnight-blue kohl lined her eyes, a complementary powder shadow covered her sur-gically created double eyelids, sculpting blush high-lighted her already well-defined cheekbones, and subtle rose-colored gloss emphasized her perfectly outlined bow-shaped lips. Even overdone, she was lovely.

Taking my hand with an enviable grace, she squeezed lightly, then let it drop, leaving me with the hope some of her self-possession had rubbed off on me. She appeared to be the epitome of the psycho-babble term *centered*.

"I am Bettina Huyn. I understand you have no time for me today," she said, her voice completely unaccented and thus unique, especially in San Antonio, where East meets West meets North meets South. Hardly anyone here has the same accent, but we all have accents. Fleetingly, I wondered if she was an actress, having had her speech sanitized by a voice coach.

She seemed a perfect lady to me; what would've made Sherlyn think otherwise?

"What is it you need done, Ms. Huyn?" I'd already calculated the time it would take me to wash, trim, and blow-dry her simple cut at thirty minutes.

"I need a style only," she answered. "But an intricate one. I need it today, by three P.M. My stylist died without warning, and now I have no one to do my hair."

Who besides Dr. Kevorkian's patients have warning of their impending death? I know fatally ill people know to expect it, but certainly not the day, definitely not the hour. Besides, it wasn't like Ricardo was ill; he was murdered! Because I couldn't read her emotions very well, I decided to give her the benefit of the doubt. Perhaps no one had told her.

"Ricardo was your stylist?"

"Yes, how did you know?"

"Educated guess. He was murdered this morning."

"Inconvenient," she acknowledged in a mildly irritated tone.

"Yeah, especially for Ricardo," I couldn't help saying as I carefully watched her inscrutable face. If Bettina was one of the select clients, she was a suspect—in my book, at least.

Sherlyn's clomps forewarned her return to her post. She and Bettina Huyn glared at each other as Sherlyn flopped into the chair at her scarred, 1850s mahogany desk. I made two mental notes to talk to Sherlyn about her dress, or rather lack thereof, and about her altercation with Bettina, even though she was indeed proving to be less of a lady by the moment.

"So?" Bettina asked, her brutally plucked bird's-wing eyebrows rising no more than a millimeter.

I couldn't resist the chance to interrogate, even if it meant I'd miss lunch—leftover taco salad, to be exact. For someone who loves food (especially jalapeños) as much as I do, that's one big sacrifice.

"I'll work you in after my henna." I paused to watch Bettina shoot a triumphant look at Sherlyn. So she wasn't so centered that she was above flaunting her success at getting an appointment. Interesting. Sherlyn, for her part, proved more mature than I'd have expected. Instead of sticking out her tongue, she pretended not to notice Bettina's arched brows, dropping her eyes to study a peeling nude on her thumbnail. I did note, however, her lower lip puffed out in a pout.

I spoke to Bettina before Sherlyn could open that mouth of hers. "Come on back and put on a smock while I rinse out a color."

After the henna had departed (out the back door, preferring to brave the dogs rather than risking another conversation with Sherlyn), Bettina Huyn sat and pulled a photo out from under her smock, leaving me to wonder where she'd been keeping it. Gingerly, I took it from her upstretched hand.

It showed the most striking woman I'd ever seen, overtly sensual even through the two-dimensional print. Her makeup was dramatic, a perfect complement for the figure-hugging gold, silver, and bronze spandex sequined dress she wore, the entire package framed by her mountain of cascading blue-black curls in an erotic style that left me in awe of the hours of work put into it, as well as its knockout effect. Madonna and Cher stood behind the woman, who was the focus of the photo.

I smiled as I handed it back. "Incredible."

"That's it," Bettina said, waving her hand at the photo in my hand. "That's the magic Ricardo made for me."

"This woman must be a star," I mused, considering the company. "He gave you her style?"

"That is me," she said with a smile that held secrets.

I did a double take then, seeing some similarity in the bone structure but none of the smoldering sensuality in the print that was very nearly smoking in my hand, not to mention none of the curves, decidedly missing from the woman in front of me. Maybe Ricardo was more talented with a brush than I'd thought. Bettina looked more Voguey vamp than his usual Pekinese.

"This is *you?*"

"Yes," she answered, rose lips spreading in a full-blown smile. "A tuck here and some padding there can do wonders."

Where she'd expertly padded prior to the photo was obvious, but I wondered what she'd need tucked. But that wasn't my problem; the two hours it would take to do her hair was. I needed to get busy if I hoped to nose around in Ricardo's life that afternoon.

"And you know Cher and Madonna?" Wow, I was getting kind of excited about the possibility of having a star-connected client. *People* magazine would be calling any day now.

"No."

I looked again at the photo. They were pretty chummy, maybe not best friends, but certainly they'd been introduced before the flash. Bettina let me entertain a few more fame-and-fortune fantasies before she burst my bubble.

"I perform at Illusions," Bettina answered as my mouth dropped open.

"I see you know it." Bettina laughed at least three octaves lower than she talked. Of course, that didn't shock me as much as it might have before she'd mentioned her work at the city's infamous drag queen club. A couple of boneheads on the city council had fought a well-publicized battle to close it down as "injurious" to the city's reputation as a family tourist destination. All the hoopla had succeeded in doing was to make tourists aware of something that was, up until then, an underground transvestite club. From what I'd heard thanks to the publicity, they were packing it in. RuPaul had nothing on the performers at this northeast hot spot. I sneaked a more pointed peek at Bettina-whose-name-was-probably-Bert to try to see what I'd missed, but I couldn't find anything masculine except perhaps in his/her hands. No matter how smooth, buffed, and nail-enhanced, it was nearly impossible to turn a man's hands into a woman's. To think I was envying her for being so centered. She was centered, all right, straddling both sexes, so to speak.

I didn't *want* to be that centered, thank you. Good

thing I'd been so blasphemous earlier, or God might have been listening to my wishing. Yikes.

After one more glance at the photo in which I tried to hide my continued amazement, I passed it back to her and watched it disappear into an undergarment beneath a fold on her dress. I couldn't help wondering if it was Hanes Her Way or His Way under there. Suddenly, my hand that had held the photo itched to be washed. I led Bettina to my wash basin, wishing the shampoo was antibacterial.

"Did Ricardo know about your, um . . ." I paused, searching for the politically correct term. "Career?"

"It's not a career," she corrected, and I expected her to brush it off as merely a job. Wrong again. Her lofty tone should've been a tipoff. "It's a divine *calling*."

"I'm glad you *heard* the ding-a-ling," I said impatiently, coloring as I heard my unintentional play on words. I rushed to cover the silence. "But you didn't answer my question."

"I can't see what Ricardo knew or didn't know, did or didn't do, is any of your business." Scythe had nothing on Bettina-Bert when it came to a poker face.

Refusing to be stonewalled by a wannabe woman who wore a fake brick house, I pulled her head back into the sink, poising the spray nozzle over her carefully made-up face, my finger on the trigger.

"Listen to me. You better answer or else."

seven

"STOP!"

I turned toward the hysterical soprano voice, although it was entirely too familiar to me and not especially welcome at the moment. Trudy had an incredibly keen sense of timing, warned divinely to pay me a visit before I cemented my trip south after death. Trudy insists God still writes my misdeeds in pencil. I'm not so sure, and if he does, he goes through a lot of erasers. It's great having such an optimistic friend, nevertheless.

Trudy, resplendent in a sleeveless fuchsia, lime, turquoise, and lemon floral rayon dress that ended with a ruffle at mid-thigh, looked no worse for wear after her morning over-the-phone faint, except for her menacing frown.

"What are you doing now?" she demanded, more exasperated than angry as she looked from Bettina to me to the spray nozzle in my hand. "This is not the best time to be threatening your customers, especially since you're a murder suspect."

"Murder suspect!" Bettina's voice began alto and

dropped to tenor. Trudy cocked her head to one side to study Bettina as Bettina studied me with decidedly more respect. Hey, maybe this bad rep would be worth something after all.

"Well, I wouldn't really call myself a suspect," I began mildly, moving my trigger finger on the nozzle and feeling a shot of juvenile satisfaction when Bettina jumped.

"Why not?" Trudy said. "The TV is."

"The TV is what?"

"Calling you a suspect. Not by name, but everybody's going to know it's you. I was watching the noon news with that stylish Amethyst Andrews. I just love her. Guess what she had on today?"

I glared. Unfazed, she looked to Bettina for encouragement and got it.

"She is *tres chic*. I never miss the news to see what she's wearing. Except today." Bettina shot me a look out of the corner of her eye as if it were *my* fault she had missed seeing the insipid broadcaster's fashion of the day. So much for my bad rep intimidating her.

"Well, maybe everyone will be so dazzled by Amethyst's couture that they won't remember I'm accused of killing a man," I offered facetiously.

"Maybe." Trudy nodded thoughtfully. "It was the most gorgeous dove-gray suit with a raw silk shell of baby pink and this scarf that—"

As Bettina oohed and aahed, I cleared my throat and brandished my water nozzle weapon. "Before I rack up another victim, maybe you'd better tell me what I'm accused of doing to the first one and why."

They blinked at me as if I were a dense child. "You don't need to get testy, Reyn," Trudy huffed. "They showed some footage of Ricardo's Broadway shop draped in all that awful yellow crime-scene tape. The reporter—I think it was that Phil Wimplepool—"

"The one with those hideous bow ties," Bettina interjected before I moved the nozzle closer and he/she shut up.

Trudy nodded and leaned in to Bettina. Clearly, I was extraneous at this point. "He had the worst of his collection on today. Would you believe pond-scum green with chartreuse polka dots?"

Bettina groaned. I think I growled.

"Don't get your panties in a wad, Reyn. Wimplepool said while police refused to say how he was killed, the case had been classified a homicide. He described Ricardo as renowned for building a beauty salon empire in the city, but a man whose past remained shrouded in mystery and who had no known relatives. Investigators were interviewing his employees, and then he said detectives had brought another salon owner and former employee in for questioning."

"Questioning?" I squawked, getting angrier with Scythe by the moment. "That *obnoxious* detective *asked* me to come down to *identify* Ricardo. I went willingly, as a favor to them."

"I'm sure that's true, Reyn," Trudy said dismissively, "but that's not what was said across the airwaves to hundreds of thousands of people. Of course, that was before it hit CNN, so I guess now we could say millions. Anyway, whatever Wimplepool said doesn't matter. The video they ran showed you coming out the front doors, looking pretty shook up and kinda green. Did you throw up?"

Okay, I am internationally accused of murder, and my best friend only wants to know if I threw up when I saw the dead body. No, no sympathetic pats on the shoulder for me, no heartfelt hugs. Somehow, the fact that she expected me to lose my cookies pissed me off more than not being consoled. She wasn't the only one today who thought I had a weak stomach.

"No, I did not throw up," I answered with deliberate delivery. I sucked in a breath and tried to lighten the moment. "Don't I get credit for my skin matching Wimplepool's tie?"

Trudy folded her arms across her chest like I was the bad kid in class. I lost whatever remaining hold I had on my temper. "Come on, how should I have looked? Happy? Skipping down the steps humming a merry tune after seeing the bloody body of my friend and mentor?"

"You could've looked less like you were facing life behind bars," Trudy advised.

"Gee, I'll try to remember that the next time a friend of mine bites it."

"Despite all that, it wouldn't have looked quite so bad for you if it weren't for the next thing."

"It gets *worse?*"

"Reporters caught an impossibly sexy detective leaving." Trudy paused, distracted momentarily by her memory of Scythe. "He wasn't classically handsome, you know. His features were a little too hard—his nose too Roman, his facial lines too deep, his eyes just too probing. But he was just so *male*. He positively radiated testosterone. It came right through the TV screen like raw heat. He's a bit dangerous, I would say."

I let her mind wander off into whatever fantasy she'd concocted. I couldn't blame her, considering whom she was married to. But suddenly, her eyes lost their faraway look, and she resumed her story. "The reporters asked him if you had anything to do with Ricardo's murder. He just looked at the camera like the cat who swallowed the canary and then said, in this toe-curling voice"—Trudy dropped her own to mimic Scythe—" 'No comment.' Have you already pissed off the police, Reyn?"

Trudy said it like it was an expected activity—that's me, always barfing and pissing people off. I bit the inside of my cheek and counted to ten before I answered. "What if the police pissed *me* off?"

"You're too sensitive," Trudy pointed out self-righteously. I would've thrown my hands up in the air, but that would've meant relinquishing my weapon, so I contented myself with tapping my left boot on the floor to a ten count.

Never one to let silence drag on longer than a full minute, Trudy finally broke it. "The TV never said how Ricardo died."

"I'm sure the *TV* doesn't know," I answered snootily. I'm a stickler for grammar, but the real motivation for my deflection was also that I didn't want to tell her in the presence of Bettina and all the other ears in the salon.

"Smarty pants," Trudy mumbled, but blessedly got the message. "Another thing I was wondering was why the place was crawling with city cops when I thought the salon was in Alamo Heights."

"Ricardo built that salon just outside the Alamo Heights city limits because he wanted to be in a school district that needed the revenue. He wanted to help kids who weren't spoiled and didn't live in half-million-dollar homes." I hadn't thought about that in years, but it had struck me odd at the time, because Ricardo was never one even to notice children, much less have a soft spot for them.

Bettina watched me closely. "You sure know a lot about Ricardo's business."

"Not as much as I want to know." I pressed down on the trigger, letting a little water trickle onto his/her left cheek.

"Please don't!" Panic shined in her obsidian eyes. "It takes me an hour and a half to get this makeup right."

"Hon, if you don't mind me saying so," Trudy interjected, "with skin that beautiful, you don't look like you *need* any makeup."

"You'd be surprised," I muttered snidely.

Bettina managed to glare at me and flash a radiant smile at Trudy in practically the same instant. I was impressed. He/she might have the woman thing down after all, I realized, as Bettina demurred prettily. "I have to be at work by four."

I trickled water down her other cheek. Bettina's newest best friend put her hand on my forearm. "Have a heart, Reyn."

"I have no heart." I sneered, increasing the water flow. "Only a burning desire to clear my name and avenge my mentor."

Bettina bought my sorry Clint Eastwood imitation. "Okay, okay. You can come to work with me. We'll ask around about what the other girls know about Ricardo. Some of them knew him better than I did. He only did my hair."

Wow. What did he do with the other "girls," then? I wondered.

"Great!" Trudy trilled. "Where's work? Where are we going?"

I smiled my own cat-who-got-the-canary smile. "You'll see."

• • •

While Bettina, her head sporting ten pounds of curlers, sat under the dryer reading Dr. Laura's *The Ten Stupid Things Women Do to Mess Up Their Lives,* Trudy and I made a list of motives Ricardo may have given someone to murder him. I don't recommend this activity unless it's absolutely necessary, because it inevitably leads to introspection, and you're left pondering the reasons your friends and enemies have to murder *you.* I could concoct a long list without much thought. It leaves one feeling especially vulnerable.

"It's well known Ricardo was a ladies' man," Trudy began, dipping her hand into the bottomless bag of trail mix I kept at my desk and munching thoughtfully. "Maybe it was a jealous husband."

"Or a jealous lover."

After pausing for a second with a cashew half past her lips, Trudy finally popped it in, chewed, and shook her head. "No, I don't see that. Ricardo had a way of charming women no matter how mad they might be. It must've been a pheromone thing. Remember the time you told me about that high-society babe who came in to get her hair done for her daughter's wedding, and Ricardo turned her hair pink? He couldn't fix it, so he convinced her it was the "in" thing. As soon as she was out the door, he was calling the florist to make sure all the arrangements matched her hair, the photographer to make sure he had lights to play down the pink and the society columnist to ensure a positive spin on the press coverage."

"I remember." Ricardo's secret of success, which he shared with me, was creating a labyrinth of favors owed him, carefully culled from select members in all facets of society and business. He knew gangbangers from the barrio and the head of the richest telecommunications company in the country. The key, though, according to Ricardo, was to make sure never to stay in the red too long when it came to favors, because the longer they remained unpaid, the bigger the payback.

Maybe he'd forgotten a favor. I shivered at the thought of the payback being his life.

"Somehow, I don't think it was a crime of passion," I said, my train of thought leading me to a conclusion I couldn't substantiate beyond intuition. "The scene didn't feel chaotic. It felt cold."

"Hey, you never told me how he died." Trudy dropped her voice to a whisper.

I pushed away from my desk to check Bettina's curls, partly because I needed to make sure no one was eavesdropping and partly just to bug Trudy. I'm petty that way. Bettina was reading chapter three ("Stupid Devotion") of Dr. Laura's book. I was afraid to ask, so instead I lifted the dryer helmet. A trace of dampness lingered. Five minutes, and the curls would be cooked. Trudy and I didn't have long to finish hashing this out.

Passing my chair, I reached into a cabinet for a notepad a client gave me one year for Christmas. It was neon orange with "Hairdressers Do It with Style" written diagonally across the upper left corner—not exactly the most subtle investigative accessory, but it would have to do. Seeing the clutter behind the door, I felt my throat swell with the memory of Ricardo's disapproval only twenty-four hours before. Funny how death puts criticism in a different light. He cared. I should have appreciated it more at the time.

Returning to my desk, I whispered in Trudy's ear,

"The murderer stabbed him in the back with the pick attached to a metal round brush."

Shock paralyzed her for a moment, but as soon as I saw her open her mouth, I clamped my hand over it, muffling her exclamation. "Muz if da bursh ee burd firmyu lisnit?"

It would've been *Was it the brush he borrowed from you last night?* at ten thousand decibels had I not been a quick draw with my silencing hand. With a nod in answer, her eyes begged me to let her loose. Mine warned back to shut up. She nodded. I let my hand drop, wiping her spit and lipstick on my black synthetic tunic.

"Holy water and horny toads, this isn't good," she couldn't help interjecting. Trudy is fond of stating the obvious. "Do you have an alibi?"

"Chardonnay, Beaujolais, and Cabernet will vouch for me," I said, avoiding mention that the only human who could swear I was home in bed was now dead. Trudy looked close enough to turning me in to the police even without that choice bit of knowledge.

"That badge-carrying hunk-of-the-month didn't look the type to consider dogs reliable witnesses," Trudy said dryly, then brightened. "But he *did* look the type to be swayed by a roll in the sack."

"Trudy!" This time, I hit ten decibels and compounded my sin by blushing.

"Okay." She held up a hand in surrender. "How about a blow job, then?"

I stood up, more horrified by the blush that heated my face than by her suggestion. "Get out! I can't believe I consider you a friend."

"Hey, I'm your best friend, the one who was—until you so gravely insulted me—trying to save your butt from being put in a sling."

"I don't think sex will keep me out of the sling."

I saw the look in her eyes just in time.

"Don't say it," I warned with a shake of my head.

"Oh, all right," she muttered, disappointed that she couldn't give me ideas about sex in a sling. "But maybe when this whole thing is over, you and Detective Gorgeous can have a nice candlelight dinner."

"Right now, he's probably doing his damnedest to picture me in handcuffs instead."

Trudy was getting that look again.

"In handcuffs, fully clothed in an unattractive orange jumpsuit, and behind bars," I clarified. "So, it's probably a little early to be making us dinner reservations."

"Okay, but it will give me something to shoot for," she said, "if you promise me you're interested and will go out with him if I can arrange it."

Trudy was a tireless cupid; if this was the incentive she needed to help me do some digging for information about Ricardo, so be it. Her career as an interior designer left her a lot of free time. I could use an extra hand. Mario's lucrative position as an underwriter for an insurance firm afforded her the ability to choose to work for whom she wanted, when she wanted. I wanted her to work for me. It wouldn't be for free. But I doubt I'd ever have to pay that bill.

"A rendezvous with Scythe." I ripped off my smock. "In a sling." I pulled the left shoulder of my bodysuit down. "In handcuffs." I hiked my skirt up over my thigh. "Or at a table. You help me, and it's a deal."

I didn't know Trudy's eyes could get that wide. Why was she so shocked when this had been what she was after? Her gaze drifted past me and back again.

I felt a presence behind me and turned around.

eight

"HOW MUCH DID YOU HEAR?" I DEMANDED AS I wiggled myself back into my clothes. Scythe, who was leaning against my office doorjamb, reached over and slid his forefinger under the Lycra at my left shoulder that had wound itself into an impossibly tight wad. With a flick of his finger, he popped it loose. I yanked out of his reach, just as the electricity from his touch zinged home to every erogenous zone I possess. How did he do that?

"I heard enough to make me glad I carry protection," he answered with that damned poker face.

The blush on my cheeks immediately suffused my whole body before I saw he was patting the bulge at his side that under the black leather jacket would be a gun. My lust-laden embarrassment morphed into fury.

"I'll make you glad," I muttered, moving to the farthest corner of the office, which wasn't nearly far enough.

"Promise?" The great stone face softened into a smile. No, a *leer* is more accurate.

I narrowed my eyes, crossed my arms over my chest,

and considered how much violence I could get away with before he threw me into the slammer. I could hear Bettina's soft alto beckoning me from the dryer. I ignored him/her.

Trudy's head was bobbing back and forth to look at Scythe and me, her goofy grin making her resemble a garish back-window auto ornament. I took my fury out on her.

"What are you smirking at?" I snapped.

Before she could answer, a clear tenor called from the hallway. "Reyn! I think I'm ready."

Bettina had lost patience and had resorted to testosterone to call my attention. Trudy's brow wrinkled. Scythe looked confused.

"Coming!" I hollered.

"I didn't see a man when I came in," Scythe observed suspiciously. "Who's that?"

"My sweetheart, and he's real jealous, so you'd better go."

"Claude?" Scythe guessed, part sarcastic humor and part uncertainty that Claude might really exist. Good, let him wonder.

Now poor Trudy's forehead looked like a road map. If she drew her brows together any harder, she'd have one long, well-plucked, copper caterpillar eyebrow. She opened her mouth to ask who the hell I was talking about and who the hell Claude was (not that way, of course, as, despite her reference to oral sex earlier, she is very pious). But without letting her get a word out, I stomped to the doorway, slipping through the space between Scythe's body, his arm, and the doorjamb. He smelled of freshly cut wood, although I couldn't place what kind. I had the urge to step back to get another whiff but resisted. Marching up to Bettina, I flipped the dryer off and whispered a warning to him/her as I unrolled one bouncy curl. I was betting she wouldn't be inclined to be too friendly to Scythe as the cops' recent hobby had been hassling Illusions.

I was right. Bettina glared at Scythe, who'd followed me out of the office and now was peeking into Daisy Dawn's nail haven as he stalked down the hall toward the room with Justine's and Alejandra's chairs.

"You better not scare the customers," I warned as I herded Bettina to my chair.

"Don't worry," he threw over his shoulder. "If they're *your* customers, they don't scare easily."

Behind me, Trudy blew a chuckle out her nose. So much for friends. Although I itched to follow Lieutenant Nosy down the hall, I began whipping curlers off Bettina's head, flinging them into the tray with a necessary speed. As heavy as her hair was, if any curl hung loose for too long without maximum chemical support (i.e. mucho hairspray), the style would droop pitifully. Despite what I'd told Ricardo last night about not wanting to own an empire, I *was* ambitious. I didn't want to be shown up in my chosen profession by anyone, dead or alive.

"So, who's Claude?" Trudy asked, pulling up a stool. She perched on it, crossed her legs, and bounced her sandal-clad foot up and down.

Scythe reappeared, industrial steno pad in hand. His gaze lingered on Trudy's legs, proving, I suppose, that he was a real man. I hadn't found one yet who could resist staring at Trudy's gams. She had the best pair I'd ever seen; long, perfectly shaped, tan, and—the true crime—without a trace of cellulite. Even her knees were pretty. She was truly inhuman. I considered it a credit to my character that I could be best friends with a woman with legs like that, especially since mine were best hidden under nothing less than ankle-length denim.

So I didn't blame him for what had now lasted long enough to be considered ogling, but I didn't especially like it, either. In fact, my stomach twisted in an odd way. I gripped the brush tighter to get a grip on my weird reaction.

"Ouch," Bettina protested, in her alto, not her tenor.

Apologizing, I tugged through her hair more gently and bit my lip instead.

"So, you don't know Claude?" Scythe, whose eyes had traveled back up to her face, asked Trudy. Cutting me a confused look, she shook her head wordlessly. Scythe picked up on the undercurrents and read way too much into them, as usual. He cleared his throat. "Are you someone who *would* know him?"

That did it. Trudy was insulted. She planted her hands on her hips.

"I guess so. I'm her best friend. I know everything about Reyn," Trudy announced.

"Then you and I need to talk," he said, flashing a grin so inviting it sparked a girl's imagination. How come all I got were frowns, groans, eyebrow hitches, laser-beam stares, and leers?

"Jackson Scythe, SAPD," he said, offering his hand.

"Trudy Trujillo." Trudy's affront visibly melted as she took his large hand in her fine-fingered one. I noticed with a small degree of satisfaction that he was the one to drop the handshake. Good thing, too, because from the looks of Trudy, they might still be standing there at the turn of the *next* century. I was in real trouble if these two talked. Scythe had Trudy so under his testosterone spell that he'd know everything about me—even about the boring underwear. That thought drew me up short. I have bigger secrets than that; I don't know why that particular one came to mind first. As if he were reading my mind, Scythe threw me a look, then half hitched his left eyebrow. I thought about my toad-green bra and had a sudden urge to run to Victoria's Secret.

"If you have time, I have some questions now," Scythe said to Trudy.

Uh-oh.

I heard the front door open and prayed it wasn't the *National Enquirer*. After all, if I was tromping around all over the TV, it wouldn't be long before the media figured out who I was and where to find me. *Argh.* Sherlyn was taxed to her limit by having to answer one phone call every half hour and greet an occasional transvestite customer. How was she going to be able to hold the press at bay? With her iridescent tennis shoes? I'd probably have to close up the shop. *Damn.*

"Miss Sawyer, none of your employees saw Mr. Montoya come by the salon last night."

I looked at Scythe, whose hard face told me he'd taken a time-out from charming Trudy to harass me. "First of all, the only employee is my receptionist, and she goes home at five. The rest are independent contractors and go home whenever they choose. Yesterday, they were all gone by seven-thirty when Ricardo came by."

"How convenient," he murmured, noting it on his steno, "for you to be all alone."

"But she wasn't alone, *señor*," Mario interrupted as he loped his lumpy body down the hall. "I was here, along with *mi cara*." He kissed each one of Trudy's knees and

then peppered her face with kisses as she cooed in pleasure, Scythe's dry-ice blues apparently forgotten for the
moment. Bettina viewed the scene with mushy tender-
ness. Scythe looked like he needed to use his own barf
bag. Maybe we had something in common after all.

"And you are?" Scythe tapped the butt of his Bic on
the pad.

"Mario Trujillo," he answered between smooches.

Scythe shot me a questioning glance. I shrugged. Nobody ever understood. It was like finding Nicole Kidman
married to Danny DeVito. No, that wasn't it, either, because Danny was funny. Mario didn't even have a wicked
sense of humor going for him.

"Excuse me," I interrupted, my left hand cradling
Bettina's curls like a baby, my right hand wielding an
industrial-size can of style freeze. "I'm about to spray."

Nothing got men out of the room faster than threatening hairspray. Mario and Scythe rushed out to stand
by the sinks, where Mario began regaling the detective
with the events of last night without being asked. Bettina closed her eyes. I pressed the trigger, meeting
Trudy's eyes over the fountain of black curls. She cocked
her head toward my office and disappeared. I remembered why she was my best friend: her ability to read
my mind. I heard the squeak of the door that led to my
living quarters. I described the way out the back to Bettina. She nodded silently and waited until I moved to
stand in front of the chair, where the men could see me
but not anything else in the room. I could hear Mario's
emotional description of his fantasy hairstyle to a visibly
dismayed Scythe. I bit back a chortle; they'd be there
awhile. I couldn't think of a better torture for the arrogant detective. After a parting shot of hairspray that

would repel them a little longer, I slipped out of sight, through the door, and into my den.

Illusions, here we come.

Fortunately, Bettina had parked halfway down the block. Unfortunately, what she'd parked was a minuscule Karmann Ghia painted saffron.

"Love this color," Trudy said as she slid into the passenger seat and looked at me like I'd better prepare to ride on the roof.

"It's custom," Bettina answered proudly.

"It'll be great for losing that police tail," I observed.

"Tail?" Alarmed, Bettina looked in the rearview mirror.

Trudy waved off her concern. "There's no tail. It's just Reyn's pessimism talking. She always thinks the worst."

Except when my friends are dying. I thought Ricardo was looped and getting a quickie when he was really bleeding to death. The reminder forced me to squeeze into the passenger seat with Trudy. We grappled for position until Trudy insisted that, being taller, she deserved the seat, and I, the shrimp, had to sit in her lap.

"Just call me the human air bag," I muttered.

"That wouldn't be accurate, hon, your breasts aren't big enough," Bettina corrected.

"Thanks a lot."

"Remember, hon, God wouldn't have given us the gift of plastic surgeons without intending us to use them," Bettina pointed out.

That appealed to Trudy's warped Catholicism. "Wow. I never thought of it like that. You think I should get my eyes done?"

"No," I answered sourly. Trudy was only thirty-three and looked twenty-five.

Bettina assessed Trudy with a serious look. "Maybe not for a year or two. I'll give you the name of a great surgeon." She turned the ignition and adjusted herself carefully in her bucket seat. When I remembered what on her needed tucking, I felt a twinge of pity for how dicey a proposition sitting might be.

Then, with a lurch that sent my forehead cracking into the windshield, Bettina popped the clutch, and we were off.

"I'm so glad I talked you into that perfume, Reyn," Trudy said, giving my neck a sniff as I rubbed the egg on my forehead. "It's sexy."

Now, I knew she meant sexy to, perhaps, Lieutenant Arrogant, but the sidelong glance Bettina slid us told me she thought different.

"I know a great club you two might enjoy. After my show, I'll take you there."

I held up a hand. "No, thanks."

"It's very discreet," Bettina insisted.

Trudy, oblivious as usual to nuances that didn't have to do with shape or color of furniture, rugs, or window treatments, shoved my shoulder as punishment for what she perceived as rudeness. "That's very thoughtful of you, Bettina. Maybe we'll have time."

Shaking my head, I let it go. The silence dragged on for a few minutes before Trudy couldn't stand it any longer.

"You said you did a show, Bettina. What can we look forward to seeing?"

Considering my position, which would likely soon be catapulting out the windshield if Trudy got the whole truth at this moment, I answered before Bettina could, "She's an entertainer at Illusions."

"How exciting," Trudy enthused. She never read anything beyond design magazines and books on feng-shui and antiques. She carried a copy of *Color Me Perfect* and color swatches in her purse. A night out for her and Mario would be to Bible study or salsa dancing (scary thought, I know). So, if she hadn't decorated Illusions herself or been paying attention when her idol Amethyst Andrews mentioned the city council debate over the club on television, Trudy would have no idea what we were walking into. In fact, I couldn't swear she knew what a transvestite was.

That was probably for the best.

As we passed through the stately but overpriced homes in staid Olmos Park, then the more modest circa-1950s neighborhoods on our way to the freeway, I couldn't help having an out-of-body image as I sometimes do. What if I were that slightly dumpy yet very normal-looking bottle blonde pushing a baby stroller on the sidewalk there, and what if I knew that a transvestite, a murder suspect, and a model-beautiful airhead married to a troll were the trio speeding through my neighborhood in a little off-yellow bullet?

I'd probably run screaming for the house, lock the doors, and hold my baby close.

I sighed. What had happened to my life?

"So, what's the plan?" Trudy asked.

I resorted to the technique my sister Pecan uses with her passel of preteen kids when they ask a question: Answer them honestly minus the details. Only supply those, one at a time, when pressed. In other words, make them work for it.

"Bettina was a client of Ricardo's."

"Three days a week for five years," Bettina put in.

"Really?" Trudy gave Bettina another once-over. I

knew what she was assuming. Rumor was Ricardo liked his dalliances beautiful and busty. Bettina was currently one of the two. Just wait. She'd be both before long.

"So, why are we going with her to work?"

"She says he frequented her, uh, place of business and was closer to some of the other . . ." What did I say, girls? Boys? "Some of her colleagues than he was to her. Maybe they can give us some clues about his killer."

"Oh." Trudy looked disappointed that Bettina wouldn't be able to give us details of Ricardo's sexual performance, details I'd rather not know but probably would by the end of the evening.

McCullough Avenue brought us to Loop 410 East, the road noise reverberating around in the almost-car-size tin can preventing us from furthering our conversation until we pulled off I-35.

Illusions was set discreetly off the access road, on a side street, behind a stand of ten-foot-high bamboo trees that hid everything but an asphalt driveway and a small gold-lettered sign. One would have to know where it was to find it, which had been one of the owners' arguments before the city council. They weren't trying to lure in unsuspecting youngsters looking for a good time. The club was members-only, with a strict carding policy. They didn't convert, apparently, only admitted the converted.

What would they make of us?

I suddenly wasn't sure I wanted to know.

"Wow," Trudy exclaimed, wide-eyed. "I didn't know this was here. I've gotta get Mario to bring me here one night."

That thought brightened my day.

Bettina whipped into the only reserved slot left behind the gray stucco building and pulled the parking brake before she took the car out of gear. I would now have matching lumps on either side of my forehead.

"I'll take you backstage, then get one of the boys to get you front-row seats," Bettina announced. She peeled off her espadrilles, fit her size nines into the four-inch gold pumps she pulled from behind the seat, and clipped up a short flight of stairs to an unmarked door. In her rush to follow Bettina, Trudy plastered my face up against my intimate friend, the windshield, as she wriggled out of the seat and ran to catch up.

"Will you hurry up, Reyn?" Trudy shouted as Bettina held the door open.

I considered a proper rejoinder but bit it back when I remembered Trudy would be getting her comeuppance once she stepped inside the club. Impatient, Bettina entered and left Trudy holding the door. She did so only as long as it took me to reach the steps, then she let it go, chasing after our reluctant hostess and leaving me to dive for it or be locked out. The muscles on the right side of my spine seized up again as I propelled myself into the half-lit hallway.

I must have moaned, because Trudy poked her head around the corner. "What is it?"

"My back."

"Horn-rims and hot dogs, don't be such a wimp about a little twinge, Reyn. Get your priorities straight. We're on the trail of a killer."

Showing great restraint in not reminding her that her husband was the cause of my "little twinge," I followed her through what felt like a neon tomb. The rhythm of rock music from deeper inside the building shook the walls. The labyrinth of hallways were painted black matte, carpeted in a low-pile black, both blacks reflected in mirrored ceilings. Was this where Ricardo got the idea for his office? I tried not to think about why or how. The blackness was periodically broken up by closed doors outlined in neon lights, labeled in glittery gold. We passed one marked OFFICE, one marked STAGE LEFT, one marked with a star whose name was lit in colored neon, RANDIE REDEAUX. Other stars glittered down the hallway, but Trudy had stopped in front of the fourth door, marked G DRESSING ROOM. The G being general purpose, girls, or gents, take your pick.

"Bettina said we could go on in," Trudy said, the haughty lift in her chin surely a sign she thought we were hot stuff to be admitted backstage to a semi-star's dressing room. Feeling guilt knocking, I opened my mouth to warn her, but she opened the door faster.

And, a second later, squealed and fainted.

nine

THOUGH MY BACK SCREAMED OVER SUPPORTING HER dead weight, I couldn't blame Trudy for going limp. I knew what to expect, and I still felt a little woozy. A dozen drag queens in various stages of undress buzzed around like colorful, happy bees in falsies. Of course, some of the breasts were real, which was more than I wanted to consider at the moment. Elbow to elbow at the counter, some wearing only bras and girdles, they applied false eyelashes, rouge, and lipstick. At our end, one hiked up a skirt to slather body glitter on a bare, curvaceous thigh.

I envied that thigh. Even men had better women's legs than I did. How depressing.

The blonde (courtesy of a custom-made wig) in the corner finally drew my attention. Ripping duct tape with his teeth, he stuck his hands down the front of his black French-cut silk undies in a delicate operation that left him with a profile as feminine as mine.

Or maybe more so.

Yikes.

Bettina was nowhere to be seen. She'd directed us to

the dressing room to shock us, perhaps scare us away. I wondered if it was just for sport because we'd become tedious or if she wanted to hide something. Hmm.

The chaos and chatter in the room had kept anyone from noticing us, two real women in the doorway, one of whom was unconscious. That just goes to show how frenetic and loud it was in the G dressing room. Before I'd decided how to announce our presence, Trudy began slipping out of my arms. The blonde with the awesome legs looked up and rushed over.

"Oh, *girlfriend!*" He (while I'd reconciled myself to calling Bettina a her, I couldn't help thinking of the blonde as a male, considering I'd watched him shape his him-stuff into her-stuff) reached over with one arm, Lady Godiva tresses draping over Trudy's face as he dragged her to the couch in the middle of the room and laid her down. Another performer, this one dressed in fluffy mules and a pink sequined and feathered robe—with no telling what underneath—put a damp washrag on Trudy's forehead.

"What happened to her?" Lady Godiva asked.

"Low blood sugar." Not true, but easier than saying they'd scared the consciousness out of her. Trudy moaned; her eyelids fluttered open just long enough to take in Lady Godiva's five o'clock shadow before they snapped shut again.

"Hand me those Calorie Cutter Caramels, LeDonna." Lady Godiva grabbed them out of LeDonna's hand and regarded what must have been a skeptical expression on my face. He patted his flat, hairless stomach, smoothing his hand around the swell of his hip. "A girl's gotta watch the fat intake. This figure's not easy to keep."

Understatement of the year, I thought as I watched him/her (damn, I was back to that!) unwrap a caramel. I took it, feeding it bit by bit into Trudy's mouth, which—as I knew it would—brought her around better than smelling salts. Trudy despises caramel; her mother hid her childhood medicines in melted caramel.

A wet brown wad shot out of her mouth, sending the "girls" scattering. The candy stuck in a neon-green feather boa, dragging it off its hanger and onto the floor. Someone gasped in horror. Gagging, Trudy sat up and batted my hand away. "Yuck. What *are* you doing, Reyn?"

"Just getting you back on your feet." I grinned, biting my lower lip to keep from laughing.

That familiar light in Trudy's eyes told me I was in trouble. "On my feet? I need to be on my knees—"

"Ooo lala, baby," one of the "girls" sang out. An odd mixture of baritone, tenor, and falsetto giggles rippled through the room. Trudy glanced around, a bit dazed and not cluing in to what everyone else in the room took to be a double entendre by one of their own.

"On my knees to pray for your salvation," Trudy finished a bit righteously.

"Bible thumper, huh?" LeDonna commented, leaning over to zip up knee-high red leather boots. He really was a dead ringer for Tina Turner. It almost made me want to stay for the show.

"Buffet Catholic, more like," I responded.

Trudy put her hands on her hips with a huff.

"You two new hires?" Lady Godiva asked, glancing appraisingly at us—appreciatively at Trudy, askance at me, especially in the general vicinity of my chest. It was heartening to know I wouldn't make a good transvestite. See, small breasts *can* be an asset.

"He's got Nicole Kidman down cold." LeDonna crooked a little finger at Trudy, a little jealously.

"What?" Trudy squawked, sitting up straighter. I patted her shoulder. *Down, girl.*

"Actually, we're not here to work," I began. "Bettina brought us."

LeDonna rolled her eyes and returned to the vanity counter, where she picked up a bottle of blue mascara. "Bettina knows she ain't supposed to bring anybody backstage. But a big star like her, she don't need to follow the rules."

Most in the room had gone back to their preparations, but I noticed a redhead in a violet lamé sheath listening silently but closely to our conversation.

"Well, since you're here, I'll take you up front, get you good seats," Lady Godiva offered. "Just let me throw on a robe."

"Don't rush," I put in quickly. "I was hoping any or all of you might be able to help me."

"Help with what?"

"Ricardo Montoya was murdered last night."

"You the cops?" LeDonna asked, her eyes, no longer friendly, drilling mine through the conduit of the mirror.

The atmosphere in the room, which had gone from comfortable chaos to friendly tolerance since our arrival, now chilled to stone cold. Trudy shifted on the couch, digging her fingernails into the flesh of my inner forearm.

"No, I'm not a cop; I'm a hairstylist. Ricardo was my friend, my mentor."

"You're the one on TV," a buxom curly-headed blonde in a cowgirl outfit spoke up, pointing. "I saw you on the noon news. You're a suspect."

So much for viewers being dazzled deaf by Amethyst's fashion sense. But apparently, having a possible murderer in their midst was preferable to a cop, because suddenly the temperature in the room warmed several dozen degrees. Trudy relaxed.

I nodded at the cowgirl. Who was she supposed to be, Mae West? "Which is part of the reason I'm here. I didn't kill him," I said, playing up an animosity that might work in my favor. "But the cops are putting on the heat anyway."

A few under-the-breath, especially creative epitaphs were muttered in sympathy. Then Lady Godiva turned back to me. "We're happy to help you if it means screwing the cops. What you need?"

"I'm looking at each part of Ricardo's life to find a motive. I heard a rumor this morning that he liked to, ah . . ." I paused, grasping for my rusty repertoire of political correctness. If I ever needed it, I needed it now, with approximately two thousand pounds of man in drag staring me down.

Trudy apparently didn't trust me to come up with anything delicate enough. "What Reyn's trying to ask is, did Ricardo experiment sexually?"

The chuckles, shaking heads, and hands waving off the rumor told me it wasn't true. "He might have liked to experiment, but with real girls, not boys playing at it," LeDonna answered. "We know, cuz lots of us tried. He was one fine-looking man. What's happened, such a hot piece of ass whacked, well, shit, that's a shame."

It occurred to me Ricardo spurning any of their advances could be considered motive for murder. Of course, the scenario more likely to me would've been Ricardo—the suave yet macho friend I thought I knew—murdering any one of these guys who'd approached him about sex. Maybe, though, he so insulted the provocateur that he/she held a deadly grudge. Glancing around the room, I could see that many of them might have had the strength to bury the pick in Ricardo's back. Bettina's disappearance and the silent, watchful redhead in the corner made me wonder all the more whether there was more here than just a lot of duct tape and falsies. I tried a different line of questioning.

"Did any of you notice if Ricardo got friendly with any of your customers?"

"Club members," Lady Godiva corrected as the temperature dropped again. "You're crossing into territory we can't cover now, girlfriend. We all signed a confidentiality agreement when we join the club. That's what our members pay for, to see a good show and never be seen here."

"Surely you have a list of club members," I began. "I could get it from your manager."

"You'd only get it over Gregor's dead body."

Trudy and I cringed, but, looking around, we saw no one else thought it a bad choice of words. Apparently, Gregor's homicidally protective nature was accepted and respected. Perhaps I'd hit on something. Had Ricardo threatened to expose Illusions' clientele? Last night, he'd talked about a windfall—had he tried to blackmail Gregor?

"Where is Gregor? Do you think he'd talk to me?" I asked, batting my eyelashes innocently.

The temperature dropped near blizzard level again. Lady Godiva smiled, though, showing a row of blinding capped teeth. "We like you, so I don't think we want you talking to Gregor. He's out of your league, girlfriend. Trust me, leave it alone. Plus, he was here all last night."

"Between two and five A.M.?" I'd extrapolated the time of death from my fuzzy view of my digital alarm;

one of the three digits I'd seen in triplicate had to be the hour of Ricardo's call, as he was bleeding to death. If only I had gone down to the salon to see what was wrong.

"Yes, we were choreographing a new group routine. We're not morning people, so we always work after closing." Several nods backed up Lady's Godiva's statement. But, of course, these were people who lied to protect their customers—why not their boss?

Everyone froze at a pounding at the door that sounded like the Incredible Hulk was on the other side. "Get out here, you pussies! What are you doing? Ten minutes to show time!"

Just as Lady Godiva started to shoo me and Trudy toward the walk-in closet, the door burst open, and an incredibly short, furry-armed man with a bald pate stomped into the dressing room. Aiming his middle finger at us (I tried not to take it as an editorial comment), he glared through little eyes that were so light blue they were nearly colorless. "Bettina told me about you two. Get the hell outta here. Ricardo paid his dues for a year, cleared his bar tab every visit, and never hassled nobody. I got no beef with him except his croaking is causing me a hassle right now. You can fix that by getting lost."

"I was going to take them up front to see the show," Lady Godiva said, rather bravely, I thought.

"Not unless they sign a membership contract and pony up two thousand bucks, you're not."

Trudy's eyes widened as they met mine, and we both shook our heads. Intrepid investigators too cheap to go where we needed to go. James Bond needn't worry.

"Then get scarce," Gregor boomed, leading the way out the door. I noticed black hair crawling out from the collar of his tacky white satin shirt. Ick. No wonder he had an anger management issue; being saddled with both a small man and a hairy man complex was no picnic. It was amazing he could get himself up out of bed every day. I flirted with the idea of mentioning electrolysis, then thought better of it.

"Thanks," I said softly to Lady Godiva as we left. The strains of "When a Man Loves a Woman" filtered into the hallway from the club. Despite having been bounced out of the joint by someone who looked like he'd rather stuff us in a trunk than show us the door, I twitched my lips into a brief smile. Maybe Gregor had a sense of humor after all, twisted though it may be. So he wasn't completely unlikable. Short, Hairy, and Menacing paused outside the Stage Left door and hooked a thumb toward the exit sign. It suddenly occurred to me that we didn't have a way back to the salon. I paused. Those colorless eyes glared. Oh, well, nothing ventured, nothing gained my gran always said.

"We don't have a ride," I told Gregor.

"Like I care?"

"I guess you don't mind us hanging around, then, as customers start coming. No telling how long it will be before we can manage to get a cab."

Grumbling obscenities, Gregor yanked his cell phone out of his pocket and demanded the salon number. I gave it to him, his stunted forefinger stabbed it out, and I noticed that even he winced at Sherlyn's grating greeting. Maybe this was one receptionist I'd fire before she quit. Gregor growled into his Motorola. "Yeah, you. You send somebody over here to Illusions club to get your boss and her pal before I put 'em to work." He paused to listen to Sherlyn. The veins on his neck started to bulge. He cut

her off. "Tough shit. I don' care it's five and time for you
to clock out, you answered the fricking phone, didn' ya?
Get your boss to pay you overtime." This time, Sherlyn
cut him off. Beads of sweat popped out on his forehead.
The volume of his growl rose with each word. "No, bitch,
you can't stay for the happy hour show. You got ten minutes to haul your boss's ass outta here before I throw that
ass and her friend's sweet one *in* the show. Understand?"

Swell. Now I was a murder suspect and a transvestite. How long before the media got hold of that? Probably just long enough for Sherlyn to hang up the phone.
Trudy gasped, which thrilled the sadistic Gregor no end.
He stretched his lips open in what I guessed was his
version of a smile, thrust the phone back into his pocket,
and took an obscene inventory of Trudy's legs, leaving
his hand in his pocket. I didn't want to think of what he
was doing in there. "Ever danced before, babe?"

Emitting a choking sound, Trudy grabbed my arm,
pulled me to the exit, and shoved me out the door. The
door clicked shut. We both jumped when we saw the
silent, watchful redhead from the dressing room leaning
against the wall of the building, cigarette dangling from
one broad hand. Close up, I could peg his color as the
unusual Egyptian Plum. He wore a black cotton outfit
that looked like a cross between medical scrubs and pa-
jamas. He must have noticed me studying them. I
needed to work on subtling my method of visual detec-
tion, which consisted of a hard stare, often accompanied
by a dropped open mouth.

"I teach karate for fun and do this"—he waved toward the interior of Illusions—"for a living."

He took a long drag and blew out the smoke before
he spoke again.

"Gregor's a prick. But he's no killer. He doesn't have enough imagination for that."

I thought anyone who could run a drag queen show probably had more imagination than the average Joe, but I didn't argue, for fear it would shut up what might be our best source of information so far.

"Listen," the redhead whispered, looking off into the bamboo as if he expected a panda to jump out any minute. "Ricardo came in a couple of times and seemed to enjoy the show, but he was more being polite, I think, than being a real fan. He talked to us, sure, about all sorts of stuff—politics, sports, hair. He treated us like we were his equals, never looking down on what we are or what we do. He was a class guy. But I think his visits were part of a plan. He was staking out the place."

"For what?" Trudy interrupted. I stepped on her foot to shut her up. She kicked me in the shin.

"For a meeting about a week ago that he had with another guy. Ricardo had come lots of times before. See, the way I figure it, by then he'd satisfied himself that he could be safer and more invisible here than anywhere in town. No one will admit to seeing someone else here. How could they without incriminating themselves by admitting to being in a transvestite club?"

"Ingenious," I whispered, and meant it. This guy was smart, and so was Ricardo, although not smart enough, apparently.

"Yeah, plus Ricardo then had insurance—the knowledge of the power brokers who come here."

The source of many of his owed favors, no doubt. Perhaps I was off-base when I thought it was Gregor out for Ricardo. Maybe it was a member of the club who wanted his secret kept, wasn't willing to pay, but was willing to kill.

"What power brokers?" I couldn't help asking.

Long Egyptian Plum's hair rippled as he shook his head decisively. "No way. I'm not stupid. But I will tell you the guy Ricardo met that night looked familiar to me, not because he comes here regularly but because I saw him somewhere on TV or in the newspaper. He wasn't someone I'd know to name, though. And he never came again."

"When was this?" I asked, instinct telling me to follow this.

"Maybe a month ago."

"What did he look like?"

"Improved average."

"What's that supposed to mean?" Trudy interjected, clearly more interested in the term as a general cosmetic description than as a way to find this man for our case.

"A middle-aged guy, average height, average weight, who wouldn't attract attention except for the tan he bought, the pricey jewelry he wore, the expensive highlights in his hair, his clothes."

"What clothes?" I asked.

"Tennis whites." Redhead blew out another mouthful of smoke. "We see a lot of weird getups in here, but tennis whites? It's not something you wear to be incognito, which people tend to want to be in Illusions. So, this guy either has the balls not to care if he's recognized, or he thought he was meeting Ricardo at a club where they swing rackets instead of both ways."

"Did you hear what they talked about?"

"No. They knew each other, but they weren't friends. Body language told me that."

"Who left first?"

"The tennis guy, tense and angry, kind of like he had a stick up his butt."

"Would you recognize him if I showed you a photo?" I asked. Trudy looked hopefully at me, as if I might know who Ricardo's mystery date had been. I had no clue.

"Sure." He let the glowing butt fall to the ground. The roar of a car engine pulled my attention to the parking lot as a dark blue late-model Crown Victoria with tinted windows squealed around the corner of the building.

It must be our ride, I thought, though come to think of it, no one at the salon drove a Crown Vic. Sherlyn's Escort was often on the blink, and she probably had to call a car service. As the car lurched to a stop at the base of the stairs, the driver's side door flew open. I reached inside my purse for my wallet.

"Freeze!"

The voice and the command were familiar but terribly out of context. Shocked, I looked up to see a big black gun trained at my forehead.

ten

"WHAT IS THAT?" I DEMANDED AS SOON AS MY EYES defrosted enough to see the frowning face behind the gun. For once, Scythe's emotions were easy to read—he had none. His laser-light blues trained on me like I was a cardboard cutout at the firing range.

"Police-issue nine-millimeter Glock."

My tongue was feeling a little thick, what with my adrenaline all going to my lower intestines, but I forced it to work anyway. "What are you doing with it?"

"I'm going to use it to shoot you unless you take your hand out of your purse very slowly and very immediately."

"You know just what to say to make a girl go weak at the knees," I muttered, while obeying Scythe's order, though I was sorely tempted to pull my checkbook out and aim it at him. Only problem was, it wasn't loaded with much.

A smile muscle twitched at the corner of his unforgiving mouth. That left eyebrow half hitched. His eyes thawed by about ten degrees. While common sense told me to be nothing but grateful, I recognized that look. I'd seen it on my brother Chevy's face when, as he changed a diaper on his firstborn, the brand-new baby boy had used his dad's head for target practice. It was that combination of disgust and grudging respect I now saw on Scythe's face.

Wow, what a way to impress a man. I really had a touch, now, didn't I?

Trudy swaying next to me drew my attention away from both my lack of sexual charm and impending mortal harm. "We're going to die!" Trudy exclaimed with a squeal as her eyes began to roll back into her head. Only then did I notice that Redhead had at some point disappeared back into the building, no doubt having sagely recognized the squeal of police tires. He won the IQ test of the day.

I slapped Trudy across the face. Her eyes snapped back to reality. One problem solved.

"Hands back up over your head," Scythe commanded, what little emotion he'd displayed fleeing his face. My mouth went dry. I did as I was told. I didn't think being shot by a man with the body of a Greek god and the charisma of Houdini would be a consolation when I was bleeding to death in the parking lot of a transvestite club. My mother would never forgive me. I wonder if I would care about that from heaven. Optimistic thinker that I am.

Shaking sense back into her head, Trudy leaned her hip against the metal railing for support as her hands joined mine in the air. "Thanks, Reyn, but I'd rather you'd have let me faint. I don't want to see my best friend gunned down."

"I'm not going to gun anybody down," he said, reluctantly letting exasperation creep into his tone, which gave me a little shot of perverse satisfaction. He slipped his sleek black gun back into the shoulder holster hidden under his blazer. "Is everything always so chaotic with you two?"

Trudy and I seriously considered the question with a long look at each other, finally nodding at the same time as we turned our wide-eyed attention back to Scythe. He shook his head with a grunt.

The passenger door opened, and for the first time I saw we had more unwelcome company. Crandall, shaking and red in the face, looked like he was having a heart attack as he struggled to unfold his blocky body from the seat. Scythe's eyes cut to his partner for a second, his frown deepening. How insensitive, I thought, for him to find his colleague's discomfort irritating. Tears began rolling over the paunchy dunes in Crandall's cheeks. Only then did it dawn on me that the old guy was laughing, albeit with one hand resting on his shoulder holster.

So my prospensity for inducing hilarity wasn't taking much edge off their perception that I was potentially violent. How much more insulting could this get?

I was about to find out.

"I guess we oughta search her." Crandall punctuated his lackluster tone with a gummy snap.

Scythe shot another look, this one completely unreadable, at Crandall. Trudy, reviving miraculously from her near faint, bobbed her head up and down. "Yes, I think you *should*, Detective Scythe."

Hands still up in the air, I balanced on my left leg in order to stomp on Trudy's foot with my right, but Scythe caught my eye and shook his head once, decisively. I put my boot back down on the concrete reluctantly, settling instead for mumbling under my breath what I'd do to Trudy when we were no longer in the presence of the law. Her grin just widened. Bitch.

Scythe sighed laboriously and cocked his head at his partner as he approached. "Do you have reason to believe that Miss Sawyer is carrying a concealed weapon, Mrs. Trujillo?"

"A concealed weapon? No." Trudy started to laugh. I was insulted. Did she not think me capable of being armed, of killing? I was tough stuff. Suddenly, Trudy cut her laugh short. She cocked her head and drew her expertly penciled eyebrows together. "Except . . ."

Everybody froze; Scythe and Crandall pinned stares on me. I gawked at Trudy. What on earth was she up to?

"Except?" Scythe prompted tensely from the bottom of the six stairs. His hand was back on the butt of his damned gun.

"Except her pepper spray," Trudy announced with a bob of her head, obviously proud she possessed such intimate knowledge of her best friend's belongings. I just wished she possessed some common sense. Oh, no, she wasn't done yet. "Not to mention the hair dryer she carries in her purse. *And,* I suppose if someone just used a brush to kill Ricardo, you police officers would consider a curling iron a weapon, now, wouldn't you?"

With friends like these, who needs enemies?

Scythe sighed again and looked to the sky (for heavenly guidance or for a weather update, I wasn't sure) before he motioned to me. "That doesn't leave us any choice now, Miss Sawyer. Come on down and get searched."

An electric thrill zapped through me at the uncontrollable image of his fingers exploring all the places on my body that might be concealing a weapon. Then reason prevailed, taking the thrill and turning it into fury. I jammed my fists onto my hips. "Now, just a minute—"

"Hands back up, and take the stairs slowly," he ordered, pulling handcuffs from an interior pocket of his jacket. "Or I can come up there and get you."

The temptation of having him exert some extra effort rivaled my need to be independent. Independence won. I descended the stairs, but ever so slowly, pleased to see Scythe's eyebrows begin to draw together in irritation. If *I* was getting some additional wrinkles out of this encounter, he would, too. Of course, the way the world worked, his would be written off as character lines, while mine would just make me look older.

I finally reached the pavement.

"Come on down, Mrs. Trujillo," Scythe ordered in a much gentler tone than he had used with me. She skipped down the stairs, forcing me to move to let her pass, putting me way too close to Scythe, who wouldn't clear away from my right side and give me my space. I could feel his body heat through the denim at my hip. He jangled the handcuffs. Turd. I hugged the wall. Trudy hipped her way past me, something sticky on her catching on my bodysuit.

"What the hell?" Trudy grabbed hold of the metal stair railing with her right hand, her left arm still up over her head, and began twisting at odd angles. I heard a brutal rip as she clawed at it with her right hand, then she waved a piece of duct tape under my nose.

"Where did this come from?" she demanded.

I pulled a face and pushed her hand away, remembering what Lady Godiva had been doing with tape before coming to Trudy's rescue. "You don't want to know, trust me."

She raised her eyebrows.

Crandall smacked his gum and snorted, cocking his head toward the club building. "If you got it inside there, I can tell you what it was used for, darlin'."

Trudy gave me a black look before smiling winningly at Crandall. "How sweet of you."

Scythe looked at me. "Is she really that naive?"

"Worse."

"What's she doing hanging around you, then?"

"Everyone needs a little corruption."

"A little?" Scythe asked, deadpan. I glared.

"Well, handsome?" Trudy prompted Crandall.

"The freaks use it to make their hot dogs look like pussies." Crandall's mouth spread in a gap-toothed grin that showed his sadistic side.

Blinking rapidly, Trudy sucked in enough air to fill a hot-air balloon, then swayed. This was no dress rehearsal. I leaped forward, knocking Scythe off-balance with the purse I had slung over my shoulder as I reached out to catch her. Scythe spat out a rather creative invective as he ripped my purse off my arm. Then I felt long, strong fingers clamp down on my right hand, yanking it back into a circle of steel that snapped shut. My back wrenched as my left arm moved to break Trudy's fall, which never came because Scythe had grabbed her around the waist with *his* other hand, tucked her under his arm, and used both hands to fasten a handcuff around my other wrist. Superman from hell.

Crandall watched, snapping his gum, as Scythe sat a woozy Trudy on the bottom step.

"Keep an eye on her," Scythe ordered as he dragged me by my handcuffed hands, backward over the blacktop to his Crown Vic.

"What's your problem?" I demanded, trying to maintain some dignity as I scuttled, hunched over, gritting my teeth against the clenching pain in my back.

"My problem is you."

"That makes us even, because my problem is *you!*" I returned.

"No." He stopped me long enough to fling open the back door to his car. He shoved me in headfirst. Just like they show on prime time. And they say TV is unrealistic. "*Your* problem is you need Ritalin. You can't stay still for one second."

"And *you* need some common sense," I fired back, some of my fury diffused by my face being buried in the worn fabric seat cushion. I felt a bit of a draft on my rear end and wondered how high my skirt had been hiked up in my current unladylike position. I wedged my feet under the seat and tried—with my hands still bound together behind my back—to winch my upper body into a semi-sitting position. I wiggled my rump inch by inch until it was almost underneath me again. I looked down to find my skirt bunched up at mid-thigh. I bounced up and down, moving the skirt lower, in order to prevent the jerk from seeing my unflattering underwear. Why did I care? He deserved to see the world's ugliest panties for his shoddy treatment of me. I looked up to see him leaning into the car, dangling my heavy purse from one hand, the corner of his lip twitching. I let him have it. "For your information, the reason I had to move so fast was to prevent my best friend from smacking her head on the pavement in a dead faint."

"You are so unpredictable that for all I knew you could've been going for the concealed weapon—blow-dryer, curling iron, one of those coloring squirt guns—that you keep hidden in your friend's cleavage."

"What are you doing looking at her cleavage?"

"Who said I was looking at her cleavage?"

"You knew she *had* cleavage."

"Yes, which is more than we can say about you."

"Don't try to distract me with insults. What makes you think I'd be concealing a weapon, anyway? I haven't shown you any propensity for violence."

"I wouldn't put it past you. I wouldn't put anything past you, Reyn Marten Sawyer."

I shoved my chin up with pride. "I'll take that as a compliment."

"I wouldn't," Scythe pointed out drily as he eased down in the backseat next to me.

Obviously surprised I had no comeback, Scythe half hitched that right eyebrow before continuing. "Let me let you in on a little investigator's secret. We usually narrow our list of suspects down by ability, opportunity, and motive. You and I agree on your ability."

He paused. I slid him a sideways glance. The backseat of the sedan wasn't made for a man with legs as long as his, so it forced his knees up about chest-high. He had those unfortunately incredible hands wedged between his thighs, three fingers of his left hand extended, the pointer on his right counting off the reasons I should be locked up for Ricardo's murder. I sucked in a deep breath to fortify my resolve and only ingested air laced with musky wood. My brain clicked. Mesquite, that's what kind of wood it was. Did he wear a subtle cologne, or did he just naturally smell like the signature tree of the dry West Texas desert, the one with the long thorns on its trunk, the tree so tough it was impossible to kill?

"Since the invisible Claude isn't going to be able to provide you an alibi, *and* you used to work at the murder scene, *and* you likely still have a key to the lock that hasn't been changed since he built that chrome palace, you clearly had opportunity. The motive remains to be explained, but we're ready to run through several tried-and-true options, including greed, jealousy, and revenge."

My instinct was to jam my hands on my hips in indignation. I tried, only to have the handcuffs stop me all too cruelly. I winced. His lips thinned. What did *that* mean? Was he feeling guilty? Well, he should. I glared at him. "Talk about revenge! I'll have a case for that against you, not Ricardo."

Scythe's hands balled into fists. "Your mouth is going to get you in serious trouble one day."

"If my mouth's so lethal, why don't you cuff it instead of my hands?" I pointed out sourly.

His jaw clenched as he stuck an open hand out the car door and addressed Crandall. "Hand me some of that duct tape."

Ee-yew. I shook my head violently as Scythe turned back to me. I forced a semiapologetic smile. "Never mind. Just joking."

"This is no joke, Miss Sawyer. This is murder, and you are a suspect."

"What's my motive?"

"Jealousy," Scythe said. "Ricardo was an infamous ladies' man. Or considering where you've just visited, maybe he was a man's man, too. At any rate, he had the gall to come borrow a brush to use on the latest piece of ass he was balling, and you couldn't take it anymore. You snuck up on them last night, and once his lover left, you made sure he couldn't cheat on you ever again."

I squirmed in the seat in fury. "Is that the best you can do? Sounds like a tired soap opera episode."

"Hey, it's not my fault people are generally stupid and uncreative."

"Are you calling me stupid?"

Shockingly, he laughed. It was low and rumbly and took way too long. I felt my toes curl. Fortunately, he spoke again, and what he said cured the curl.

"I can't believe you're more up in arms over being called stupid than being called a suspect. That's a new one on me."

"Nobody calls me stupid and lives to tell about it," I shot back without thinking. Duh.

Scythe's eyes glittered. "Is that what Ricardo called you right before you stuck the homemade pick in his back?"

"No, Ricardo knew better than to call me stupid. He might have teased me about my business acumen or my boot collection, or any number of things, but he would've never called me stupid. Besides, I thought you were stuck on the jealous lover angle."

"I'll work whatever angle gets you to give us more information. Or confess. Or get out of our way."

"Well, you're about to work a whole geometry lesson full of angles with no results, because I didn't do it. Ricardo might have tried to get me to sleep with him, but I didn't go for it."

"I see." I saw a question flash in his eyes before he extinguished it. "So maybe you were fighting him off when you accidentally stuck the pick in his back."

"Not hardly. Ricardo was so arrogant he would never have pushed himself on anyone. He was more like, 'Here I am, baby, come and get it.' He thought himself too irresistible to chase anything. He expected to be chased, by every woman. It was more the fact that I didn't find him sexually attractive that kept him half-heartedly teasing me about a liaison. He never found *me* irresistible, I can assure you."

"I can believe that," he put in.

"What? Why wouldn't he find me irresistible?"

Scythe cocked his head thoughtfully and paused—a little too long, in my opinion. How long could the list be? He shook his head. "You just don't seem like his type."

"Whose type am I, then?"

Scythe shrugged. "Maybe a deaf mute's type. You're not bad on the eyes, and he wouldn't be able to hear you or fuel your unflagging ability to argue."

I narrowed my eyes. "You just hate a woman who always has a comeback."

"You're right about part of that statement."

"Which part?"

"You're so smart, you figure it out."

"I'm not the one who should be figuring anything out. You are. Instead, you're wasting your time trying to pin the murder on me when you should be out finding the real killer."

"As soon as I eliminate all your potential motives, I can move on," he said airily.

"What's left? Greed?"

He held his palms up.

"That's easy. Just check my finances. I am a conservative spender, don't gamble, don't have any outrageous expenses outside of one too many pair of cowboy boots and a fortune spent on Eukanuba dog food. My business is in the black, moderately successful—"

"But not a major moneymaker like Ricardo's Salons is."

"So what?"

"So, it might be nice to have the cash flow from a couple dozen salons instead of just one."

I slid a glance at Trudy, who was accepting a stick of Juicy Fruit from Crandall while still managing to talk a mile a minute. While she might be spilling the beans to the old guy about Ricardo's weird offer to me right now, Scythe didn't find out from her, because she'd been with me almost all day. Who did that leave? Mario, who was, if humanly possible, an even bigger blabbermouth. I grimaced. "I don't need the cash flow from a couple dozen salons."

"There's a fine line between need and want. And when one crosses that line, one embraces greed."

"Okay, Psychologist Scythe," I said. "I don't *want* the income from a couple dozen salons. How about that?"

"So, what are you going to do when you get them in his will? Give them away to charity?"

"I doubt I am going to get anything in his will besides a lump of coal. He was just talking off the cuff last night. He was in a bizarre mood. Even if he were serious, I can't see that he had time to change his will between his visit to me and the hair appointment he was so frantic to get to in time."

"Maybe he'd already changed his will," Scythe offered as he pulled my purse up from between his feet onto his lap. He pried open the snap and looked askance into the dark, overfilled depths.

"Without telling me? Right."

Tentatively, he put a hand into the purse. "Happens all the time. Will readings are rife with happy and, more often, unhappy surprises for those concerned."

I shrugged—or, rather, tried to. Considering my

handcuffed wrists and tightening back, it probably looked more like a hunchback having a spasm. "You'd know better than I would. The only will reading I've ever been to, my great-grandma gave every heir one plastic flamingo from her front yard, a pie plate, and a hundred bucks. We were all pretty satisfied with that. Well, except for her favorite grandson, who actually got her most prized possession."

He was clearly resisting the invited question. Finally, he gave a small, indulgent groan. "Which was?"

"A pair of ornamental yard deer that Jackie Dean from two streets down had welded into the, uh, breeding position."

"Your grandmother kept that in her front yard?"

"Well, until some city slicker got elected sheriff and gave her so many tickets for public indecency that he threatened to take her to jail unless she moved them. That's when we really knew Great-Gran was sick. She moved those deer without another word. If she'd been feeling up to par, she would've called his bluff and gone to jail."

The corner of his mouth twitched. His hand felt around inside my purse. "Sounds like you have an interesting family."

"I'm the most ordinary member of it," I said proudly.

Scythe whistled under his breath. "Remind me to come armed to the Sawyer family reunion."

"What reunion?" I demanded. I didn't think he was joking anymore. His voice had gotten hard and very sure.

His laser-sharp eyes met mine as he pulled out a black leather case, extracted what was inside, and flicked it open.

"The reunion at the county jail when they have to

come bail you out. Maybe trouble with the law runs in the family."

Light from the setting sun winked off the razor-sharp edge of the steel blade as the rock in my stomach hit bottom and bounced.

eleven

OUR GAZES WERE LOCKED FOR WHAT SEEMED LIKE a minute but was probably only a second or two. Still, those damned dry-ice lasers made their point. Finally, I had to swallow, which of course meant he'd won, didn't it? I parried by using the only weapon at my handcuffed personage's disposal: my tongue

"What will you arrest me for? Not having a permit to carry a concealed hairdresser's razor? That will certainly make you hero of the SAPD," I quipped.

"Just because you don't need a permit doesn't mean you ought to be carrying something like this around."

Scythe snapped the razor shut and put it on the seat between him and the car door, as far away from me as he could. As if I could pick it up with my teeth and lash him with it? Get real. His oversized hand reached in and pulled out the battery-operated mini-hairdryer, the battery-powered curling iron, the three different sizes of brushes, the hairspray, piling them in his lap. Twisting the cap off the tube of hair gel, he smelled it appraisingly and frowned. What was wrong with cucumber mint, anyway?

He then pulled out the teasing comb and tested its point with the pad of his forefinger.

"What are you, the purse police?"

"I'm the everything police, since somebody killed your pal with a brush instead of something reasonable like a gun or a knife or even poison, for God's sake."

I didn't have a comeback for that one. I hate it when that happens.

He cleared his throat. "Where's the pepper spray?"

I blinked at him.

He sighed. Heavily. That damned eyebrow half hitched. "Little canister, defensive weapon, shoots out liquid pain? Your pal Mrs. Trujillo said you had some . . ."

"It's in there somewhere." I tried not to sound churlish. From the look on his face, I failed.

"*Somewhere* being the operative term," he shot back as he flung out my key ring, my checkbook, my calendar, my thesaurus. Pausing there, he retrieved the three-by-three-inch book, held it up, and looked at me in question.

"Is this so you'll never be speechless?"

"I hate to be stuck anywhere without something to read, so I always carry a book or a magazine. This week, I decided to improve my vocabulary."

"Lucky us," he muttered under his breath.

"Excuse me?"

"I said, 'How admirable,'" he deadpanned, loudly.

Sure. My common sense told me to keep teeth firmly on tongue.

"Like the new word I learned today," I blurted out, ignoring my common sense.

He sighed but couldn't resist biting. "Which is?"

"*Vainacious.*"

"That is *not* in there."

"Well, every now and then, when properly inspired, I took in the thesaurus for a word, and I don't find one that quite does it, so I embellish. *Vainacious* is a perfect description."

For what, is all he had to ask. *You* is what I was dying to answer. Instead, he dropped the thesaurus onto the seat between us, along with the subject in general, and looked askance at the bag. I could tell he was considering sticking his face into the black, cavernous hole but thought better of it. He shook his head instead. "Better not go there. Something might bite me."

"Very funny." I strained against the handcuffs. "If you'd just undo these, I'll find it myself."

"Good try," he muttered as he dumped my purse upside-down on the floor between his feet. Wadded-up receipts, three pens without caps, my wallet, an all-in-one screwdriver set, scissors, a pair of orange socks, and four dog biscuits cascaded out.

"Interesting taste in snacks." He picked up a dog biscuit with a thumb and a forefinger and sniffed. This was obviously a man guided by his olfactory nerves. Before I could properly wonder what I currently smelled like, he dropped the biscuit onto the seat between us and conducted an exaggerated visual review of the assembled mess. "But no pepper spray."

Then I remembered. "Uh-oh."

He rolled his eyes. "What now?"

"I was running about ten minutes late for my first appointment this morning, so I was racing up my porch steps, when Jolie, my seven-thirty, came hurtling around the corner and bashed into me. Jolie is a little high-strung anyway, and my being late just—"

Scythe interjected. "Please get to the point."

"Don't be in such a rush. You want to know about Jolie Dupont, anyway, she might be a suspect." I paused for dramatic effect.

Scythe ignored the drama. "Okay, why would this Jolie be a murder suspect?"

"She used to be a client of Ricardo's and was acting weird this morning, like she didn't want me investigating his murder."

"If that's what putting her on your suspect list, put me on it, too."

I kicked at his shin with my Justin. He moved it out of the way just in time.

"Do you want to be arrested for assaulting a police officer?"

"If I'm gonig to be arrested for that, take off the handcuffs so I can do it right."

The edge of his mouth twitched. He glowered to try to cover it up, but it was too late. "You're lucky I have a sense of humor, or you'd be sitting in a cell block right now."

"I'm shaking in my boots. If you're done wasting your time trying to scare me, do you want to know what happened to my pepper spray or not?"

He pulled his eyebrows together in an exaggerated thoughtful expression. "I'm not sure now."

I glared and pursed my lips.

"Okay, okay, what happened to it?"

"Well, I don't know to swear on Grandpa's grave, but my purse went flying. I thought we got all the stuff back in, but I didn't have time to inventory everything, so I guess maybe some could have skidded into the front flower beds. I didn't look there."

Shaking his head, Scythe blew out yet another sigh. If

I speeded up the irritating comments, I'd have him hyperventilating in no time. Then he'd pass out, and I'd find the handcuff key, free myself and find Ricardo's killer before he came to. He reached into the pocket of his jacket, pulled out a cell phone, punched in a number, and KO'd my escape fantasy. "Soila, will you let the doc BOLO for traces of pepper spray on the Montoya body when he does the post? I'd like to be there, too. Call me when he starts, okay? Thanks, darlin'."

"What?" My legs straightened so much in shock I nearly banged my head on the ceiling of the Crown Vic. "You think I shot Ricardo with pepper spray?"

Scythe flipped his phone closed. "I don't believe in coincidences, and one of your weapons of mass destruction is missing the day after your mentor is murdered with your other one. Seems like a logical thing to do, to check for the pepper-spray traces."

I had to admit to myself it *was* logical. Fruitless but logical. "You're wasting your time," I advised sourly.

"Thanks to you."

"What do you mean?"

"I mean that you're withholding information and then proceeding to get in our way as we try to find out who killed your pal, which gives more opportunity to the real killer to get away with it. Why don't you give up the hunt?"

"No can do."

"Come on," Scythe insisted in a tone I recognized as nearly desperate. "What if I agree to concentrate on some other suspects if you go back to cutting hair?"

I narrowed my eyes and winced at the handcuffs scraping against my wrists as I tried to jam my hands on my hips. "Are you trying to tell me you've been turning the heat on just to get me to lay off the investigation? All this was pure intimidation?"

"Look, we checked phone records, and a call was placed from Ricardo's Broadway salon at two thirty-four that lasted about three minutes. He could've pissed you off. You could've gone down to meet him and killed him in a crime of passion, but I doubt that you would've used your own brush to do the deed. Still, maybe you're that stupid or got that blinding mad. But then this morning, we get an anonymous call on our info hot line that claims you're asking lot of nosy questions about Ricardo. And now, you're at this drag-queen club, a place an informant tells us Ricardo began to frequent recently. Either you're looking for someone else to pin the murder on so you stay in the clear, or you're a busybody with misguided loyalty to your friend. Frankly, I'm betting on the latter, but you know things you're not telling us, and you're meddling to the point where I might just have to lock you up. There's a lot of media heat on this case, and the police chief is not going to be patient. Why don't you just come clean? Then you can go back to your job, and we can do ours."

Even though I knew how much that honest speech cost him, I shook my head.

He blew out a sigh and laid his head on the back of the car seat. "Why?" he muttered, more to the car ceiling (or maybe God) than to me.

"Because I owed him."

"With a shift in attention that was simultaneously lazily slow and intensely focused, he turned. That torpedo gaze got me in its sights again. "*Now* we're getting somewhere. What did you owe him?"

I shrugged, trying not to show how those eyes affected my insides. "I owed Ricardo like one friend owes another a favor. Ever since I went to work with him, we kept a running tally of who owed whom. You see, I was just about the only person who worked with him who would actually treat him like a person rather than some kind of demigod. We joked, and I talked back to him sometimes . . ."

"I can't imagine," Scythe threw in under his breath.

"And," I said, with a defiant head toss, "I think he liked it."

"Whatever you say."

"What's that supposed to mean?"

"It means that all pushy women think men like to go toe to toe, while in fact we might like our women soft and feminine and agreeable, not tough and smart-mouthed and difficult."

Just barely managing to remember that he had the power to throw me behind bars, I swallowed the growl that rose in my throat, making it sound like a gurgle. Cool, I know. "I hope you're speaking for yourself and not trying to burden the entire male gender with your small-minded insecurities."

He turned his palms up. "See, that is what I'm talking about. How attractive is this?"

"Pretty attractive to a man who would rather have a woman who can beat him at Cranium than beat him off."

"Who's that? A gay man?"

I let the growl out this time. He looked unrepentant.

"I'm finished talking to you. I refuse to answer any more of your questions, you chauvinist pig." I leaned over his lap and hollered out the door. "Crandall, get in here. I want you to continue my interrogation. I'm not saying anything else to your partner."

Crandall and Trudy exchanged a look that might be interpreted as one of shared long-suffering. After a moment or two, Crandall snapped his gum as he ambled over to the car, hiking up his polyester slacks. I straightened up and focused out the windshield, ignoring the gaze I could feel burning into the side of my face.

"Used your charmer routine on her, I see, hotshot." Crandall chuckled.

"I'm finished with her, anyway," Scythe clipped out as he reached between the seat and my lower back to grab my wrists. His knuckles brushed my hip. I doubled over, face on my knees, to avoid his touch as he unlocked the handcuffs.

"Yeah, you macho guys, use your women, abuse them, then you're finished with them." Even as I said it, I knew I shouldn't. I mean, here I was being questioned for murder. The cop—albeit one who was a *vainacious* jerk—*was*, in fact, taking off the handcuffs and letting me go. *Keep your mouth shut*, the angel on my shoulder warned. The devil on the other won. I was still boiling over his idiotic chauvinism. I wasn't *that* pushy, was I?

The cuffs came clanking off. I straightened my upper body and surveyed the scene of the crime against my purse. The truth was, I wanted to avoid the arctic torpedoes, because I can hide behind the bravado of my mouth just so long before my eyes give away everything I'm thinking and feeling. Especially to those eyes. I gathered what was on the seat cushion, jamming it back into my bag. I paused. The items on the floor were going to be a problem, because the only way I could reach them was by sticking my hands between a pair of muscular male legs. Hmm. Maybe I could accidentally drop something heavy on his *cojones*. I wanted him to hurt.

He saved himself by reaching down before I could and scooping up the junk on the floor. I opened the purse so he could dump it by handfuls. I only thought I was safe, though. He paused at my billfold and opened it up.

"Hey," I protested as he scanned my driver's license photo.

The twin torpedoes met mine, their power softened by amusement. "You're not very photogenic, are you?"

"What does it matter to you? I have a brain, and I'm not afraid to use it and therefore qualify as unattractive in your book, camera or no camera."

Scythe referred back down to the photo in question. It was two years old. In my typical expedient fashion, I'd swung by the license office after spending an entire weekend with my nutty relations at Mom's surprise birthday bash. My big brother Chevy's two kids had come down with chicken pox (what kind of parents are conscientious objectors to a vaccine for a childhood virus?). Chevy developed shingles as a result, leaving me mostly in charge of the itchy, speckled crew as his wife, Barlow, was off on a "girls' weekend" in Aruba with her friends. My sister Pecan's on-again, off-again boyfriend drove his Harley-Davidson up for the event and kept getting run out of town by a small but energetic group of born-again Baptists who thought he was a drug-addict member of a motorcycle gang intent on selling the two children into white slavery. Dallas announced he was having an early midlife crisis and decided to quit his job as a stockbroker and join the Marines, only the Marines wouldn't take him because he was too old, so he was going to take them to court on principle. Charade had just had her chakras read by a psychic who warned her not to go "into the light," so she stayed locked in a closet for two days. Gran had run off with the man who owns the funeral parlor in my hometown, and it had taken us most of Sunday to find her shacked up at a Motel Six in the nearby "city" of Bastrop, population six thousand.

So, imagine what I looked like twelve hours later, and this is the photo Lieutenant Arrogant perused now. "You used to have your hair dyed blond?"

"I am a natural blonde," I admitted grudgingly. This is not something I like just anyone knowing about, but I was secretly grateful that he'd commented on that instead of the dark circles or crow's feet.

"That explains a lot."

"Like what?"

He regarded me for several long moments. "Never mind."

"Chicken," I murmured.

He slowly pivoted in the seat and stretched those long, long legs out of the car. He stood, leaving me with an eye-to-waist view of his cowboy belt with a silver buckle and conchos. Did everything about him have to be so male? It hit me like a blast furnace. Suddenly, his face obstructed my view just as it was about to get interesting. He leaned back into the car.

"Just for the record, you weren't just used and abused, no matter what you may think. When you've been used and abused by me," Scythe warned, those torpedoes firing full force, "I promise, you'll know it."

twelve

"YOU GUYS HAVE SOME MAJOR CHEMISTRY GOING."

I grimaced. "Like seventh-grade lab all over again—baking soda and vinegar in balloon. *Kaboom!*"

Trudy giggled and wiggled in the passenger seat of my truck which we'd picked up after Sherlyn rescued us from the cops in the Illusions parking lot. She'd been late because Daisy Dawn had been fixing the peeling nude on her fingernail. "Sounds fun to me. I guess you'd be the vinegar, and he'd be the baking soda."

"Why?" I slid her a suspicious glance and reached over to turn JoDee Messina singing (appropriately) "Bye, bye, my baby, bye, bye" down on the radio. I wanted to hear Trudy's recipe.

"Because you're sour, and he's gritty."

"Oh, Trudy, enough already. Even if I found him irresistible—which is a joke, since he's as appealing to me as a slab of cold bacon—I'm not his ideal woman. He likes them deaf and dumb in all senses of the word. What are the chances I would ever be that?"

"Ohhhhh," she moaned like a terrier in heat. "For

that man, I'd cut out my tongue, rupture my eardrums, and get a lobotomy."

"How could anyone who'd make a statement like that be my best friend?"

I glanced askance at her for a moment before letting my gaze lock back onto the two-lane highway. I was headed north on U.S. 281, bound for a little place in the Texas Hill Country called Sisterdale. Zorita lived there, and I hoped to hell I could remember exactly how to get to her odd house on the hill. Zorita (I was never told her last name or if the first name was her real one) had been one of the reasons Ricardo had been so financially successful. It takes money to make money, and Zorita told Ricardo where to put his money to make it multiply. She wasn't a stockbroker; she wasn't a financial advisor; Zorita was a psychic. I was probably the only person who knew Ricardo consulted her, and, as usual with my life, it was probably an accident and an unfortunate one at that. I'd been at the salon one day about six years ago, when Zorita called and demanded money immediately. Ricardo was busy, and I wasn't, so I was dispatched to deliver the greenbacks after swearing never to tell. I hadn't. After all, whom would I tell that my boss often banked small fortunes on the whims of astrological configurations and visions as interpreted by a woman who read more auras than books? I always thought the people you choose to work for reflect on you. This revelation about a man whose revered business acumen won him dozens of small-business association awards would not reflect well on me, so I kept my mouth shut.

Frankly, it really showed the chaotic state of my mind since Ricardo's demise that I had forgotten all about Zorita. She was not a person easily forgotten. I was reminded of her during my latest confrontation with Lieutenant Loser. He'd looked at that driver's license photo, which made me think of my sister who had her weekend ruined by a psychic, which made me think of Ricardo's fortune-teller. That's how my mind works mostly—these gazelle-like mental leaps. You never know where those damned things are going. That was why people couldn't always stick with my train of thought—I was way too far ahead of them.

I could hear Sarcastic Scythe's answer to that thought. *Right*.

Who cares what he'd say, anyway?

So, here we were buzzing up to see a woman who could see the future. Did she know we were coming? I didn't know much about Zorita's so-called abilities other than the fact that my buddy credited her with his fortune. Wouldn't it be convenient if she could see back in time as well as future dollar signs? She could tell us whodunit, and we could take that back to Señor Skeptical, who'd arrest the fiend forthwith. Yeah, right, even if Zorita gave us the goon on a silver platter, Scythe would still need some damned evidence, now, wouldn't he?

Well, it couldn't hurt to ask. I'd try. If she was really that good at seeing into tomorrow, couldn't she just end it all right now for us and tell us whose face she saw behind those iron bars? I felt a shot of hope that Zorita could have us wrap this up in time for me to make my five o'clock highlight who was a really good tipper.

I might have finally broken my promise to Ricardo (what good would the secret do him now?) and told Scythe about Zorita if he hadn't been such a complete jerk. On top of his chauvinistic remarks, he announced as they left that they were on their way to Ricardo's million-dollar Dominion manse, and I'd better stay out of their way. If he even smelled (there was that again) a trace of me within a ten-mile radius of the exclusive enclave which was off Interstate 10 just outside the city limits, he would order an APB out on me so fast heads would spin. Oooh, scary. I'd show him. So, with his attitude getting my hackles up, Scythe effectively dried up any more information he might have gotten out of me. I'd smiled sweetly and promised easily, knowing Trudy and I had someplace infinitely more productive to go than Ricardo's house, which I suspected would be as devoid of clues as a *House Beautiful* feature. The cop had narrowed his arctic blues at my acquiescence but drove off with his gum-smacking partner without saying another word.

"I bet Scythe and Crandall are already there, hoping Ricardo's sofa will tell them a story, while we're minutes away from getting the real scoop from his soothsayer," I mused as I changed lanes to pass a truck and a horse trailer.

"I wouldn't get so high and mighty yet, because, no matter what Zorita says, I won't help you keep digging into Ricardo's murder unless . . ."

I threw a glance right. Was that my raspberry-lipped Watson delivering an ultimatum? What was it about me that drew out the pugilist in people today?

"Unless what?" I asked after a ten-second pause, which Trudy uncharacteristically refused to fill.

"Unless," she said, dropping her sparrow soprano to a threatening middle C, "you give me your word you'll go on a date with Lieutenant Luscious."

"We've been through this."

"We were interrupted. You didn't give me your word."

"That's easy, since I feel reasonably certain he will never ask me on a date."

"If somehow he is persuaded to ask you, I want a promise that you will go. With him. Out. Somewhere." She paused, her shiny, fruity lips spreading in a mischievous grin. "Or *in* somewhere."

"Ha ha. You oversexed married women have to turn everything into potential nookie."

"Reyn." Trudy assumed her lecture tone reserved for times when she was about to quote one of the many women's magazines she memorized every month. "It's a fallacy that as a rule married women get more sex than unmarried women. Sex in marriage is only less complicated and more available, and hence only seems more frequent."

"Where'd you read that? In the latest *Cosmo?*"

In that new magazine *YOU!* as a matter of fact." Trudy's lower lip pooched out. I'd hurt her feelings. She was always so proud of her newly garnered facts, whatever they may be. I felt a little guilty, if only briefly.

"Well, you can tell *YOU!* that your informal survey shows that if you've had sex even one time in the last six months, you have not only had it less complicated and more available but also more *frequently* than your unmarried friend."

"The article also said that contrary to popular belief, women get just as irritable as men when forced to be celibate for a long period of time."

"Oh, please. Everyone's ill temper can be blamed on lack of sex? What man wrote this article?"

"If you're going to be so hard to get along with, I'm going to need to get you a dildo."

"Trudy!" I shouted. From the backseat of my crew

cab, Beaujolais woke and stretched over the seat to lay her black head on my shoulder. Chardonnay groaned. Cabernet rose, sighed, turned once around, and settled back down. I took one hand off the steering wheel and patted Beau on her sleek black head. "It's okay, girl. Go back to sleep." After licking my earlobe, she retreated to her place, where she leaned her head against the window.

"I don't know why you insist on bringing those damned dogs with you everywhere you go." Trudy tolerated my Labs, and they ignored her. Most of the time, anyway. I looked in my rearview mirror to see Cab tilt her head that was lying on her paws, open one eye, and glare at Trude.

"I feel guilty when I limit their entire lives to my house and the yard. How would you like to live like that?"

"I wouldn't mind if I was a *dog*," Trudy retorted. "You know, this could be another reason you never have a date. The percentage of men who might be attracted to you and *not* repelled by dog slobber is probably lower than the percentage of men merely attracted to you."

"I wouldn't want a man who didn't love my dogs." The vitamin salesman had a dog—a yappy, pin-headed toy fox terrier—but at least it proved he liked pets. "Listen, Ricardo is more dead than my love life." I ignored Trudy's challenging stare. "So, can we just concentrate on finding his killer this week and a date for me next week?"

"Promise?"

"I promise anything just to keep you on the subject at hand."

"Goody, goody." She clapped her hands together so enthusiastically that I wondered just how much she's worked Scythe already. I felt a brief pang of panic at the thought but then brushed it off. After all, Trudy was an eternal optimist. Which was why we made the ideal pair—I was an eternal pessimist. The two of us together were perfectly balanced. Although I have to point out that I consider *pessimism* another word for *realism*. I pressed the volume on the radio back up to one of the Dixie Chicks begging for a cowboy to take her away. Oops, springing into my mind's eye came the image of Scythe in his way-too-talkative Wranglers. Quickly, I switched the station to one where Faith Hill was whining about her lover putting her through emotional torture. *Ah.* I relaxed. If that didn't just justify my celibate lifestyle, I didn't know what did. The only torture my life partners put me through was some occasional bad canine gas, which I seemed to have evoked with the simple thought. Trudy made a gagging noise. I rolled down the two front windows to clear the air.

"You know," Trudy shouted over the radio and the whistling wind. I braced for the worst, but she surprised me by changing the subject as I'd requested. "We haven't gotten very far, besides figuring out that Ricardo was meeting on the sly with a prepster in tennis whites at a transvestite club."

"I think that's a pretty big clue. It's more than the police know, anyway," I added defensively.

Trudy laughed. "You are so competitive, Reyn. You'd think you had something to gain from beating the police on this investigation. But no, you just can't stand to lose, at anything."

Sometimes my sweet but dimwitted friend could read me so sharply it hurt. Or maybe I was just so damned easy to read anyone could do it. Ouch.

"It's not that at all. I owe it to Ricardo."

"Whatever," she answered with a knowing smile.

We lapsed into silence for a while as we left the San Antonio city limits, climbing in elevation as the terrain began to change dramatically. San Antonio sits on the cusp of four different topographies. South of downtown was flat, sandy prairie. The farther east you went from the Bexar County Courthouse, the more rich red-clay farmland you'd find. Westward travelers on Highway 90 toward the Mexican border encountered limestone-imbedded mesquite that eventually gave way to desert, and due north, the direction we were headed, became a hilly limestone, cedar-dotted, aqua-crystal-stream-lined paradise known as the Texas Hill Country.

Being 180 miles from the Gulf Coast and the center of all these geographic patterns made our weather changeable, to say the least. Winters could be hot and humid one day and ass-chilling cold the next. One esteemed politician who was running for governor in the nineties likened Texas's weather to rape, recommending that if people didn't like it, they might as well sit back and enjoy it. Charming, huh? Well, he didn't win the governor's race, if that is any consolation. And, though his comment was in extremely bad taste, he was right about the weather in the Lone Star State.

Still, most of us sit back and *complain* about it, instead of enjoying it.

The four-lane highway narrowed to two, and I had to slam on my brakes suddenly to avoid the ten-point whitetail buck that picked that moment to visit the ranch across the street. My bumper missed him by inches. The girls were thrown into a whining, scuffling, growling heap on the floorboard. I'd glanced back to make sure they didn't need help untangling their legs, when Trudy screamed. I looked up and swerved, barely missing an 18-wheeler that had drifted a few feet across the solid yellow lines into my oncoming lane. The girls were left to themselves as I waited for my blood pressure to return to normal. Trudy's knuckles, which had wrapped around the grab bar at the dashboard in front of her, had just begun to look flesh-colored again, when a big black cloud came out of nowhere and dumped grape-size raindrops on our front windshield. Just as I began to wonder if nature weren't conspiring against us, I recognized the small clearing off to the right that was Zorita's driveway. I cranked the wheel, and the truck bounced down the gravel road into a patch of cedar trees, unseating the grumbling dogs yet again.

We hadn't gone a hundred yards when the rain stopped as suddenly as it had begun. The sun's rays shone through the trees in long, thin, illuminated paths that made the close, low woods seem otherworldly. I looked at Trudy, who met my expression with her own raised eyebrows. Were we being weird, or was there something weird going on? I checked the dogs. Animals respected that sixth sense that we humans probably all still possess but tend to overanalyze or completely ignore. Maybe it was nothing more than the survival instinct we think we don't need because we're so smart. Anyhow, mine was definitely too hard to read, so I was relying on the girls to tell me. All three dogs held their ears pricked and their necks stiff, and their eyes roamed out the windows with obvious purpose.

Trudy still wasn't talking, which for her was sign enough of trouble.

The wind picked up; branches shook; shadows danced.

My foot had eased so far off the accelerator that the truck was barely crawling down the driveway.

I shook off the shiver that was slithering down my back, blew out a breath of frustration at my ridiculous imagination, and pressed on the gas. Too hard. The truck leaped forward, spewing white gravel in our wake and scattering whatever spell we'd put ourselves under. Trudy wrapped her raspberry talons around the grab bar at the dashboard and held on tight as her cotton-candy-colored booty bounced wildly on the seat. The dogs, knocking heads against the windows and each other, alternately growled and moaned. I gunned it more as the driveway headed in a sixty-degree angle up a hill. Whatever might have been eerie in the woods would have to chase us. I pressed harder on the gas, and now the truck complained with a suspicious engine whine. The cedars ended abruptly, and we climbed to the pinnacle of the now bare hill, where a structure stood.

"Wow," Trudy intoned, wide-eyed. "Weird."

I'd remembered Zorita's house as odd, but it was worse than that. Worse than weird. It was bizarre. The last time I'd come, I'd only seen it from the driveway, where Zorita had met me. Close up, it looked to be about a thousand square feet built in a circle. *Would that be circular feet, then, instead of square feet?* I wondered. My gazelle mind in action. Anyhow, the shape wasn't the bizarre part. The walls were glass from three feet up to the ten-foot ceiling. All the way around. From ground to three feet was limestone and mortar, an attractive complement to the sandstone-colored tile roof, so someone had taste that took a big detour when it came to the glass deal. No curtains of any kind lined the windows, which made the contents of the home visible from where we stood. There were no in-

terior walls. A single beige parson's chair sat squarely—
and it seemed especially square in that round environment—in the middle of the room.

Okay.

Trudy had been watching my reaction, I suppose, because she looked a little impatient when I finally turned
to her.

"Does she really live here?" she asked.

I shrugged, glancing around for another building. *Nada.*
I began walking toward the house, stepping over stray limestone rocks, cedar bark, and a baby prickly pear. So much
for landscaping. "Maybe it's some kind of observation hut."

"A hut that costs more than my retirement fund."

"I thought you used up your retirement fund with
your boob job."

"Mario's got to have something to look at when the
rest of me goes. I call that a retirement fund," Trudy returned rather defensively—for her.

I slid her a look. "So why didn't he use *his* retirement
fund for it?"

Trudy glared. We didn't fight often, but when we did,
we went for the jugular—the advantage of knowing
someone as well as you know yourself. "What's your
point, anyway?"

"Everybody has different priorities, that's all," I offered judiciously as I approached the front door. Or side
door or back door. The house was round, after all. The
door was beige. I knocked. Somebody really liked beige.
That occurred to me only because I absolutely despise
beige. It's such a gutless color.

"I didn't see anyone home," Trudy stage-whispered.
"And it's not like they could hide real well."

"Then why are you whispering?" I asked loudly.

The door flung open. Trudy jumped and knocked me off the limestone rock on which I'd been balanced. Zorita stood—all four feet, ten inches, hundred and eighty pounds of her—in the doorway, dressed in a beige rough-weave linen shift. She wore beige Birkenstocks on feet that looked like a pair of rolls that had been left to rise too long. Even her feet were beige. Her long, straight hair was beige—no kidding. That had been no easy task for her stylist, either, because her skin tone told me she was a natural black-brunette. I could understand why, as a psychic, she'd beiged herself—it drew all attention to her dark eyes. I resisted their hypnotic effect, because all the beige was beginning to piss me off.

"I saw that red spike, so don't try to hide it," Zorita directed at me, left hand extended, fingers wiggling, off to my right about a foot. Instinct won over intellect, and I glanced into the space indicated. I saw nothing but more beige—beige rock, beige sand. Of course.

"Where?" Trudy twisted her body around mine so she could see in the space beyond me. "Oh, yeah . . ."

"Oh, yeah, what?" I followed her searching gaze. More beige.

Poker-faced Zorita was nodding sagely, the lowest of her three chins echoing the gesture. She had been looking at me. Rather, not precisely at me but near me, all around me. It was disconcerting.

"You see it, then?" She turned her face and looked directly at Trudy. Why did she rate the direct treatment and I got the dog-searching-where-to-pee look?

"I think I do. A red flash . . . there! Another one, coming from her chest!"

"Oh, come on. Now I'm Supergirl about to be transformed into my costume to save the world?"

Trudy and Zorita both ignored me. At least half a minute ticked by before Trudy finally shook her head. "That's it. I don't see another one. What did it mean?"

"A red spike like that is the sign of sudden deep emotion. Did you notice it being dull red or vibrant red?"

Trudy was thinking so hard she looked like she might hurt herself. A raspberry fingernail tapped her temple. "Dull, I guess. But deep, rich."

Zorita nodded once. "Excellent! A spike of dull, deep, or, as you said, rich red indicates a sudden flash of anger. Spikes are showing us only a temporary emotion, but if it had been brighter, it would've revealed sudden violent tendencies. Like those of a murderer."

Trudy's eyes nearly bugged out of her head as she looked back at me. I narrowed my eyes at her. "Notice Zorita said *would've*." *Listen to me, it sounded like I was buying into this crap. Argh.*

"I'm going to have to watch you a little more closely from now on, Reyn," Trudy warned, suddenly the expert.

Before I could properly unleash some of those vibrant red spikes on my best friend, Zorita stepped back and swept her pudgy arm to grant us entrance to her human fishbowl. "Please, come in."

We stepped onto the pine hardwood floor, which— surprise, surprise—was beige and completely bare. I finally noticed the top of a ladder peeking out of a four-foot circular hole in the floor next to the right wall—or the right side of the circle—and what looked like a double handrail, sort of like what helps heave one out of the deep end of a pool. *Okay.*

Zorita followed my glance or else read my mind. "That's where I live. The basement contains my living area, kitchen, bedroom, and bathroom. Here is where I work."

"Ah-ha," Trudy murmured, impressed.

"I sit on the highest peak for miles. Nothing distracts me from reading my clients' auras or seeing through the sky into their future."

"Oooh, can you tell me my future?" Trudy asked.

"Of course, my dear. As soon as we've done our business, it would be my pleasure. I'm sure you have a happy road ahead; your wonderful blue aura is that of a healing, spiritual teacher." She slid a sidelong glance at me before bestowing a beatific smile on Trudy. "And with that confident, affectionate pink in your aura, it's a good thing *she* has you at her side."

Spiritual? Trudy? Maybe the fashion spirits. Teaching what? The survey results from women's magazines? "What's that supposed to mean?" I demanded.

Zorita waved both hands as if to clear smoke. "With all your green and yellow—"

I'd had about enough of this. "Don't forget the red."

"Yes, and the red." Zorita nodded grimly. "Spikes."

"What's green and yellow?" Trudy asked.

"A light green indicates the potential onset of injury. She should be careful for the next few days—"

"Too late. I already hurt my back." I grimaced. "Helping Miss Pinky Blue's husband, it just so happens. Big help she is."

Zorita looked unconvinced, pausing just a second before she continued to answer Trudy's question. "And the yellow, well, that can denote intelligence, success or creativity . . ."

I grinned self-righteously.

". . . Or jealousy, selfishness, or negativity, depending on the shade of yellow it is."

My grin faded.

Zorita clapped her hands. "But let's get on with it. I know why you've come."

"You do?" I blurted. *Well, good,* I thought, *that will spare me all those tedious questions. She can just come out and tell us who killed Ricardo. Or, sparing that, maybe she'll hint at the evil forces around him so we can get busy ferreting them out.*

"Yes." Zorita nodded, then rudely interrupted my grandiose plans. "You've come to pay his outstanding bill."

"What?" Trudy and I said in unison, although I must admit I sounded much more distressed than she did. With good reason, it turned out. I was the one getting the shakedown.

"I'll just go downstairs and get the invoice for you." She leaned her round body toward the hole in the floor.

"Wait." I put a hand on her doughy arm. She looked at my fingers like they were hateful vermin.

"Please remove your touch. You have a very powerful personality. It interferes with my psychic abilities."

I felt a shot of perverse satisfaction and battled with the urge to grab her with the other one and maybe breathe on her real hard or shoot her with some red spikes. Instead, I remembered we needed to use her psychic abilities, so I dropped my hand. "I just want to know why you think I'm going to pay Ricardo's bill."

"Because you're inheriting most of his estate, that's why."

I snorted in disbelief. "I don't think so."

"I know so."

"You have a copy of his will?"

"No!" Her hand flew to her chest like I'd aimed for her heart. "I don't need one."

"Okay, so you're guessing."

Trudy, who'd been watching our conversation like it was the final round at Wimbledon, gasped. I suppose I'd hit one into the net. "Reyn, that's blasphemous. Psychics don't guess."

Zorita threw Trudy an approving look before shaking her head at me. "She's a skeptic, my dear. Don't try to protect me. We deal with this every day."

"Yes, but not from someone who wants your help," Trudy pointed out all too accurately. Damn her. She could be such an airhead and then with no warning act like she belonged to Mensa.

"My help?" Zorita asked, stunned.

Trudy looked from Zorita to me and back again. "Yes. We want you to help us find out who murdered Ricardo."

Zorita swallowed hard, closed her eyes, and began hyperventilating. Sweat beaded on her upper lip. I thought she might be having a heart attack, so I took a step forward. Her left arm flew up, hand splayed out in front of her. "Stay back."

Yikes. I got the creepy-crawlies up and down my arms. Trudy looked completely—and happily—entranced.

After about a minute, Zorita's eyelids lifted with the speed of a sloth on quaaludes. Sweat now dripped down the corners of her mouth. Ick. Her dark eyes widened until we could see the whites all the way around. "You do not want to know who killed Ricardo."

"Why not?"

"Because when you take that dark road, I don't see you coming out."

Then, with a quickness that was stunning for one so heavy and short-limbed, she spun and disappeared down into the hole.

thirteen

I IMAGINE THAT TO ANYONE PSYCHICALLY TUNED, I looked like a human firecracker right about then, what with my aura all green and yellow and red spikes flying out with lightning speed. Zorita had never reappeared, having hollered up through the hole in her floor that she would forgive "my" bill if we would just leave. My bill, my rear. I guessed that by predicting I was about to inherit Ricardo's estate, she was trying to get me not only to cough up the money for his last reading but to beg her to read my future as a millionairess as well. She predicted the future wrong there, didn't she? I wasn't going to ask squat.

I was going to let my faithful assistant ask instead.

"Zorita," Trudy cajoled, perched on her spike heels on the edge of the hole in the floor. "We *so* need your help. The police really don't seem to be on the right track, and we'd hate to see the person who did this to Ricardo get away with no punishment."

"We all will meet divine punishment for our sins one day," came the response from the hole. "The guilty one will pay that way."

Great, a Bible-thumping psychic. I thought those who relied on otherworldly talents were supposed to be the spawn of Satan or some such. At least, that's what Great-Granny Penscik always warned me about. My luck to have encountered the only psychic in this zip code who wanted to let divine redemption instead of mortal law deal with a homicidal maniac.

"All we really need is a list of Ricardo's clients. Not for all the salons, of course, what a chore that would be," Trudy explained patiently. "We would so appreciate it if you could pass along just the names of the women he still personally serviced."

Trudy caught my jolt and blushed, stammering down the hole. "I mean, I mean, you know, the ones he still did the hairdos for."

"I know what you meant, Trudy," Zorita sent back up the hole. "With your truly good heart, you aren't the kind of woman to imply otherwise, although your friend is. However, you are a good enough friend to *her* to do whatever she wanted you to do. And to say whatever she wanted you to say."

She was right, of course, on both counts. Maybe there was something to this psychic stuff, after all.

"Hey!"

Trudy was mad now, spitting mad, as we call it back in Dime Box. It didn't happen often, but I loved to see it happen when it did. I had the short fuse, she had the long one. It took a lot to push her over the edge, and Zorita just had. No doubt, there were red spikes shooting out at that moment amid all her placid blue and pink, although it would take someone more psychically tuned than I to ascertain them. Imagining them was enough for me. I grinned.

Trudy stomped over to the edge of the hole and hollered at the top of her lungs. "If being a good friend is a bad color aura in your book, then you can have it, lady, because I will keep being a good friend no matter what color it turns my aura. Right now, you ought to be reading whatever is the most threatening color to you, because I am about to crawl my heinie down there and get the list of Ricardo's clients from you, whatever it takes. So what's the color for stubbornly persistent and fiercely loyal?"

I was impressed.

So was Zorita, apparently. Because within a minute, a sheet of what looked like hand-beaten papyrus decorated with dried violets appeared at the hole's opening. A list of about a dozen names and corresponding addresses had been written down on it in a crooked mess amid the squashed stems and petals. What was the purpose of paper like this? *Hmmm.* Before I could entertain too many thoughts of the deep meaning of violets and the scary curses they might represent, Trudy plucked it out of her hand and mince-marched on her spikes toward the door, cocking her head at me to get a move on. She *is* a bossy britches when she gets mad.

I followed. She had gotten the goods.

"Before you go off on this ill-advised journey of discovery," came Zorita's disembodied voice rising from the hole, "I have to warn you . . ."

Trudy paused in mid-mince. I kept going. My hand was on the doorknob when I realized Trudy just might not be able to resist asking the question Zorita wanted asked. I spun and tried to get Trudy's attention with my zip-the-lip motion, but her gaze was glued to the hole in the floor.

"Warn us about what?"

I groaned.

"You must know, Trudy, not everyone on the list is a client. They are the names that came to me. And holding that list is shaking hands with fate."

"Uh-huh," I muttered. "A fate named Violet."

Shooting me a glare, Trudy put her finger to her lips. "Whose fate?" she asked the hole.

"The fates of six people. Leave the list here, it goes one way. Take the list with you, it goes another."

"Which way is it supposed to go? One way or another?"

"Ah, Trudy," she said, buying time as Trudy's insistence clearly surprised her. "The age-old question."

I silently mimicked what she'd said so pompously. Trudy glared. We waited. When Zorita added no more, Trudy asked, "Okay, I guess what you're telling me is we don't know which way fate is supposed to go. Which are the six people, then?"

"I don't know."

"No duh," I said under my breath. Trudy threw me a warning look.

Zorita wasn't finished. "But I do know that many things die in the face of truth."

I grunted. "Yeah, like lies."

"Lies and more," Zorita intoned, having heard me, apparently. "Happiness, peace, and, often, lives."

Trudy gasped. "Someone's gonna die?"

I rolled my eyes, reached over, grabbed the violet papyrus, and pulled open the door. "Turn on your brain, Trude. Someone's *already* dead."

"I mean someone else besides Ricardo," Trudy snapped at me as she made a dive for the list. I held it up over my head, wrenching my back but successfully keeping it out of her hands. I dashed for the truck.

"If we take this list, Zorita, is someone else gonna die?" I heard Trudy call back into the house.

The front door banged closed in Trudy's face, and the dead bolt shot. Now, I never saw Zorita's rotund shape rise up out of the hole, but that doesn't mean she didn't, right? And I wasn't telling Trudy the windowed room backlit with the setting sun looked empty when I jumped into the truck, cranked the engine, and honked her out of her daze.

We didn't talk much on the way back. Trudy was so spooked she could hardly put a sentence together, and I was so frustrated that I wasn't able to answer one as sensitively as I should have for my pinky-blue friend, anyway. Our one attempt to converse went something like this.

"Trude, can you read me the names on the list?" I reached to retrieve it from the side pocket of the truck door.

"I, I'm not . . . ah . . . I don't think we should have it."

"Trudy, please! I am dying to know who's on it."

"Reyn! Don't . . . I mean, you can't . . . say *that* word."

"Word? What word?" I really was stumped for a moment, before bursting out, "Dying! Dying! Dead! Die! Died! Maybe I'll really do it, and then all the suspense will be over, and you can snap out of this trance, you freak."

Then she started crying. "I'm (*sniff*) . . . I'm sorry I care (*snort*) about you. Finding Ricardo's killer isn't worth losing your life."

"Maybe not, but is it worth getting me hooked up with Detective Darling?"

A glimmer came into her eyes then, and I thought I had her back, but her eyes filled up with tears. "You can't date him if you're dead (*intense sobbing*)."

I stopped trying after that. Dusk fell fast, and the stretch of Highway 281 we were on was so busy I couldn't even turn on my interior light and take a look at the violet-pitted page. It would have to wait until we got home. I weaved in and out of traffic, knowing the girls must have their legs crossed in the backseat. I'd intended to let them out to relieve themselves on the top of Zorita's hill before we started back to the city, but, considering the way our close encounter had ended, I had a vision of them coming out of the woods as a trio of horny toads or armadillos or something worse, so I decided they could hold it until we got home.

Chardonnay was whining in my ear by the time we turned into my driveway. I parked, snatched up off the console the damned barf bag Scythe had slipped me at the crime scene, stuffed the violet list in the rear waistband of my skirt, opened the back door for the girls, and walked around to the iron gate at the side of the house to let them into the backyard. Trudy had gotten out and walked around the left side that front McCullough, where the salon parking lot is, presumably to get into her car and go home to Mario. Just as well. I wanted to review the list alone and collect my thoughts about it before I got her input. I crunched my way across the grass, littered with the hard, waxy leaves of the three-hundred-year-old oak trees in my front yard. They were evergreens that molted spring and fall, and I thought with some sense of relief that it would be pretty hard to sneak up on my house while the trees were shedding their leaves. See, sometimes it pays to be a lazy gardener.

I heard Trudy talking to someone in the parking lot. A baritone someone. Not the flasher, I hoped, especially hoping it was not the murderer. My heart pounded.

As I was about to round the fat, blooming gardenia bush that sits at the southeast corner of my house, I heard Trudy giggle. "Lieutenant Scythe, you rascal."

Not the flasher; not the murderer, much, much worse.

"Just telling the truth, ma'am, that's all."

That again. Did he know the truth can kill? Zorita told us so. I leaned into the gardenia bush and peeked through the leaves. He'd shed the sport coat, and his baby-blue knit shirt fit a little too tightly across the chest and biceps and a little too loosely at his abdomen. They need to redesign polo shirts to fit his body type.

"I just don't think I look all that good," Trudy was saying modestly. "I mean, after Reyn dragged me all over the county and beyond today."

"I've just never seen a woman look so pretty and fresh at the end of the day like you do," Scythe lied.

Didn't Trudy realize that it was night, and night meant it was dark? The security light over the salon's front door was about fifty watts shy of doing any good and only highlighted their shadows. I leaned deeper into the bush. What was Scythe up to?

"To look so good (*tsk*), especially after all your cross-county adventures," he added, saccharine-sweet. "Where all did you say you'd been?"

Ah-ha. The light might be dim out there, but it lit up in my head. How could Trudy not know he was pumping her for information with his lame flirting? He wasn't even any good at it. The flirting, that is, although there was no proving that by the way Trudy giggled again. Maybe she was just trying to be polite.

She twisted a lock of hair around her forefinger. "We went—"

"Shopping." I extracted myself from the bush and swung around the corner very suavely and just in time to stop the blabbermouth from spilling our secret.

They both turned to me. Trudy blushed. "We *did?*"

"Shopping for what?" Oh, but that Scythe was quick. Damn him.

"Uh, baby clothes," I blurted. Well, I figured the only three things I might know more about than he did were salon products, feminine hygiene products, or baby stuff. I discarded the first one, since he might know more than I thought he did, considering it was his business because of Ricardo's murder. I discarded the second, because I didn't want even to mention anything that remotely had to do with sex in front of him. So that left the third. And, yes, I did consider all this in the approximately five seconds it took to answer his question. As I said, a chaotic mind but a swift one.

Clearly too chaotic.

"Baby clothes?" He sounded skeptical.

"Yes, rompers, jumpers, and those cute little onesies . . ." Thank the good Lord for big families, especially the mini-humans, my nieces and nephews.

"Onesies?"

"Brilliant inventions." I smiled, nodding idiotically. "Cotton knit deals that button . . ." I started to demonstrate, Scythe's gaze following as my hand went to my crotch. I blushed and dropped my hand. "Between their, uh, legs." That one eyebrow half hitched. I rushed to fill up the air. "Kind of like the leotard I have on."

Both eyebrows shot up. He smothered a grin and looked studious. "Now, with the babies, I could understand that the design is one of convenience. For diaper changing, of course. For you, however, I fail to see the advantage of extra buttons. Unless it is some variation on a chastity belt," he offered, glancing at Trudy in exaggerated question.

Trudy looked at me thoughtfully. "Maybe *that's* why you don't get dates. You need to be more accessible!"

"Trudy!" My face was blazing hot now, and I never blush. I didn't even feel like myself. My tongue felt thick. My mind felt loopy. Zorita must have put a curse on me. Either that, or I wasn't cut out for this investigating stuff.

"So, who are you shopping for?" He'd had his fun. He was focusing back in on his prey.

"Oh, one of the girls at Illusions." Trudy jumped right in.

"Is that right?" The corners of his mouth were dancing again. "I wasn't sure those 'girls' had quite the right equipment to give birth."

"Just because you're not equipped doesn't mean you can't be a parent." I jutted my chin and met those laser eyes in challenge. "Bettina was such a help to us that we thought we ought to get her a little thank-you. And then Trudy remembered her talking about adopting a baby, and we thought that might be a way to show our appreciation."

Both Trudy and Scythe stared at me.

"What did you decide on?"

Trudy and I shared a look. *Uh-oh*, it said. "We couldn't agree."

"No." Trudy laughed. "One argument after another."

"Over onesies," Scythe deadpanned. He was on to us but couldn't prove it. *Ha!* Us 1, Them 0.

"Oooh." Trudy glanced from me to Scythe to her Seiko. "Look at the time. Mario will be missing me. I have to run, Reyn."

"Not so soon." I grabbed her left upper arm with two hands, hard, leading her to the back door, which takes me straight into the kitchen. "Come in, have a glass of cab. We can talk about what gift to get Bettina, and I'll run pick it up tomorrow."

Prying my fingers loose, she backed toward her car. "I'll have to take a rain check."

"But I won't," Scythe said. "I have time for a glass of wine."

Trudy couldn't have smiled bigger if she'd just found out they'd discovered a cure for cellulite overnight. Not that she had any, she was just obsessed with it. I glared. She ignored me as she deactivated her car alarm and slid behind the wheel of her lime-green VW Bug. "Thank you for the compliment, Lieutenant."

"You're welcome, Mrs. Trujillo. Please call me Jack."

"Only if you call me Trudy," she returned before buzzing off down the street.

How cozy.

Speaking of cozy. "Now, about that wine," Scythe purred.

"I thought you cops aren't supposed to drink on the job." I stood my ground. I didn't trust this cat.

"I'm not on the job."

"Right."

"What's that supposed to mean?"

"From what I understand, detectives can be called

twenty-four hours a day. Besides that, you don't seem the type able to leave a case at the office. I bet you hang on to an investigation like a pit bull."

"I see. You're an amateur psychologist in addition to being an amateur detective?"

"Touchy, aren't we? What happened, did I hit close to a nerve?" I flashed a grin and let myself into my house. I felt a surge of confidence. I could deal with him. If he wanted to follow me in, well, he'd just better watch himself.

I threw the keys and the barf bag onto the kitchen table. "Don't you want to take that back, since I didn't need it?"

"Not yet, you haven't."

What did that mean? I didn't bite, though. Instead, I walked straight to the pantry, although kind of sideways like a crab, since I didn't want him to see the list sticking out of my waistband. Then I flung open the pantry door like I was intent on dinner and he was imposing. He looked over my shoulder.

"You aren't the world's skinniest woman, but there's no way you can eat all the crap that's in your kitchen." He read off some labels. "Lemongrass sauce. Dark chocolate layered truffles. Bayou Beef in a can. What gives?"

"I'm not the world's skinniest woman, huh?" I jammed my hands on my hips. You certainly have a way with words. A bad way."

"Your friend didn't think so."

"Ha! You were just trying to butter her up for information."

"There's all kinds of ways to get information," he said with a sly shift in that right eyebrow.

"What way would you say you're using with me,

then? The insulting method? Do they teach that at the
police academy? The piss-them-off method?"

"Who says I'm trying to insult you? Who wants to be
the world's skinniest woman, anyway?"

"Ninety-nine percent of the female population."

""Really?" He looked interested in understanding the
female psyche for a nanosecond. That quickly disappeared. "Well, that just shows how stupid women are.
Have you ever slept with a really skinny woman?"

I probably looked like I was going to hurl. I mean, it
was one thing to rub elbows all day with transvestites,
but I had to draw the line at imagining myself in bed
with a skinny woman.

"No. Have you?"

Scythe looked a little disgruntled at my ability to
reply. "None of your business."

"You made it my business when you brought it up."

"Now, about that wine." He smoothly tried to change
the subject, wandering over to the refrigerator. Who
keeps cabernet in the refrigerator? I realized he must
be a Bud man, because otherwise he'd be checking
countertops.

I was mulling over this likelihood so hard that I failed
to remember that my refrigerator hadn't been cleaned
in at least six months. Once I did, I jumped up and tried
to block him from getting the door all the way open.
Too late. He stood staring into the chilling recesses of
the Whirlpool. After what seemed like ages, he looked
down at me.

"I see your next murder weapon."

fourteen

"WHAT ARE YOU TALKING ABOUT?" ALL SORTS OF scenarios ran through my head. Had the murderer broken into my house and planted a murder weapon in my refrigerator? Had Zorita hexed me, turning a pickle into a pickax?

Scythe, looking especially grim, reached onto the second shelf, extracted a clear Tupperware container, and held it between us. "This is what I'm talking about."

Something green and fuzzy was growing on an unrecognizable mound.

"Penicillin cures," I pointed out, folding my arms across my chest. He was standing a little too close for comfort. I had the list of suspects in my waistband to protect. I inched closer to the refrigerator door and away from him.

"Do you realize how many people are allergic to penicillin?" Scythe countered. "Slip this tasty morsel to someone like that, and he'll go into anaphylactic shock. It's all over."

"When I do, I'll make sure they hunt you down as

accessory to murder." I narrowed my eyes. "You *know* what they do to policemen in prison."

He raised both eyebrows. "No. What? Care to describe it to me?"

I felt my face growing hot. I was not a prude. Why was my body doing this to me? I turned away, reaching to the wine rack on top of the refrigerator. "How about that wine?"

"Thought you'd never ask."

I discerned a chuckle in his voice but did not turn around to see if a grin accompanied it. The Us-Them score was even now, with that comparing-my-leotard-to-a-baby-onesie trap I set for myself, walked in, and let him spring. I'd have to stop doing that. Running my fingertips over the tops of the bottles, I debated my options. I didn't want to go too expensive; that would seem like I was trying to impress him—wrong message. I didn't want to go too cheap, because that would make me look, well, cheap. Why was I thinking about this so hard for a man I'd already decided was someone who wouldn't know a pinot grigio from a Popsicle?

I paused at a mid-range French bordeaux. Nope, those French could be just too upright.

I drummed my pointer finger on a Chilean malbec. Oh, no, those South Americans were known for being hot, spicy, sexy. Another mis-message.

Still without looking at Scythe, I slid a bottle of Australian shiraz out of the rack—a mid-range import from a country that wasn't passionate, wasn't snobby. Nice, firendly, down-to-earth people, those Aussies. Besides, the wine tasted good.

After all this, he probably wouldn't notice, and I'd given myself an extra gray hair for nothing. Trying to act nonchalant, I spun around and set the bottle on the counter.

"Where's your corkscrew?" he asked.

Ah-ha, so he knew about corks.

"It's in the drawer to your right." I answered as I retrieved a couple of everyday wineglasses. Didn't want to use the crystal. Wrong message again.

I tried not to watch as his hands worked the corkscrew, but I couldn't help an occasional glance. Exceptional hands. As he slid the cork out, I found msyelf beginning to forgive his irritating habit of homing in on my vulnerabilities. Then he opened his mouth. "I can see why you didn't use going to the grocery store as your excuse."

"My excuse?"

"For not telling me where you really went."

I didn't try to deny it. I didn't lie well on the spur of the moment, or even with a lot of prior planning. Obviously. "As if it's any of your business *where* we went."

He poured the wine without responding. His face was unreadable. My chaotic mind finally zeroed in on the insult he'd intended. "Hey, what do you mean?" I demanded. "Why wouldn't I have been to the grocery store?"

"Because." He put the bottle down on the counter and opened the refrigerator again. "You have an entire grocery store in *here*. What single woman eats this much food?"

"Remember, now," I said acidly, "I'm not the skinniest woman on earth."

"Even a six-hundred-pound woman couldn't eat all this stuff. Portabello mushrooms, Havre cheese, an entire beef tenderloin, kalamata olives, New York cheesecake, even kim-chee, for God's sake. Unless, of course, there really is a Claude living here; he might be able to mow through all this." Leaving the refrigerator standing open, he made a show of leaning into the stairwell that led upstairs to my bedroom and living area.

Ignoring the Claude comment—*let him wonder*—I tackled the criticism head-on. "In my family, we are taught to be prepared. We're big—"

"Yeah, especially if all of you eat this way."

"Very funny. I'm a member of a big, extended family. Every one of us has to be prepared for invasions—"

He looked askance into the refrigerator again. "Invasions of what? Dozens of Italian-Greek-Dutch-Koreans from the Bronx?"

I jutted my chin. "If you were hungry, you would be glad I had all that."

"Who says I'm not hungry?"

"It doesn't matter if you are. You aren't inviting yourself to dinner, too." I slammed the refrigerator door shut and grabbed my glass, sloshing just a tad over the rim as I sat down on the kitchen window seat I'd cushioned with an old Chihuahuan woven blanket. I was careful to sit squarely in the middle so he couldn't get a wild hair and sit down next to me. Then I swung my feet up to the chair closest to me, crossing the right Justin over the left, leaving him no choice but the chair at the far end of the butcher-block table. I glanced out the window, watching the fruit bats swoop at mosquitoes in the ocher light of fading dusk.

"At this rate, we might both starve to death before I get what I came for."

Huh? I met his laser stare and resisted the urge to swallow hard. I knew the only thing he wanted from me was information. I knew he was using innuendo to throw me off-balance.

My turn.

"You'll go first, because I have more fat stores than you do and can live without food longer, as I'm not the skinniest woman in the world."

"Would you drop that, already?" He ran his fingers through his hair in frustration. *Ha!* Score one for Reyn. He blew out a breath. He picked up his glass and promptly put it down again. He stalked to the kitchen table and looked down at me. "Good God, you're like a dog with a bone. Give you a description made without really much of a thought, and you're going to carry it around with you for the rest of your life?"

I tried not to let him see how smug I was about disturbing him. "Maybe."

"Are you like this with everything?"

"Yes."

"Great. So you won't be letting go of this investigation unless I knock you over the head with a club."

I jumped up, rose onto my tiptoes, and tried to meet him eye-to-eye. I narrowed mine. "I knew you were a Neanderthal."

He reached into the breadbasket on the counter, grabbed a baguette, and held it over his head, waving it threateningly. In all fairness, he didn't know I'd bought the bread a week ago, and it might be more harmful than he realized. "I'll show you Neanderthal."

Behind me, my kitchen door burst open, and a two-hundred-fifty-pound, five-feet-tall ball of fury dressed in rainbow spandex flew into Scythe with fists pounding. I recognized the bouffant snow-white hair and jumped out of the way as she pinned him against the windowsill, her hands wrenching the baguette away from him and jamming it up against the underside of his chin. I heard his head cluck against the window glass and cringed. Scythe had gone completely still, and I knew it was one of the only times I would ever see him truly surprised. I have to admit I took a moment to enjoy it.

"Mama Tru!" I admonished, only slightly belatedly. Mario's mother lived catty-corner across busy McCullough Avenue. Her neighborly connection was the reason I got my house and at such a good price. But nothing in life is free. I consequently have no secrets and frequent interventions from the Trujillo clan.

"*Cállate,* Reyn," she ordered without taking her glare off Scythe. "I won't let the murderer kill you, too. It looks like I got here right in time. Hand me that butcher knife, and call the police."

"Mama Tru, the police are already here," I explained patiently. Mario's mother tends to overreact.

"Why don't they do something about this devil, then?" She paused to glance around while I hid a grin. "Where are they, Reyn?"

"You've got him pinned against the window."

She shot me a look. "Yeah, sure. Don't worry, I get it, Reyn. You *have* to say that. His accomplice is hiding in your pantry with a gun trained on you, right?" I opened my mouth to speak, but she soldiered on, jamming the bread farther up, clunking his head against the glass again. "*Escuche, hombre,* and whatever *amigos* you brought with you. Now there's two of us here, and one is a tough old lady who's not afraid to go to heaven if her time's come. If I have to die to save my Trudy's *amiga mejor,* then it's God's will. So bring it on!"

Oh, Lord, Mama Tru was watching too much cable.

Scythe looked from me to Mama Tru and back again, silently pleading with me to do something. I gave him credit for respect for his elders, because he was easily strong enough to brush her aside with the sweep of a forearm, yet he didn't move. I didn't, either. He looked kind of cute with a petrified loaf of bread under his chin. Besides, until he got over his good manners and told Mama where to stick it, I had him where I wanted him.

Scythe must have seen it in my eyes, because for the first time, he looked scared. "Miss Sawyer . . ." he warned.

I smiled and sidled up to him. "We'll let you go, Lieutenant, once you answer a few simple questions."

He groaned.

"Where did *you* spend the afternoon?"

He squirmed a little. Mama tightened the baguette. Scythe gave up. "Searching Ricardo's house."

"What did you find?"

"That Ricardo was a clotheshorse, had expensive taste, and not much company unless he wiped down his house regularly. There was only one other set of fingerprints besides his. Are they yours, Miss Sawyer?"

"Good try, Lieutenant. They are mine only if they are the only pair to have survived from a big Christmas party there five years ago. My guess would be they belong to his maid. Ricardo is—was—an extremely private man. He told me that he'd never entertain again, that people were way too nosy, even with nothing to smell. If he did any entertaining, it would've been at someone else's house."

"Whose?"

"If I knew that, that's where Trudy and I would've gone this afternoon."

"So, where did you go?"

Uh-oh, I stepped right into that one, didn't I? How

could I throw him off the scent? I smiled. "To see a psychic."

He rolled his eyes toward my second story and tried to shake his head, but my granny muscle tightened her grip and wouldn't let him. He settled for another groan. "A psychic? You've got to be kidding."

My smile widened. "Nope."

"So, I suppose she told you the identity of the murderer?"

"Not exactly." I had to be careful here. I didn't want to lie to the police. That could get me in worse trouble than I was already in. By the same token, I didn't want to give it all up. I could feel every petal and stem in the violet paper tucked into my back waistband. I wondered if he could see it with that damned laser vision of his.

"What does that mean?" Scythe paused for a moment, and I might have answered him with more than I wanted if he hadn't sneered condescendingly and continued, "Did she give you the murderer's astrological sign and favorite color? Did she tell you the killer was a cockroach in a previous life?"

"You have it backward," Mama Tru interrupted. "I think if he killed Ricardo, he would be a cockroach in the *next* life."

Scythe tweaked his eyebrows at Mama, and I could see he was reaching the limit of his patience. "I stand corrected, ma'am."

I needed a distraction before Scythe pursued the psychic angle any further. Perhaps gratitude for saving him from the clutches of a senior citizen on a mission armed with week-old bread would do it. I put a hand on Mama Tru's shoulder. "Maybe we should give the detective a break and let him get back to investigating, Mama Tru."

"Is he really the police?" Her liquid brown eyes turned to me and looked so disappointed that I was tempted to lie. I swear, Mama Tru had that Catholic guilt thing down to an art form.

"I'm afraid so, Mama Tru. But you know how much I appreciate you being here in case the murderer *was* after me."

"You know, Reyn, I was watching that pretty little *gringa* anchor lady on Channel Thirteen, and she made it sound like you were a suspect. So, if they want to lock you up"—she gave Scythe a suspicious look—"the police might be as dangerous to you as the murderer."

Scythe's whole body sighed. I watched his bicep dance at the cuff of his knit shirt as he reached up to rub the back of his neck. *Hmm. He might be dangerous to me, all right, dangerous to my chastity.*

"Don't worry, ma'am," Scythe said wearily. "We just want a little information from Miss Sawyer."

"Really?" Brightening, Mama Tru cocked her head sideways. "What kind of information?"

Uh-oh. Mario got his blabbermouthity from somewhere, and it wasn't his dad, for whom an entire sentence was a rare speech.

Scythe, no dummy, recognized an opportunity. He took one of Mama Tru's soft, round hands in his, introducing himself. Mama Tru, coming under the spell of his charm, returned the introduction. Then he reached for the bottle of malbec and a glass, a crystal one. *Ah-ha,* so he had noticed my omission. "Can I get you some wine, Mrs. Trujillo?"

"*Sí,* Lieutenant. And, please call me Esmeralda."

"You can call me Jackson, Esmeralda."

Mama Tru was practically purring.

I should've been grateful for the distraction, but it ticked me off. How come she got the chivalrous knight, and I got the laser-beam hard-ass? I gave myself a mental slap. As they sat at the kitchen table, I weighed my options in escaping just long enough to hide the violet paper. I could excuse myself to go to the ladies' room, but how would I explain having to back all the way there?

"How long have you known Ricardo, ma'am?" Scythe said in an exaggerated version of his dry West Texas accent. He was shifting into his interrogating-old-ladies mode.

"Oh, I didn't know him."

I could see Scythe visibly deflate.

"But," Mama Tru added, "I do know a lot about him."

"The police aren't interested in rumors, Mama."

"Wrong, Miss Sawyer," Scythe corrected. "Many rumors carry a grain of truth in them."

"Ha!"

"Ha what?"

"I guess you've never known a teenage girl. They can make up stories out of whole cloth without even a speck of truth, much less something as substantial as a grain."

Scythe looked a little funny for a moment, but it might have been my imagination, because by the time I blinked, he had his game face on—unyielding. "We aren't talking about teenage girls, are we, Esmeralda?"

"No, Jackson, I hear things about Ricardo from my son and from Delia Bonita."

"Who used to be a teenage girl," I pointed out.

"Who used to be a teenage girl? Mario?" Scythe slipped in.

I glared. He obviously didn't appreciate my help, so he could do this on his own.

"Delia," Mama Tru was saying, "still went to Ricardo for her hair. You know, he only did that for very special customers, ones he'd had around a long time."

"I talked to Mario earlier," Scythe said. "So I probably know all you can impart from his end. But what has Delia told you?"

I resisted the urge to pull out the paper to see if Delia's name was on the list. I hoped so, or the whole Zorita thing was a hoax.

"Many, many things over the years. I can't remember most of these."

"That's fine. What you do remember is probably what will be most important to me." Scythe was endlessly patient. With her, not me.

"We went to Judy's Tacos over on the south side after the last time she got her hair done. We go eat somewhere after her appointments, then run around shopping at the thrift stores."

That explained the funky caftan. I'd thought they stopped making those things in the seventies.

Scythe laced his hands togther, probably to prevent himself from a dozen impatient gestures he was dying to make to get Mama to the point. His knuckles whitened. He nodded to encourage her to go on.

"We were at Neighborhood Thrift, going through the women's dresses, looking for something for her granddaughter to wear to her cousin's *quinceañera*, when—"

"Just a minute." Scythe held up a hand. "You're telling me that Delia pays how much to get her hair done?"

"Two hundred sixty dollars."

"And," Jackson continued, "shops for her family's clothes at a thrift store?"

Mama Tru tsked. "Jackson, have you ever been to a thrift store?"

I resisted the urge to grin as I tried to picture Scythe picking through racks of jumbled clothes in a warehouse. He wouldn't do it unless he were looking for a clue. In fact, I doubt he ever shopped for clothes, period. Maybe he got his girlfriends to do it for him. "No, I haven't," he answered.

"Last week, I found a silk organdy dress, brand-new with tags from Neiman Marcus, for nine dollars and ninety-nine cents. And it was senior citizen day, so I got twenty-five percent off that. No matter how rich you are, Jackson, you can't pass up a deal like that. Besides, someone as cultured as you should know that sometimes the rich are the worse for being cheap."

I threw Jackson a sidelong glance. He looked duly impressed with Mama's insight but still impatient for the good stuff. We'd been talking fifteen minutes and had only found out the places to shop and eat on the south side.

"Did she happen to mention Ricardo while you two were out finding deals?"

"Oh, yes." Mama nodded and took a swig of wine. I think she thought it was *sangria,* becuse she made a face like she'd been expecting the sweet watered-down drink and got dry tannin, thirteen-percent alcohol instead. "We passed a billboard for one of the open city council seats, and Delia mentioned that Ricardo seemed especially distracted by the local political race. She said in all the years she went to him for hair, he'd never even mentioned politics, but this time he was different. She said Ricardo was always so cool and smooth, but that day he as *un hombre del fuego.*"

"A man of fire? Why?" So Jackson knew some *español*.

"She didn't know. It surprised her. You see, she's the secretary—or what do they want us to call them now, executive assistants? Anyway, she is the executive assistant for the chairman of the Bexar County Republican Party. She said something to Ricardo she shouldn't have, she said. Told him about someone who was about to announce to run in one of the races. She felt guilty about it, because Ricardo, he got a little passionate."

My fingers wiggled. *Down boys, you can't pull out that list to check just yet. Patience is a virtue. Wait until the nosy policeman is gone.*

Scythe shrugged. "People get passionate for all sorts of reasons. Did Delia happen to say which race Ricardo was focused on?"

She shook her snow-white head. *"Lo siento.* I didn't ask. We started talking about the *mariachis* her daughter-in-law's sister hired for the *quineañera.* They aren't very good, and they are very expensive, and—"

Scythe stood up and stuck his hand into his back pocket, extracting a card from his business card case. He took her right hand in his, put the card in her palm, and covered it with his left. "Thank you so much, Esmeralda. Please call me if you talk to Delia again or think of anything else. You've been a great help."

Had Mama Tru run Scythe off so soon with her promise of endless chatter? If that was the case, I would have to keep her around.

Scythe looked down at the beeper on his belt, and I realized he was being paged. He pressed a button, obviously recognizing the number displayed. "I apologize, ladies, that I have to leave so soon."

He carried his half-drunk glass to the sink, then walked to the back door. I jumped up, careful to follow behind him so he couldn't see the paper. I was almost home free.

I thought.

"Reyn." Mama Tru was looking at my back. She leaned forward with her hand outstretched to grab the paper. "You have something—"

I jumped and narrowly missed banging into Scythe. "Something to make for dinner. Oh, yes, Mama Tru, I do. I hope you'll stay."

"How about a thousand somethings?" Scythe muttered derisively. I knew my distraction technique would work. So much for my pride.

He had a hand on the doorknob when he turned, surprising me. This time, I did bump into his chest. *Oops.* He steadied me with a hand on my waist. There was a second I had to hold my breath. I decided it was because two inches to the west, and he would be touching my big clue. Although I might have been lying to myself, because for that second I forgot about the damned paper.

"Don't think you've wriggled out of talking to me," he said quietly. "I'll be back."

"I'll be asleep."

"Oh, Claude like to tuck in early?"

I grinned. "That's right."

"Guess I'll have to wake you up, then."

With the ghost of a grin, he was gone, leaving me to wonder how he was going to wake me and when. *Damn.*

fifteen

I MET THE DAWN FEELING WORSE THAN THE MORNING before, probably because I'd woken a dozen times waiting for Scythe to make good on his threat. Or promise. Or whatever it was. One time, I woke up thinking I heard the telephone ring. Another time, I thought I heard the *ping* of a rock hitting my windowsill. I shot out of bed in a cold seat after a nightmare that he'd sent the SWAT team in after me—with me wearing only my somewhat holey "Fat Babies Have No Pride" T-shirt. After slipping on panties for some peace of mind, I finally got back to sleep, only to have my subconscious embellish the previous nightmare, imagining what Scythe would do to me once the SWAT team had me caught. *Hmm.* I was sweating again when I woke, but I wasn't cold.

I beat James Brown to the punch again, hearing my alarm as I was winding up an extra-long shower. I actually shaved my legs two days in a row. A record, I believe. Reviewing the contents of my closet, I decided that today called for a more take-charge outfit than the one I wore yesterday. Skirts made me feel feminine, but they also made me feel vulnerable—the last thing needed around Scythe. Not that I thought I would see him today, understand. I just wanted to be prepared for any eventuality.

After slipping on utilitarian white cotton panties and a white cotton bra, no padding, no underwires, which somehow today seemed inadequate, I chose a chic pair of flat-front black combed cotton slacks and started to reach for an emerald-green shirt, one of my favorites. Remembering the red spikes and how much they seemed to intimidate Zorita, I snatched off the rack a rayon three-quarter-sleeve button-up-the-front blouse in a deep ruby, instead hoping to accentuate my red spiky aura and scare off any potential trouble, especially of the tall, brunet, and badged variety.

Black lizard Luccheses and a black leather belt with a silver horny toad buckle completed the ensemble. I shoved some plain silver loops into my earlobes, tucked the violet paper, which I'd read and reread dozens of times before going to sleep, into the front left pocket of my blouse, and buttoned it shut. Then I cocked my head at the assembled trio.

"How about some breakfast, girls?"

I didn't have to ask twice. They were off, down the stairs, a chorus of clicking nails and excited yips. All that for a can of the same dog food they'd eaten for years. That's why I think dogs—really, animals in general—have so much to teach us humans. They take absolutely nothing for granted. Every treat, every pat, every second of attention, is appreciated. I told myself to go through the day remembering their lesson. Ricardo didn't have the chance, but it wasn't too late for me.

With my positive attitude firmly in place, I fixed the dogs their bowls and made myself a cheese *quesadilla*, smothering it with sour cream and *jalapeños*. I could eat

Mexican food three times a day—not real Mexican food from across the border or the stuff they serve in any other state in the United States—I'm talking about the Tex-Mex food San Antonio is famous for. *Tortas, gorditas, chile rellenos, lingua, cabrito,* and—when I forgot my hind end had to fit into a pair of Levi's the next day—*barbacoa,* that decadently high-fat meat.

Even just thinking about *barbacoa* made me feel dietetic for only eating *queso blanco,* flour tortilla, and a fatty cream product. Hey, I forgot the vegetable. *Jalapeños* are a vegetable, right? I really had a complete meal in front of me. Better than Cap'n Crunch, anyway. One day when I had more time, I'd compare the fat content of those two so I could feel even more pure.

Char, Beau, and Cab were finished before I was—another reason I love these dogs, they made me seem so civilized—and asked to be let out in the backyard, where they stay most of the day unless I have an exciting outing like yesterday, when they sat in the car for hours and just escaped being turned into toadstools or worse. I glanced at the clock as I sat back down on my bar stool and took another juicy bite of the *quesadilla.* It was seven forty-five. My eight o'clock had canceled so I planned to go into the office and use that hour to work on my books. I never seemed to get caught up. I really needed to hire a full-time bookkeeper, but I just couldn't quite afford it. Six more regular clients would do it, but it seemed I never could hit that magic number. Every time I'd get close, one client would drop me, bringing me back down. I was just stubborn enough not to adjust my number down according to the circumstances, as Trudy always insisted I do. I wouldn't rely on the other stylists and nail techs in the shop to put me over the top, either. As soon as I did, one would disappear, taking his or her portion of the rent and the percentage on their gross intake with them. They were the gravy, I was the meat loaf, as Gran would say.

With a self-pitying sigh, I cleaned up breakfast and headed down the hall and into the salon. I never failed to get that surge of pride when I first walked into my very own shop each morning. I guess the morning I didn't feel it was the morning to close the doors for good. I straightened a painting on the wall, a large landscape with a melancholy romantic atmosphere. I'd actually been tempted to look for Heathcliff on the rolling berms. I'd bought it at a starving artists' sale and got home before I saw it had the art teacher's grade of A-minus on the back. I sometimes wondered if any of my highfalutin clients—the ones who had original van Goghs, Rembrandts, and Monets on their walls (I did have a few of those clients)—could see the minus in my humble oil.

I thought of Ricardo's shops, where he had a single commissioned modern chrome sculpture—a different one in each shop—in the center of the lobby. Just one of those sculptures cost more than my house, not to mention the art in it. One time, while I was still working for him, the receptionist caught a client's five-year-old son climbing the sculpture. She went to Ricardo in a panic. He calmly told her to leave it be, that if the mother let the boy destroy the artwork, she certainly had enough money to replace it. That's called having balls. And there was more. He had nothing on the walls but mirrors, which any hairstylist would consider extremely brave. In our business, you don't want the customer to look too much at herself, or she'll start finding fault in what you've done. It worked for Ricardo, but he was charmed.

Well, he was until yesterday.

After I unlocked the front door, I took my philosophical, nostalgic attitude into my office, leaving the door open so I could hear any arrivals. Sherlyn was supposed to start work at nine but she rarely made it before nine-thirty. The stylists and nail techs were allowed to start booking clients as early as six-thirty A.M., but it was rare to have any of them before nine. I could go check their books, which I required them to leave out for me to see, but I didn't feel like it. I sat down at my desk instead and was met with a framed photo of Ricardo in front of the Broadway salon with his arm around my shoulders, me holding my first State of Texas cosmetology license, grinning like a goofball.

I looked young and stupid. He looked proud. Or maybe he was just photogenic.

Sighing heavily, I opened the April books. After a few minutes, I realized I was seeing not the numbers but the list on the violet paper. In my mind's eye, I saw the names again. Three men and seven women. I knew about half the names because they were in the news on a regular basis—doctor, lawyer, Indian chief (politician)—or they were friends of friend (such as Delia). Of the five remaining, I knew three because I'd worked at his shop. They were an heiress to a salsa fortune, a sister to a past president of Mexico, and the owner of a feminine-products manufacturing company. That left only two who were a mystery. I reached for the yellow pages to see if it could be that easy and was just thumbing through to find the first name when my telephone rang. It was eight-thirty.

"Transformations, more than meets the eye," I answered automatically. I hadn't been paying a receptionist for long, and I was still the best one so far. I was dying to be stripped of the title, but I doubted Sherlyn would be the one to do it, since it was her fourth day in a row to be late to work.

"May I speak with Miss Reyn Marten Sawyer?"

"Speaking."

"Ah, Miss Sawyer, I was informed you were early to work, and I'm thankful that information was correct. I was a little apprehensive."

"Yes?"

"My name is Rita Gibson. I was retained by Mr. Ricardo Montoya to represent his estate."

"Yes?"

"As I'm sure you know, Mr. Montoya had no living relatives—"

"None he cared to claim, anyway," I clarified.

"Yes, well." She cleared her throat. "I will be planning the memorial for him. Or, I should say, I will be carrying out his instructions for his memorial."

"I see." Of course. It was just like Ricardo to plan his own funeral. "I'll do anything to help."

"Good thing, too," Rita Gibson said. Was that a hint of a chuckle in her voice? "Since you're required to."

"Required to?" I felt my hackles rising. "What are you talking about?"

"I don't know how much of this Mr. Montoya apprised you of."

"Try none."

"All right. He's left a list of detailed instructions for his funeral and burial, including scripts for the eulogy. You are the only one who will be speaking who isn't a hired actor or priest. Mr. Montoya must have thought highly of you."

Ha. "I still don't see how I am *required* to do this?"

"If you don't speak at his funeral, then you won't get your inheritance."

"Inheritance? What inheritance?" I had a funny prickly feeling at the back of my neck. Zorita couldn't have been right. Ricardo had been joking. This was all a nightmare.

"You really don't know?" It was the first time she really sounded like this whole affair was giving her a headache. I could hear her asking herself, *Why can't some people just write a normal will, give their money to those who expected it, and be tucked away neatly in the ground?* I might have appreciated Ricardo making his attorney reach for aspirin first thing in the morning, except that the whole affair was giving me a bigger headache. Rita Gibson had regained her frosty professionalism and moved on. "Mr. Montoya left all his salons to you, albeit with *extremely* detailed provisions on how they should be run, but first you have to speak at his funeral. Or you don't get anything. Not even his firstborn child."

"What did you say?"

"I'm just quoting what Mr. Montoya wrote in the will. That's how he put it: 'If she failed to perform said requirements, she will get nothing, not even my firstborn child.' "

"He doesn't have any children," I paused. "Does he?"

She was about to lose her patience with me. "As I told you, Miss Sawyer, he told me he doesn't have any family."

"Okay." Was this whole thing Ricardo's idea of a joke, or was he trying to tell me something. I wouldn't ever consider myself his best friend, but I couldn't name anyone he was any closer to. The vice president of Ricardo's Realm, Inc., would be a natural choice, but Ricardo always told me Gerald made a wonderful soldier and would fail as a general. Gerald was a man made to take orders. Was he giving me the salons because he thought I would make a great general or because he knew I had an insatiable curiosity and he wanted to invest my emotions in finding out who killed him? By now, I'd convinced myself Ricardo knew he was a marked man.

"Mis Sawyer?"

"I'm sorry. I was thinking."

"Yes. Take your time."

As if I needed a lot of time to grease the wheels in my dull, nonlawyer brain? She only wished. "When did Ricardo write this will?"

"He redrew his will about a month ago."

"What did the old will say?"

"I can't tell you that."

Can't fault a girl for trying. That's one thing I promised myself when I turned thirty: never be afraid to ask a question. It's amazing the information you can get that way. I'm constantly surprised at the questions some people answer. Sometimes all it takes is changing some words. "And you can't tell me who might have been a beneficiary in the old will who was cut out of this current will?"

"No, I can't." Did I hear some grudging respect in her chilly voice? Maybe I was imagining it. I wasn't imagining the tinkle of the bell on the front door. Sherlyn must finally have deigned to grace the place of employment with her presence. "Miss Sawyer, as you are the sole beneficiary of Mr. Montoya's will, I don't see a need for a formal will reading. I do need you to sign some papers following the memorial service. As for the salons, I will inform the vice president, a Gerald Akin, of the contents of the will. He will report to me until you sign the papers. If you anticipate that this information will be difficult for him to accept, we can arrange a joint meeting . . ."

Gerald and I always got along great. In fact, I bet he probably spent the last twenty-four hours popping Tums at the speed of light at the thought of having to make all these decisions himself. "No, I think Ger will be okay with it. He's not going to lose his job."

"I'll let him know of your intentions. But you understand you can't make any decisions until you deliver Mr. Montoya's eulogy and you sign these documents. This is a company worth—"

"Whoa." I put up a hand. As if she could see it. Maybe it gave my voice more authority. "I don't want to know."

"Excuse me?"

"I don't want to know how much the company is worth."

"B-But—" I'd finally rendered Ms. Gibson speechless.

"But nothing. I have enough rattling around in my head without those numbers."

"That's very strange, Miss Sawyer."

"This whole thing is strange, Ms. Gibson. And I intend to get to the bottom of it." I unbuttoned my pocket, removed the violet paper, and smoothed it out on the desktop. "I'm going to find out who killed Ricardo and why, before I sit on any corporate throne."

"Oh, dear." Wow, maybe she did care. "Please don't do that until you've accepted ownership of the salons."

She did care, all right. About herself and the pain in the ass the paperwork would be if I got killed and she had to track down my heirs.

"Listen, I said, as she was no doubt already searching her lawyer brain for some obscure statutes that would apply to the death of an heir before the transfer of property. "If you would be so kind as to get me copies of the scripts of the actors so I won't be repeating all the wonderful things they're going to say about Ricardo in the service, I'd really appreciate it." Truth is, I really wanted to see if there would be any more clues in what he had to say about himself. I was honestly considering not speaking at the funeral. I'm that perverse. I hated it when people manipulated me, even from the grave. I might have relayed this information to Ms. Gibson, but it probably would've given her a heart attack.

"Of course. I'll have them messengered over immediately."

"You don't have to be that quick about it."

"Yes, I do. The service is today at four o'clock."

"Why so soon?" I squawked.

"Ricardo's stipulation was that his memorial would take place within forty-eight hours of his death."

"But wasn't he Catholic?"

"You're his friend, you should know that," she snapped. Maybe she was human after all. Not very, though, because she got herself back under control again. "The service is at a nondenominational church. The burial will take place privately and separately after the body has been released. That can take a while in a case like this."

"Okay." I sighed. What else could I do?

"And if you'd like, when it is convenient, you can have your attorney contact me regarding the dispensation of the will."

If *I'd* like? She'd like, that was for sure. She'd rather do the lawyer-speak thing with her own kind than have to translate it all to me. I almost told her to forget it, until I remembered the attorney on the list Zorita gave me. I could call him on the pretense of looking for a recommendation for an attorney. What a great excuse to weasel information out of a weasel. "I'll do that," I told her.

"One more thing," she said. "Ricardo's instructions are to tell you, 'I've made two mistakes. The first was the best thing I ever did. The second was the worst thing I ever did.'"

"What!?"

"That is a direct quote. That was the last thing I was to tell you in this phone call," she said, and hung up before I could ask more.

Huh?

I stared at the receiver in my hand a few minutes before I replaced it. Grabbing the frame in front of me, I stared at the photo of Ricardo, hoping to see the key to all this in his eyes. If he'd felt threatened, why hadn't he told me? Why hadn't I probed his odd attitude the night he died instead of pelting him with sarcasm? Why hadn't I rushed right over when he called in the middle of the night, instead of going back to sleep?

What the hell was I going to do with Ricardo's empire? I didn't want it. That might seem crazy, but I always liked to do things the hard way. My goal in life was to make a name for myself, and I couldn't do that by taking over a company emblazoned with someone else's name, built on someone else's blood, sweat, and tears. Money didn't interest me nearly as much as success did. Well, I'd do a Scarlett O'Hara and think about it tomorrow. It wasn't mine yet, anyway.

"You're a big help," I told Ricardo's image as I moved to put it back.

"Seems to me you'd be a little more grateful to the man who's made you a millionairess."

The frame slipped out of my hands as I spun around, sending it flying against the wall.

Jackson Scythe was leaning against the doorjamb of my office, arms crossed smugly across his chest, unsmiling, laser beams turned on high. This was a man who relished the sneak attack. He didn't even flinch with the shattering of glass.

"Seems to me you'd be a little more polite and not eavesdrop on other people's conversations."

"Seems to me you'd know that eavesdropping is Chapter Four in the detectives manual."

"Very funny."

"Is that your default comment when your brain can't catch up with that mouth of yours?"

"Only with you. I'm trying to make you feel better about your complete lack of good humor."

His lips thinned, and his eyes narrowed. Just barely but enough for me to know I'd hit a nerve. Was he a little sensitive about his hard-ass attitude? I'd have to file that one away in his list of vulnerabilities. A list of one. He probably already had a list as long as his arm of mine. I can't help it that I'm easy to read.

"You think you're going to get away with it?"

"With what? Insulting you? Well, I *was* hoping—"

"With killing Ricardo Montoya and walking away with his multimillion-dollar fortune."

I started laughing. A combination of lack of sleep, the shock about the will, and the repeating vision of Ricardo lying there with the brush sticking out of his back had made me semihysterical. Or maybe it was the overly serious way Scythe had delivered the accusation, like he'd stun me into confessing right then and there. Or maybe it was the absurdity of the notion—of me killing my mentor to walk away with something I didn't want.

Whatever the reason, I couldn't stop laughing. Scythe had gone from ominous to bumfuzzled in two seconds flat.

The bell on the front door tinkled. "Reyn? Reyn Marten Sawyer, is that you?"

"Back here," I sputtered, and struggled to compose myself. I recognized the soprano as one I'd heard before, but I couldn't place whom it belonged to.

Wedge heels clunked down the hardwood. I swallowed another laugh that rose in my throat. Scythe, having recaptured his menace, glared. The broad, smiling face of number eight on my violet paper list peered around Scythe's right shoulder.

"Reyn, is there any way on God's green earth you could squeeze me in today? What with—"

"Of course," I cut in before she could let on she was one of Ricardo's clients. "How about right now?"

Scythe's eyebrows drew together in frustration.

"Ms. Janice Hornbuckle, meet Jackson Scythe." I introduced then, knowing my next comment might just send him flying. They shook hands. "Mrs. Hornbuckle owns My Mother Earth, maker of feminine-hygiene products."

"Really?" I could see a flash of panic in his eyes.

"Oh, yes, young man." She turned back to me, excited. "And Reyn, I can't wait to ask your opinion about a new product we have under development."

That did it. Scythe ran his hand through his hair. "I'm sorry to have to leave you ladies."

I decided to ignore the sarcastic inflection he put on the last word for my benefit. I didn't mind. I'd gotten rid of him. Hee hee. I almost started chortling again, until I saw his laser beam catch sight of the violet paper on my desk. *Damn.* I'd forgotten it was right there in plain view. "What's that?" he asked, nodding toward it, eyes narrowing.

"Oh, that? A recipe a friend passed along." Well, I wasn't lying. It was a recipe of sorts. Recipe for finding a killer, right? I coolly tucked it in between hairstyling books on the shelf.

"A new recipe. I'll just have to stop by for dinner, then, won't I?"

"You won't."

"I will."

Mrs. Hornbuckle's head bobbed back and forth between us like a tennis ball on match point.

I smiled suddenly. "Great. Make it a little early, so I can give you a hair trim first to thank you for all your kindness."

The panic flashed again. Before he mouthed a smile that didn't even get close to his eyes. He made a visual pass over my hairstyle. Okay, so the asymmetrical bob wasn't my most flattering style ever, but I figured it would grow out. Story of my life.

"A trim won't be necessary," Scythe forced out.

"Oh, of course it will. You really need your hair cut. It's starting to curl around your ears and cover that sexy neck of yours," Mrs. Hornbuckle put in with a wink.

I could see Scythe fighting the urge to look into the mirror to check out his sexy neck. Gag. What a big head.

"See you tonight." I pulled a pair of scissors out of my tool cart and tested their sharpness with my index finger. Shaking his head slightly, Scythe turned away and let himself out.

Janice Hornbuckle looked at me over the top of her wire-rimmed eyeglasses. "I'm so relieved we finally got rid of him. I have something important to tell you."

sixteen

I SILENCED JANICE WITH A FINGER TO MY LIPS AND stalked over to the front door. I didn't trust Scythe. I could imagine him making sure we heard the door shut while still standing in the foyer with his ear pressed against the wall. I guess it takes a sneak to know a sneak. I ducked behind the ficus I kept in the corner of the lobby as I saw a Crown Vic, with Crandall at the wheel, make a U-turn on Magnolia and head west. I swear, I could feel Scythe's gaze burning through the dark-tinted windows of the sedan. Where were they off to now? I couldn't worry about it right now. I had a hot one in my salon chair.

"Coast is clear," I told Janice as I strode back into my room. I motioned to her naturally wavy hair, which she wore surprisingly long—to her waist. It made me think of peace signs and tie-dyed shirts. "What do you need done?"

"Just a trim, Reyn. It's the same style I've had for fifty years. I do hope I can start coming to you now that Ricardo is in another dimension."

Like the Twilight Zone? I fought to keep my face neutral. "Of course you can. If you'd like a regular appointment, we can work you into my book after we're finished." I threw a smock around her shoulders and ran my hands through her fine salt-and-pepper hair. Her style was unusual for a middle-aged CEO dressed conservatively in khaki trousers and white silk blouse. It would take me ten minutes to trim it, if I stretched it out. "Let's go ahead and wash and condition first."

As we walked to my sink station, Janice shook her head. "I just wish I could have done something."

"What could you have done?"

She shook her head again and seemed lost in thought. I counseled myself on the benefits of patience as I leaned her head back and washed, massaging her scalp, hoping to rub the secret out like Aladdin's lamp. When I was finished and was wrapping the towel around her head, she sighed heavily. "I think if I would've pried a little more, he would've opened up to me, and maybe all this could've been avoided. Ricardo might be alive today."

I swallowed the *What?* and led her to my room, settling her in the chair. I tried to imagine myself like the cool psychologist who listens to Tony on *The Sopranos*. You know she wants to lean over and shake him sometimes or have her mouth drop open wide enough to admit a semi, but she just sits there. Calmly. Waiting. My hero.

I waited.

I bumped into my tool cart and sent it crashing into the wall.

Obviously, not calmly.

I righted my cart, chose a comb and some scissors, and willed her to start talking before I started snipping so she wouldn't need stitches by the time I was finished.

"Why don't you tell me about it?" I said to Janice. Very cool.

"I met him last night about nine."

Ah-ha. She was the mystery customer.

"I was scheduled to get my regular trim and condition," she continued, watching my poised scissors rather nervously. "First he tried to talk me into going shorter. He showed me photos, a shag, like we had back in the sixties. But he started waving this weird-looking brush around, and I realized this shag was going to need some twenty-first-century styling, so I said no."

At least that answered the question of why Ricardo needed the brush. Janice paused. I started snipping so she'd keep talking. "His cell phone rang, and you know how he is, he ignores it if he is with a customer. I imagine he doesn't turn it off because he wants to know he's had a call, but I've never known him to allow an interruption when he's with me—or, I assume, with any other client."

"That's right," I confirmed. That was part of Ricardo's deal. Two big ones for—I looked again at Janice's hair—a twenty-five-dollar cut, but you would have his undivided attention.

"This time, he excused himself and walked to his bathroom, but with all that tile and mirror and chrome, it's like an echo chamber. I heard everything he said."

I held my breath so I wouldn't blurt anything out, like *What the hell did he say?* Instead, I smiled and nodded.

"I really shouldn't tell you." She mulled.

My fingers tightened around the handles of the scissors. Janice swallowed hard.

"You just said you should've said something last

night. Now is your chance," I reminded her, exchanging my scissors for the comb and beginning to work it through her hair. She winced. This might be better than the scissors for extracting info.

"Too late to save him." Was she ever stubborn. I had to admire that.

"But maybe not too late to find his murderer."

"You're right. Protecting his privacy now won't help him, will it?" She paused, watching a woodpecker choose just the right piece of oak tree outside the window.

I marveled at Ricardo's privacy even beyond the grave. How did he instill this powerful instinct in all his friends and customers to keep our mouths shut about his business, when human nature is the complete opposite? Of course, with our tongues quiet, our imaginations went into overdrive, and we made up elaborate scenarios miles from the truth. I know I did in the beginning. He'd threaten to pluck me bald if I told anyone he was going home early. It was probably just to watch *Oprah*, but I assumed he had a hot rendezvous until I got to know him better. He cultivated that air of mystery, though.

Janice sucked in a breath and finally gave it up. "He told the person on the other end that if 'he' didn't do what Ricardo asked, Ricardo would tell everything he knew."

"Blackmail?" I was shocked.

"It sounded like it."

"He was talking directly to the person he was blackmailing?"

"Oh, no. I'm sorry. He was talking *about* the person he was blackmailing. He referred to 'he.' I got the impression he was talking to a woman. He called her '*mi cara*' once and then cautioned her to keep calm, that everything would work out for the best."

Best for whom? Not Ricardo, obviously. "Anything else?"

"No. It was a short conversation, whispered. And I missed the end, because he flushed the toilet and drowned out whatever else I might have heard. When he came back to me, his hands were shaking so badly that I told him I had a dinner date I'd just remembered, and we could reschedule my trim for another time. He agreed, obviously relieved. I've never seen him so distracted."

I wondered if the police had already traced the call and were on the hunt for another suspect I didn't know about. That bugged me.

"Have you told the police?" I asked.

"No!" Janice almost shouted. Her hand flew to her throat protectively. "I won't talk to police. Not voluntarily. Not ever."

"Why?" I tried to hide my shock at her reaction

"I have a distrust of governmental authority. I demonstrated against the war in Vietnam in the sixties and seventies." That explained the expensive fringed purse and hairstyle—holdover hippie. "I've seen the view from behind bars. I think politicians are more corrupt now than they were then, only now I'm more selfish, too. I have a company to protect, women who rely on my products. Besides, the IRS audits me every year. One visit to the fuzz, and they'd find some reason to close me down for good."

Wow, was she paranoid, or did Big Brother really lean on her that hard? After thirty years? She must have been a pretty big thorn in their side. I admired her for that, but looking at her now, I realized no matter what she had been and the trappings she tried to hang on to—the long hippie hair that she had expensively cut, the Sandra Acuna fringed pouch purse that was retro-sixties but cost in the neighborhood of two hundred dollars, her talk of the "other dimension"—Janice now was really no different from any corporate stooge. Protecting what she had was more important than anything—like truth, justice, what was right.

That scared me. I hoped age would make me wiser, not clinically cautious.

Then I thought about my gran and relaxed. If genetics had anything to do with it, I'd be okay. Gran was anything but cautious.

"I appreciate you telling me, Janice," I said as I retrieved my scissors and began snipping.

"What are you going to do?" she asked.

"I'm just checking around, doing things the police don't have the time or the inclination to do."

"You won't tell the police about me, will you?" She gripped the armrests so tightly her knuckles went white.

Man, I really wondered what she'd done in her past to warrant this kind of paranoia. Or *was* it all in her past? "No, Janice, I promise your name won't pass my lips, even under the influence of thumbscrews. I'm not on the best terms with the police, anyway."

"Don't get hurt. I don't want your blood on my conscience, too."

What an odd choice of words. Or was I becoming as paranoid as she was, suspicious of everyone who mentioned Ricardo's name? "Don't worry about me, Janice. I can take care of myself."

"With a little help from her friends," Trudy chirped

as she swung her head around the doorjamb. I saw she was doing lime green today as the rest of her body encased in silk and spandex danced into the doorway. She'd even changed her fingernail polish, although I wasn't entirely sure that ice blue was the perfect complement to lime. Trudy made it work somehow. She always did.

"And her friends' mothers-in-law," I couldn't resist adding.

Trudy hung her head for a moment, then put her hand on my forearm as I replaced my scissors on the cart, picked up a brush, and reached for my blow-dryer. "Reyn, I'm sorry about Mama Tru."

We shared a moment of silence, during which I realized that despite all her faults, Mama Tru was another example of a geriatric with spunk. Okay, so I didn't have to dread my twilight years anymore. I looked at Trude, about to forgive her for the family she married into, but she ruined it by breaking into a lascivious grin.

"But I hear that you were tight with Policeman Perfect, sharing a glass of wine, cozy in the kitchen. I want the skinny."

That's all Janice had to hear. She jumped up out of her chair, ripped off her smock, and swung her half-dry hair out of her face. "Reyn! You're involved with a cop? You lied to me."

"I did not. It's not what it sounds like. Not even close." I spared a glare at Trudy before focusing back on Janice, who was now grabbing her fringed bag on her way out the door.

"I just hope you don't betray my confidence. I don't want to wear black-and-white stripes again."

I wanted to tell her they dress you in orange in our

county jail, but it probably wasn't what she wanted to hear. I listened as she nearly stampeded down the hall and slammed the front door on Sherlyn's good-bye. I might be wrong, but I don't think she took the time to schedule her next appointment with me. There went another potential regular customer thanks to a Trujillo big mouth.

I turned to my erstwhile buddy, whose mouth was actually looking the part at the moment, hanging wide open in shock. "You already found the killer?"

I snorted as I put the blow-dryer and brush back on the cart. "Not hardly."

Trudy followed me into my office. I plucked the list out from between the hairstyle books, smoothed it out on the desk, and made a check mark by number eight. I scanned the other names. Was Ricardo's *mi cara* on here, or was she merely a confidante?

"But she said—"

I waved off the rest of her statement as I closed the office door. "Paranoid ex-hippie."

"Oh. I thought she was trying to be pop with the peace ring, the purse, and the platform sandals."

"No, she's just hanging on to the wrong parts of her past."

"I'll say," Trudy intoned. A fashion faux pas was the biggest sin in her book, although sometimes I wondered if she ever looked in the mirror. Of course, when I looked at fashion magazines, I rarely looked down past the shoulders, and my own fashion consisted of whatever I chose to go with cowboy boots.

Trudy read the list over my shoulder. "You really think one of them did it?"

"I don't know, but it's a place to start." I told her what

Janice had overheard. "So, all we know now is that Ricardo was apparently blackmailing someone, met a guy in tennis whites at a transvestite club, was inordinately interested in one local political race, and—" I paused. I wasn't ready to tell her about my potential inheritance. I wasn't ready to accept it, and I knew if I told Trudy, it would be in the newspaper tomorrow morning. I love my friend, but she doesn't know how to keep her mouth shut, especially about things that need to be kept secret. "And last night, while he was cutting Janice's hair, he talked to someone who knew about the blackmail and called her *mi cara.*"

"Could *mi cara* be a man?"

"I don't think Ricardo was gay or swung both ways. It's just an instinct, and we have to rely on that, since we have little else to rely on at the moment."

"If Janice was the appointment he had last night, you don't think she did it?"

I shook my head. "It just doesn't make sense for her to come here and offer the information willingly if she killed him."

"Okay. What's our next move?"

I considered our options. We could go systematically down the list, paying visits one by one. But first, I thought we needed to go to Ricardo's house. Perhaps there was something the police missed that a friend would see as odd or out of place. But surely it was still sealed as an extension of the crime scene, and I doubted the cops would invite us in. Unless we had an official reason to be there. Perhaps on an errand for the man who was running Ricardo's salons? "Let's go see Ricardo's right-hand man," I told Trudy. "Then we'll tackle the rest of the list."

● ● ●

Gerald told me on the phone that he was working from home since the police wouldn't let him back in his office located at the rear of the Broadway salon. We followed his directions to a tiny but well-kept gray asbestos-siding house in a lower-middle-class neighborhood built in the fifties off Vance Jackson Road. As we pulled into the concrete driveway, I decided my first act as head of Ricardo's, Inc., would be to give Gerald a raise, because he was either grossly underpaid or was socking away a ton of money.

He met us as the door wearing a navy-blue suit, white shirt, conservative tie, and that deep side-parted, Ward Cleaver hairstyle he used Dippity Do on to keep motionless. The hand that shook mine was damp with perspiration. He flashed a shy smile. Poor guy was nervous. I wondered if the attorney had passed along my message. I wanted to reassure him but remembered I had to be careful because I still didn't want Trudy to know. "How are you holding up, Gerald?"

"Great, just great," he stuttered, then caught himself, obviously wondering if that sounded too crass. "I mean, I have so much work to do that I haven't had time to really think about losing him. I mean, there's just so much to get arranged, and there's the daily crises that crop up that take my attention. I mean—"

I put a hand on his shoulder. "We know what you mean. It's easier to keep busy. I imagine it will really hit you hard once you get back to work at your Broadway office and he's not there."

It sounded a little awkward, but he got my message—he wouldn't be fired. His eyes brightened, and he smiled a little more confidently. "Thank you, Reyn."

Trudy's eyebrows drew together. She knew she was

missing something but wasn't sure what. I moved out of the small foyer and into the living room, choosing the worn but clean plaid love seat. Gerald had to be on Scythe and Crandall's suspect list, but I didn't see him ever having the balls to bury a brush in his boss's back. I knew from reading enough true crime that a meek personality often hid homicidal tendencies, but I couldn't make the stretch in Gerald's case. Ricardo's murder was obviously a murder of the moment, using a weapon of convenience. What would have tripped Gerald's temper? Love or money? I couldn't see him harboring a secret crush on Ricardo all these years, then finally coming out with it. Even if he had, Ricardo was the kind of man who, despite his machismo, would've dealt with it kindly. He genuinely liked and respected Gerald. I'd seen it every day at work for years. On the other hand, if Ricardo had made an unwanted pass at Gerald, I saw Gerald being embarrassed, not bloodthirsty. If it had been a money issue, Gerald finally having enough of his millionaire boss taking advantage of him, I saw Ricardo not realizing how cheap he was being and easily increasing Gerald's salary. Ricardo had such tunnel vision that I doubted it ever occurred to him that he was underpaying the man who was keeping his business running on a daily basis. No, I'd bet Gerald had never asked for a raise in his life.

I just couldn't make it fit. Or maybe I didn't want to.

Trudy and Gerald were making their way slowly into the living room. Trudy was asking him how he had found out about Ricardo's murder.

"I went into work that morning, and the police stopped me." He sat on a recliner while Trudy sat down next to me.

"I'm sorry, Gerald, I didn't see you there," I said,

racking my memory for something other than the sight of Ricardo's bloody body.

"I was sitting in a police car when you came out of the salon. I knew when I saw your face how bad it must be. The police wouldn't tell me. I guess they think I might have done it."

Gerald stared at his hands, which he'd clasped between his knees.

"Well, if it's any consolation, you're below me on the suspect list."

"I suppose you have more of a motive than I do," he commented.

Uh-oh. Trudy looked at him sharply, then questioningly at me. I forced a smile. "You're right. I was well known for locking horns with Ricardo a lot more times than you ever did. I suppose the cops would look there first, huh?"

"But that's not what I mean—" Gerald drew his eyebrows together in confusion. He must have assumed I'd told my best friend about my inheritance.

"Oh, don't try to excuse my bad temper." I waved my hand at him, hoping to wave away any more that he might say. "You saw it enough times when I worked at Ricardo's."

Gerald smiled then. "It was good entertainment."

Oh, swell. If I ever got tired of styling hair, I could just sign on as entertainer on my prickly personality alone.

"Maybe they'll hire you at Illusions," Trudy put in with a cruel grin. She was mad at me.

"I think Ricardo really missed you when you left. He'd comment on how calm and quiet it was every day for nearly a year," Gerald reminisced.

A lump rose unexpectedly in my throat. Tears welled

up in my eyes. Why this would make me want to cry when his dead body didn't, don't ask me. A forgiving Trudy patted me on the shoulder. That took care of it. I hated to show weakness, and crying was weak in my book. I blinked the tears away, then focused back on how I could get the key to Ricardo's house from Gerald without letting Trudy in on the inheritance deal.

Trudy did it for me. "We're trying to find out who killed Ricardo," she said to steer the subject away from emotions to action. Every now and then, I was glad I dragged her along.

"Really?" Gerald moved his hands to his knees and leaned forward. "Isn't that dangerous?"

"I'd call it defensive," Trudy put in smartly. "Since they really think Reyn did it."

Oh, good, Trude. Now Gerald was really going to want to slip me the key so I could cover up my murder tracks. My gratitude toward her dissolved.

"Why? What evidence do they have besides the obvious motive of—"

"Professional jealousy? None, really."

Gerald looked terribly confused now. "But you weren't jealous."

"How right you are. Besides which, they'd have to draw a list of the hundreds of salon owners who were professionally jealous of Ricardo."

"But don't the police know that you—"

"Used to work for Ricardo? Of course, that's why I'm first on the list."

He opened his mouth, but I jumped in before he could say anything more.

"Gerald, did Ricardo ever mention pudding to you?"

"Pudding?" Poor man's head was about to start spinning on his shoulders, I was jerking him in so many different directions. He glanced at the bottle of Mylanta on the kitchen counter we could just see through the doorway. "What flavor?"

"Any flavor."

Gerald shook his head, completely dumbfounded by my nonsensical line of questioning. "I don't recall him ever eating pudding or talking about it."

"How about political races?"

"Pudding in political races?"

"No, just any political races."

Gerald paused to think. I appreciated that. Maybe I should do more of it. The pausing, that is. Suddenly, he brightened. "As a matter of fact, lately he'd been a little worked up over the race for the state representative's position that's going to open now that Juan Sifuentes announced he's going to resign due to illness. It surprised me, because Ricardo never really cared about politics. As a small-businessman, he donated to some races when his customers or acquaintances were running, but it was very hands-off. He'd tell me to send a modest check here or there. He'd attend the parties for his own PR but he never actively campaigned for anyone."

"What makes you think this state rep's race was different?"

"He just talked about it a lot. Asked me and people around the salon questions, like what kind of person they'd vote for. Now that you're making me think about it, he tried to make it sound casual, but there was something urgent underlying it all."

"Who's running in that race?"

"I don't think anyone has declared yet."

"None of his clients was getting ready to run, were

they?" I racked my brain for anyone on the list who might be a potential candidate.

"Not that I know of. But you know, Reyn, Ricardo kept his client list private. No one really knew it. They went in and out the back door and often were there after hours."

We three sat in silence for a moment, not knowing what all that meant, if anything.

"Did Ricardo ever mention two big mistakes he made in his life?"

Gerald laughed at that. "Ricardo didn't have any flaws, much less did he ever make a mistake."

I smiled. That was the Ricardo we knew and loved. Gerald clearly wasn't Ricardo's confidant, but I remembered what Janice said about *mi cara* and thought I'd give it a shot. "Gerald, did Ricardo have any woman who was special to him?"

Gerald didn't even pause. "Not ever. He dated, as you know, but he never got serious with any woman. If she tried to, that was the end of her."

"You don't think that he might have been secretive about a woman, taking her only to out-of-the-way places and his home? He could've been in a passionate affair and no one would know?"

"No. He dated, sure, lots. But there was no special woman now. I think he gave his heart away a long, long time ago and never got it back. Never wanted it back, really."

"Why do you think this?"

He shrugged. "An impression. An instinct."

"Or experience," Trudy put in after remaining uncharacteristically silent through my interrogation. Now she smiled gently at Gerald. "You know because you gave your heart away a long time ago, too, didn't you?"

Oh, my Lord, now my romantic friend was going to turn this into *True Confessions*. Gag.

"Maybe," he answered, reclasping his hands at his knees.

I had to get out of there before they got too mushy. I excused myself to go to the bathroom, and they barely noticed. After I'd washed up in the bathroom that was tiled from floor to ceiling in 1970s avocado green, I ambled through the kitchen, taking my time to avoid the lovey-dovey conversation. The kitchen was extremely organized; even the sugar, coffee, and flour canisters were labeled. Each copper canister was marked with electrical tape regarding its fullness level. It made my cozy kitchen seem haphazard and cluttered. In my peripheral vision, I took in the keys on a rack by the garage door, a rack for baseball caps, and a rack for umbrellas. Keys? I felt temptation drawing me to the wall. If the flour was labeled, wouldn't he label keys, too? The concept seemed foreign to me. I had reams of keys, and if I didn't know what they went to, well, too bad. Sometimes when I had to let myself into my sister's house, I had to try a dozen different keys first.

I listened for their conversation and heard that he went to the same church and saw his long-held love and her family of four every Sunday. What torture. *Why do that to yourself, Gerald?* How would I know, I'd never been in love, and from the sounds of it, I didn't want to be.

Those keys were calling me from the rack. I ambled back there and looked from afar. I saw each key had a colored tag. Maybe they were just color-coded, with Gerald being the only one who could break the code. I squinted. I saw words. I took a step forward. I saw "Broadway salon," "Thousand Oaks salon," "1604 salon" on red tags. "Ricardo's office" was attached to a silver tag. *Hmm*. I looked for another silver tag. *Bingo*. "Ricardo's house, back door." My fingers wiggled. This had to be a sign. It was meant to be.

Should I?

This way, Gerald wouldn't be implicated if we were caught, I reasoned. I was doing a humanitarian thing by borrowing the key.

Okay. I snatched it and tucked it into the front pocket of my blouse, buttoning it carefully.

They were quiet in the living room. *Uh-oh*. I walked back into the room, probably too quickly. They both looked up.

"What took you so long?" Trudy asked.

"Just giving y'all time for your love talk. You know I don't know anything about that stuff."

They shared a wiggly eyebrow look.

"What?" I demanded. They both shook their heads in pity. I cleared my throat. "We'll let you get back to work, Gerald."

Trudy was looking at my chest. She cocked her head. "Reyn, why are you lopsided?"

Big mouth. My hands flew to the pockets that did ride right over my barely-B-cups. "Uh . . ."

"Did you just stuff your bra?" Trudy asked, voice of experience, apparently, although why she'd ever have to stuff hers with the puppies she possessed, I had no idea.

I could feel my face burning. Oh, well, an excuse was an excuse. Anything but admitting I stole Ricardo's key. "How did you guess?"

"Thinking you might run into Lieutenant Scythe, huh?" Trudy winked at Gerald, and I wondered what Big Mouth had told him as he winked back. "Why don't we

stop by Victoria's Secret and get you one of those padded
jobs you can cinch up? I've even seen A-cups get cleavage
out of one of those."

"Great idea." I grabbed for her elbow and hauled her
upright. "I can't wait to get there."

Trudy knew now I was lying. She looked at me suspiciously. "But—"

"But nothing," I said as I hustled her to the door.
"I've got a man to catch."

At least, I thought it was a man. The killer, that is.

seventeen

AS WE EXITED THE INTERSTATE, WE BEGAN TO SEE
the multimillion-dollar homes dotting the cedar- and-oak
covered limestone hills to our right. Trudy and I went
over the plan for the tenth time. We were zipping along
in her bubble-gum blue Miata convertible because she
said that my "old" truck would stand out in this new-
money neighborhood, drawing unwanted attention.
Mine was the vehicle of a maid or a construction worker,
she said. They really got eyeballed. Her little Miata
wasn't a Mercedes, but it might pass for a car one of the
poorer residents might buy his children, who, in my opinion, probably deserved more eyeballing than the above-
mentioned categories, but I wasn't going to split hairs
with Trude. She was doing me a favor.

Trudy had come up with the perfect way to get past the
guard gates. She'd called an interior design customer of
hers on the excuse that she'd been to an antiques auction
preview and thought a piece there would be ideal for
them. She just wanted to make sure it fit before she bid on
it. Once we measured, we could go on to Ricardo's house.

"The only hitch is, Reyn," Trudy explained, "you have to act like you're my assistant."

Humph. "Can't I just be a friend along for the ride?"

"Um, no. These people are picky about who they let into their home."

"Yeah, but you don't have an assistant."

"Xylophones and Xeroxes, Reyn, why do you have to worry everything to death? They don't know I don't have an assistant. I did this house three years ago and have come up in the world since then."

"How on earth do you remember their décor three years later? Aren't they going to be suspicious? How are you going to explain seeing some antique and placing it only in their house?"

Trudy shot me a sidelong look that made me nervous. "Their décor is, um, unique. You'll see. You'll never forget it, either."

I doubted that. Décor really wasn't something that stuck with me, no matter how expensive it was. We turned at the massive stone marker announcing "The Dominion," passed the expensively verdant golf course with its palatial country club, and neared the guard gate. The waiting line was five deep. We crept along.

"What do they ask for, a complete financial statement before they let you in? The measurements of everyone in the vehicle?"

"Well, if that were the case, it might have helped get us in quicker if you'd agreed to stop at Victoria's Secret on the way," she pointed out, looking askance at my chest hidden beneath the ruby rayon. "If they find out you buy your underwear at Dora's Discount Deals, they probably won't let us in."

She grinned. I groused. Finally, she pulled up to the

guard's podium standing in front of a control room that looked like it might pilot the starship *Enterprise*.

"We're going to the Strake home."

The guard shook her stern head. "I don't think so."

Trudy's mouth dropped open. "What? They called ahead, I'm sure of it."

The guard pointed at someone in the control room, who dialed a phone. "Mr. George Strait did not call us today about anyone visiting."

"George Strait lives here?" I blurted out. Normally, I am very cool when it comes to men, with two exceptions: country-western singers and bull riders. I lust after them with no shame. I just hoped I wasn't salivating.

Trudy waved me silent, throwing me an aggravated look.

"I said," Trudy enunciated each letter carefully, "Strake, with a *k*, as in *kill*."

The guard's eyebrows flew up under her bangs. *Oh, great, Trude.* It was my turn to glare. Between the two of us, we were certainly slipping in unnoticed.

The guard on the phone was turning bright red, apologizing into the receiver to George, I assume. A third guard stepped out of the control room with a clipboard and nodded once.

The guard at the podium was writing down our license-plate number.

"Do you know your way?" she asked.

"Yes," Trudy began.

I cut her off. "Actually, she's terrible at directions. If you could just give them to me once, I'll make sure she doesn't get lost."

I was sure the guards didn't want anyone wandering around lost inside the gates, making the high-priced residents nervous. The guard explained how to get there. She asked for Trudy's driver's license and said she could have it back when we left. As we wound our way up the hill, we argued about whether it was my George comment or her kill comment that warranted holding her driver's license hostage. At any rate, if anything went amiss in the Dominion that day, we were toast.

"Next time, we're driving your truck," Trudy muttered.

She pulled up the driveway of a three-story house that looked about a mile high. It was stucco, and it was painted black. Okay, so maybe I would remember some of their décor. As we got out and walked toward the front door, a little white truck with an amber light on the roof and "Security" lettered on the doors passed slowly on the street. I hoped it wouldn't wait for us. We didn't have a plan for getting to Ricardo's house under Rent-a-Cop surveillance. Smoothing down her neon mini-dress, Trudy rang the doorbell. I expected Morticia to answer, but instead, a very ordinary-looking middle-aged brunette wearing forty-thousand-dollar diamond earrings greeted us. Her dyed sienna hair was cut to chin length in the latest star style with long, eyelid-dusting bangs. Those bangs told me this woman was bold, liked to make a statement, and thought of herself as sexy. Boy, I was about to find out how right I was.

Mrs. Strake and Trude air-kissed. That phenomenon still amazes me. I can never get my smooch and my cheek approach timed just right. I end up either puckering up right in someone's face, which sends them reeling backward in abject terror, or actually making contact with their cheek, which, of course, is the biggest no-no because the whole idea behind the air-kissing business is not to touch.

I stuck my hand out so Mrs. Strake and I could shake as Trudy introduced us. That's when I caught sight of the sculpture in the cavernous foyer. It was a life-size bronze pair of nudes—a man and a woman in the most unusual sexual position I have ever seen. Could she really get her leg up like that and her hands there while he was doing that to her? I cocked my head to the side. It looked like it might hurt unless one was a professional contortionist. Lucinda Strake was trying to peel her fingers away from our shake. *Oops.* I'd been a little distracted. Trudy stabbed a fingernail into the small of my back as we stepped into the foyer. I guess I needed to take this all in stride like the lackey I was pretending to be. Perhaps erotica was décor number 403 taught in interior design school. We passed a mirror. I took a step back. Its frame was wooden, carved with monkeys with very human-looking faces in a hundred different sexual positions. At least, I thought there were a hundred. I didn't have time to count.

Trudy caught my elbow with her talons and dragged me along with her.

"I still haven't found anything just right for this space, Trudy," Lucinda was saying as we neared the double doors to the dining room. Our host kept glancing at me suspiciously. Could it have been my mouth dropping open with each bizarre piece of erotica we encountered? As we passed the dining room, I tried to slow down to fully take in the ten-foot-by-sixteen-foot oil painting on the wall, but Trudy hustled me along so fast all I caught was a flash of tangled legs and bare fanny.

We got to a small room at the end of the hall that I suppose one would refer to as a lounge. Wallpapered in a deep crimson velvety fabric, it had a half dozen of those one-sided lounging chairs that reminded me of

Roman orgies and a small built-in bar. The glass table in the center was held up by a metal labyrinth of bodies I resisted looking too closely at. I'd just gotten my mouth to stay closed, after all.

Lucinda and Trudy were standing at an open space on the wall next to the bar, discussing the antique piece in question, which existed only in Trudy's imagination. I glanced at the highball glasses reflected in the mirror behind the bar. I caught sight of a penis and a pair of breasts. What they were doing, I don't know. I looked away and tried not to imagine what her dinner guests did on those lounging chairs, sipping out of *those* glasses.

I couldn't believe my good Catholic friend was behind all this. Wait till I told Mama Tru. On second thought, I thought I'd save it to hold over Trude's head as potential blackmail material the next time she pissed me off. The thought of blackmail sobered me up. I hadn't had time to mull over Ricardo's potential dealmaking. I wouldn't have bet he'd be so underhanded and dirty, but I wouldn't have bet he'd be murdered, either.

"This massage table is in very good condition," Trudy was telling Lucinda. "Eighteenth-century Thai. Apparently, it's straight out of Bangkok."

"As long as it fits, you can go as high as forty-two thousand," Lucinda Strake said.

I coughed. That was the annual salary of one of the richest natives of my hometown. Trudy glared. I cleared my throat.

"Allergies," I explained with a weak smile.

Trudy snapped her fingers and held open her hand. I wondered if she wanted a low five, then I remembered she'd handed me a tape measure in the car. I took it out of the pocket of my blouse, trying not to smack it into her hand too hard. I was supposed to be subservient. She snapped it open, pulled out a bit of the metal tape, then zinged it shut. What was this? Checking to make sure I hadn't tampered with the numbers on the inch markers? She dropped it into my hands with her thumb and index finger, then pointed at the wall. *Grrr.* I scuttled as best as my pride would let me over to the wall and measured the height and width of the space, calling out the numbers, which she entered into her PalmPilot. She *hmm*ed and sighed as she reviewed data on the tiny screen, tapping the little wand against the side thoughtfully. Lucinda, her hands clasped in front of her chest, was holding her breath. She blew it out suddenly.

"Okay, go to fifty thousand if you need to."

Wow, I didn't know Trude was this good. She'd built the suspense so high without saying a word that the lady was about to hand her a blank check. She even had me on edge, and I knew the piece wasn't going to fit because it didn't exist.

"I'm sorry, Lucinda." Trudy finally shook her head sadly. "This piece is just not going to work."

"Oh, no." Lucinda looked like she would cry.

Trudy patted her on the shoulder as we walked back into the hall. "I'll keep looking."

"With all this talk, now I'm eager to have this space filled. We'll double your fee if you find something before the month's out."

"I'll find something," Trudy promised as she ushered me out the front door.

"She won't say anything," Lucinda said with another glance at me. "Will she?"

I bristled. Trudy stuck another fingernail into my back and twisted. "Would I hire someone indiscreet?"

Lucinda smiled gratefully, and I smiled back, teeth clenched. Trudy, feeling I was going to tell her client where to go, quickly air-kissed her and dragged me to the car. I was so mad I almost forgot to look for the security truck. It was gone.

We started down the street and stopped just short of the intersecting street that would take us to Ricardo's house. Trudy edged the little sports car in front of a thick mountain laurel tree, which would hide the car from the house we were parked in front of. First, she put up the top so we could squeeze into our exercise wear. It involved a lot of grunting, groaning, swearing (only on my part), and looking up and down the street for cars. And just to make my day complete, as Trudy and I were maneuvering the cramped space and trying not to put each others eyes out, I heard a loud rip. Of course it came from my jeans, not hers, which were left without a crotch. Good thing I didn't need them anymore.

Just as we'd planned, Trudy popped the hood. I got out, glanced around to make sure no one was looking, lifted the hood, pulled the cable loose from the carburetor, and let it hang. I eased the hood shut. Now, if anyone asked us what we were doing there, we could say we had car trouble. And my sister Pecan said all those months chasing Hervey Keil my junior year were a waste of time. She thought I was only watching his butt every time he bent over the hood. Wait till I told her it enhanced my investigative technique.

I cocked my head north, and we started out. I wished we were there already, not so much because I thought someone would stop us on our nefarious mission but because I was wearing spandex. This was Trudy's idea. She said the only way we wouldn't be noticed walking in the Dominion was if we were power-walking in overpriced exercise wear. Since I don't own any, I stuffed my tree-trunk legs (I refer to them as "muscular" in public just to show I don't have a self-esteem issue) into a pair of Miss Exquisite Hams' skintight leggings. The fact that she got to wear the black ones and I got the fuchsia just proves life's not fair.

The road to Ricardo's house rose at a sixty-degree angle in front of us. As we huffed and puffed our way up, several cars passed, everyone doing double takes—the men at Trudy's legs, the women at my bravery for wearing pink spandex. Finally, we approached Ricardo's house, which seemed a lot closer to the intersection when we were driving, and I was surprised to see it looking the same. The first time I'd seen it, the nondescript rock one-story hidden among the oaks had surprised me. His ultra-modern salons screamed so for attention I'd assumed his home would, too. But the better I got to know Ricardo, the more it made sense—the salons were PR, his home was his private enclave. I looked both ways before we power-walked down the driveway and slipped behind the cover of a sago palm to the front door.

Trudy had extracted from Crandall the jewel that the police had deactivated the alarm system so they could come and go during the investigation. If she hadn't done that, I would've had to drag Gerald into the whole deal, and that wouldn't have been pretty. He broke out in a cold sweat if Ricardo's bank account didn't reconcile by ten cents. What would breaking and entering do to him? I popped my heel out of my shoe, recovered the key from my instep, and fit it into the lock. Holding my breath, I turned it, trying not to imagine the alarm going off and me trying to run away through the woods behind in shiny fuchsia. Scary.

Silence greeted us as I eased the door open. We both let out our air and stepped over the threshold. I could see everything was as I remembered, except for the sprinkling of fingerprint dust on every surface. I resisted the impulse to clean it up.

"Don't touch anything," I told Trudy. What kind of criminal was I to have forgotten gloves? "We need to find something to wear on our hands so we don't get fingerprints everywhere."

Every hairstylist uses thin rubber gloves to apply chemicals. As a rule, we are vain about our hands for good reason. Our customers look at our hands while we do their hair, and no one wants someone with nasty-looking fingers going through their precious locks. That's why most of us use gloves for other chores, such as washing dishes and cleaning house. Ricardo's hands were the most beautiful I'd ever seen on a man. He had to have a box of gloves here somewhere.

It struck me as we tiptoed from the foyer to the kitchen that this looked like a model home, and, in fact, he may have bought it as one, furnished and all. He agonized over every small detail in each salon, but at his home, I doubted he agonized over anything. The greasy dust covered the emerald-green marble countertops and an island big enough to house my entire kitchen. I'd bet he had rarely cooked in there. The pantry, whose door I opened using a kitchen towel, held a bare minimum—a box of crackers, a can of salmon, ultra-virgin olive oil, a can of Rotel tomatoes, a box of Grape-Nuts. No pudding. None was to be found in the refrigerator, either, which held a few vegetables, fruit, and a package of gouda cheese. I got lucky under the sink, where I found not pudding but the box of gloves. I handed two to Trudy and snapped on a pair myself.

We moved from room to room, whispering. Why we whispered, I don't know, since the nearest home was a half-acre away. Still, our stealthy mission seemed to call for it.

"You know, it doesn't seem lived in," Trudy observed. "Yes, the décor is vanilla, but even the worst décor gets a personality from its owner. I don't feel anything here. No personal photos are out. Even the art on the walls is motel bland. I wonder if Zorita could feel anything if we brought her through here?"

"Zorita would feel the presence of greenbacks if he had any hidden away."

"You're so callous, Reyn. Speaking of green, you need to remember the green aura she saw around you. I've been reading up on auras, and that's a real warning sign that you're going to get hurt."

"I've already been hurt. My back. Your husband tried to cripple me."

Trudy shook her head at my aura ignorance. "I'm going to hate to have to say I told you so."

I moved to the final bedroom, which Ricardo used as an office. Only it didn't much look like he used it. Of course, the space where the computer had been was empty, the police no doubt having taken it for evidence. Damn, I wished I could see if he had any files that referred to any of the ten names in my pocket. Except for the fingerprint dust, the desk was pristine clean, with not even a scrap of paper or a stray pen. The drawers were perfectly organized with office supplies.

Disappointed, I closed the last drawer and turned away. I guessed this was a big waste of time. Scythe and his crew had swept out anything that was potentially useful. I moved back to the master bedroom and went through the bathroom drawers and cabinets. No revelations there, beyond the fact that he preferred Rembrandt toothpaste and Charmin toilet paper. A weird-looking brush sat next to a pile of fingerprint dust. The handle read "SAPD". It looked like one of the evidence techs had forgotten it.

Determined to find something, anything, I went to his walk-in closet and began searching the pockets of the pants hanging there. I looked around. If anyplace in the house showed Ricardo's personality, it was here. The clotheshorse owned a six-figure wardrobe.

I could hear Trudy opening and shutting drawers in the bathroom. "Where do you think he kept his condoms?"

"Who says he needed any?"

"Come on, Reyn. Every single man should have some. *Modern Sex* magazine says that the percentage of men who contract a disease from sex is—"

I stuck my head out of the closet. "Trude, how many magazine subscriptions do you have?"

She jutted her chin in the air. "None of your business. Besides, I'm just trying to help."

I went back to my search. At slacks number twenty-one, I found a business card from a Mexican food restaurant on the near west side, with "3/tacos $1.99 before 10:30 A.M." written on the back. Probably not the case breaker, but I slipped it into my shoe anyway. Never know when one might get the munchies.

The alarm pad on the wall beeped. The alarm was deactivated, but it still announced when a door or a window was breached. *Uh-oh.* I grabbed Trudy and dragged her into the closet, closing the door softly and switching off the lights.

"Do you think it's the killer?" Trudy whispered.

Holding my finger to my lips, I shook my head hard. No, I did not think it was the killer, although he or she was better than the alternative. The alternative being the police. I had a momentary flash of hope that it was Gerald. But then I remembered I had his key. *Damn.*

In the pitch dark, I searched my visual memory for the best places for us to hide should whoever it was open the closet door. I shoved Trudy into the corner behind a long alpaca coat. Her skinny black legs would blend into the shadows. My pink ones were an issue, though. Eye-catching, to say the least. Listening for the intruder, I slid two plastic storage bins off the top shelf, put them against the wall behind the shirts, and stood on them, crouched in a semifetal position. *Uh-oh.*

"Ack," I moaned.

"What?" Trudy whispered.

"Shut up," I said through clenched teeth. "It's just my back. I don't know how long I can hold this."

As I began to catalogue every nerve in my lower lumbar region, we heard voices. A man and a woman passed the closet door, grousing about detectives.

"They can leave doors to vics' houses unlocked, and they don't get any heat, but we leave one small tool and get an ass chewing. Is that fair?" the man said.

"Crime scene is what solves the case, and they get all the credit," the woman agreed. "Their heads are so big it's amazing they fit through the doors every morning."

Thank the good Lord for professional jealousy and office politics. I heard them pick up the forgotten dusting brush and walk back out, passing the closet door again.

"Whose the worst, d'ya think? That Scythe?"

I nearly fell off my perch, I was nodding so hard.

"Oh, no," she said. "He can be a little brusque, and

some things he says come out wrong, but he's just really driven to solve cases. And every now and then, he can be so charming. One time, before you started, he brought flowers to all the women in our department and the receptionist on his floor."

Huh?

"Aw, he'd just dumped his last Flavor of the Week and was looking for a new one."

"You're just jealous because girls don't swoon over you like they do him."

"Yeah, they swoon, and even before they're done fainting, Scythe's through with them and, *bash*, they hit the ground."

"You should be grateful he leaves something for you to pick up."

"Hey! I'm not that bad!" the man shouted after her. The front door opened and shut.

We waited what seemed like an eternity but was probably only a few minutes. It wasn't long enough to be safe but, damn, my back was killing me. I unfolded myself from my position of torture and opened the closet door. Trudy left the alpaca with a good-bye pet.

"You shouldn't listen to that guy about Scythe"

"Yeah, I'm sure I want to be his flavor of this week."

We'd turned the corner, and Trudy started to argue, but instead, she looked at the wall, then at me and back again. "Something's not right. That wall is a little too thick. There's not enough room in the closet to account for the design on this side. Let's go back in and check it."

I never guessed that a Watson with an interior design degree would be the one to break the case, but she was. When we went back into the closet, I pulled the Prada lavender silk shirt back from the wall on the fat side, and there was a framed photo of a handsome teenager, his black hair moussed into spikes.

"He looks familiar somehow," Trudy murmured.

I wasn't distracted by the kid but by the fact that it was the only framed photo in the house, and it was against a wall that Trudy said was too fat. I carefully took the photo off its hanger, but the wall was blank. No secret door. Not even a safe that we probably couldn't have cracked. I knocked all along the wall, but all sounded the same. It sounded like Sheetrock, and it felt like a piece of it dropped in my stomach.

"I guess I was wrong." Trudy sighed. "Sometimes contractors make mistakes and then cover it up. The owners never catch it."

Reluctantly, I went to replace the photo. As I ran my hand along the back of the frame to line up the nail with the hanger, my fingers caught something square on the back of the frame. I turned it over. A flat magnet was taped there. I peeled it off and stared at it, wishing it could talk.

The whole purpose of a magnet was to meet another magnet. I held it flat against the wall, starting as high as I could reach and working down in grid fashion. On my last pass, next to the baseboard, I heard a crack and felt the magnet pull. Slowly, I drew the magnet off the wall, and a one-foot-by-one-foot piece of the wall came with it.

eighteen

THE DOOR HAD BEEN CAMOUFLAGED BY USING AN uneven edge that blended with the texture on the Sheetrock so well it was invisible.

"Wow," Trudy said, more impressed with the secret hidey hole than with her expertise in finding it.

We could see nothing but a dark space and the shadows of the frame and pipes. This time, I didn't let myself get disappointed. Not yet. I stuck my hand into the hole and felt, trying not to imagine how many brown recluse spiders lived there. This would be their textbook favorite environment. I'd take on a thousand rats over one brown recluse. The tiny, unassuming arachnids abounded in South Texas, and one bite was so poisonous that at worst it shut down human organs and at best rotted away the skin and muscle surrounding the bite. It was not pretty. The gloves only covered my hands, leaving my wrists and forearms feeling very vulnerable, and who's to say brown recluses couldn't bite through thin plastic? After a few seconds of morbid contemplation, my curiosity won over the potential for being permanently disfigured. I reached in farther. My fingertips made contact with cold metal. They followed it around a rectangular container about the size of my aunt Big's toolbox. I extended my arm around the space surrounding the box and felt nothing. I wished we had a flashlight, but I didn't want us separated in case the cops came back. I made a mental note that the next time I went breaking and entering to pack some *luz* or take a smoker who'd at least be equipped with matches.

"I think that's the only thing in here," I muttered, extracting my arm, which was now dusty and trailing cobwebs.

Cobwebs?

I swallowed my terror and wiped my arm clean with only a minimum of heebie-jeebie shivers.

"What's the only thing in there?" Trudy demanded in a whisper.

"A box."

"Let's see it."

"It's too big to take through the hole. Ricardo must've put it into the wall when he had the house built and accessed it through the hole. I just hope it's not locked."

"Locked? Wouldn't that be a little paranoid?"

I craned my neck to look back at Trudy. "Isn't having a metal box hidden behind the Sheetrock paranoid enough?"

"Not really. I'm thinking I need to get some kind of secret compartment to hide the things I don't want to come out when I die."

"What things? The sex house you designed isn't a secret anymore. How much worse can it get?" I grinned.

Trudy raised her eyebrows, crossing her arms over her chest. "Don't you wish you knew?"

"I will know. Look at how hard I'm poking around in Ricardo's life, and he wasn't as good a friend to me as you are."

A flash of fear reflected in Trudy's eyes for a second. *Hmm.* I'd only known Trudy for five years this week. We'd been best friends for four years, eleven months and 364 days. Ours was just one of those relationships that clicked from the very beginning. She was a little dingy, too fashion conscious, a lot of fun, and loyal as a dog, and sometimes we could read each other's mind. We were very different, but I'd never gotten along better with anyone in my life. Still, I didn't know everything about her. Obviously.

"Hey, I've got a deal. I'll promise not to stick my nose into your secrets after you die if you stick your hand in there"—I nodded toward the hole—"and get out whatever is in that box."

Trude, nose wrinkled, was already shaking her head. "There's spiders. Plus, I'll get dirty."

Okay. I guess her secrets weren't *that* incriminating. *Darn.* So, I would have to risk my life instead. I held my breath and reached back in, feeling for the latch or, worse luck, a lock. After imagining at least half a dozen encounters with brown recluses, I found it on the short side. It was my lucky day—a simple, unlocked latch. My heart pounded. I popped it and lifted the lid. Tentatively, I tiptoed my fingers inside, remembering the bowls of peeled grapes that felt like eyeballs at the haunted house the Daleys ran in Dime Box every year in high school.

My hand shrank back for a minute.

Sometimes I wished I didn't have such a good imagination.

Eyeballs and spiders shoved out of my mind, I made contact with the contents—slick photo stock and newsprint. Something that felt like hair.

My hand had already drawn back instinctively, scraping my forearm along the top edge of the hole. *Ouch.*

"What is it?"

"I felt hair."

"Hair, like on something alive?" Trudy grimaced and backed up a few steps. Guess I couldn't talk her into grabbing whatever was in there. I should've said it felt like a silk negligee trimmed in fur. Maybe then she would've reached in to get it. I wished I thought faster on my feet.

"Hair like on something that used to be alive, anyway. It didn't move when I touched it." I drew in a deep breath and stuck my hand back in, gathering up as much as I could in one handful. As I was drawing it out, I felt tiny feet crawling on the back of my hand. *Ack.* My elbow flexed faster than the hammer of a gun, dumping my booty all over the floor. Dozens of photos and a news clipping scattered. No hair. Great. Before I could think too long about it, I stuck my hand back in and grabbed the hair, throwing it out of the hole.

It was a nine-inch lock of straight black hair—human—tied with a purple bow. It smelled like lavender.

I looked up at Trudy. Her eyebrows hovered around her hairline. She looked at the mystery hair and at me and back again. "This is weirder than a dead rat," she observed.

"Yeah, who would've guessed we'd be wishing for a dead rat," I said as I stared at the odd collection of things at my feet.

I rolled off my haunches and onto the floor. Trudy

joined me. The newsprint was yellowed. I unfolded it carefully and read the date aloud. "It's twenty-four years old." The article was about the death of a local scion of San Antonio society, sixty-one-year-old Paul Johnstone. He resembled a toad dressed in a monkey suit. Not a handsome man but apparently a generous one. The article described him as one of the city's premier philanthropists—seemingly supporting every nonprofit artistic enterprise in town at the time—from museums to dance troupes to botanical gardens to choirs. The directors of such were quoted as saying art in San Antonio was much poorer with his loss. I guessed so. Literally and figuratively. Especially since his wife was quoted as saying her husband had been in the process of reviewing the allocations of his donations. She hinted the recipients in the past might be disappointed because the money would be going elsewhere.

"Elsewhere," I muttered aloud. "Yeah, I bet right in her pockets."

The story continued on a page stapled to the first, including a three-year-old wedding photo of the couple. He looked the same as he did in the first photo. His pretty blond wife, Sarah, looked about eighteen.

"Talk about May-September romance," Trude said with a little giggle-snort. "Try January first–December thirty-first romance."

"It wasn't that bad," I admonished. "Besides, I'm sure it was love."

"How did he die?" Trudy asked.

It was a carefully written obit, which made me wonder if Johnstone had supported the newspaper as well. Finally, we found it buried on the back of the second page, barely escaping the city editor's scissors to make the page.

"He was found unconscious in his study near midnight, his brandy half drunk. It doesn't say who found him. We can assume wife, maid, or butler. He died en route to the hospital."

"It sounds like a heart attack or maybe a stroke."

"It sounds like an episode of *Murder, She Wrote*. Maybe the butler did it."

"Quit being so suspicious."

"Well, why did Ricardo have it in here? You think he was good friends with a member of high society two and a half decades ago? That was before he started his first salon." I did some mental math. "He started his first salon the next year. So, at the time this was written, he was still a south side nobody."

We stared at the article in silence for a few minutes. It didn't make any more sense. I reached for the stack of photos. One was a snapshot of a dark-haired woman in her twenties who was looking at someone away from the camera. The wind blew her hair back from her face. She was laughing and glowed with happiness. She looked familiar to me, but I couldn't place her.

"This could be her hair," Trudy pointed out, wagging the lock at the photo.

I nodded and gathered up the rest of the photos, all of which were smaller. There were at least two dozen of what looked like school photos of the same black-haired Hispanic boy from kindergarten to high school. It was the young man whose framed photo hid the secret compartment in the closet wall. Why did Ricardo have a photo history of a boy? Handsome but serious, he looked like he carried the world on his shoulders.

"You think this is her son?" Trudy asked, holding the photo of the woman next to the photo of the boy at maybe twelve.

"Yes, he looks like her through the mouth and the eyes," I agreed. "Although maybe that's just what we want to believe. Then at least two of these three things would have some connection to each other."

"I think I know who she is," Trudy said, cocking her head as she studied the photo of the woman.

"Who?"

"She looks like a younger version of Senator Villita's wife. I just saw her on the noon news doing a piece on fashion in Washington, D.C. She was saying that they really are going more for the traditional lately. What with the ecomony in a slump and the threat of terrorism, we as a nation need to feel some security. My new *Girl's World* said the same thing about skirt length."

"Trudy," I snapped, "enough about the fashion." I squinted at the photo. Celine Villita was my client Jolie Dupont's best friend. I'd met her a couple of years ago, when Jolie had brought her in for an emergency 'do since her regular stylist was ill. I certainly hadn't seen her smile—the woman was way too uptight for that—but it could be the same person twenty years later.

Why did Ricardo have an old photo of another man's wife? Long-lost sister? Long-lost lover? Current lover?

Was this the reason Jolie didn't want me digging into Ricardo's past? To save her friend from an embarrassing revelation or worse? "How long have the Villitas been married?" I wondered aloud, not really expecting an answer from the heavens.

"Oh, oh!" Trudy chirped. "I know that because Gigi Gleason asked her that in the interview I watched. They celebrated their twenty-fifth anniversary last year."

"So all this"—I waved my hand over the photos and the newspaper article—"happened about the same time.

Some old rich guy dies. Some one-day-will-be-a-senator's-wife laughs in a picture. Some little kid is born. A boy who has grown up to have his photo hung in Ricardo's closet on the wall."

"Maybe Ricardo swings both ways, and this is his young lover," Trudy offered with a quick grin.

"Okay, you made your point. I'm doing too much guessing. I need to go see Celine Villita."

"If she'll see you."

"If she won't, then we know we're barking up the wrong tree and this photo is not of her. Because she's got to be nervous as a cat in a room full of rocking chairs wondering if the police are going to stumble upon whatever is the secret she and Ricardo shared."

"But even if we can make Celine Villita and Ricardo fit somehow," I continued, "I still don't see any middle-aged Anglo man who'd wear tennis whites and meet Ricardo at a transvestite club. Do you?"

Trudy thought for a while. It was so scary-looking I almost made her stop. "Just Paul Johnstone, and he's dead."

"Maybe his ghost came to Illusions," I offered under my breath.

Trudy brightened. "Maybe. Let's call Zorita and ask her."

"Enough with her, already!"

"She'd probably be able to help more if you'd just let her." Trudy pouted.

"Probably. My loss."

Rising up on my knees, I put everything back, latched the box, and replaced the hole covering.

"Are you crazy? Aren't we going to need that in our investigation?" Trudy asked.

For all my rebellious nature, I was raised a rule follower. "If we really do find who planted the brush in Ricardo's back and this stuff is vital to proving it, the fact that we removed the evidence will give the defense a big enough loophole for the killer to step through. I don't want that. We can ferret out the killer, let the police do the catching, and let the lawyers keep him—or her—behind bars."

"Lieutenant Scythe would be very proud of you." Trudy winked at me.

"Ugh, that almost makes me want to take it." I straightened up—or, rather, tried to. My back clutched up, and I stumbled into the rack of clothes, my tennis shoe stomping on something in the dark space underneath that crunched like paper. I held on to the rack and tried not to cry. "Trude, reach down under my feet and get whatever I just stepped on."

She bent her perfect nubile body down and collected what looked like another old newspaper clipping. "This will teach you to get things out of secret compartments in an orderly manner. It must've flown out without us seeing when you were doing your hurricane imitation."

"Very funny. Let's see what it says."

It was an old wedding announcement—a photo of Paul Johnstone's widow and a man more her age, dated just two years after Paul's death. Mike Van Dyke was a tanned bleached blond, handsome as a movie star, with eyes as dead as a shark's. Or maybe that's just what I wanted to see, I cautioned my overactive imagination.

"I don't understand why Ricardo had this squirreled away, but at least we know Sarah Johnstone's new last name."

"And we might have found the guy who likes to wear tennis whites," my fashion maven friend pointed out. "He'd look pretty damned good in them."

Could it be? But why? Mike Van Dyke wasn't on the list of clients Zorita had given us. What was he to Ricardo? Another husband of an old lover?

But the biggest question was, who knew that the fashion-conscious interior designer would be the one to make the two biggest breaks in the case? I was still mulling that over as I replaced the wedding announcement in the hidey hole.

"What time is it?" I asked Trudy as I clipped the box shut.

"Wow, time sure flies. It's already three-thirty."

Uh-oh.

Before I panicked, I reminded myself that Trudy only wore a watch as a fashion statement—this one an elaborate number with a couple hundred colored stones—so I couldn't be sure it was even set to the right time. I double-checked Cinderella on my wrist, but, sure enough, her hands were pointed due north and slightly south of west. She was smiling. Bitch.

Okay, now I could panic.

"Damn," I swore, calculating our travel time to the church. It would take us at least ten minutes to get back to the car at a dead run and twenty to make it to the church. This wasn't counting traffic. "I'm going to miss the memorial service if we don't hustle."

Trudy looked from my Nikes to my fuchsia legs to my bare midriff to my sports bra and back down again. "Are you going to give the eulogy in *that?*"

"What choice do I have?" I grabbed her arm and prepared to drag her back to the car.

Trudy planted her feet, cocked her head, and swiveled her gaze across Ricardo's wardrobe.

"No, absolutely not." I shook my head so hard I felt my brain ricocheting off the sides of my skull. "I will not wear a dead man's clothes to his own funeral. No way, no how."

Famous last words.

nineteen

I MIGHT HAVE BEEN ABLE TO SLIP INTO THE CHURCH
unnoticed if it weren't for the sound of the Miata's tires
squealing as Trudy laid about a hundred feet of rubber on
the asphalt in front of the building. I might have been
able to overcome the initial curiosity of the third of the
congregation that was either still on its way in or came out
to check for an incoming missile if I hadn't been wearing
every color in the rainbow.

Speaking of might-have-beens, I might have been
able to arrive on time, in a dignified manner, wearing
black, and delivered a well-studied, socially acceptable
speech about the life of a good, if slightly selfish and
more than marginally narcissistic, man, if I hadn't been
so damned curious and driven to find his killer. And if I
hadn't forgotten to keep an eye on the time when I was
breaking into his house.

So much for might-have-beens.

Instead, I was striding down the center aisle of the
Clear Creek Church in scuffed-up Nikes (I fell once in
our dash back to the car), a silk Aloha shirt with a wild

print of palm trees, hibiscus flowers, flamingos, exotic and scantily clad buxom bathing beauties (it was the only shirt in the closet that had any fuchsia in it, which was Trudy's requirement, and it covered my heinie, which was my requirement), my hot pink legs flashing with each step. In this get-up, I didn't think it mattered if my speech was so socially acceptable. I knew Ricardo wanted a sendoff fit for the Salon King of San Antonio, but I'd bet he didn't expect to be offed with a brush. I felt compelled to change the plan for him.

The minister was trying—and failing—to hold the congregation's attention with a passage from the Bible. I'd like to think that the ear-piercing tire squeal was what woke up every news photographer in the place, but this was a jaded bunch, so I imagine my first step in the door was what did it. From wars to wrecks, I'd bet they hadn't seen anything like me before. At any rate, all the red lights were on and the film running as I plunked myself down in the first pew next to one of the hired actors.

Father Gallego passed the service off to one of them, who, in a slick script, sprinkled with Bible verses, outlined Ricardo's perfect life, from his privileged upbringing in Mexico to his success as owner of a small empire. Lies, mostly, but they sure sounded good and made us all wish we could have such a perfect life. Then a delicately beautiful Hispanic actress got up and delivered a heart-stopping description of the lives Ricardo had changed with his support of children's charities in the city. Much closer to the truth, but it made me wonder why he couldn't have had one of the organization's presidents give the speech. Probably because they wouldn't have made such good sound bites for television.

I could tell it was nearly my turn, because Father Gallego was glancing nervously my way, hoping, no doubt, that I would disappear before he would have to introduce me. Too bad. He said my name like it tasted rancid, so much for "love thy neighbor as thyself." Even without the love, I rose bravely and marched to the podium.

I almost lost my nerve when I saw half my clients and old coworkers in the pews. I regained it suddenly when I caught sight of Scythe and Crandall in the back. Crandall was shaking with pent-up laughter. Scythe was scowling ominously. He'd better not think of telling me what I could and couldn't do. I'd show him.

"Today is a day to celebrate." I paused as a collective gasp ran through the crowd. "That's why I'm dressed this way. I want to celebrate the life of Ricardo Montoya, businessman, benefactor, and friend. He would want us to remember him with pleasure instead of tears. Think of the legacy he leaves behind—every day, hundreds of men and women will have their self-esteem boosted and, through that, their lives improved in countless ways. So smile when you leave here today, smile every time you leave one of his salons, and thank him for what he has done for you.

"But what can you do for Ricardo? You can help find the one who took him from us by sharing his secrets. I know Ricardo was a private man and never wanted his privacy breached. But did you ever wonder if that was because he was protecting someone or being threatened in some way? Maybe keeping secrets is what got Ricardo killed. What if what you know about his life could get you killed, too?" Another gasp rose, followed by jagged whispers.

I pointed at a man sitting in the third pew. "What you know might not seem like much, sir, but . . ." I pointed at a woman on the other side, in the twentieth pew. "If you combine it with what she knows, it might just solve the puzzle that Ricardo's left with his murder." The sound of whispering was rising, and I was about to lose them. Scythe stood, and he and Crandall moved to the back wall of the church. Scythe's laser blues caught me in their sights and pinned me with an intensity that stopped me for a moment. Hey, just watch, he was going to thank me for this later. "I know enough to see some of the patterns on the puzzle but not the whole picture. Help the police get the whole picture. Tell them what you know about Ricardo. Before it's too late for one of you here today."

All hell broke loose, with everyone talking at once. Father Gallego cued the organ player, who banged out a dirge but failed to drown out the crowd. Reporters were reaching out and grabbing people willy-nilly; the poor cameramen didn't know whom to film first. I slipped behind the organ box and down the hallway behind the altar. As we'd planned on the way over, Trudy was outside with the engine running. I was to find a way out a back door, and she'd pick me up.

I turned the corner down a darkened hallway. "Just where do you think you're going?" I recognized Father Gallego's voice.

He stepped out of the shadows and looked pretty scary. My heart thumped hard in my chest. I had nothing to be ashamed of, but I'm sure glad I wasn't an acolyte who'd lit the wrong candle.

"I, uh, am trying to get out of here."

"Thank the good Lord for that." He nodded at a door at the end of the hallway. "Go out there. Once you are through the small garden, you will be free of the grounds."

"Bless you, Father."

He crossed the air as I passed. "May the Lord forgive you for turning my sanctuary into a circus."

The Lord? He knew my intentions were honorable. I was more worried about Ricardo not forgiving me. But if my old boss and buddy really thought about it, wherever he was, he'd realize that he'd gotten just what he asked for. He wanted a funeral San Antonio would never forget. The one he'd scripted was too much like a thousand other funerals. The one he'd gotten would never be outdone. They'd be talking about Ricardo's sendoff decades from now.

I pushed my way out the door. As it closed, so did a hand on my right wrist. Yikes, was the air cross not enough, did the good Father want to dunk me in the sacred water, too?

"What in the hell's wrong with you?"

I'd know that baritone anywhere. I turned just as Scythe pulled me with him until we were behind a tall banana tree. By then, I'd found my voice. "You tell me. It seems to be your favorite pastime."

"Don't sulk. It doesn't become you." I could almost hear him counting to ten in his head for patience. "Would you *please* tell me what you think you're doing?"

"I *think* I'm going back to work."

"Back to work as a hairstylist or as a wannabe murder victim?"

"Hey, no need to be nasty."

"Hey, no need to be stupid." Scythe sucked in a deep breath, and I saw for the first time how upset he was. He was angry, all right—I could feel it emanating from his body. Talk about red spikes. But there was something else there, too. Worry, maybe? But why would he be worried about me? Worried about his job, more likely. "Why did you just load the gun for the murderer and point it at yourself? All he's got to do is pick the right time to pull the trigger. The sooner, the better."

"Come on, aren't you being a little melodramatic?"

"I'm being realistic."

"You think you'd be grateful that I sent all those informants your way. It's a lot easier than searching them out, I bet."

He snorted in disgust. "That's a whole other thing that I'm not going to get into with you. After this, we'll have to assign at least two extra guys just to handle all the wack-jobs who'll be coming in with useless information."

"Oh, I didn't think of that."

"I wonder if you think at all." He finally noticed he was still holding my wrist in his hand. He let it go and looked at my fuchsia legs. "Like this outfit. What led up to it—and don't give me that bullcrap about celebration."

"I was just running a little late, and this was handy."

"Handy where? In Ricardo's closet?"

That got me. I met the laser blues head-on in surprise. He stared right into me as no one ever had before. I bet he got people to confess to all sorts of things they didn't do with that look. My brain refused to offer a quick rejoinder. I blinked in answer.

He half hitched the right eyebrow. "You didn't find anything, did you?"

Ha! My blank look was just what I needed now. What a good defense. I blinked again.

"And you would share anything you might have found or might find in the future, right?"

I smiled. His eyebrow hitched higher. So, despite all his criticism of my investigative technique, the lieutenant was a little afraid that I might be on to something.

I recognized the purr of a Japanese engine. Saved by my faithful redheaded Watson, I patted Scythe on the arm and slipped past. "Gotta run. Keep in touch."

"Oh, no need for that," Scythe said airily. "As of thirty minutes ago, you're under twenty-four-hour SAPD surveillance. For your own safety, you understand."

"As if you guys care about my safety," I returned, noticing for the first time the unmarked dark blue Crown Victoria fifty yards behind Trudy's car. I sulked. "You still think I did it."

"Technically, you are still within the suspect radar now that you're Ricardo's heiress, having delivered your eulogy." He paused to pull a face. "Such as it was."

I guessed Scythe had talked to the frosty Ms. Gibson, who was likely thrilled to throw suspicion my way. From the way my stomach clutched, my bizarre inheritance still made me feel icky. What was I going to do with the salons? I pushed that problem aside and dealt with the live one behind me. Throwing him a huffy look, I walked toward the passenger side of the Miata. "You're not too observant if you've discerned that I'd kill for money."

He shrugged. "Everyone would kill for something. It's just finding out what that something is."

I turned, ready to call his bluff. "What would you kill for?"

"A night with one of the girls on your shirt." He winked and, with a wave at the cops behind us, disappeared back into the church.

Trudy had done her homework while I was inside creating havoc. She handed me a slip of paper with the Villitas' local address that she'd gotten from a friend of a friend of a cousin of a client. In the small-town society labyrinth of the big city of San Antonio, it's not what you know, it's who who-you-know knows.

"My client says Celine and the senator are in town right now doing some campaigning for their son, who's getting ready to announce his intention to run for the state representative seat being vacated by Sifuentes."

I was watching the Crown Vic in the rearview mirror. It was behind about three cars but changed lanes with Trudy. "What did you say?"

"Their only kid is about to run for office. The political couple is in town to help Junior gladhand. Got it?"

What had Mama Tru said? Her Republican Party girlfriend had given Ricardo some inside information about a political race. Gerald had mentioned Ricardo being suddenly politically conscious. Something niggled at me. "Is Villita a Democrat?"

"Yes."

"Who is running against him?"

"I didn't ask. And if you actually ever read the newspaper that you insist on subscribing to and never read, you might know without asking. Just like if you ate all the food in your refrigerator, you'd . . ."

"Weigh three hundred pounds. Just like too much information would make my head heavy. I prefer to operate on a need-to-know basis."

Trudy shook her head. "Can anyone ever have the last word in an argument with you?"

I frowned. Scythe always seemed to have the last word, like that shot about the girls on my shirt. *Humph.* Was he really attracted to exotic-looking half-naked nubiles with big bulging breasts? He was a man, of course he was. Why did this irritate me so much? Because I was an ordinary-looking, fully, if oddly, dressed mature woman with practically no discernible breasts? Why did I care what he thought, anyway? He was an arrogant . . . no, I'd use my new word. He was a *vainacious* jerk.

"I think we're being followed," Trudy said.

"We are."

She looked at me nonplussed. "You know?"

I nodded. "It's the police."

"The police?" Trudy veered into the middle lane of the three-lane highway, sending the car that had been about to pass us on the left squealing into the far left lane, sending the surveillance cops whose Crown Vic had been in the left lane onto the shoulder and into the back of a stalled truck. *Oops.*

Trudy and I cringed. She smiled weakly. "I got rid of them."

"Yeah, you sure did. What technique." *Oo-ee.* I didn't want to be around Scythe when he found out about this one. "You might want to take the next exit, in case they put an APB out on us."

She swallowed hard. "We can take the long way to Terrell Hills."

"Good idea."

We were still at least ten miles from the Villitas' Guaraty Street address. Since few roads in San Antonio were actually straight and even fewer ran through without being broken up by a stream, drainage ditch, sudden one-way access, or road construction, it took a while to wind our way there. Thank goodness Trudy grew up in the city, or we'd still be wandering around.

The drive did give us time to review what we'd learned in the case. Ricardo was interested in a political race, presumably the one in which the Villita son was running. Gerald thought he nursed a decades-old broken heart. He and Celine Villita might have a history. Or he and the Villita son might have a history. What we still didn't know was what proof was in the pudding. Or what the Johnstone-Van Dykes had to do with anything. Or what two mistakes Ricardo made—besides borrowing my brush, that is.

The Villita estate was grandiose even on a street lined with stunningly expensive old homes. Set back from the street, behind a rock wall and iron gates, its green-tiled roof rose above the oak trees. Trudy stopped at the intercom box and pressed the button.

"*Hola?*"

Trudy looked silently at me. I'd do the talking. "Hello, *habla inglés?*"

"*Sí.*"

"Please tell Señora Villita that I'd like to see her."

"You don't have appointment."

"No, tell her I'm Trudy Trujillo, a friend of Jolie Dupont's."

I shoved my hand over Trudy's mouth before she could get it all the way open.

"*Sí.*" The maid sounded like her going to fetch the *señora* would be a waste of her time.

Trudy finally shrugged in acceptance, and I dropped my hand from her mouth. Just then, the maid's voice crackled again over the intercom, surprise and curiosity evident in her voice. "*Entrase, por favor. La señora* will be with you *pronto.*"

"*Gracias.*"

The heavy gates opened at a ponderous pace. I worried for a moment that it would give Celine time to escape out the back, but I reminded myself if she hadn't wanted to see us, she wouldn't have let us in and would have sent some goons with baseball bats out to pound a warning on Trude's car. The maid waited at the front door of the three-story rock mansion. It was as imposing as the senator himself. His presence in person was larger than life; the power of his political office only multiplied the effect. I hoped he wasn't at home this evening, or I might just lose my nerve.

"Come." The uniformed maid beckoned as I got out of the Miata. Trudy sent me a smile as the maid shut the door behind me.

The maid escorted me to the sitting room just beyond the foyer, which seemed unusually small for a home that had to be at least ten thousand square feet. As I settled in the sitting room, I realized that it had been renovated that way on purpose. The sitting room had been part of the foyer at one time and had been built in. Perhaps these people didn't want anyone lingering, as company tended to do in foyers. A guest was to be put in her room, a compartment, dealt with, and then sent on her way.

I wasn't left to mull the issue long. The maid hadn't been gone thirty seconds when Celine Villita appeared in the doorway, shutting the double doors behind her. Dressed in an expensive black-and-white St. John knit skirt suit, panty hose, and Via Spago pumps that likely cost more than my annual dental plan, she looked pale and tense. Even a facelift couldn't hide the unhappiness in her thin face; her brown eyes reflected it. Her thick hair, recently dyed Amazon Midnight, was drawn back in a French twist. This woman was trying hard to be sophisticated and controlled. She might once have been the carefree young girl in the photo, but I was far from certain. I stood, racking my brain for a way to get her to smile.

We shook hands—hers was limp, apathetic. She smelled like lavender. But I cautioned myself—it was a common scent.

"You say you're a friend of Jolie's, but do I know you?"

"We've met. I styled your hair once a long time ago. I am Jolie's stylist. I have a shop in Monte Vista."

"Oh, yes." She gave my hairdo a once-over. "Your hair. It's different."

I sighed internally. Couldn't anyone notice anything else about me? "It's been different probably three dozen times since I saw you. I like to change it every month or so."

Suddenly, realization washed over her face. "You're not a Trujillo, you're Reyn Marten Sawyer. You're the one they say killed Ricardo!"

If it was an act, it was Academy Award winning. It took a lot of a package this carefully presented to show real emotion. She was clearly horrified; her hand was at her throat. She swallowed several times and fought to retain her composure.

I had to admit I was disappointed. I didn't want to take her off my suspect list completely. After all, guilt and the emotional defense necessary to get away with murder could make a person act all sorts of funny ways. Still, my intuition told me while she didn't do it, she might be the key to finding who did.

"I don't know which 'they' you are referring to, but if it is the media, then you ought to know a lot better than I do how 'they' might create a misleading perception. Tell me they've never done that to your husband?"

She nodded once, crossed her arms over her chest, and moved to the picture window that overlooked the elaborate gardens sloping down the property to the right. As she gazed outside, she asked, "You're telling me you didn't kill him?"

I really wanted to answer, *What's it to you?* but bit my tongue. The conversation felt precarious, as if choosing the wrong word would get me escorted back to the Miata at warp speed. She was the one who opened the conversation to Ricardo; if I treaded carefully, I might be able to learn something. I was close, I just didn't know to what. I remembered when I was about ten, trying to get a rattlesnake to leave its hole without coiling and striking me. Why I wanted to do this, who knows. But I had a stick and poked all around it without ever touching the snake, and finally, maybe an hour later, it slithered away. Perhaps if I used this technique with Celine Villita, the truth would come slithering out.

"I didn't kill him. He was my friend and mentor for years. I'm trying to find out who did kill him."

"What brought you here?"

Uh-oh. This was a tricky one. Perhaps telling her I'd broken into his house and found a secret compartment with a photo of someone who might resemble her with a lock of hair that might be hers would be a little too direct. I went for the jugular instead. "It's really about your son."

She spun then, facing me, a fierce mother tiger. "What about him?"

"I understand Ricardo was getting ready to make a big donation to his campaign."

Celine relaxed slightly. "Ricardo donated to a lot of political campaigns."

"Did he?"

Oops. She realized she might have let too much go

there, but her years in politics allowed her to cover it smoothly. She rubbed her left hand up her right arm. Over and over again. Nervous gesture? "Oh, come on, Miss Sawyer, he was well known as a philanthrophist. San Antonio will really miss him."

"I didn't realize politics was the object of philanthropy."

"It is when the representative supports important charities with his legislation."

"I'm sure that's why Ricardo was so interested in Jon's campaign."

Celine's arm rubbing was getting almost manic. "Maybe. After all, Jon's father is a champion of minority charities."

There was something eerie about her saying that after the accolades issued to Ricardo at the funeral for his support of minority children's charities.

"But I wonder how Ricardo heard about Jon running. Even the newspapers don't have wind of it yet, do they?"

Celine would have no hair left on her arm at this rate. She wasn't surprised. She knew Ricardo knew, which meant either he told her, or someone who told him told her. "A few connected people knew. I guess they were so excited by Jon's candidacy they jumped the gun."

She'd stopped the arm rubbing and stood unnaturally still. I was getting too close to something. She was about to coil and strike me right out of there. Time to lie. I smiled. "I know that must be it. I've heard wonderful things about your son. He must be exceptional."

Her chest puffed a little with parental pride. She turned to me, relaxing in a beatific smile. Suddenly, the years fell away, and she was the girl in the photo in Ricardo's wall. "He *is* exceptional. So caring and sensitive to the concerns of the community. He will make a wonderful representative. Jon is a gentle, wise soul, despite his youth."

Gentle? He'd be eaten alive in the world of Texas politics, where it was still the Wild West with a cutthroat cowboy culture despite the suits. Surely, Celine and her husband knew that; they'd lived it long ago, before he made it to D.C. Perhaps they had cautioned Jon about the dangers and were just being supportive of his decision to run.

"We would be lucky to have him in Austin."

"Yes," she said, distracted by the entrance of a Mercedes sedan that pulled through the gate and down past the garden to the garage. She looked at me. "I'm afraid I'm out of time. I wish I could help you in your search for Ricardo's murderer, but I really can't. It doesn't have anything to do with Jon."

She was suddenly anxious to get me out of there. Who was in the sedan? Even though I was afraid it might be her powerful husband, I stood firmly rooted at the window. "So, how did you know Ricardo?"

I'd caught her off-guard. For half a second, she looked afraid but again covered well. She waved her hand in the air. "Oh, we'd known each other since high school. He was an old acquaintance. That's all. We knew each other way back then. We hadn't talked in years."

She was lying, then; her eyes slid from mine just before she spoke her last sentence. Was she Ricardo's *mi cara*?

A dark-haired man got out of the sedan, talking on a cellular telephone. Even from a distance, I recognized him as the young man from the photos. He gestured as he talked and began walking toward the garden. I gasped. It was Ricardo's son. The photos could not capture what was so obvious in person. There was no denying it. He moved with that casual elegance I'd never seen another man exhibit. His gestures were Ricardo's. His profile was Ricardo's.

"It's time for you to leave," Celine snapped.

Maybe I shouldn't have gasped. Not out loud, anyway.

twenty

Since Celine was already teetering off-balance and I was already an unwelcome guest, I proceeded with Plan B: Forgo politeness, and get as much information as I could before I was thrown out.

"Does anyone call you '*mi cara*'?"

A flush flew up her neck. "I don't think that's any of your business. In fact, none of this seems to be your business."

"Actually, it is," I said, "because Ricardo in his will seems to have left his salons, all of Ricardo's Realm, to me."

"Congratulations," she said bitterly.

"No, your sympathies is more like it. I don't want the salons. I have my own life."

Her gaze flicked to the young man, who sat down on a concrete bench next to a yellow rosebush bursting with blooms. "Then get on with it, and leave us alone."

I followed her gaze. "Is that Jon?"

"Miss Sawyer." She faced me. "I hope you don't go off in the wrong direction in your investigation, no matter how well intentioned it may be. Involving yourself in other people's lives can be very dangerous. Someone is already dead. I would hate to see you get hurt as well."

The words were vague, the tone pointed. I knew when I'd been threatened. Unfortunately, it made my perverse nature try to get a more direct threat out of her. It worked.

"Mrs. Villita, I am loyal to a fault to my friends, and Ricardo was one of my good ones. I was once described as a pit bull. When I get something in my mouth, it takes knocking me in the head to get me to let go. It's going to take a pretty big stick to stop me from trying to find Ricardo's killer."

"Don't make me tell my husband you've been here. He is as much of what you call a pit bull about his family and his career. Just having you here at his home threatens us both."

"How so?"

"There's no need to play games, Miss Sawyer. Just know that you need to redirect your investigation, or you will be hurt."

"I'm not afraid of that."

"Not afraid of losing your reputation, your business? And how about your family?" She saw that took me aback. "There are more painful ways to hurt than your body, trust me. Stay away from the Villitas. I will have Rosa show you out."

I heard the ringing of a telephone as she flung open the double doors and marched down the hall to the left. With her tied up hunting down Rosa and handling the phone call, I estimated that I had about thirty seconds to find my way to the garden and Jon Villita. I went straight across the tiny foyer and down the hall that ran parallel to the one Celine had used. I slipped through the first doorway and into an office, which fortunately had French doors to the outside. They were locked. I checked the top drawer of the desk, found a set of keys, fumbled for a moment with a few of them, and finally fit the right one into the lock as I heard the squeak of Rosa's rubber-soled footsteps.

I left the keys in the lock as I eased the door shut. I picked through the rosebushes, letting the thorns scrape across my skin as I made my way through the garden without the luxury of the path. I hid underneath one as I heard a door at the house open.

"Jon, *mi hijo*."

"Yes, Mother?" He called about fifty feet ahead and to the right of me.

I reaimed myself and waited.

"Come inside now. I need your help."

"I'll be right there."

What else could she say? *The woman who figured out your real parentage is skulking around the grounds?* The door shut, reluctantly. Even as far away as I was, I heard the sigh Jon blew out. As I searched for the path, so I wouldn't leap out of the bushes and scare him, I wondered if he knew Ricardo was his father. I'd bet not. Had Senator Villita found out and killed Ricardo? Had Ricardo threatened to tell Jon, expose his heritage? And how did the other news clipping fit in?

I rounded a corner and saw Jon, still sitting on the bench, leaning his elbows on his thighs, staring at his hands laced between his knees, cell phone beside him.

"Mr. Villita?" I called softly.

He looked up, surprised, but he stood graciously and held out his hand. "Please call me Jon."

I hesitated for just a moment as I got over the shock of his voice sounding exactly like Ricardo's. I put my hand in his, and we shook. "Reyn Sawyer."

He looked like he was doing his best to try to place me. "Have we met? I used to pride myself on never forgetting a face or a name. But I'm sorry, with this campaign I've met so many people. They say as a politician, I need to find ways to talk around not remembering someone, but I can't do that. I prefer to be honest."

"I prefer that, too," I said with a smile. I liked him immediately. There was a weariness about him unusual for someone so young, but also a genuineness that was refreshing. "And you haven't forgotten my face or my name. We've never met before."

"Well, I promise not to forget your name, Reyn. It's just unusual enough for me to remember. And your hair, that I won't forget."

I smiled back at his grin and resisted the urge to return the good-natured jibe. His hairstyle was the height of aged conservative—a side-parted medium-length that was what a sixty-year-old politician might wear.

"Ah, now, memorizing my hairstyle won't help you, since I change my color and style almost as often as my clothes," I told him.

"A master of disguise?"

"No." I laughed, feeling a small twist in my gut as it occurred to me I might have to become a master of disguise if Celine sicced the senator on me. And what about my mom and dad, my sisters and brothers and nieces and nephews? "It's nothing so dramatic. I'm a hairstylist, and I like change."

"Hairstylist. I bet that's a fun job, making people feel better about themselves."

He gets it! I looked at Jon Villita more closely. I wondered about how much genetics play a part in how we turn out. Maybe more than I ever thought, if a man with the blood of a beauty salon magnate and raised by a U.S. senator still found hairstyling a high calling.

"I like it," I admitted. "But the job you're running for is an important one. Maybe it's better to be important than to have fun."

"You think so?" he asked. "Even if you're miserable while you're being important?"

"Politics isn't your thing?"

He glanced guiltily at the house. "Are you a friend of my mother and father?"

"No, just met your mother, never met your father, and don't especially want to."

He laughed. "I don't blame you. He's a good man, don't get me wrong. But we're just two different people. I respect what he's accomplished and what he enjoys. But he doesn't offer me the same respect."

The way he was talking about the senator, I guessed Jon didn't know about his parentage. I went fishing just to be sure. "Sometimes being a parent is a difficult thing."

Jon didn't bite. He truly didn't know anything about Ricardo. "Are you a parent?"

"Oh, no, haven't even gotten to first base. I need to find someone to love first."

"That's another thing. Anyone I'd fall in love with wouldn't be good at politics, which would mean I wouldn't be allowed to marry her without a lot of pain and suffering. You know, I'd rather fall in love with a nice girl and have an ordinary job than be groomed for the White House at twenty-five." He paused and sighed. "I guess that sounds whiny."

"No, it sounds like you know yourself better than most twenty-five-year-olds do. That's pretty wise, if you ask me. Have you told your parents?"

"I have, and they don't think I'm old enough to make a life-changing decision like that. I'm old enough to represent an entire constituency and make decisions for them but not for myself?" He blew out another sigh. "I guess it doesn't matter. I don't have another option. I refuse to use my father to get a job, but where could I go in this town where they wouldn't know the name Villita?"

He sounded so trapped my heart went out to him. Before I could find comforting words, he blew out yet another sigh and struggled to change the subject. "Did you know that hairstylist who was murdered?"

"Yes. He was a good friend of mine."

"I'm so sorry." Wow. He really was.

"What do you know about it?" I was fishing again. Maybe Daddy had brought it up at the dinner table. Maybe I'd get lucky, and Jon had heard the senator discussing the murder plan with the brush-wielding hit man.

"Not much," Jon admitted. "My dad told his speechwriter to use it in a speech she wrote for me to give today at the Rotary Club. It was an example for the need for better crime control. It seemed so cold to use this poor man's death in a political platform when he wasn't even memorialized yet. I left it out. Got in trouble, too."

Good for him. The boy had balls.

"Jon!" Celine called from the house. Surely, she'd seen us sitting there by now, but what could she do other than drag him away like a five-year-old or get me in the sights of her rifle and take me out like a sniper? The frantic note in her voice worked better than anything on this sensitive young man whose spirit was about to be trampled to death in the political arena.

"Mom sounds like she's about to lose it." Jon stood and shook my hand. "She's been on edge the last day or so. I'd better go see what she needs. Nice to meet you, Reyn. I hope we get to talk again one day."

"Me, too," I said as I watched him go. I resisted the urge to back all the way to the Miata. Of course, even if I saw the bullet coming, what would I do—duck? Karate chop it? Besides, if they were going to silence me, I figured it would be an "accident" that would not happen on the grounds of their pristine home. That would leave too many people asking too many questions.

Trudy had the motor running, but I forced myself to almost meander to the car. I looked over the grounds, fingered the leaves of bushes as I passed, smelled the pungent blossom of a jasmine vine. I knew Celine was watching, and I didn't want her to think I was scared.

My nose started running before I got to the Miata. The sneezing began before I opened the passenger door. Who says I'm not a good detective? I've discovered I'm violently allergic to blooming jasmine.

With snot cascading down the back of my throat and my nostrils in gallons, we made our less-than-dignified exit from the Villita estate. I searched my purse for anything to use to stem the flow, but I never seem to have any tissues. I was going to make a terrible mother one day. The good ones always seemed to have a tissue handy. I had to settle on the sock. Hey, it was clean.

Trudy looked at me. "Your cell phone rang while you were in there."

"Yeah?" I fished out the phone. It didn't show I had any missed calls.

I looked at her in question. She looked at me in apology. I had a bad feeling about this.

"I answered it," she said as she headed east on Guaraty. "I thought it might be someone who heard your challenge at the funeral and wanted to give us a tip."

I couldn't argue with that one. It was a smart move. "Okay. I still hear a 'but.' "

"It was Jackson." She looked at me quickly, then back to the road. "Lieutenant Scythe."

"Uh-huh."

"He wanted to know where we were. I explained that the mishap on the freeway with the other police car was an accident. He didn't seem mad about it."

Sure.

"You didn't tell him where we were, did you?"

I looked in the rearview mirror and saw my nemesis four car lengths behind. Scythe looked ready to bite a nail in two. Could it get any worse?

I knew better than to ask myself that question.

"Don't worry, Reyn, I didn't give away our location for free. I made a deal."

twenty-one

"A DEAL?" I TRIED NOT TO SHRIEK, BUT I THINK I failed, because Trudy swerved and nearly hit a light pole. Behind us, Crandall honked. "I don't like the sound of that."

"Neither do I. Do you think he's making fun of my driving?" Trudy huffed into the rearview mirror.

"I'm not talking about not liking the sound of the honk, Trude. I'm talking about not liking the sound of a deal."

"How do you know you don't like it when you don't know what the deal is."

"I know you, and I know Señor Sneaky Snake, so I don't like it."

"Sneaky Snake. Ooh, that sounds sexy. I'm glad to know you're thinking along the right lines."

"What lines are those?" I demanded, openly shrieking this time. "Are you pimping me out to Scythe for some information?"

Trudy grinned as she negotiated a turn going about twenty miles an hour too fast. I think she was angling to get pulled over by the pair behind us. The only thing she'd forgotten was that we were still in Terrell Hills, which is a two-square-mile incorporated, *muy* expensive enclave with its very own police force whose members will pull anyone over because they are simply bored. I saw the flashing lights coming at us as we whizzed past a cross street. I didn't warn her, that's how mad I was at her. I prayed they'd throw her conniving heinie in jail.

The Terrell Hills patrol car wheeled around the turn so fast I wondered if the cop thought we were bank robbers. The guy even had his siren on. Maybe Scythe had put an APB out on us and it was still hot. Well, swell.

"Witches' tits and bats' butts," Trudy swore under her breath as she pulled over. When she used vulgarities with body parts, she was mad.

I watched the Crown Vic ease in behind the patrol car in my rearview mirror. The officer got out. She was pretty and slightly built but posturing like a bulldog. Uh-oh, this would be worse than a short cop with small man complex. And she still had the siren on. It was giving me such a headache, I felt like getting out and turning it off for her. Before I could follow through, Scythe appeared at the woman's side, flashing his badge. It was as if she were butter and someone turned the burner on high. Copette melted. She cocked her head and her hip; her hands fell to her sides to mold to her waist. She smiled sweetly. Ugh, couldn't she see how damned arrogant, uh, vainacious, he was? Couldn't she see that whatever charm he was using, it was to get something from her?

I was almost so distracted by their body language that I forgot to wonder what their voice conversation could be about. It had to be about us. It couldn't be good.

Suddenly, the Miata lurched forward, nearly giving me whiplash. Even whiplash would've been worth the

look of surprise on Scythe's face right before he spun
and ran back to the Crown Vic. Hee hee.

"What are you doing, Trude?" I screamed as she
cranked the wheel to the left and the Miata leaned hard
on the two right wheels. Before I could get my seat belt
buckled, she took a hard right straight into what looked
like no more than a space between two wisteria bushes.
I closed my eyes, envisioning being buried in the brick
of someone's historic mansion. All I felt was the flap of a
wisteria leaf on my face (so much for the allure of a convertible) and the bumps of a bad road. Slowly, I opened
my eyes. We were headed down a secret lane that cut
behind a row of estates.

I heard the zoom of a souped-up V-8 engine passing
behind us. We'd lost the cops. Again. I looked at Trudy.

"Way to go, girl. I didn't know you had it in you."

Trudy looked at me in surprise. "What do you mean?"

"I didn't think you were devious enough to run from
the cops and succeed."

She looked confused for a moment. "I'm not running
from the cops. I just looked at the time and realized I've
got to get home. I'm doing *carne guisada* for dinner for
Mama Tru and Daffy. I'll be dog meat if I'm late."

"You're serving dog meat, why not be it?" I shook my
head. I couldn't believe she'd lost the cops twice in one
evening *by mistake*. Only Trudy.

"I know you don't like *carne guisada*, which is why
you're not invited."

Carne guisada aside, if Daffy were coming, I was
eternally grateful to not be invited. Daffy was Trude's
mother, and if anyone ever lived down to her name, it
was Daffy. She made Trudy look like a Rhodes scholar
on Trude's worse day.

"How did you know about this shortcut?" I asked as the Miata poked its nose out on North New Braunfels between two white-bloom-filled crepe myrtle trees.

"One of the drapery seamstresses I use told me about it."

"How does she know about it?"

She dropped her voice. "She had an affair with one of the famous residents."

I held up my hand. "Don't tell me what guy it is. I can't handle any more intrigue right now."

Trudy flashed a grin. "It wasn't a guy."

"I lead a sheltered life," I muttered.

Trudy snorted as she snaked through another back road on the way to my neighborhood. "Right. One of your best pals is murdered with a brush, you stick yourself in the middle of the investigation—"

"Hey! The cops did that by calling me to identify him."

"And instead of sitting back and letting them do their job, you have to threaten a psychic, break into the victim's house, taunt the killer into coming after you at the funeral, and accuse the wife of one of the most powerful men in America of having an illegitimate child. This is all pretty extreme just to get some attention from a cute cop."

We'd arrived at my house, Trudy having used so many shortcuts even a bird couldn't have flown a more direct route from the Villita house to mine. I was sure we'd beaten Scythe and Crandall, who no doubt would be showing up in minutes. I'd pretend I wasn't home. Trudy pulled into the driveway.

I glared at her. "I'm not the one obsessed with him, you are."

"Methinks you protest too much."

I was caught. I couldn't protest now, could I, or I'd be proving her right. *Bitch.* I got out of the car. "Okay, so I can obsess some more—what's the deal you made with him?"

"You'll know soon enough," she said as she backed out without waiting for me to close my door. It swung open, then shut as she floored the gas and zoomed up McCullough.

I considered going through the salon just to check that everything was hunky-dory but decided I would just get distracted by the paperwork there waiting for me. I wanted to concentrate on the killer. Daisy locked up on Wednesdays, and she was the most reliable one I had working at Transformations, so I didn't worry about the lights and fans being turned off and the alarm set. Instead, I walked around to my kitchen door, running through the conversations I'd had with Celine and Jon. The girls came up, Cab sniffing me over to see where I'd been, Char whining because she'd been abandoned all day, Beau rolling her tongue out to show how starving she was.

I was so busy placating them I didn't see the man waiting in the shadows until it was too late. I jumped, spun, and would've run except he wrapped one arm around my waist.

He whispered roughly into my ear, "No way you're getting away again. Not even if I have to tie you up."

"Promises, promises," I muttered. I couldn't believe he caught me.

"Ah, so your *compadre* told you about our deal?"

"I didn't agree to any deal. Especially anything involving being tied up or whips and chains!" I shouted.

Scythe put his hand over my mouth. "Hush, Big

Mouth, or I'll shoot you with a stun gun just to shut you up until I can get you into the house."

I struggled, but it was like fighting a brick wall. He used his body to push me forward past the dogs and up the stairs. I burned a reproving look at the three canine faces. Only Char had the grace to appear embarrassed that they'd let Scythe trespass. Cab and Beau were too busy panting adoringly at Scythe. Usually, they were first-class watchdogs—strange men always sent them into peals of threatening barks. He must have bribed them with doggie treats or something. See, I knew he was sneaky.

"Open the door," Scythe ordered.

"You wish," I said into his palm.

"While I would love to be a gentleman and open the door for you, I don't seem to have an extra hand to dig up your keys. Of course, I can call to action my trusty handcuffs, and that would free up one of my hands."

"We can talk out here," I told his hand. It sounded more like "Wick and tackle ho," but he seemed to understand, not that it did me any good.

"No, we can't, because I don't want any witnesses when I collect on my end of the deal."

Gulp. "What if you don't collect?"

He'd leaned down near my mouth to hear what I said behind his hand. He smelled like fresh-cut cedar. "Oh, don't worry, I always collect. Remember, I carry a gun."

The adrenaline was wearing off, and I was beginning to feel the contours of his body along my back and rump. *Uh-oh.* Time to go inside so I could get some space.

"Come on now, Miss Sawyer. Don't make me employ my favorite method of torture."

"What's that?" I imagined thumbscrews and guillotines.

"Tickle torture."

I found my keys in record time, shoved the right one into the lock, and twisted so hard I nearly bent it. As I turned the knob and pushed the door open, he let his hand slip off my mouth, a half second too slowly. I broke his grip on my waist and fell into my kitchen. He followed, shooting the dead bolt behind him.

I hated to admit it, but it was the sexiest sound I'd ever heard. I was in real trouble. I'd tell him anything to get him out of there before I made one *muy grande* mistake.

"What'd you do that for?"

"I'm trying to save the world by keeping you inside."

"Ha. Ha. Ha," I deadpanned as I moved as far away as possible from him without actually leaving the room. I needn't have bothered, because he walked straight for the front door, where I heard him check the lock, then into the salon, where I presume he was checking the doors were locked there, too. He certainly was making himself comfortable in my home. It grated on my already frayed nerves. Sexual electricity will do that, you know. Maybe I needed to get a vibrator so every time I got near a halfway decent-looking man I didn't get all goofy about him just out of hard-up desperation.

It was full dark by now, and I reached up to flick on the homey Tiffany knockoff I have to light the kitchen. His hand closed over mine to stop it. I jumped.

"You nearly gave me a heart attack," I scolded.

"Use your head, would you, before someone uses it as target practice?" he snapped, dropping my hand.

"I think you're being a little melodramatic again." I

walked over to the refrigerator and yanked open the door, because I needed to do something to keep my mind off its sudden penchant for various sexual positions. My distraction failed when he suddenly reached around me, brushing me in all the wrong places, to get his finger on the button at the door junction that operates the light. It went dark again, blinding me until my eyes could adjust after the brief flash of sixty-watt light.

"Don't tell me," he finally said in the silent dark, "that you're *hungry?*"

Oh, dear. It was the way he said it. And he was way too close. And it was way too dark. And it was way too hot, even with the forty-degree air blowing on us from the refrigerator. He kissed me. Okay, maybe I kissed him. Well, we kissed each other.

Oh, boy, did we.

I'm not sure how long it lasted, because I stopped thinking for a while. That's hard for me to do. I can't remember when it last happened.

At some point, his finger came off the refrigerator light button and moved with the rest of his hand to my right breast, because that's where it was when I started thinking again. I did that only because he said, "What the hell is this?"

His hand was molding my breast, and we could hear the crunching of paper. He ran his thumb back and forth. *Crunch. Crunch. Uh-oh.* With the speed of light, his fingers unbuttoned my pocket and extracted Zorita's list. I tried to escape, but as his other hand had been cradling my head and now grabbed my hair, I couldn't go far.

"Would you please let go of my hair, you Neanderthal?"

In all the nonthinking activity, my hands had some-how migrated to his chest, which I now pushed at with all my might, then swiped for the list. He held it easily out of my reach, while trying to read it.

I got fixed with the twin torpedoes. "What is this?"

"A list of Ricardo's customers he did personally."

"Gerald Akin couldn't tell us whose hair Ricardo styled. His receptionist said Ricardo handled that all on his own, and most of them came in after hours. Where did you get this?"

"Ricardo's *cunandero.*"

"I didn't know he had one."

"You didn't ask."

"Listen, Smarty Pants, you don't treat a cop that way and expect to get away with it."

"How about kissing a cop that way and expect to get away with it?"

"Oh, no, no, no." He shook his head and pinned me so hard with those blue eyes that I thought I might have to step back. "Don't even get started. That was a mistake."

"You can say that again." Crossing my arms over my chest, I glared right back.

"I don't have to say it again. Because it won't be dis-cussed again ever. It didn't happen."

"Fine by me."

"Good."

"Good."

We stood there not speaking—I'm not sure I was breathing—for at least a full minute.

Scythe seemed to make some internal decision, be-cause he nodded to himself and then looked over the list again. "I don't see any of the Villitas' names on this list."

"No."

"Why did you go see them?"

I decided not to lie, because Scythe expected me to. "She's an old friend of Ricardo's. I thought she might be able to shed some light on his past."

Scythe looked at me like he wasn't sure I was telling the truth. "And did she?"

"Not exactly. She was threatened by my questions, though, so she's hiding something. Then I met her son. I think Ricardo is his biological father. Jon doesn't appear to know that, however."

"Come on. You think one of them killed Ricardo to keep a twenty-five-year-old secret? This is the family of a U.S. senator. Something like this nowadays wouldn't prevent him from being reelected."

"I don't know what to think."

"What did the *cunandero* say?"

"She said I have lots of red spikes in my aura that make me really, really scary and dangerous, so you'd better watch out." I narrowed my eyes and tried to look bad-ass.

Scythe blew out a hard sigh. "Dangerous to yourself," he muttered. "I need to talk to this *cunandero* myself. How do I get to her house?"

Goody, was I really going to get rid of him? I pulled open a drawer and scribbled the instructions on a piece of notepaper. I held it out to him, careful that we didn't accidentally touch.

"If we're exchanging information, what do I get from you?"

"I didn't know it was an exchange."

"Well, I have been very cooperative and forthcoming with you, seems you could have something for me."

His smile developed ever so slowly. I tried not to let

it affect my erogenous zones. "What do you want from me?"

Uh-oh, I stepped right into that one, didn't I? I cleared my throat to get our exchange back on a business footing. "I want to know what the autopsy said."

"Dead from a pierced aorta. He bled to death. Of course, the collapsed lung didn't help anything, but it didn't kill him, either."

"Could he have lived if someone would've gotten to him sooner?"

Scythe was watching me carefully. "Maybe if that someone was right outside the door and called 911 immediately. It doesn't take long to die with a hole in the biggest artery in the body."

I nodded, but I wasn't buying it. I think he knew I felt guilty and was bending the truth to make me feel better. Probably just because he didn't want to deal with an emotional female.

"Any mention of pudding in his stomach contents?"

Scythe gave me a funny look. "No, only the remnants of what the coroner surmised was a Cajun blackened tuna, some kind of roasted potatoes, green beans, and coffee. Why?"

"Just wondering. Ricardo mentioned pudding to me on the phone that night."

"What about pudding?"

"He said, 'The proof was in the pudding.' "

"What is that, some kind of code between the two of you?"

"We had no code. I don't know what it meant. I thought he was drunk and goofy." I sucked back a sob that threatened to erupt. I swear, I never knew when I'd go all mushy over Ricardo. I hated it.

Scythe strode to the door, pretending not to see the glimmer of tears in my eyes. He put a hand on the door-knob and turned. "Lock it behind me. I'll be back later to collect on my deal."

I still didn't know what the deal was, but I wasn't about to beg right then. I jutted my chin out. "Maybe I won't be here."

"Don't worry, I'll know where you are. We've as-signed two teams to your tail. One's parked out front, the other out back."

I smiled. I knew they wouldn't keep me from doing what needed to be done next.

twenty-two

I DON'T LIKE CLIMBING TREES, NEVER DID, EVEN AS a kid, even as a self-professed tomboy. So scaling a tree to get out of my house showed just how badly I wanted to get to Illusions that night. I could've tried to waltz right out of the house and hope the cops stationed outside would let me mosey on over to the transvestite club at midnight. They might have, I don't know, but I didn't want to take the chance that they would stop me from finding out what I needed to know.

Scythe hadn't returned, and was I ever relieved. That kiss was going to complicate an already complicated relationship. I know he thought it was a mistake, and I said it was a mistake, but while I didn't think at all during the kiss, ever since our lips came unlocked, I couldn't think about much else. I finally told myself that in a couple of days, when I had the case all solved for them, this badge-slinging cowboy could ride off into the sunset in his black sedan, never to be seen again, and I could go back to fantasizing about the vitamin salesman.

It would be ever so much safer.

Speaking of safe, I was sitting on an oak branch looking at a ten-foot drop and wondering how hard the ground was. It's really cool to live in a hundred-and-fifty-year-old neighborhood with trees that are taller and older than the two- and three-story houses, until, that is, one is sneaking out of one's house and needs a low branch to carry one safely to the ground.

I'm not a complete idiot. I had tried to go out the front door; the cop out on the street had waved through his car window. I tried to go out the back door, and the cop who sat with a view of the salon door and the kitchen door waved. I opened the upstairs window, and no one waved, so I turned on my bathroom light, set up my Spurs' Tim Duncan bobblehead doll behind the frosted glass window, and turned a box fan on high to keep the bobblehead bobbing.

Looking up now, I realized it might not fool Scythe, who expected me to do stuff like this, but it was probably good enough for these guys.

I sucked in a deep breath, wiggled my heinie off the branch, and dropped to the ground, rolling to a stop in an ungraceful heap. I have to admit I worried about my back, but, amazingly, the jolt seemed to pop something back into place, and I walked a little more freely than I had before. Maybe my luck was turning.

I hoped it was dark enough in Illusions so the grass stains on my jeans and T-shirt wouldn't show. I tiptoed over to my next-door neighbor's house. Rick Ugarte is a songwriter whose muse is only awake from midnight to five A.M. and only when nourished by fresh air. I know this because when he and his attorney wife first moved in, I had a little trouble sleeping, what with his office being right below my bedroom window and some of his songs being hard rock boosted by a synthesizer. Rick and I had a little talk, and I told him I'd try to be tolerant if he'd try to write country music to a guitar. The next week, he sold his first song—to an up-and-coming country music star out of Austin. I haven't heard the synthesizer or hard rock since. If I'd known it was that easy, I might have bought the damned song the week before.

Anyhow, I hunkered down next to Rick's open window and waited for him to finish his verse. "You lost him today . . . but girl it'll be okay . . ."

"Ricky," I whispered.

He looked up, completely unfazed by a face in his window. I love creative airheads. "Reyn, what's up, girl?"

"Can I borrow your van?"

"No *problemo*." He reached into his pocket and threw me the keys.

"Thanks, I'll have it back in a little while."

"Whatever. Just don't transport any dead bodies in it." He grinned.

"Ricky, you know—"

He waved off whatever denial I would've delivered. "What I know is, you're famous. Infamous. Like Jesse James. I think I'll write a song about you. 'Reyn on the Run' . . ." He started to sing in his halfway decent tenor, "She couldn't stay, because the cops thought she oughta pay . . . or take a roll in the hay . . ."

Uh-oh. I looked over my shoulder. Rick had a direct view of the kitchen, although it was dark, so he hadn't seen much. In fact, he might not have seen anything but Scythe accompanying me through the door. He was probably just guessing. "Listen, about that . . ."

"Hey, girl, I say get yourself some. You're way overdue."

He laughed as I shook my head and retreated toward the carport behind their house. Even my neighbors were keeping track of my celibacy. Maybe I was getting ready to set a world record. I pulled a face at my borrowed transportation. It was going to be tough being inconspicuous while driving a big eggplant, but on the bright side, the cops wouldn't be expecting me to drive a purple minivan, so I'd probably slip by unnoticed.

I tucked my hair under one of their kids' baseball caps, jammed it down on my head, and put on a too-small orange windbreaker with "Toby" embroidered over my left breast and the name of some Little League team emblazoned on the back. Sure enough, the cop on the street barely looked up as I passed and waved nonchalantly.

As I neared Illusions, I debated how best to slip in unnoticed, get my information, and slip out again. Unfortunately, I didn't have the advantage of Bettina taking me through the back door. I couldn't just waltz in the front door, because I wasn't carrying two grand on me. I could either loiter at the back door, hoping someone came out for a smoke, or I could bum admittance by cozying up to someone entering the club. I almost opted for the latter as I followed a Jaguar into the lot and parked next to it. The silver-haired driver looked like a sharp-dressed businessman until he got out of his car and I saw that the lower third of his pinstriped three-piece suit was a black leather miniskirt complemented by fishnet stockings and patent-leather pumps.

Okay, loitering sounded like a great idea.

I didn't have to hide behind the Dumpster long before a stagehand with a sweaty forehead and dirty jeans came out the door, propped it open with a chunk of wood, and lit a cigarette. I pressed the alarm button on Rick's key ring, and the van's horn started honking. From the front door, the no-neck bouncer went to investigate, but when he saw the stagehand smoking outside, he hollered at him to come check it out. Perfect. The guy ambled over there. I tripped up the stairs and into the dark hallway. "She's More Than an Angel" poured through the speakers. There was a crowd down near the G dressing room, maybe a passel of VIPs with backstage passes. Sighing, I headed down the hall the opposite way, which would take me past stage right and into the audience. I had no doubt that Short, Hairy, and Menacing wouldn't appreciate my return, but I was hoping he didn't spend much time mixing with his customers. And anyway, I was wearing my disguise, which, upon review via the mirror on the wall, made me look like I was trying to be a ten-year-old boy. He'd never recognize me once I got in.

As I slunk my way past stage right, I could see Bettina performing a sultry number. Her alto was good enough to do a musical in a small-town dinner theater, I thought. Once on the floor, I tried to edge up to the stage without attracting any attention. Maybe she could slip me into the dressing room, and I could talk to Redhead and be out of there before Gregor saw me.

I tried not to stare at the patrons. There was a share of glassy-eyed and panting weirdos, but I was more surprised by how many normal-looking men were in there. Scary. A few stray women sat with their dates, trying not to appear uncomfortable. A table full of giggling middle-aged women in their cups were whooping it up, and that's where I caught sight of Gregor. Should've figured.

Well, maybe they'd keep him distracted. Bettina finished with a flourish. I had to admit her hair still looked fabulous. I was admiring my handiwork so thoroughly I almost forgot to call her name as she passed. She looked down and dismissed me. "Sorry, I don't do little boys. Try little girl in a frilly dress next time."

Gross. That was TMI for me. I struggled to get back with my program. "Bettina. It's me, Reyn Marten Sawyer."

She paused. I pulled off the baseball cap, unzipped the jacket, peeled it off, and called her name again. She looked back, recognized me, but then her gaze drifted past me, and she scooted backstage.

Uh-oh.

Before I could turn around, a hairy hand clamped down on my elbow. "This ain't a strip joint." Gregor hauled me around in front of him. "You!"

I smiled big. "Nice to see you again, Gregor."

"I told you to get the hell outta here and stay out."

"I will, I promise, if I could just show one of your, uh, performers a couple of photos. I'll never come back again."

The next performer, who was dressed up in a schoolgirl's uniform, peeked around the edge of the stage. Gregor waved her on, and the music started. He looked back at me, squeezing my elbow harder.

"You're nuts, you know that? I saw you on TV tonight, what you did at that funeral. You better not have dragged that killer here to shoot the place up; not the cops, neither. You're trouble."

"Nobody followed me. But the longer I'm here, the more risk you're in, you're right. If you let me talk to that, uh, employee of yours with the long red hair, I'll go. But if you don't, I'll hang around outside until closing."

"No you won't, ole Tiger out front will bounce your ass down the road."

"And I'll call 9-1-1."

He was caught, then, and not smart enough to figure out that the cops were the last ones—well, maybe second to the last after the murderer—I wanted to see right then. Squeezing my elbow until I knew I'd have bruises and glowering so hard he had one eyebrow, he dragged me through an unmarked door and down the dark hallway to the dressing room.

It went from chatter to dead silence as he opened the door. What the hell did he do to keep them so scared of him? Maybe it was his BO. That was pretty damned intimidating.

He pointed his short, hairy middle finger at the redhead sitting at the mirror. "Phoebe, get your ass out here and talk to this bitch, or I'll fricking kill you."

Oh, the charm.

Phoebe looked thrilled to see me, glaring to beat the band. He he was dressed in fifties garb and looked like my niece's Lucille Ball Barbie doll. I wondered what she was going to sing. Gregor dragged me down the hall and shoved both of us out the back door.

"You have two minutes. Then I'm sending Tiger around. He'll break your phone first, then your face."

He slammed the door shut. Phoebe-who-was-probably-Phil pulled out some smokes and lit one quick. His/her hand was shaking, crimson-painted acrylics clicking together.

Out of my pocket, I pulled the picture of Senator Villita I'd printed off the Internet and showed it to Phoebe. "Is this the man who met Ricardo?"

"No way." He/she started to reach for the handle of the door.

"Wait." I'd found an old photo of Mike Van Dyke,

Sarah Johnstone's tan, handsome second hubby, in the newspaper archives on the Web. I pulled it out and unfolded it.

Phoebe did a double take. He/she grabbed the paper and looked closer. "Yeah, it could be him if this is an old picture. The dude with Ricardo was like in his fifties. This dude looks like his younger brother, maybe." He/she turned and opened the door, ready to scurry in.

Before the door shut, I asked, "Why are you so scared?"

"Because there was a note on my car when I left last night that warned me to keep my mouth shut or else. I guess that's what I get for talking to you. Or else."

The door banged shut before I could tell Phoebe to call the cops about the nasty note. Shucks, our business was done in well under two minutes, so I wouldn't get to meet Tiger up close and personal. I returned to the eggplant on wheels and got home less than an hour after I'd left. Rick quizzed me about where I'd been, and when I told him a transvestite club, he decided to change the second verse of the "Reyn on the Run" song. He said he'd have it finished the next time I was in the news, which, I warned him, at the rate I was going, would be the next morning. He was sure it was going to be his big hit, his ticket to Nashville. I just wanted to know if I got any nookie in it. He smiled and said it was a mystery.

Just what I needed, another one of those.

I was too tired to climb the tree back into my house and figured the cops couldn't do anything about me leaving after I'd already done it except be pissed off, so I went to my back door and reached for the key I kept hidden in the fake rock in the flower bed.

"Hey!" the cop yelled. I glanced over my shoulder and saw him looking from me to the bobblehead's shadow in the bathroom and back to me again. "How'd you get out?"

"I'm her twin sister. Reyn's still in there." The uniform looked simultaneously relieved and confused and was silent long enough for me to slip into the house. The girls mobbed me as I came through the door. Since I had practically no social life, they were not used to me up and leaving at midnight. It had them a little worried.

"Never fear, girls, I'm not turning into a vampire."

They still looked at me expectantly. I sighed. "And I didn't get any nookie, okay?"

All three drifted away then. Cab nosed her empty food bowl, Char sniffed my jeans leg, and Beau flopped onto the floor. So even my dogs were disappointed in my love life.

On that happy note, I stripped and dragged on the once black, now gray "Buck Off" T-shirt that my horse-crazy niece sent me for my birthday years ago. I crawled into bed.

The cacophony was deafening.

I pulled the pillow over my head and tried to ignore it. I was bound and determined to get the first uninterrupted night of sleep I'd had in three nights. Some people might call this stubborn, I call it focused. At any rate, I was so focused that I really didn't consider for several minutes why my three Labs would be having fits in the middle of the night. It was still dark; I registered that before the pillow came down. When I finally began to feel uneasy about the barking, I assumed it must be the cops doing a perimeter search. But then I asked myself why. They hadn't left their vehicles since they'd driven up, as far as I could tell.

Then I heard dog toenails scrambling across my hardwood floor and the screech of nails being dragged across said hardwood floor. Ouch, that was going to leave a scar.

"What the hell are you girls doing?" I yelled. I don't often swear at the dogs, but that floor represented every drop of blood, sweat, and tears I put into this damned house.

As I threw the covers back, I heard a thump and a whump. And two yips.

It was only then that I considered I might have an intruder.

Okay, so I'm not the sharpest knife in the drawer when woken from a deep sleep.

I jumped out of bed and proved I had a modicum of brainwave power by pulling on the smelly gray gym shorts I had left lying next to the bed several days before when I'd gotten a wild hair to exercise.

As I descended the stairs, I realized I should have a weapon. Besides my morning breath, that is. So I grabbed the girls' leashes with their metal-link choke collars that I had wrapped around the bannister at the base of the stairs and envisioned myself swinging them like a lasso above my head, ready to strike the bad guy in one fell swoop.

I was too late. Three hundred pounds of frustrated dog came at me as I reached the first story. They scrambled for purchase on the hardwood floor and bashed into me, barking and baying. But as soon as they stopped, they were off again, leading me to the scene of the crime, I presumed. I followed them to the kitchen door, which was standing wide open, having been wrenched that way by a crowbar. I know that because the crowbar was sitting right on the steps outside. The door looked like it hadn't put up much of a fight. There was a small dent in the hundred-year-old wood, and that was it. The lock still even looked intact. I guess I needed to move to Fort Knox if I was going to keep nosing around in Ricardo's murder.

Char came up and nuzzled my hand. I patted her head and reached down to cradle her muzzle to thank her for protecting me. That's when I saw the six inches of black material hanging from her left canine tooth. *Hmm.* Can we say *clue?* I felt the shiny material. Lycra. I grabbed her collar and visually inspected the other two. They didn't get a piece of him. Or her. I hated to be sexist, even when someone was trying to get me.

I kicked the door the rest of the way open and marched barefoot to the SAPD car still sitting out behind my house. Now, granted, it was a bit of a stretch for the guy to see both doors, and he'd really have to be up patrolling all night and still not be able to swear he never saw anyone at either door, but he couldn't argue it to me, because when Char and I walked up, he was asleep. I tapped on the window. He jumped. Poor guy. He looked about thirteen.

"Hi. I just wanted you to know someone just broke into my house, and my dog got a piece of the intruder's clothing."

"Uh." He cleared his throat and sat up straight. "How did that happen?"

"You tell me, Officer Norland," I said, reading his badge. "You're out here."

"Ma'am . . ."

"Don't call me ma'am. I'm not old enough for that."

"Of course you're not," he agreed, not believing it for a minute.

"Call your *compadre*," I recommended, "and we'll go inside and figure this out."

"Yes, ma'am," he said as he reached for his radio.

I led Chardonnay back to the house, giving up on him having the wherewithal to think of saving the material as evidence. I saw slobber dripping off the tip of the Lycra and hoped she didn't swallow real hard between now and when someone with a Ziploc came along.

Norland and the cop who had been sitting at the front walked up to the kitchen door just as two cars pulled up into the salon parking lot. One turned out to be the burglary detective, who tried to make me feel like he was doing me a favor. The other was the fingerprint tech, who dusted the door. Someone, I'm not sure who, put the Lycra in an evidence bag, but the detective downplayed its importance and told me we'd have one in a million chances of ever finding a suspect from a generic clue like that, unless, of course, my dog had drawn blood.

Twenty minutes later, as I was trying to figure out how to keep my wrenched door shut for the night, I heard, then saw, a four-wheel-drive diesel Ford truck— all shiny black paint and chrome—roar up. Jackson Scythe emerged from the stud mobile and started talking to the surveillance cops, who'd gone back outside to check for clues at the perimeter. It was the first time I realized I might not be dressed appropriately for company—with no bra or underwear and a holey oversize T-shirt that hid rather ripe shorts. I considered going upstairs to put more or better clothes on, or at least underwear, until I saw how hard Scythe was chewing out the poor young guys.

"Hey, you!" I shouted out onto the lawn. "Try picking on someone closer to your own age."

Baby-blue chips of dry ice found me. Boy, were they ever smoking. "And where would I find that?" he asked.

I shrugged. I pegged Scythe for around forty, though I never was good at guessing ages. It didn't matter, I was after the insult. "Happy Trails Retirement Home? AARP membership roster?"

The two officers who were about half his age bit back smiles. The dark-haired Antonio Banderas lookalike Scythe had been chewing out particularly hard looked like he wanted to kiss me for the distraction. Cradle robbing had its appeal. I'd have to take a rain check. Scythe was already stalking my way.

"Why didn't you call me?" he demanded in that low, quiet voice that was tight with fury.

"What for?" I answered. "The police were already here."

That set him back a moment. "But I'm in charge of the Montoya case."

"Who says this has anything to do with Ricardo?"

"Don't be stupid, Reyn," he snapped.

He was being his bossy self, which never failed to raise my hackles, but just as I was about to tell him where to go, he'd used my first name. He had never done that before. It distracted me from my counterattack just long enough for him to get in another verbal jab.

"Where did you go when you snuck out?"

"To see my boyfriend."

"You don't have a boyfriend."

"How do you know that?"

"The same way I know you don't have a twin sister."

"You've investigated *me*?"

"You're a suspect. How good a cop would I be if I didn't?"

"I guess you think you know everything about me, then."

"Not hardly," he admitted, shaking his head in obvious bewilderment. "I don't know why you're the only one of five kids to have a halfway normal name."

"Because I'm the only one that's halfway normal. I'm the white sheep in a family of black ones."

He shook his head, completely flummoxed. "That is unbelievable."

"It's not my sisters' and brothers' faults. Mom and Dad named us after something that happened during our conception. They were in Dallas; they were in the back of a Chevy; they were feeding each other pecan pie; they were playing a game of buck-naked charades."

"And they couldn't remember with you, so they pulled out some old family name?"

"No, they went bird watching and saw a wren and a marten before they couldn't keep their hands off each other, apparently."

"Wow, I guess they were really hot for each other."

"Still are. It's very embarrassing." I pulled a face. "Anyway, my parents' naming strategy is well known in our little town, and the nurse assumed that *wren* was short for *Reynolds wrap,* about which she'd drawn her own kinky scenario. Hence the *Reyn* on the birth certificate. I send that nurse a thank-you card on my birthday every year."

The corner of his mouth was twitching. "So, I guess you really like birds."

"I hate them with a passion. That's one thing I would murder."

"Don't joke about murder." He was back to dead serious. I think he allowed himself amusement only ten seconds at a time, stopping it before it got way out of hand and he might have to smile.

"Who's joking?"

"You are, most of the time, usually to avoid a serious conversation." He seemed to see what I was wearing for the first time. I fought the urge to squirm under his laser vision which zeroed in on the "Buck Off" on my chest. "Like that shirt, for instance. How do you expect to get a date wearing that?"

I raised my eyebrows and crossed my arms over my chest. " 'Buck Off' could be interpreted a lot of different ways. It could be a warning. It could be a challenge."

I turned then and began tidying up my kitchen. I could feel him come up behind me. A little too close. "So maybe your parents passed down some of their sexual adventure to you?"

Just then, we heard the slamming of car doors out front. We hurried to the living-room window to see Trudy and Mario get out of the Miata and head for the house.

Once inside, they fussed, kissing and hugging until I waved my hands to get some space.

"Rick called us," Trudy explained.

"Big mouth," I muttered as I wandered back into the kitchen to make coffee.

"He told me to tell you he's already working on a third song, and at this rate he'd have a whole Reyn album by the end of the week. What did that mean?"

"Never mind," I said, spooning the Kona coffee beans into the grinder. "Everybody want a cup?"

"Thank you," Scythe said, "but I can't. I have someone waiting in the car."

"Bring Crandall on in," I threw out.

"It's not Crandall," Trudy observed as I followed her gaze out the window and to his car, where a willowy blonde had rolled down her window and was preening in the rearview mirror.

He'd been flirting with me with a *date* in the car? Did he never fail to surprise me with how low he could go?

"Better not keep her waiting," I said.

"I suppose not," he admitted. "It looks like she's getting restless."

Scythe turned to Mario and Trudy. "You all will take her home with you tonight?"

"The hell they will. I'm not going anywhere."

All three sighed simultaneously. Trudy shook her head and patted Scythe on the arm. "We'll stay here."

"Thank you," he said as he headed for the door.

"Hey," I called. "You have any luck with Zorita?"

He half turned as he went out the door. "Yeah, I'm orange."

"Wow." Trudy breathed as she watched him go. "Orange is passionate, creative, adventurous, ambitious." Then she turned to me. "Since he's leaving looking dissatisfied, I guess you didn't deliver your end of the deal?"

"I still don't know what the deal is. You won't tell me. He won't tell me."

"I guess he will when he's ready."

twenty-three

WE DECIDED WE WERE HUNGRY, AND EVEN though I knew if I ate at two o'clock in the morning, I'd be sorry, I threw together some *chorizo* and egg breakfast tacos anyway. I was piling on *jalapeños* and *tomatillo* salsa as I watched Mario insist on preparing Trudy's tacos for her. The girl couldn't do anything on her own when he was around, not even take off her own shoes. There he was rubbing on her feet as she ate. It made me sick, and I wondered why. Every woman should want such fawning attention from her man. I must be a masochist, because all I could do was think about the biggest jerk on the planet and the way he kissed.

Maybe I needed therapy.

Maybe the vitamin salesman would rub my feet when I ate. I could rub his bald head.

I turned back to the phone book. I was hoping I wouldn't have to call on the who-knows-who-from-whom-I-knew strategy for finding out where the Van Dykes lived. It ate up too much time and required me to dish out too much information to people who didn't need it. No luck in the Metro phone book. I tried the supplement for the outlying suburbs. Bingo. There it was. So one thing in this whole mess had been easy.

"They live in Fair Oaks." A suburb slightly north of where Ricardo had lived.

"We're going to break in?" Trudy asked, excited.

"No, Trude. What would that accomplish? You think we'll find the blood-splattered clothes just lying around? Or maybe a confession note pinned on the refrigerator?" She looked hurt, and I felt guilty. "I need to talk to the Van Dykes and get whatever I can out of them. I just wish I could even guess at what their connection would be to Ricardo."

"Maybe Ricardo was the paramedic who answered the call when her first husband died," Mario said, chewing a mouthful of taco.

Trudy and I both stared for a moment, my taco poised halfway to my mouth. "What?"

"Well, Trudy told me that the newspaper article you found said an ambulance responded when Johnstone collapsed. That was around twenty-five years ago, right? Remember the night Ricardo died—when he fixed your shoulder, he let it slip that he'd been a paramedic. I thought that was too cool. And it might have been around the same time."

Now I was really embarrassed. First Trudy finds the secret compartment, then her ding-a-ling husband remembers a major clue.

"Okay, say Ricardo was the paramedic who answered the call. So what? Why keep the article?"

"Maybe Ricardo was in love with this Sarah woman just like he was with Celine Villita. Maybe it was his chest of forgotten lovers," Trudy mused as she chewed.

Mario cooed, "Oh, you are so romantic, my sweetness."

Trudy blew him a kiss. "Maybe Sarah had a love child of Ricardo's, too."

I shook my head. "Then where are all the pictures of him or her? There weren't any in the box, and he sure kept enough of Jon."

"Maybe Sarah wasn't as accommodating as Celine was about photos."

"It just doesn't feel right," I said, finishing off my taco but not really tasting it. "If that was the case, are we looking at one of the two husbands who found out about his kid's true parentage and offed Ricardo because he's pissed? Or Ricardo two decades later finally decides he wants the kid to know he's his?"

"What if Ricardo was the paramedic who went to the Johnstones' that night, and he made a mistake that ended up killing the guy?"

"And the widow waited twenty-some-odd years to blackmail Ricardo?"

"Well, he is famous now. And rich."

"But so's she."

"Oh, yeah."

We all stared at the center of the table, deflated. Nothing seemed to make sense.

"Okay, what if Johnstone was murdered and Ricardo had proof?" Ricardo telling me the proof was in the pudding kept ringing in my head. But so did the two mistakes. Was one a mistake that killed?

"And he waited twenty years to blackmail the murderer?" Trudy took over as devil's advocate. "Why now, when he's rich and famous, instead of when he was struggling with his first salon?"

"Do you know how he really went from being a paramedic to a hairstylist?" Mario asked. "I think those paramedics make pretty good money."

"No. Ricardo always carefully deflected talk about his past. I just assumed he started at one of those five-dollar haircut places here in town, then scrimped and saved or found an investor to start his first salon."

"Maybe that's it," Trudy put in. "He screwed the investor out of his return."

"And the investor's coming at him just now? Ricardo has been successful for a long time."

We stared off into the silence for a while again. The rap at the kitchen door made all of us jump. The Antonio Banderas lookalike whose badge read "Espinoza" opened the door and peeked in. I beckoned, and he entered. "Our relief is here. They'll stay on until the seven o'clock shift change." He paused for a moment, seeming to search for the right words, then he stretched out his hand to shake mine. He handed me two business cards with the SAPD emblem. "Miss Sawyer, thank you for what you did with the lieu. I think he was getting ready to write us up. Now he's not, and that means a lot to me and Pete, the other officer on tonight. If there's anything you ever need, you can give us a call, and we'll do our best to help you."

I considered the kiss; the kid was damned cute. But I sacrificed spicing up my love life for the sake of the case. "I might need some help tomorrow."

"Yes, ma'am?"

"You know anybody who has access to twenty-five-year-old records in the medical examiner's office?"

"A guy in my rookie class, his girlfriend works in the ME's office."

I wrote down Paul Johnstone's name, the date of his death, and my fax number on a scrap of paper. "If you can swing it without getting anyone in trouble, I'd love to see the ME's report on this guy. Or, at the very least, notes on the report with cause of death, stomach contents, and the names of the paramedics who brought him in."

"No problem." Espinoza nodded and pocketed the paper. "My classmate owes me. I saved his butt when we did our shooting test."

"Thank you."

"I'm glad to help. And I'm glad you're okay. We're sorry we let that intruder get past us."

"He nearly got past my dogs, and that's practically impossible, so don't worry about it."

Espinoza looked around the table as he backed for the door. "Hey, where's your sister?"

Oops. I didn't want to embarrass him with the truth, especially since he was about to do me a huge favor, so as Trudy and Mario looked at each other, perplexed, I forced a smile. "Uh, she's gone to bed already."

He nodded and made for the door. "It's late. Good night."

We wished him well, but as soon as he was out of earshot, Trudy gave me a quelling look. "Which sister is here? Pecan or Charade?"

"My twin sister?" I smiled sheepishly.

Mario and Trudy shared another look, this one exasperated.

"It's a long story," I began.

Trudy held up her hand. "Everything's a long story for you, Reyn Marten Sawyer. You complicate life without even trying."

With that, my best friend and her husband rose.

Holding hands and giggling, they were off to my spare bedroom. I dragged myself, my girls following, up the stairs. I fell into bed wondering if I'd be awakened this time by a drill, dogs, or a dream.

It was none of the above but the insistent tapping on the door to my bedroom that woke me. I thought for a moment that it might be the murderer after me. But by the time my heart's beat accelerated and my fingertips tingled with adrenaline, I'd already convinced myself that the killer wouldn't be so polite.

I sat up. The tapping continued. "Yes?"

"Reyn?"

It might be worse than the murderer.

"Come on in, Mario." I'd tried to keep the resignation out of my voice and failed.

"No, no. You sound tired. I'll come back later."

Later? For the first time, I noticed the sun was up, too far up. I was beginning to remember throwing my alarm clock onto the floor at some point. I looked on the nightstand. Sure enough, it was gone. "What time is it?"

"Nine-fifteen."

I jumped up, swallowed the scream when I saw myself in the mirror, and ran for the bathroom. I had a nine-thirty appointment coming into the salon. The girls yawned. Char followed me, looking guilty that she'd let me sleep so long. The other two snuck up on my bed, completely unrepentant.

"Sherlyn's canceled your morning appointments because we told her you needed some rest."

"She can't cancel Miss Olive. She's ninety, has a bad heart, and it'll kill her to miss her weekly 'do. I draw the line at one body a week."

Mario was still wheedling outside the door. "Trude's gone to work and left me to keep an eye on you. I was wondering . . ."

"Wondering what, Mario?"

"Would you cut my hair?"

I met my own eyes in the mirror and shook my head at myself. Just say no. "No, Mario."

Proud of myself, I stripped off my T-shirt and got into the shower. In a minute, I was out and clean. After spraying some root lifter along my crown, I ran the blow-dryer over my hair as I toweled off. I considered shaving my head, too, as the drying took way too long. Finally, it was dry but not sleek the way it was cut to be. It looked tousled. I used some shaping wax to make it look like it was supposed to be that way. It still didn't look quite right, so I grabbed some scissors and point-cut the asymmetrical style into a short symmetrical mess. This would be much easier to keep. Too rushed to agonize over my wardrobe, I yanked on discount-store underwear and shrugged into my only padded bra, stuck my legs into some Levi's, pulled a black silk T-shirt over my head, and stepped into a pair of gray and black ostrich boots. I was cinching up a black leather belt studded with silver and brass as I opened the bedroom door.

"Aack!" I knocked my head against the doorjamb as I jumped back from Mario, who was lurking just outside.

He didn't seem to notice he'd scared three years off my life or that my hair was shorter. "But Reyn, I was just watching Kelly and Regis on TV, and George Clooney got this buzz cut. Trudy loves George Clooney."

"Go rent her some old *ER* episodes."

"But he doesn't have the hair buzz in those."

Was I going to have to listen to this all day? I would

have to ditch him at some point. What better way than to get the clippers and make him so embarrassed he wouldn't be seen in public? I reminded myself of the consequences as I skipped down the stairs—Mario's whining, Trudy's certain retribution. But on the upside, I would be free today, and I wouldn't be bothered about doing his hair again until the quarter-inch buzz grew out.

It might be worth it.

The clock read nine twenty-five. I let the dogs out into the backyard and pushed the button on the coffeemaker, which I so handily set up the night before and forgot to turn on for my company. Mario followed me like a fourth dog. Since the *chorizo* still sat in my stomach as if it had re-formed into the pig overnight, I eschewed breakfast and went straight for the door that led to the salon.

My hand was on the knob when Mario started whining again. "Please, Reyn, just consider it."

"Come on, Mario, let's do it."

His mouth opened and shut a few times. He shook his head before a sound finally came out. "Really? You mean it?"

"Yup. Get into position, and make it snappy. I'll be ready to start when I get there."

He lumbered off.

Behind me, a familiar and unwelcome bass said, "Just what I like, a woman who takes control of her sexuality."

I turned around to see Scythe, arms crossed over his chest, eyebrow hitched, at my office door.

"You know, I'd always heard when one was oversexed, it meant you didn't have to think about it all the time. Guess you blow that theory."

"Who says I'm oversexed?"

"Well, you're more sexed than I am, since you've had more dates than I have in the last twenty-four hours."

"Who says that was my date? That could've been my sister. My *twin* sister."

I glanced into my office and saw a few pages on the fax machine. The autopsy results on Johnstone?

"You're having sex with your *sister*?" I said a little too loudly. Heads popped out of the rooms where Daisy Dawn was doing nails, Alejandra was foiling a highlight, Autumn was trimming a bob, and Enrique was finishing a flat-top. As Scythe waved at the audience, I scooted into my room and grabbed the clippers, hoping he'd be distracted enough to pass my office without looking inside.

I started at the hairline and ran up to the top before I realized I had the number two blade in. Okay, it was going to be a little shorter than he'd wanted it. Mario screamed, "Wait! Wait! I changed my mind!"

"Too late now. But the good news is, it'll grow out. Even faster than you think, because summer's right around the corner, and hot weather makes hair grow faster."

Scythe finally meandered in and stood off to the right of my chair. He looked pained as he watched Mario's black hair falling to the ground. I had the nearly uncontrollable urge to shift the clippers to *his* head. Maybe I was a sadist, after all.

I was finished in record time, and I spun Mario around and ran my hand over his scalp to make sure his peach fuzz was even. Damned if he didn't look almost handsome. Trudy was going to thank me.

Mario was blithering so hard he couldn't look in the mirror. Super, guess my babysitter was out of commission for the day, or at least until enough people told him he looked good. I had to be out of there ASAP. Mario rose and went sobbing down the hall.

Now, to get rid of the badge.

"What'd you do to your hair? Stick your finger in a light socket?"

I wanted to tell him where to stick his finger but decided to be cool-headed and mature instead.

"What can I do for you?" I asked, clippers poised invitingly.

"Uh." Scythe shifted on his toes. I finally had knocked him off-balance. Did it only take a hairstyling tool? Next time, I'd try snapping scissors when he got smart-ass. He cleared his throat. I tried to look earnest. "I came to find out why you were at Illusions last night."

"Who's the rat?"

"That's none of your concern."

"Well, then, why I was there is none of your concern." I started the motor on the clippers on the pretense of oiling them. Scythe shivered.

"The informant likes to dress like a schoolgirl," he blurted.

Now I knew whom to avoid, as if I would ever again need the services of a transvestite club. I really had just wanted a concession from him. He gave, so I should. "Okay, I was there to show one of the performers two photos to see if they could identify whom Ricardo met at the club recently."

I had Scythe's full attention now. It also looked like I had earned a modicum more of respect and a modicum more of irritation. Probably a wash all around. "The two photos were of . . . ?

"Senator Sal Villita and a Mike Van Dyke."

I'd shocked him. Boy, that felt good. "And was it either man?"

"The redhead couldn't be sure it was Van Dyke. But it certainly wasn't Villita. Ricardo met with a middle-aged *gringo* tennis player."

The relief was palpable. I imagine dealing with a political bigwig was one of the cops' biggest headaches. "Why did you even consider Villita?"

"Because his son is really Ricardo's biological child."

"What?" Scythe looked pained instead of amazed. "How do you know this?"

"I haven't gotten a DNA sample, if that's what you're asking. But I talked to Celine Villita and met the son, Jon, and his speech, mannerisms, walk, and profile are dead ringers for Ricardo." I left out the part about her threatening me. I thought it might make him so mad that it would distract him from the important information.

"And you knew to go nosing around at the Villitas' why? Because you picked the highest-profile family in San Antonio and decided to make life difficult for yourself, or what?" He was getting angry. Aw, I didn't know he cared.

"Ricardo kept a photo of Celine and photos of Jon."

"You saw this where?"

"At his house."

"We didn't notice them," Scythe muttered to himself, running his hand through his hair. Then he got back into laser-vision mode and tried to extract honesty out of me. "And you got into his house how?"

"I had a key."

"You didn't tell me you had possession of a key." Scythe looked a little suspicious. I think he still entertained the idea that Ricardo and I did the nasty. Well, let him think it.

"I borrowed the key." I didn't want Gerald to get in trouble. "Without the owner's knowledge."

"Okay." He put one hand up. "I don't want to know. Don't try to tell me. Just tell me who this Mike guy is and why you had a photo of him."

"He's a rich scion of San Antonio society. I'm ashamed of you that you don't keep up with the Who's Who around here."

Laser blues heated a hole through my head. "And the second part of my question? Why you had a photo of him?"

"Oh, because Ricardo did."

"House, too?"

"Right." He moved toward the doorway. "I'm gone. And remember, you have a tail. Don't lose it, it's for your own protection."

"Being a devil is protection in and of itself," I agreed.

It took him a few seconds to process my rejoinder. Then he shook his head but couldn't stop the smile. Wow. Good thing he didn't smile often. I wouldn't have many pithy comebacks with that looking me in the face. I stopped thinking again. Just briefly, because as soon as it appeared, the smile was gone, and so was Scythe.

He hadn't seen the fax. And I was dying to see it, only I had Miss Olive coming unsteadily down the hall at me first. This investigating stuff was going to teach me to be patient whether I wanted to be or not.

twenty-four

AS I DROVE DOWN THE SHADED STREETS OF FAIR Oaks, I tried to get my thoughts in order. I glanced in the rearview mirror and saw the dark sedan that had followed me since I got on McCullough still behind me. The police tail, no doubt. It should've bugged me, but it was actually a comfort. Things were coming together too fast for me to assimilate. The report that Espinoza's friend's *sancha* had faxed told me Johnstone had some high-dollar vodka, steak, potato, butter, sour cream, asparagus, and geranium pudding in his stomach contents. Geranium pudding? I'd called a chef friend of mine, who said that geranium desserts were a gourmet food. That fit for a rich man, I supposed.

Hey, Ricardo, what proof was in this pudding?

The cause of death was officially listed as massive loss of blood. Paul Johnstone suffered from ulcers, and one had burned a hole in his stomach, so he bled out internally. The medical examiner had made notations that it seemed the victim's apparent recent vomiting (according to the widow) had exacerbated the situation and could have caused the hole in his stomach to split wider. There was no cause listed for the vomiting. His arteries were clogged but not enough to kill him. His liver was compromised but not enough to shut down completely. He'd had enough alcohol in his system to dull the pain of his bleeding ulcer and have him shrug it off as a bout of the flu.

The guy was a mess, but something told me it probably wasn't an accident that he'd died that day. The problem was, that something was nowhere in print.

A Ricardo Montoya was listed as one of the paramedics who transported Johnstone.

So now I had more pieces, but they had yet to fit together. Ricardo had a secret, out-of-wedlock love child raised by the most famous man in San Antonio. He was a penniless paramedic who answered the call on a wealthy man who died. Not long after, he gave up one career and bought a business, with which he became a smashing success. Twenty-five years later, he was stabbed to death with a brush pick. The child he never claimed may run for political office.

I sighed. How did it all fit together?

I was going to have to go shake the Van Dykes' tree and see what fell out.

I felt a bit claustrophic for a moment and wondered why. I glanced into the rearview mirror again and saw the sedan was riding a little close to my bumper. Jerky cops, what were they trying to do, intimidate me on the isolated stretch of two-lane road that fell off into ten-foot-deep ditches on either side? Before I knew it, the sedan pulled next to the truck on the left and swerved, banging into the front panel. I slammed on the brakes, countered the swerve, narrowly avoiding the ditch. The car sped ahead.

Then a bubble-gum blue Miata appeared seemingly out of nowhere, buzzed past me, and chased the sedan.

Yipes. I guess Mario got over his hair after all.

Before I could get back on the road, another dark sedan (I could've sworn it was a Crown Victoria) zoomed past after the other two.

Now, maybe a bunch of people were running really late to work today and I just got in the way, but I doubted it. I flirted with the idea of going after Mario to stop him but realized we'd be going around in circles, as the bad guy after me would have found me and started chasing me again. Instead of going to Mario's rescue, I dialed his cell phone.

"Hola!" I could hear the screech of tires.

"Mario, I thought you were supposed to be baby-sitting me?"

"You left me! You butchered my *pelo bonito,* and then you left me!"

"Yes, and now you've left me."

Screech. *"Dios mío! Es claro. Espera.* Wait for me, Reyn. I'll turn around. *Ai-ee.* Someone is after me now. A big black car!"

"Mario, that's the police. Get out of their way, and let them catch the guy."

"Hokay. I'll be back to you in a few minutes."

"No, Mario, that scared me nearly to death. I'm on my way home. I'll meet you there."

"Promise?"

"You're breaking up, Mario. See you at home."

I cut the connection just as the Van Dyke house rose above me, a pinky-peach stucco monolith on the hill, with a driveway that wound its way up ostentatiously, lined by atrociously expensive transplanted palm trees. Most of the estates in Fair Oaks went out of their way to blend in with the Hill Country scenery of craggy limestone, sprawling live oaks, and patches of cedar. This one looked out of place—as if it belonged in Miami, above the coast at Cabo San Lucas, along the French Riveria, not just off a two-lane road in a small, albeit wealthy, community just north of San Antonio with no water in sight. I stopped at the gate and pressed the intercom button. I hadn't pondered how I was going to talk my way in. With my luck, I knew whatever plan I fashioned would come apart at the seams. I decided to put one together as I went along instead.

"Oh, you're early," a terribly affected female voice blared over the speakers. "I'll buzz you in, dahling."

"Thank you."

Wow. That was easy. Wonder who I was supposed to be?

Dahling? Uh-oh. I remembered Trudy's client in Terrell Hills and who her darling was. Mixing with the moneyed set without the convenience of hiding behind my blow-dryer was making me nervous. Maybe I should've had a plan.

The gates opened with the speed of a sloth, and I wound my way quickly up the limestone-studded driveway before she realized I wasn't who she thought I was.

I passed a gardener planting gold columbine under the palm trees. I waved. Mouth open, he looked at me as if I were landing a spaceship on the property. Guess not too many of the Van Dykes' guests acknowledged the help. As I parked, I saw another gardener up in a palm, trimming a loose frond. I decided not to call a greeting to him for fear he'd lose his grip on the trunk and fall to the ground in shock.

Sarah Johnstone Van Dyke must have been watching my approach, because she opened the door with practiced panache as I hit the top porch step. *Porch* really wasn't a good description of what was an *Entrance* with a capital *E*. It was meant to impress. So was she. Sarah was a perfect high-society specimen with her just-past-shoulder-length, fourteen-karat blond hair straight side-parted and drawn back in the newest sleek look (à la Gwyneth Paltrow) held at the nape with a jeweled barrette. The style, which was calculated for a cosmopolitan image, set off a sharp-featured (almost ferretlike), approaching-fifty face that had been carefully preserved by a Dallas plastic surgeon. I wonder if they know plastic surgeons leave their mark as well as artists do if you know what to look for. I'd done the hair around enough of his faces to know one on sight. Her body was a petite model size two, including surgically enhanced breasts, dressed in a flowing floral print blouse with peasant sleeves, white linen capris, and rainbow-patten leather sandals straight out of last month's Neiman Marcus catalogue.

She was so perfectly presented she could be mistaken for a mannequin, except for the eyes. Her green eyes glittered with cunning. Cunning isn't necessarily smart—cunning is knowing how to manipulate people to get ahead, cunning is knowing how many lies to tell to get what you want, and cunning could be more dangerous than smart any day.

I guessed that her cunning was dulled by her immense wealth, and that was in my favor.

She introduced herself, for which I thanked God that she hadn't embraced me in a steamy kiss. I would've been out of there without the information I sought, that was for sure.

"I am so honored to meet you," I said, groveling. She preened for a moment.

"I'm so glad you're here," she gushed. "I think it will be such a tremendous article."

Article? So I was a reporter. And she was welcoming, so it was going to be a feature. "It should be," I hedged.

"This strategy should really work, slipping the fact that Mike is going to run for the state representative seat into an article about our home."

Ah-ha. Did Ricardo know? Did he meet with Van Dyke to tell him to lay off the challenge against Jon? But why, then, would he have the twenty-five-year-old article about Johnstone's death? He must have had something to blackmail Van Dyke with. But what? Maybe he'd known sweet Sarah had knocked him off with pudding and could prove it. But how? There was no trace of poison in his system, according to the autopsy. But then, coroners in the late seventies didn't have the technology they did today . . .

"It will really turn the tables on the media, have them thinking they've uncovered some big secret, and they will be all over it like mud on a pig."

Oops, she was showing her common roots? Was she a farm girl turned society matron? Sarah caught herself and smiled. "Instead of a simple declaration that's turned into nothing but a sound bite at ten, Mike's campaign will be off with a bang. CNN or Fox might even pick it up."

"Hopefully."

"My husband is down at the tennis courts. He practically lives in his tennis whites . . ."

Double *ah-ha*.

"So I'll take you down there after we talk, and you can meet him."

"Perfect."

"Where's your photographer?" She looked around.

"We come separately. I get the copy and scout things out for him and then make recommendations about what to shoot."

"I see. What do you want to do first, look around or do the interview?"

"Let me get some background first, then I'll look around, then we can talk some more."

"That will suit," she said expansively. "I've canceled my masseuse for today."

"How fortunate." I smiled. "Tell me, how long have you lived here?"

"Nearly twenty years. Right after we got married, we tried living at my estate in Terrell Hills, but it was difficult for Mike to make it his own. And it was difficult for me with all the memories."

I nodded. "I understand completely. That was the home you lived in with your first husband, Paul Johnstone?"

She stepped back, surprised. "You've done your research, haven't you?"

"That's my job."

Sarah seemed satisfied, but I would have to tread carefully from here on out. "Paul died in the house, and I couldn't go into that room again without remembering how horrible it was that night."

"What happened?"

"Paul had been complaining of stomach pains for weeks. His color was bad. I thought his ulcer was getting worse, and his food experiments weren't helping matters."

"What food experiments?"

"Somebody had talked him into this gourmet dessert discovery using everyday plants and flowers—so he had the gardeners bringing him geranium, rose petals, lavender—depending on what he talked the cook into making that night."

"How did they taste?"

"Truly awful, like rancid lemons, most of them. I don't know how he choked them down. Of course, he chased every bite with a mouthful of Absolut. I think I tried two, and that was it for me. I stuck with Godiva chocolates from then on."

Had the gardener brought in a poisonous plant accidentally a time or two? Or was it on purpose? I racked my brain for plants my sister told her kids to stay away from when they had their poison plant drill at home (Pecan is very militaristic in her parenting)—azalea, poinsettia, oleander.

"So poor Mr. Johnstone just keeled over, and you called for an ambulance?"

"Why are you so interested in this?" She stepped back, suspicious. "I thought the article was about the house and the campaign."

I leaned into her like I had a confession to make. "I'm sorry. I'm freelance for other publications, and I've been hired to do a big spread on the history of paramedics for *Parade,* you know, that insert that goes *nationwide* in newspapers on Sundays?"

She nodded eagerly, cunning glittering to attention in those green orbs.

"And I thought I might be able to put in a quotation from you. The editors might want a photo, too, since I'd guess that cameras love you." I waved off the idea. "But never mind, I apologize for bringing it up."

That did it. Her greed for publicity won out over suspicion. "No. I suppose I could help you. What did you need to know?"

"How were the paramedics who responded to Mr. Johnstone?"

"They were fabulous, so soothing in my time of need, I just couldn't have gotten through the ordeal without them." *Me, me, me.* Her husband might have died of medical neglect. She probably mobbed them before they could get to poor Paul.

"In fact, one of them was so considerate that I took care of him as a little thank-you."

Uh-oh, here it came, she did the nasty with Ricardo, and they had a love child, and . . . what? The jealous ghost of Paul is the one who killed him? Mike Van Dyke finally found out and blew a fuse twenty years later? Maybe she and Ricardo had a long-standing affair, and he found out, but, geez, I couldn't see Ricardo with this affected mannequin of a woman. Celine Villita was more like it, because she was human under her veneer. Sarah Johnstone Van Dyke's only sign of humanity was selfishness.

I sucked in a deep breath and went for the details. "Took care of him?"

"Yes." She was obviously proud of herself. "A, uh, friend, recommended that it might be a nice gesture to thank the paramedic with a monetary gift. Kind of like a tip."

"A tip."

"Well, maybe more than a tip, it was fifty thousand dollars."

"Fifty thousand dollars?" I blurted, trying not to choke to death on my tongue.

"Oh, please don't print that. You don't think the man will get in trouble for accepting it, do you?"

"Not now."

"What do you mean?"

"Not after all this time."

"Oh, good."

"You don't happen to remember his name, do you?"

Sarah narrowed her eyes. "Why do you want to know that? It doesn't seem like something you'd put in the article."

"I might want to find him and talk to him," I clarified by the seat of my pants. "For the article."

"My husband said we shouldn't have anything else to do with him." She crossed her arms over her chest.

"What does your husband have to do with it?"

She realized her mistake too late. "He, uh, was the friend I was talking about. Mike helped me through that difficult time so well, that's how we became so close and fell in love. Living through a hardship will do that, you know. Look at the movie *Titanic*."

Yeah, murdering your husband so you could marry your "friend" was real hardship, all right. This was the scenario beginning to form in my mind. I seriously doubted that Mike encouraged his "friend" Sarah to gift Ricardo with such a large sum out of the goodness of his heart. Ricardo knew something and promised to keep it a secret with a sudden influx of cash that he turned into an empire. It took me a moment to come to grips with the fact that my longtime mentor could be so calculating and amoral, but I'd always known Ricardo to be oppor-tunistic. I just didn't know it was to this degree.

A deadly degree, apparently.

Sarah was watching me suspiciously.

"Oh, *Titanic*, I just love that movie," I lied. The guardedness in her face cleared somewhat, and she picked up the movie and went on about it ad nauseam.

I nodded at times I hoped were appropriate and thought more about what her revelations meant. My instincts told me Sarah was in the dark about any murder. Yeah, she married the old codger for money and might have been doing a "friend" for fun, but I thought Mike was behind any nefarious dealings. To give Mike the benefit of the doubt, I could say that maybe he and Sarah were just caught fooling around by Ricardo, and that's what the hush money was for. But $50,000 was a lot of money in the eighties (heck, I thought it was a lot of money now), and why would Ricardo be dead twenty-five years later if the secret he was protecting wasn't against any law but a biblical one?

The political race and the apparent coincidence that Van Dyke chose to run against Villita's (Ricardo's) son bugged me.

I looked at Cinderella on my wrist and exclaimed at the time. "I guess we'd better get back to the original reason for my visit."

Sarah nodded, only slightly disappointed to be derailed from describing Leonardo di Caprio.

"Does anyone know your husband plans to run for office?"

"I don't see what this has to do with—"

I held up a hand. "I just need to know how big a revelation this will be. The bigger the story, the better placement in the magazine."

"Oh, of course," Sarah agreed. "The only person who knows is the chairman of the county's Republican Party."

Whose wife is the friend of the friend of Mama Tru's. The friend who gets her hair done by Ricardo and must have told Ricardo that Van Dyke planned to run against

Jon Villita. What did Ricardo do with that information?

"It'll be a big surprise, then."

"Oh, yes!" she breathed.

"Señora!?" A maid called out to us from one of the thousand glass doors along the back side of the house.

"What is it? Didn't I tell you I wasn't to be disturbed?"

The maid looked secretly pleased to have pissed on her patron's parade. She hid it well, though. "But, Señora, there is someone at the gate who says she is a reporter."

Uh-oh.

Sarah looked at me and blinked. The liar in me kicked in just in time. "Maybe the media's found out about Mike's run. Do you think?"

"It certainly is possible." She was already calculating the degree of attention the media would be paying her. She was bursting with excitement and hid it poorly with a big sigh. "I suppose we're about to be mobbed with cameras and reporters and live TV vans. I must go and deal with this. Why don't you go down and talk to my husband, and I will join you as soon as I can?"

"Good idea."

"I can get Isadora"—she waved toward the maid—"to take you down there."

"No, no need to take her from her work. I can find the tennis courts." The hell I would. I was out of there. I had a feeling Mike Van Dyke knew exactly who I was and might make it a mission to see I never got out of there.

Sarah hustled off in her pencil-heeled sandals, and I looked for a way back to the driveway that would keep me hidden until she and the reporter got out of sight. I was picking my way through a patch of tropical bushes when a man with a machete jumped out from behind a hibiscus.

"Ack!" I screamed as my heinie got friendly with the pointed end of a bird-of-paradise leaf.

"I'm sorry." The gardener I'd waved at earlier put down the machete and helped me out of the bird-of-paradise.

His face was weathered from being out in the sun for years, but it was warm and inviting.

"No, I should say I'm sorry, because I think I startled you earlier."

"Oh, you did. We don't get many folks up here who pay us any mind. Sometimes I go home wondering if I'm invisible."

I shook my head. "Worked for the Van Dykes long?"

"Nearly thirty years. Mr. Johnstone was first class. Van Dyke, now, he's been a Stalin since he moved from the cabana into the big house."

"What do you mean?"

"He worked here, was one of my assistants."

"He was? I heard Mr. Johnstone liked to use plants from his garden in his menus. Did Van Dyke happen to help compile the mixings for those gourmet desserts?"

The gardener wrinkled his already wrinkled brow. "You know, he did. He actually talked Mr. Johnstone into it."

"Geranium isn't poisonous, is it?"

"No, ma'am." He warmed quickly to the subject of the garden. "You know, the only plant we had that was poisonous on the place back then was oleander. Another one of Mike's projects. He talked Mr. Johnstone into planting a whole row of it along the back fence. Pretty blooms in the spring, but I'm not terribly fond of it myself. I've got grandkids. I know the sap of the leaves is bitter, and they wouldn't eat much of it, but you don't like to take chances with that kind of thing."

"No, sir," I agreed as my heart pounded in my chest. "So the sap's bitter, kind of like rotten lemons?"

"Yes, ma'am, just like that, but it would take more than a bite to kill you, and they say that the taste of the cardenolide glycoside toxin would stop anyone with sense, but . . ." He shrugged.

"Better safe than sorry," I offered. He nodded. I held out my hand and thanked him for saving me from my leaf stabbing. He retrieved his machete and went back to work. I turned and had made my way through the grounds and almost to my truck, when I saw a flash of white out of the corner of my eye. I knew without looking that I should hurry.

"You!"

It was the same greeting I got from Short, Hairy, and Menacing, but I didn't think Van Dyke was going to be quite as nice as the Illusions manager had been. I ran, leaped across the massive porch, and made it to my truck just as the front door opened. Sarah and the real reporter walked onto the porch. Mike Van Dyke collided with the reporter as I zoomed down the driveway, trying not to go up on two wheels as I skidded around the ridiculous hairpin turns.

As soon as I was out of the gate, I dialed my cell phone. I blew out a breath and started to think about how far I'd misjudged Ricardo's character. I didn't have long to come to grips with it, since Gerald answered on the second ring. "Hi, Boss."

"Don't call me that, Gerald."

"Oh, okay," he said, resigned. "I knew you'd want someone else for the job eventually."

"No, that's not what I mean." I rolled my eyes skyward. "I mean, just don't call me Boss. I can barely boss myself, much less anyone else."

"Are you all right, Reyn?"

"I'm great. I just need some information from you about Ricardo. It goes back a ways."

"I've got everything computerized, and here I sit. So go ahead and ask."

"Can you find out how much money Ricardo used to set up his first salon?"

"Hold on," Gerald said. I heard the computer keys tapping. "He set up an account in the Ricardo's, Inc., name in 1979 with fifty thousand dollars."

"Cash?"

"I don't know, Reyn, that detail isn't in here. But, you know, that would be a lot of cash for someone to have on hand. Unless an investor gave it to him that way, which would be a little fishy. I have to dig through some file boxes, but I'll check for you. By the way, when you were at my house, do you remember seeing a set of keys to Ricardo's house lying around anywhere?"

"Uh-oh, Gerald, you're breaking up. I'll call you back when I have a better signal." I hung up. I kept an eye on the rearview mirror as I took an unusual route home. Celine Villita had threatened me, I was being followed, and Mike Van Dyke looked like he'd wanted to get his hands on me, and not for an autograph. For the first time since I'd started my crusade, I felt I was in too deep with no way out. That's when I swallowed my pride and dialed a number I thought I'd never call.

twenty-five

THE CELL PHONE NUMBER SENT ME TO THE VOICE mailbox. I dialed the office number.

"Scythe's desk." I'd know that gum smack anywhere. "Crandall here."

I greeted Crandall. "Scythe's not around?"

"No, Sherlock, he's not. What can I do for you?"

"He wasn't by chance following me earlier, was he?"

"He has better things to do than babysit you, Sherlock."

"Hey, Crandall, I've got a copy of the limited edition of Cher's smash hits if you tell me where Scythe is."

The long pause told me he was tempted. Finally, he smacked his gum. "No can do, Sherlock. You'll have to wait to jump his bones."

"That's not what this is about!"

"Sure, then tell me what it's about."

I knew I should go ahead and lay out all I'd learned that morning to Crandall. After all, a cop was a cop. It wasn't as if Scythe took me so seriously, but Crandall took me less so.

"Come on, you're burning daylight," he said.

I went through the autopsy result and being followed, my visit to the Van Dykes' house. I told him I'd narrowed it down to Villita (rather, a hired hit man) or Van Dyke. He listened until I finished, then he laughed.

"You're telling me you think a U.S. senator killed the Salon King to keep him from ratting out about whose DNA the kid carries because the son's running for office and that might damage his campaign?"

"Or . . . it was Van Dyke," I began.

"The lawnmower-turned-million-dollar-check-casher killed the Salon King to protect a secret that might be (a) that he and the wife were playing hide the salami decades ago or, worse, (b) that he killed the wife's husband to get the moolah. Or both. The Salon King took money to keep his trap shut a long time ago but was about to renege on the deal. We don't know why, but it could be because the rich ex-weed-puller is about to take on the Salon King's secret son in said political race."

"Right, sort of." His sarcastic delivery made it sound far-fetched.

"And we have zero evidence of all this."

"Well, you could probably get Sarah Johnstone Van Dyke to admit on tape that she gave Ricardo that money."

"I hate to tell you this, Sherlock, but monetary gifts aren't against the law."

"But—"

"Sorry to say." He paused to smack his gum. "I'm not buying this, but *As the World Turns* might, unless they've already used it as episode 454. The fact is, I think you've listened to the gossip of one too many bored housewives. That and all those hair chemicals you snort every day obviously form a potent combination."

"Except—"

"Here's some advice. Let us do the investigating. You go back to cutting hair. I hear you gave yourself a new 'do. Why not try another one if you've got some extra creative energy on your hands? I'll tell Scythe you called. Try to stay out of trouble, would ya?"

He hung up in my ear just as I'd opened my mouth for my counterattack. Sure, he'd tell Scythe. And why did Scythe tell him about my new hairstyle? I could just see the two of them yukking it up. Muttering to myself, I threw my phone onto the passenger seat and checked the rearview mirror as I turned into the salon parking lot. I couldn't see any dark sedans. Still, I leaped out of the truck and hustled to the salon door, wincing as I passed the dent on the panel, wincing again when I passed the bubble-gum blue Miata.

With the weekend approaching, the salon was buzzing with activity. Every stylist had a customer. Daisy Dawn had one set of nails in her chair and two waiting. I had appointments booked until six o'clock. I figured I was safe from bloodthirsty killers until evening. I didn't think whoever was after me wanted to take on handfuls of women in perm curlers, foiled chemicals, and wet acrylics.

Or Mario.

The hero in question was regaling the lobby with the harrowing version of his narrow escape from death and how he saved me from certain doom. When I walked in, he nearly killed me with a bear hug.

"Where have you been? We've been so worried."

The two women in the love seat whom I didn't know nodded, eyes wide. Sherlyn had her thousand-pound shoes kicked off and was reviewing her pedicure.

Strangers were terrified for me. Employees could care less. How heartwarming. I turned back to Mario. "I took the long way home to make sure I wasn't being followed."

"Oh. It seemed like forever. I was about to come looking for you again."

Darn. Lost opportunity.

"Thanks anyway. I'm home now to stay." I left him to finish his tale.

One of the women sighed. "I think you look just like George Clooney. You know, he was on Regis this morning."

I paused a step. Who was the hero now?

All my appointments wanted to talk about Ricardo. If they hadn't seen the snippets of the funeral on television, then they'd heard about it and thought I was brave. I wasn't sure if the bravery was for wearing the fuchsia spandex in public or for my challenge to uncover his secrets. Maybe a little of both.

I was blowing dry my last appointment—a point-cut wedge I'd dyed a lovely shade of R-3—when the phone rang. I'd sent Sherlyn home already when the salon cleared out, and Mario had gone into my house to make himself a snack. Scythe had never called, and I was tempted just to let the damn thing go to the answering machine. In the ensuing hours since my chat with Crandall, I'd decided that I shouldn't share my theory with Scythe after all. It did sound ridiculous. Mike Van Dyke probably recognized me from TV and newspapers and hadn't wanted a rabble rouser poking around his precious tropical garden. The car following me was probably just a heavy for Villita, there to tell me to lay off the little woman so she didn't cry and run her mascara. He was probably the same guy who'd broken into my house and was likely behind bars right now, caught by the cop who'd been tailing us.

"Transformations, more than meets the eye."

Traffic noise blared into the phone. "Reyn? This is Mama Tru. Is Mario there?"

I sucked in a breath to answer, but she went on before I could. "My Trans Am is broken down here on Loop 410 and Nacogdoches and—" *Honk!*

"Mama Tru?" I yelled.

"Asshole!" she screamed. "Not you, Reyn dear. I'm sorry."

"Mama Tru, you just sit tight, you hear? I'm sending Mario to get you right now."

"No, no. I know he has to protect you from getting killed—" *Zoom. Beep.*

"It sounds like you're in more danger of that than I am, Mama." Mario walked down the hall, half a sandwich with what looked like olives and portabello mushrooms hanging out of his mouth. "He's on his way."

I filled Mario in and shoved him, protesting, out the salon door, down the steps, and into the Miata. "Trudy and I will be back in a little while," he said out the window. "She's probably almost done at her job. Once I get Mama taken care of—"

"Don't worry about anything, Mario. Look." I pointed at the front of the house, where I could see a marked police car. I waved at the officer, who looked bored out of his gourd. He waved back. "I've already got company."

"Okay." Mario didn't look too sure, but he drove off anyway.

I headed back to the salon, turned off all the fans, lights, and one curling iron (I'd have to talk to Enrique about that tomorrow). I set the alarm and went into my house. I wondered with a tinge of pique how Scythe had made out that day. I'd bet anything he'd gone through the list I'd given him, probably found the likely suspect and put him behind bars already. I probably was off in soap opera land, and they'd have a good laugh over me. Meanwhile, I was still having trouble reconciling the friend I knew with the man I'd come to know with my digging. I guess Scythe was right when he told me to leave well enough alone. I hated that.

The girls were crying outside. I let them inside and almost immediately heard a distant boom. They ran to the right side of the house. I followed, and we saw a plume of smoke coming from down the street, out of sight.

"Geez, if it's not one thing, it's forty," I muttered amid the barking. Then I realized I sounded just like my mother and gave myself a mental slap.

I hurried to the front window. The cop car was gone. I thought he might be on top of things, but just in case, I thought I ought to call 911. I picked up the phone. It was dead. Maybe someone had hit a telephone pole. Did they still use poles, or did they bury everything underground? I guess I should be more on top of advances in general technology instead of just in hairstyling tools.

Where was my cell phone?

I remembered throwing it onto the passenger seat. Maybe Scythe had tried to call me on it. I forgave him. Sort of.

I told the girls to stay—which I doubt they heard, they were baying so loudly—then, grabbing the keys out of my purse, I went out the kitchen door. I retrieved the phone, saw I'd missed four calls, and entered my voice mailbox. Another boom echoed from down the street. I walked around the house to see if I could discern more before I called 911. Plus, I was selfish enough to want to hear my messages first. Scythe was the first call. "I don't know where you are, but get home so I can get a guy on you. I'll be there to talk to you as soon as I can."

Hmm. Sounded like he might be taking me seriously after all.

Or just wanted me to stay out of his way. A more likely scenario.

I'd reached the front porch, when I looked up and caught sight of a pair of male legs behind the gardenia bush next to the steps.

"Well, well, what took you so long?" I asked, hanging up the phone.

"I had to wait until everyone left, stupid bitch. I've been out here all afternoon."

I was just registering the fact that this wasn't Scythe's baritone—it wasn't a baritone at all but a weedy tenor—when he leaped forward and put a vise grip on my upper arm. If I hadn't been so busy assuming it was my friendly nemesis, the too-tan legs with knees too knobby to be Scythe's (remember, I'd felt those knees) would've been a dead giveaway. Bad play on words, I thought, since dead is probably just how this guy wanted me. The girls were going nuts inside, banging their noses against the window. I heard sirens down the street. Oh, if only one of the police cars or fire engines passed by my house, maybe I could get someone's attention. I struggled, kicking out and bucking with my body. He knocked the car keys and cell phone out of my hand; they both skidded across the porch and off into the flower bed. He wrapped his arms around me, and I saw he was wearing tennis whites and snowy Reboks.

Uh-oh. Maybe I shook the Van Dykes' tree a little too hard.

"Damn, damn, damn."

"Shut up," he hissed, slapping a piece of duct tape over my mouth. Shoot, he'd taken away my best weapon.

Some petunias started singing the *William Tell* Overture. Now I could tell where my phone was, if I could just get this cretin off me. I kicked him in the crotch, and his grip loosened for an instant. I dove for the petunias, hanging my torso off the end of the porch. He grabbed my feet and sat on them. I searched the flowers, beheading them with abandon. The phone, with my superior luck, had stopped ringing. I felt eyes on me and looked deeper into the bushes to Rick and Laurel's white cat, Merlin. I wondered why she wasn't heading for the hills with all this noise, and then I remembered she was deaf. I was trying to send her a Dr. Doolittle message to run for help, when my fingers touched something metal, small, and cylindrical. Not the phone. I lifted it up and saw the can of pepper spray that I'd lost out of my purse when Jolie ran into me the morning Ricardo died.

Van Dyke was dragging me toward the front door. I drew my hands up at my chest to hide the can. We'd reached the front door, with me still facedown on the porch. I could feel him grab the back of my shirt, lifting me up. His arm was wrapped around my waist; his other hand reached up to grab my hands. I shoved them down. Up. Down.

"This isn't a Laurel and Hardy movie." He swore and grabbed my hair instead and pulled hard. *Ouch.*

"Open the door," he ordered. I don't know what he'd planned to do about the dogs that were ready to rip him limb from limb, but that wasn't my problem. He wouldn't get that far. I put my finger on the trigger of the pepper spray and twisted the doorknob with my other hand, opening the door just as I aimed behind me and sprayed.

"Aaaaaa!" Van Dyke let me go and fell back as I slipped through the door, shut it, and threw the dead bolt.

The girls were drowning me in dog spit. I ripped the duct tape off my face, taking some skin with it. Worse than ouch. I don't know which of us was swearing more, me or Van Dyke. I peeked. He was writhing on the edge of the porch, trying to get his skinny tanned legs back under him, tears streaming down the right side of his face. It looked like I'd only gotten him in one eye.

Where was Scythe when you needed him?

I heard the *William Tell* Overture outside again. Damn.

I wondered if I could make it to the back of the house and jump into my truck before he got to me. The keys! They were in the petunias, too. Where was that extra set I had? Why wasn't I more organized?

"That will be my if-I-live resolution—to get organized," I muttered to myself as I ran to the kitchen. Char followed. Beau and Cab stayed at the window, barking at Van Dyke.

I yanked open my junk drawer and started throwing things out. No keys. Glass shattered at the front of the house. The dogs went ballistic, nails skidding on hardwood. Char booked it out the kitchen door to get in on the action. I was a little worried that one of them would get hurt fighting Van Dyke, but I knew they'd have him cornered in the living room long enough for me to get the phone and call the police. I ran down the hallway and caught sight of a gremlinish white ball of fur headed straight for me, right before I was nearly mowed down by my own three dogs. Legs tangled in crazed canines, I nearly fell as they raced up the stairs after what I belatedly realized was Merlin.

How did Merlin get into the house?

I seriously doubted he threw himself through the plate-glass window to save me, despite my Dr. Doolittle message. I felt a little guilty anyway, although I didn't see any blood.

I heard Van Dyke picking his way through the glass.

I ran for the kitchen door and was caught again.

This time, I felt tears welling in my eyes at the hopelessness of it all. My dogs were upstairs, cat cornered, baying at the tops of their lungs. They could stay that way for hours. The sirens were drowning them out completely, so even the neighbors wouldn't wonder about the noise. My cell phone was outside, and a murderer was inside with his tennis-fit arms wrapped around me.

Now I felt the point of a knife against my throat.

Well, I guess I could've hidden the kitchen knives while I was looking for my damned truck keys, couldn't I? This guy was an opportunistic killer, just grabbed whatever was handy. Oleander. Brush pick. Kitchen knife.

That would be my second if-I-live-through-this resolution—hide all sharp objects in case I decide to go poking around in a murdered friend's life again.

Maybe I wouldn't have any friends left. If Mario and Trudy came back any time soon, Van Dyke might off them, too. Of course, I'd bet I was going first.

Panic threatened to overwhelm me. As usual, I was

thinking way too much. I told my survival instincts to take over my brain. Screw thinking. Start doing.

Too late. I felt the duct tape going around my wrists, then taping my arms to my sides. I still had my legs, which I spread as far apart as I could. The knife then dug into the vicinity of my kidney. Have I mentioned I really hate knives—like worse than guns or snakes or needles? I could envision the blade invading my skin, diving into my organs. The vision paralyzed me. He taped my ankles together, then shoved me into a chair. And taped me into that, too.

"People can see me sitting here," I pointed out.

"Right." He looked outside and back to me like he'd had a plan all along. "And they'll think you are enjoying a nice salad for dinner."

"What salad?" I asked.

He pulled a Ziploc bag full of green leaves out of the pocket of his shorts. "Oleander salad."

Uh-oh.

twenty-six

FLINGING OPEN CABINET DOORS, MIKE VAN DYKE finally found a bowl and dumped the oleander leaves into it. Then he raided the refrigerator. "Look at this. You could open a gourmet restaurant. Radicchio. Chinese parsley. Endive. Kale. Even cilantro! How convenient. This will have the cops all over the map wondering which one of these freakish lettuces from weirdo places accidentally got packaged with some oleander. Good for me."

Ripping open bag after bag, he threw a little of each kind of green into the bowl, then he took the oleander leaves and broke them up into it, mixing it with his hands. I watched as the white sap melted into the water beading on the lettuce leaves. I was in trouble. Deep trouble.

As Van Dyke opened the refrigerator door, I finally got a good look at his hair. Yuck. It was number two clipper-cut on the sides, but he'd permed the crown sometime in the decades since his wedding and had it plastered in a mini-pouf with both gel and hairspray (control issues) like he thought he was some sort of blond JFK (ego issues). With a grunt of satisfaction, he flourished some lemon-lavender salad dressing he'd found behind the milk and doused the assembled leaves with it, chortling. "And when they wonder just why you could stomach the taste of the oleander, well, here's the answer. I bet this tastes like crap." He looked on the label at the expiration date. "I'm the luckiest man alive! It's even out-of-date."

Well, it didn't taste scrumptious, but I wasn't admitting that to him. I'd bought it on a lark a long time ago, tried it once, and never tried it again. My third if-I-live-through-this resolution—clean out the refrigerator so I won't have any extra ammunition for homicidal maniacs who happen to come calling.

The cordless phone sitting next to the refrigerator rang. We both looked at it like it was alive.

"I thought I cut the phone line," Van Dyke complained.

"So it was you, not the accident down the street."

"That was me, too, and it's no accident," Van Dyke boasted. "I paid some guy in a trench coat big bucks to throw a firecracker into a gas tank."

I guess the flasher had a place to stay tonight—the burn unit of the hospital. Nice guy, this Van Dyke.

The sirens still blared. The dogs still barked. I was still up the creek without the paddle. I looked more closely at the phone. It was the long-range cordless I'd bought for the salon. Mario had been talking on it to Trudy when he'd gone to make his sandwich. He must have forgotten to take it back to the receptionist desk. Thank the good Lord for dimwit friends.

It stopped ringing. Van Dyke looked at me.

"It's the phone for the salon."

The phone started ringing again.

"Do you have an answering machine?"

"Yes."

"Then why aren't they leaving a message?"

"Bring it to me, and I'll check the caller ID."

He showed me the display. Trudy was calling from home.

"It's my best friend." I smiled in relief.

"So?" He was getting worried, time to play on that. The phone stopped ringing.

"So, she's probably called my cell phone and my home phone and gotten no answer. If I'm not answering at the salon, then she'll get worried and rush over here. Right away. Speedy quick."

Van Dyke grimaced. "How far away does she live?"

"Not far," I lied. "Five minutes or so."

We stared at the quiet phone. I prayed as hard as I ever did for Trudy to try a third time. Ten of the longest seconds of my life ticked by. It rang again.

Van Dyke swore. He sat down next to me, holding the knife point in my back, where the brush had stuck out of Ricardo. He jammed the receiver to my ear. "Talk to her, then, but you'd better not let on that anything's wrong, or I'll forgo the nice, clean way to kill you in favor of the quick, bloody way. Remember, I've done that before. I don't like it, but I will do it."

He pressed the talk button with his thumb and leaned in so he could hear.

"Hello?" The knife point dug into skin. I winced. He dug it deeper. I felt some blood seeping out. I tried not to panic.

"Reyn! I was frantic with worry! Why didn't you answer any of your phones? Are you crazy? Don't answer that! I know you are."

"Hi, Trude, no need to be worried. I was just busy."

"Busy doing what? What could be so important that you'd give your best friend a heart attack imagining the things that could be happening to you right now?"

I paused. How could I come up with a way of telling Trudy something was wrong without Mr. Quick Stab catching on? And I didn't want her to faint if I shocked her too strongly. I went for the humor angle. Inside joke. "I was trying on some things I got from Frederick's of Hollywood for my date."

Van Dyke wiggled his waxed eyebrows. What man waxes his eyebrows? *Gag.* I might be sick even before I took a single bite of oleander.

"Date? What date?"

Oh, come on, Trude!

"The date with that tall hunk you tried to set me up with all week, of course, you silly. How could you have forgotten? What kind of friend are you?"

"What things from Frederick's of Hollywood?" She sounded suspicious now. Praise the Lord, I think she was getting it.

"Oh, you know, the leopard-print satin pushup bra with the black fur trim." I suddenly wished I actually looked at those catalogues they sent. Who knew it might save my life one day? Was Van Dyke breathing heavier? Gross. I finished my description quickly. "The red see-through negligee with the gold feathers. Those black suede crotchless bikini panties."

I know I heard Trudy swallow a laugh. *Bitch.* "Oh, yeah, those things. I remember now. Your date's gonna love them."

Van Dyke brought the knife up to make a cutoff motion across his throat. *Don't I wish he'd get a little closer to his neck.* Trudy had the message. I just hoped she had enough time to get help before I was a goner.

"I hope he does." I giggled just for good measure in case Trudy hadn't gotten it by now. I doubted she'd ever heard me giggle.

"You and the mirror have fun!"

Van Dyke cut the connection and threw the phone onto the table. "Gosh, after that, I wish we had the time to have you model those luscious items. But, sorry, got to kill you in time to make dinner at the club tonight." He glanced at his Rolex. "I might take them to my girlfriend, though, if you don't mind. Of course, you won't mind, you'll be dead. Might as well make good use of them."

He chuckled for a moment, then sobered up suddenly. "Let's get on with it."

He found a fork and stuck it into the pieces of green and shoved the bite toward my mouth. I stared at the pieces of leaves in front of me, trying to pick out the oleander from the other. It probably wouldn't matter; enough sap had gotten on the other pieces to do me in. One bite of cardenolide glycoside wouldn't kill, the gardener had said. I wished I'd asked exactly how many bites of the toxin was deadly. That knowledge might come in handy right about now.

My lips refused to open.

"Listen," he said, peeved, as he reviewed the Rolex again. "I only have an hour before I have to be at the San Antonio Country Club."

"That's only about five minutes from here," I pointed out helpfully.

"Yes, but I want to make sure you're dead before I leave."

"Oh."

He shook the bite of salad in front of my face. I shook my head. He picked the butcher knife back up off the table. "Quick or slow. Pretty soon, you won't have a choice."

I opened my lips. He shoved the bite in and pricked my jaw with the knife to get me to chew. Ick. Man, did it taste worse than dog do. And I'd know, because my thankless brothers made me eat that when I was four years old. I told myself to gag, throw up, but I didn't then, and I didn't now. Sometimes having an iron stomach is a handicap. I pretended to gag.

Van Dyke reached into his back pocket and flourished the duct tape. "I can shove a whole bunch of this in your mouth and duct tape it closed between bites."

I vetoed that idea, only partly because nothing in my life had hurt worse than ripping that duct tape off my face. The other part was, I wanted use of my tongue. I was getting a confession out of him, even if I wouldn't be alive to repeat it. Trudy's right. I am competitive, and I would beat the cops at this or else.

I was feeling "or else" right now. The far end of the kitchen was looking a little hazy. I'd better hurry.

"I'll take another bite if you tell me why you killed Ricardo."

"Because he was a stupid busybody, just like you are."

"What do you mean?"

"Why are you sticking your neck out—your life out—just to find out who killed your friend?" He forced another bite into my mouth.

I tried to act as if I was chewing. I shoved the wad

into the corner of my cheek and pretended to swallow. "Because it wasn't fair that he died. I owe it to him to find out who did him wrong."

"The only person you owe anything to is yourself. Those of us who live long lives know that. We are born selfish beings and are meant to live that way. But foolish Ricardo was just like you in the end. He thought he owed some kind of protection to a son he never acknowledged. I'm going to blow the poor boy out of the water in the state rep campaign, and Ricardo was trying to ensure his bastard son's success by forcing me out of it."

Somehow, despite the oleander, the sick pit in my stomach seemed to lighten. I didn't realize how hard the thought of Ricardo being so callous as to take a bribe hit me. That he tried to be altruistic in the end boosted my morale. I now saw two guys in tennis whites holding butcher knives, but they came together periodically. Then the whole room started to swim. "How was he going to force you out of it?"

"Blackmail. You see, he was the first paramedic on the scene and found us in flagrante delicto. The old codger was finally dying in his study and had called 911 himself. Hell, I'd been trying to poison the old boy with oleander in his damned desserts for about a week. I didn't know that night we'd hit the lotto. Ricardo went straight to Johnstone, and then his partner came in, they loaded him up, and off they went. We saw them at the hospital later, and I recommended to Sarah that she give him a "gift." It was the perfect plan, because once he accepted the money, he became an accomplice. But he didn't know an accomplice to what—just a little indiscretion or more."

"He knew it was more," I said, not able to make the two Van Dykes in my vision come together again. I smelled that bitter, rotten lemon. My stomach was cramping, but nothing was coming out of my mouth. *Thanks a lot, iron gut.*

"Yeah, I didn't know that until he called and wanted to meet me at that queer club. He threatened to come forward with proof that I'd killed Johnstone. Then his fate was sealed. I hate to be pushed. He pushed. I stewed about it long enough to realize I didn't want to give up anything I had, including my dream to be a politician. I called him and met him that night at his salon. He wouldn't compromise this time, so I killed him."

"Hands up!"

I tried to throw my hands into the air. I felt as if I was drunk on tequila in Tijuana. Nothing was focusing. I thought I heard Scythe's voice, Trudy's voice, and Mario's voice. But I also saw floating in my mind's eye suede crotchless black undies, a red and gold feather negligee, and a leopard-print pushup bra. I felt fingers slide under my jaw, I saw dry-ice eyes filled with a strong emotion—it may have been concern, but I was dying, so I couldn't be sure—and suddenly, for the first time, I felt like throwing up. I tried to reach across the table for the barf bag that had been sitting there for days and buried my face in it.

twenty-seven

I BLINKED AND SAW STARK, HARSH WHITE. FOR SOME reason, I thought heaven would be a gentler color, like butter yellow or baby blue. Maybe I was in hell. I really didn't think I'd been all that awful in my life, but I had been kind of a bitch to a couple of girls in high school, and of course I did swear. Only every now and then, but still, maybe God counted, and I'd surpassed the limit.

I hadn't gone to see my gran in about six months. I think she had major pull upstairs, so maybe she was the reason I wasn't in heaven.

Finally, I had given Mrs. Reinmeyer that mohawk. She was on the altar guild at church. I mowed her down by accident, though. Didn't that count?

"Reyn? Reyn? Oh, rednecks and rosaries, will you please wake up? I'm tired of praying, already." Trudy's voice floated my way. Oh, no, had that damned old Van Dyke killed her, too? Okay, maybe that's why I was in hell, for leading her to the gallows. But she wouldn't be there with me. She was a good Catholic.

"I think she's coming around."

That was Mario's voice. So I'd dragged everyone down with me. Oh, the guilt.

"I'm sorry," I heard myself mumble.

"What are you sorry for?" Trudy asked.

"For taking you all to hell."

"We'd better not go to hell! Or I'll kill you," Trudy argued. "I've said enough Hail Marys in the last twenty-four hours to save us, our children, and our children's children."

"I thought I was dead," I explained as I tried to sit up. It took a few tries. It seemed I had the strength of a newborn baby.

"They pumped your stomach a few times. You got a little dehydrated. They say you're going to be okay, though. Well enough to wear those crotchless undies and leopard pushup bra." Trude winked at me.

I smiled. "I'm just glad you got the message."

"Listen, I couldn't have gotten the message more clearly if you'd drawn me a picture. I called Scythe right away, and he was nearly to your house anyway. We weren't long behind. He heard the confession you got out of Van Dyke while he was trying to figure out a way inside without getting you stabbed."

"Good. So Van Dyke is out of circulation?"

"Yep, his case is already headed for the grand jury, it's so tight. His wifey is long gone, though. They think she jumped the last plane to leave San Antonio that night for Acapulco with one of the gardeners."

The more things change, the more they are the same. "So everybody is okay?"

"Everybody but Merlin, who's unhurt but refuses to

get down from the top of your wardrobe, and the vitamin salesman's Porsche, which is toast."

"Oh, no. It wasn't his car that . . ."

Trudy was nodding. "Oh, yes, it was. You're probably not his favorite neighbor right now."

So much for my love life. Even if it was nothing more than fantasy.

"Did they ever find out who was following me?"

"Scythe caught him, which was why he was late getting to your house. He was a heavy of Villita's who was just supposed to report back on your comings and goings and got a little carried away. I imagine they are going to ask you to press charges against him."

I shook my head. "I won't. I don't want to cause Jon any more suffering than he's already going through."

Mario was looking at me with pride, shaking his head in amazement. "You are so brave, Reyn."

"Really, it was nothing. I was just trying to do justice by Ricardo."

"No." Mario waved that away, then ran a hand over his hair. "I'm talking about my new style. You were brave to give me this. And so many people love it. I am *muy macho* now."

Trudy watched him, glowing with pride. What was I going to do with these two? It was that love thing again. I still didn't get it, despite my near-death experience.

"Have you guys been here since I was brought in?"

They tore their gazes from each other and looked at me. They nodded.

"Would you please go home?"

They did a visual consultation. "If you insist," Trudy said.

"I insist."

"By the way," Trudy added as they walked out. "Zorita says your green aura is gone, and she's sorry you didn't listen to her when she tried to warn you about the impending injury."

"Did you tell her her list was a bunch of hooey?"

"I mentioned it, and she said she never said the six people's fates you had control of were on the list at all."

Well, hell, Zorita was right. So much for assuming. What did Gran always say? Don't assume, it will make an ass of you and me? How many times had I proved that in the past couple of days?

"We'll send Jon in, then," Mario said, blowing me a kiss. "Jon?"

"Jon Villita wants to talk to you," Trude informed me as she exited, holding Mario's hand.

That was a shocker but also convenient, because as I'd slipped into whatever abyss I'd been in, I'd come up with what I ought to do with the salons should I live to see another day.

The door to my hospital room opened, and Jon came in. It hit me hard, because he was so much like Ricardo in the way he moved, the way he held his head, the way he smiled. He'd cut his hair to the young man's style of the moment—ultra-short with a front flip. It suited him. "I'm glad to see you made it. You had me worried."

"Why?"

"I wanted to have the chance to thank you for caring about my father—my biological father—enough to risk your own life to prove who took his."

"Oh, you know?"

"Some of it came out in the media. My mother and dad—the senator—told me the rest. Ricardo and my mother were in love, but she met my dad and thought he was a better future. When she turned up pregnant, Ricardo agreed not to fight for the right to me if they raised me right."

"Has the revelation messed up your political campaign?"

"Yeah." He grinned. "About half a dozen people have come out to challenge me all of a sudden. If I stay in it, my d—well, Senator Villita's name is going to be dragged through the mud along with mine. If I get out, his spin doctors can fix it for him."

"I'm sorry."

Jon shook his head. "I'm not. I didn't want to do it, anyway. I was only doing it to please my dad. This gives me the perfect excuse to find a job I might like more."

"I think I have one for you."

"Really?"

"I'm giving you Ricardo's salons."

He was already shaking his head. "I can't accept that kind of gift."

"It's not a gift. It's what's rightfully yours. I think Ricardo knew when he willed them to me what was going to happen and what I would eventually do with them." I replayed what I remembered of our last conversation in my mind. I nodded to myself.

"I don't know what to say," Jon began as the door opened and Scythe stuck his head in.

"Say 'Thank you, Ricardo,'" I answered Jon. "And one day, I'll tell you more about him."

"I'd like that." Jon reached down and gently shook my hand.

"You know, Ricardo said that he made two mistakes in his life—one was the best thing he ever did, and that was making you, I bet. And one was the worst thing he ever did, and that was taking that hush money from Sarah Johnstone. If you take the salons, it will be making right his wrong."

Jon nodded thoughtfully and left.

"See, I knew you'd need that barf bag one day," Scythe announced.

"Yeah, who knew you'd give Zorita a run for her money in predicting the future?"

"I didn't do too good a job, or I would've been at your house sooner."

"Oh, well, I lived," I responded lightly.

He shook his head as he strode to my bedside. He was dressed in his requisite Wranglers and a wrinkled periwinkle polo shirt. It looked like he might have slept in it or at least wallowed around in it in a hospital chair for a few hours. His rusty blond hair stood on end. I got all mushy until he finished my sentence. "Although you really shouldn't have."

"I shouldn't have lived?" Anger made me strong enough to sit up all the way.

"Right. Not the way you shook up half the city, baited the bad guy, and then set yourself up like a plate of enchiladas in the middle of a fiesta."

"But I hear Van Dyke's behind bars now, along with a confession."

"It wasn't worth it."

"It wasn't worth what?

"The headache you gave me."

"Okay, let's make a deal: I'll trim your hair, you'll teach me the proper way to investigate, so next time—"

Scythe was already shaking his head. "No next time. No deal."

"Why not?"

"You get in enough people's hair without knowing how to do it," Scythe said, easing down on the edge of my bed, laser blues turned on high. "And besides, I still haven't collected on the deal your pal made with me. It's time to do that right now. You'd better pay up . . ."

I smiled. "Or else?"

POCKET BOOKS
PROUDLY PRESENTS

Sprayed Stiff

Laura Bradley

Available in paperback Fall 2004
from Pocket Books

Turn the page for a preview of
Sprayed Stiff. . . .

One

I got on my knees, held my breath, and extended my fingers.

It was sleek and firm, but it sprang slightly at my touch. I kept my eyes closed and continued my exploration.

Smooth but growing more textured as I moved farther.

Suddenly, the surface gave way. My fingers sank through, diving into a wet, gooey pit.

"Ugh," I groaned, and squeezed my eyes more tightly shut as I extracted my hand.

"What the hell are you doing?"

I really didn't want to look at what was hanging off my fingers, and I really didn't need to open my eyes to see who was standing over me. Instead, I eased to my feet, trusted that my guest would stay out of the way, and did the blind man's grope to the sink. I cranked the handle up and slid my hand under the stream of water.

"Ow, damn damn damn damn." My eyes flew open

and took in the kaleidoscope of neon that was my best friend Trudy, which was almost more painful than my boiled skin. I danced around the kitchen shaking my seared hand in the air. I'd forgotten that just minutes before, I'd cranked the water as hot as it could go, which felt like somewhere around eighteen million degrees. That's what I got for being forgetful.

"I hate to repeat myself," Trudy said as she handed me a dish towel, "but I will anyway. What the hell are you doing, Reyn?"

"I'm cleaning out my refrigerator."

"Dun-dun-dun-dun," Trudy sang out the dirge. "Dun-dun-dun-dun."

"Very funny."

"From the looks of what was hanging off your fingers a second ago, it's not too funny. What was that, anyway?"

I peeked into the half-open hydrator. "Rotten eggplant. I wonder if I left it a little longer, whether it could ooze out of there on its own. Or perhaps be carried out by the decay expert it is currently fostering." I looked a little more closely at the gray-green fuzz near the stem.

"I'm not going to ask *why* you are cleaning your refrigerator. Obviously, it's needed to be cleaned almost since you bought it. However, I will ask why are you cleaning it *now*?"

"It's one of my if-I-live-through-this resolutions to myself."

"Wouldn't those be made *after* you survived the refrigerator cleaning?"

I glared. "I made three resolutions to myself while that maniac was trying to erase me." I swear, some people are so intolerant.

"That was six months ago, Reyn. You're just now getting around to it?" Trudy pointed out with irritating accuracy. Why couldn't I have a best friend who thought I was brave and brilliant, who never pointed out my faults and always praised my virtues? Because I'd never buy that load of crap, that's why. Trudy was shaking her head. "What about the other two resolutions?"

"Well," I began as I replaced the dish towel on its peg, "one of them I can't do yet, or hopefully ever."

"Why not?" Trudy cocked her hip and put a fist on it. Her rayon mini-dress looked like something straight out of *That '70s Show* (or, of course, the actual '70s), with its psychedelic wiggly bull's-eye business and the clash of electric green, traffic-cone orange, and spastic yellow. Its hem hit three inches below the crotch of her Victoria's Secret undies (I didn't have to look, she just didn't own anything else). People would be thrown into peals of hysterical laughter had I worn anything like this. The same people would be paralyzed by awestruck ogling when Trudy wore it. Her legs were that good. Even better now, after a summer out in the sun. The thing is, summer in San Antonio lasts until about November, so she'd still be tan by Christmas. Now, me, I never tan. I just get freckles.

I was getting an ugly ass-kissing best friend in my next life. I could get used to wading through crap. Sure

I could. I wanted some stranger to look at me first, just once.

"I can't do it because the resolution is that I will hide all my knives and other sharp, potentially homicidal objects in my house the next time I go poking around in a murdered friend's life."

Trudy rolled her eyes. "What are the odds of *that* ever happening again? I mean, how many people have friends who are murdered, and then, of course, even if that did happen—by some bizarre twist of fate—you've learned your lesson on not messing around with murder investigations because you nearly got killed. Right?"

Uh-oh. I really wasn't sorry for what I'd done about Ricardo's murder, even though my best friend and the man who occupied my dreams at night thought I was sorry. But I wasn't letting on to them. "Right. Sure. I'll never touch one of those things with a ten-foot pole again. No sirree. So, the odds are way too low ever to consider resolution number two: the hiding places for those sharp objects," I agreed, ignoring the eggplant and moving on to the jars along the refrigerator door. I cracked one open.

"And the third if-I-live-through-this resolution?" Trudy asked, not appropriately distracted by the pungent odor of apricot jelly that had fermented nearly to wine.

I closed the jar and pitched it into the garbage can I had dragged into the middle of the kitchen. Its twenty-gallon capacity was already half full. "It's a little vague."

"Vague."

"I was under a lot of stress at the time, remember? I was being pursued by a duct-tape-wielding killer who had an affinity for sharp objects and poisonous plants."

"You made this resolution before or after you were victim to the sharp object or a poisonous plant?"

"Before. But I had already been attacked by the duct tape. It tore the first six layers of skin off my face."

"Uh-huh, the excuse you used to keep Scythe at arm's length for a month." She let that hang in the air for a minute. I wasn't going to bite. Talking about the hunkamunk police detective gave me a headache. And hot flashes. I was too young to be having those. He was a helluva good kisser, that's all I knew, even after six months of pussyfooting around our sexual attraction and "the deal." Frankly, it was enough to make a woman go gay. But Trudy didn't even need to know that much. She raised her eyebrows, reached for a container of tofu, and checked the expiration date. "And the resolution?"

I lowered my head and muttered, "To get organized."

Trudy's giggle always starts like the peep of a newborn chick and gets louder and louder, until it reminds me of a violin in the hands of a three-year-old in need of a double dose of Ritalin. I saw tears in the corners of her eyes. It really pissed me off.

"What's wrong with getting organized?" I grabbed the tofu out of her hands and shoved it back onto the shelf. To hell with the expiration date, whatever it was.

Death by tofu didn't sound as bad right now as dealing with an interior designer's idea of organization.

The interior designer in question made a visible effort to sober up. "Nothing. Nothing at all. Where did you start?"

"Umm . . ."

"Okay," Trudy said patiently. Obviously, the most organized person I'd ever met wanted to encourage this train of thought in the most disorganized person on the face of the earth. "What prompted you to make this particular resolution?"

"Besides imminent death?"

"Besides that."

"I couldn't find my extra set of truck keys for a getaway."

"Okay." Trudy rubbed her hands together. "So, you found them and got all your keys set up in an organized manner."

"Umm . . ." I considered reapproaching the eggplant and toed the hydrator open farther.

"You didn't find your extra set of truck keys, did you?" The way she said it made me think the nuns at Trudy's grammar school had rubbed off on her a little too much.

"Not yet."

Ever optimistic, Trudy smiled, a little too brightly. "Instead, then, you tackled the job from a different direction. Taking on your closets, maybe."

"You think I should start there?"

"You haven't started at all?" Her shoulders slumped in disappointment. The too-bright went out of her smile. Her neon was suddenly the only thing lighting up the room.

"I wanted to do the refrigerator first, considering it involved perishables." Bravely, I swiped up the oozing eggplant and slam-dunked it into the plastic pail.

"It involved perishables, *six months later.*" Trudy threw her hands into the air and sashayed to the kitchen door. Shaking her head in disgust, she let herself out and slammed the door. My Labrador retriever trio, mother and two daughters, looked at me in question. They'd been observing the scene quietly since Trudy walked in. I think they were on their best behavior in hopes of me slipping them a molding slice of brie or something worse. You know dogs. Remember where they like to sniff.

"I'm definitely looking for an ass-kissing friend," I told Beaujolais, Chardonnay, and Cabernet. "Starting tomorrow."

I returned to my grim work in the refrigerator, and, aside from taking the time to eat two pieces of turtle cheesecake before they went bad, I kept at it for a couple of hours, until I was interrupted by the ringing of the telephone. Since I'm so supremely organized, I always put the cordless receiver back on the cradle. Of course I don't. I ran around, knocking into things, listening for the direction of the ring. I found it—slipped between the cushions of the couch in the den (duh!

The first place everyone looks!)—but not before the call went to the answering machine. I hated the sound of my own voice, so I hummed my way through my greeting, then listened to the reedy-voiced caller. "Reyn, this is Tamara (*pause*), Tamara Barrister. I am so sorry (*long pause*). So sorry to bother you so late."

For the first time, I glanced at the clock. It was 11:19.

Nine-one-one could be extrapolated here (with an extra *uno*), but of course, I didn't notice it at the time. Even thinking about it now gives me the heebie-jeebies. All I thought of at the time was *Gosh, it* is *kind of late.* But I'm a night person, so I was just coming alive, which is why I kept listening.

"If you could do me the courtesy of a return call as soon as you get this missive, I would so appreciate it. I have a bit of an emergency. An emergency. It involves Mum."

I was in a mood—I mean, who really gets off on cleaning the refrigerator? Okay, don't answer that, I don't want to know that person, if a freak like that really exists. So I picked up before Tamara—one of the most eccentric clients to cross my threshold—hung up the phone.

Travel the globe with the hilarious
PASSPORT TO PERIL
MYSTERIES
By Maddy Hunter

ALPINE FOR YOU 0-7434-5811-7
Emily Andrew takes charge in Switzerland when the randy
tour escort turns up murdered.

"If you're looking for laughter, you've come to the right place...
 sure to provide giggles and guffaws aplenty."
—*Cozies, Capers & Crimes*

TOP O' THE MOURNIN' 0-7434-5812-5
A haunted castle in Ireland is no blarney when inhabitants
get literally scared to death.

"Just as hilarious and delightful as the first one. I found myself
 laughing out loud and wiping away tears (of joy) as I quickly
 flipped the pages." —*Old Book Barn Gazette*

AND COMING AUGUST 2004

PASTA IMPERFECT 0-7434-8291-3
The passion of Italy gets in the blood of aspiring romance
authors when competition over a book contract turns deadly.

Available wherever books are sold.

10163

Find a fast-paced caper in the

Poetic
Death Mystery
Series

By Diana Killian

HIGH RHYMES AND MISDEMEANORS
0-7434-6678-0

While touring the homes of her beloved romantic poets in England's Lake District, Grace Hollister gets tangled up with a charismatic ex-jewel-thief-turned-antiques-dealer who has something worth killing for.

"A cross between James Bond and *Romancing the Stone*....
There is action, action and more action in this light-hearted tongue-in-cheek thriller."   —*Books 'n' Bytes*

A SELECTION OF THE MYSTERY GUILD

And coming in October 2004...

VERSE OF THE VAMPYRE
0-7434-6679-9

A local stage production of *The Vampyre* goes a bit too far when accidents begin befalling the cast, culminating in fatal fang marks on the neck of a society lady. Could a real vampire be stalking the English village of Innisdale?

Available wherever books are sold.

POCKET BOOKS
A Division of Simon & Schuster
A VIACOM COMPANY
www.simonsays.com

Get set for glamour

in the debut

Lauren Atwill Mystery

By Sheila York

~

Star Struck Dead

0-7434-7046-X

Smart and sassy screenwriter Lauren Atwill
sets out to solve a murderous plot when she
becomes the victim of a blackmail ring targeting
tinsel town's elite.

**"A real treat, *STAR STRUCK DEAD* offers
a stylish glimpse into the grit and glamour
of '40s Hollywood."**
–*RT Bookclub Magazine*

POCKET BOOKS
MYSTERIES
are to die for!

Curl up with a cozy...

JOAN HESS

Misery Loves Maggody	0–671–01684–9
murder@maggody.com	0–671–01685–7
Maggody and the Moonbeams	0–7434–0658–3

MADDY HUNTER

Alpine for You	0–7434–5811–7
Top O' the Mournin'	0–7434–5812–5

The Brush-off by Laura Bradley	0–7434–7111–3
Arson and Old Lace by Patricia Harwin	0–7434–8224–7
High Rhymes and Misdemeanors by Diana Killian	0–7434–6678–0
A Lady Never Trifles with Thieves by Suzann Ledbetter	0–7434–5747–1
Shadows at the Fair by Lea Wait	0–7434–5620–3
Star Struck Dead by Sheila York	0–7434–7046–X

Available wherever books are sold.

POCKET BOOKS
A Division of Simon & Schuster
A VIACOM COMPANY
www.simonsays.com